FINDING
TED JAMES

STEVEN WILCOX

Book design by Steve Mead

Published by Ingramspark

ISBN 978-0-57836-0-041 (paperback)
ISBN 978-0-57836-0-058 (ebook)

To Judy: My rock for the past 54 years.

CHAPTER 1

WINSTON THIBODEAU JAMES was sitting in a folding chair in his backyard. He was talking with his dad. It was a warm July evening, and the sun was about to set. Mack, Winston's dad, did his routine testing of the flow of beer. Always a heavy drinker, Mack's drinking had increased after Mabel left him. Mack always joked he had two jobs. First, Mack was a carpenter for his brother's construction company; This job paid the bills and kept a roof over their head. The second was more of a hobby. He checked to see how easily beer flowed from a bottle. His preferred beer was whatever was on sale.

Occasionally, Mack became wistful. This was one of those nights.

"Do you know how you got your first name?" Mack asked, slurring his words.

Winston did not want this conversation. He sat with a glazed, far-off expression. After a pause, Winston rolled his eyes at the question. "I am not sure," Winston lied.

"You got it from your grandfather, my old man."

Mack drained the beer in his hand. He tossed the bottle into the trash can, then opened the ice chest and grabbed another. Before continuing the story, Mack twisted off the lid, threw it into the can. He then fell back into his chair.

"My old man was a chain smoker. I'll never understand how he lived to be 92. Pop died with a lit cigarette in his mouth. It was a blessed miracle he didn't burn the house down." Mack paused and took a sip from the bottle. "It is a family custom the grandfather got to name the first male child. My dad's favorite brand of smokes was Winston. I still remember the slogan—Winston tastes good like a cigarette should." Mack took another swig of beer and wiped his mouth. "Yep, your grandfather named you after a brand of cigarettes."

Then he gave a gruff laugh to keep the strained conversation going and inquired, "And Thibodeau?" Winston already knew the answer.

"Unlucky, as all get out. It has been a tradition for the middle name to be your great-great-grandfather's first name, Thibodeau. Thibodeau Montgomery James, may his soul rest in peace."

The sun finished setting, revealing a blue-green tinted sky and moon was visible, as was Venus. The weatherman had predicted a thunderstorm to the next day, Winston questioned that prediction as he sat looking up into space, observing the cloudless sky.

Without a word, Mack disappeared inside. The screen door slammed behind him. Winston stayed in his chair, waiting for his dad to return. Instead, Mack's bedroom light went on. Winston understood his dad was not coming back. Winston took a deep breath. Then he sank further into the chair, never taking his eyes off the moon and Venus.

Winston hated his name. To him, neither his given nor his middle name were real names. They were mere words. Ted's sixth-grade teacher told him a common nickname for Thibodeau was Ted. Armed with this new information, Winston began forging new identity. From then on, He allowed only his family to call him Winston. To his teachers and friends, his name was Ted.

The primary problem with his first name was his grandfather. To use a brand of cigarettes to name your grandchild was, in Ted's mind, the ultimate act of stupidity. He shared his feelings with his mother. She suggested he tell everyone he is named after Winston Churchill. It would be a lie he would always carry with him.

Winston always considered his grandfather to be a jerk. It seemed no matter what anyone said, his grandfather had a pessimistic and profane comeback. Not wanting to continue that tradition, with his new identity, Ted did not cuss. Everyone around him: his dad, his mother, his friends, all used profanity. It was almost impossible for them to make a comment without it being profane. When Ted's grandfather died, Ted attended the funeral but refused the offer to eulogize him. Every memory of his grandfather was graphic or centered on an obscenity.

Ted's mother, "Able Mable," his dad's nickname for her, wasn't much of a role model either. Ted believed she was a dancer, or to be more specific, an exotic dancer. So how does someone in high school explain his mother takes her clothes off in public? It was an image too painful for Ted to conjure up. More than once, he wanted to ask her how she could degrade herself. What would she say? Would she deny it? In the end, Ted's cherished the relationship with his mother. He believed any confrontation might destroy the only sense of normality he had.

Ted did know Mable received two checks from work. Mable showed Mack her regular paycheck. The second check went into a savings account. Mack did not know about either the second check or the savings account.

From their joint checking account, Mack paid the rent and utilities. Mable paid for the groceries.

When drunk, Mack became boisterous. Mack was not violent. But one time. Mable came home from the club. Mack, for an unknown reason, was furious. Mack had finished what beer he had in the house and began searching for spare change for more beer. Then he found an envelope with Mable's second paycheck inside. The notation on the envelope had one word: "Miscellaneous." It was more significant than the paycheck Mable had shown him. So, when Mable came home, Mack confronted her.

Mack and Mable were yelling and screaming at each other, then the unthinkable happened. For the first time in Mack and Mable's twenty-year marriage, Mack struck his wife. Mack slapped her hard on the face with an opened hand. She fell and broke a tooth. She also had a red mark on the side of her face. She got up and swung at Mack, but he was too fast for her. This time, Mack punched her. The punch was a roundhouse hitting Mable in her right eye. The injury gave Mable a black eye, or what most people called a shiner. Mable could not work with visible bruises.

The fight happened on Thursday. Mack's payday was Friday. When Mack got paid, Mable assumed he would come home with a case of beer. They greeted one another, more like strangers than husband and wife.

After Mack's third beer, Ted's mother pulled Ted aside.

"Winston," she stopped. "I'm sorry, I know you prefer Ted." She looked at him

for a moment and smiled.

"I am going out for a bit. I am not sure how long I'll be gone. Do not worry or wait up for me, OK?"

"Sure, but." She cut Ted off.

Ted looked dumbfounded at his mother but did not utter a sound.

"Listen. Lois will be here in a minute. Lois and I will be together this evening. Go to a friend's house. You have the car."

Lois arrived, honked twice, and Mable was out the door. Ted did not notice the small canvass bag she was carrying. Stopping at the car, Mable opened the door, then turned and waved at Ted. A minute later, his mother and the car disappeared down the road.

That "little bit" turned into two years. Sometimes, Lois

would stop by the house when Mack was not there. She would give Ted a note from his mother. Then, after about three months, everything stopped. No letters or phone calls. It was as if his mother had vanished into thin air.

On Ted's 18th birthday, Lois gave Ted a birthday card from his mother. Inside the card was a picture of Mable and her new boyfriend. From the background, Ted guessed they were in Florida. On her new boyfriend's boat? The card read, "Getting a divorce and starting over. Get out the first chance you get. Love, Mom."

Six months later, a large envelope arrived, requiring Mack's signature. Ted signed Mack's name and took the envelope. Ted did not open it-he didn't have to. Instead, Ted saw the law firm's name, Henderson & King, in the return address. Ted understood what was in the envelope. The divorce papers.

When Mack came home, Ted gave the envelope to his father. Mack opened it and stared at it in quiet disbelief. Then, he sat down and read the whole thing. No drinking, talking, or cussing. When he finished, all he said was, "Son of a." Mack made a fist and pounded the arm of the chair. Ted knew the phrase ended with profanity, but Mack stopped mid-sentence. Mack read the documents a second time and forced a smile. It was apparent to Ted his father was fighting back the words he wanted to say.

There was a second envelope. Mack signed the documents, and then he shoved them in the second envelope. He got up and sealed the envelope before giving it back to Ted.

Ted's dad stood there for a long time. His voice strained, he added, "Go drop this at that stupid self-mail thing they have at the post office." Then, visibly shaken, Mack said to no one in particular, "I want everything reminding me of her, out of this house."

Mack opened the fridge, took two beers, and slammed the back door. Ted pried the envelope open and slipped another note inside.

"Where are you? Next month will be my 19th, and then I'm out of here. Don't care where or how, but I am gone!"

Ted planned on leaving when he turned 18. But no job, no plans, or any real ambition kept him where he was. While Ted hated Mack's drinking, he was reluctant to leave his father to his own devices. So, Ted felt trapped.

He taped the envelope shut, and instead of mailing it, he hid it in his room. The next day, he went to the lawyer's office.

Ted entered the law firm, identified himself, and handed the receptionist the envelope.

"There's a note to my mom inside. Can you make sure she gets it? It's from me.

Not my dad."

"Sure, no problem."

"Thanks," answered Ted. Then he turned and left the office.

After dropping off the envelope at the lawyer's office, Ted headed home. His dad was waiting for him. Although drunk, Mack did his best to act as if he were sober.

"Do you know where she is?"

"No."

"Win-ston?" He ordered, pronouncing his name in two deliberate, distinct syllables.

"Look, Dad. When she left you, she left me too! I have no idea where she is."

"Have you heard from her?" Mack demanded.

"Yes, a few times." They stood there looking at one another. Ted braced himself, not sure what his dad was about to do.

"Well?"

A brief look of panic flashed across Ted's face then he answered, "Lois has heard from her. She would send Lois a note for me. Lois put the note in a card. The note never said where she was."

"Is she with anyone?" Mack challenged in a tone laced with menace.

With determination in his voice, "Once. Mom sent me a picture of her and another guy. She didn't tell me where she was. She said nothing about the man. She did tell me she was divorcing you. The envelope came and I saw it was from a lawyer. I assumed what it was the divorce stuff. That's all."

Mack, fists clenched, took a step toward Ted. Ted stood his ground and never voiced a word.

Mack blinked first. He turned and left. Ted heard the door slam.

"You are on your own for dinner. I'm not hungry."

Although Ted weighed almost 150 pounds, others treated him like the proverbial 98-pound weakling. He had had a severe case of acne, and his face showed the scars. There were students Ted hung around with at school. Both boys and girls. It would be a mistake, however, to say Ted had friends. Once school let out for the day, his so-called friends disappeared.

At five-eight, he was of average height. It was common knowledge how Ted got his first name. This meant Ted got bullied. Then there was his alcoholic father and exotic dancing mother Each adding to the problem. The bullying stopped when he started hanging around a couple of delinquents. They didn't have guns or do any drugs stronger than weed. As the three walked the halls, no one paid them attention. There were two of them. They painted buildings, broke into schools, plus a few homes and businesses. They called him Teddy, and he was their lookout. He called them the dynamic duo. Ted was sixteen when he fell in with the dynamic duo. Now, the duo had become a trio.

All three had minimum-wage jobs. The criminal aspect of their lives was an adrenaline rush. There were police reports of the burglaries. However, what the burglars took had no value and no one followed-up.

The group was well known. Getting out of this situation was simple, Get a job! Most of the former members did that. None of them ever had a record except for trespassing or painting graffiti. A few found jobs not requiring a college education: truck driver, factory worker, or similar jobs. One attended college and is now a teacher somewhere. Two were forged a career in the military.

Living in a small midwestern town had its advantages. You were off the beaten path, and everyone knew everyone else. Occasionally, this was problematic. However, the police knew who-was-who. The police were more into rehabilitation and guidance than racking up arrests.

More hard-core drugs were coming into town, but they were being brought in from the big cities by kids wanting to make an easy buck. This was a blue-collar community without a lot of extra cash. So, drugs were not yet a problem.

Ted believed big city crimes were coming to his little corner of the world. Ted dreamed of getting on with his life. This was not in the plan.

"Hey, Teddy." It was Little Jimmy Dickens. Jimmy's real name was Jimmy Dickenson, and he was shorter than Ted by an inch or so. He was the current ringleader. Jimmy kept singing that old country song, "May the Bird of Paradise Fly Up Your Nose." Little Jimmy Dickens made the piece famous, so the name stuck. Jimmy was sitting on the curb in front of Ted's house. Ted did not immediately see him. Ted stopped when Jimmy called his name.

"Hi, Jimmy."

"You got a birthday coming up."

"Next month. On the fifth."

Ted studied Jimmy, who was not making much eye contact. "The big one-eight!"

"19," Ted corrected, "I'm looking for a way out of this town."

"I've heard that on the street. We should talk."

"OK," Ted responded, swaying back and forth.

"Have a seat." Jimmy point to a spot on the curb next to him. "We, Freddy and me, have a job for you."

This paralyzed Ted for a brief second. Whenever Jimmy said, "We have a job for you," it meant something bad.

Several seconds passed before Ted sat on the curb. There were several inches between the two. A casual observer would know the two were not friends.

Looking Jimmy in the eye, Ted asked, "What is it you want?"

"A simple B&E. Old man Kelley's—over on Sycamore."

"Yeah. Why the old man?"

"We have it on good authority; the old coot keeps a large stash of cash hidden in his dresser. We need cash, so."

"You want me to break in and steal his money," Ted repeated in a matter-of-fact tone.

"Not all of it. I believe it is over a grand. All we want is a couple of C-notes. The old man won't miss them."

"I have never done anything like this. I'm not sure I know how."

"Sure, you do. Remember Donovan's over on Aspen?"

"Yes, but I got in. I looked around and took a magazine. You wanted proof I had done it. I have never taken money. Or anything else that was valuable."

"Same plan. This time, a couple of bills. He'll never miss them. Promise."

Ted's face glazed over. He focused on a parked car across the street.

"Look, it will be simple," Jimmy continued, bringing Ted

back to earth. "Freddy does the old man's lawn. The key is under the flowerpot."

Ted gave him a "you have got to be kidding," look.

"Yeah, just like in the movies. Can you believe it? Seem like everyone knows he keeps a key under the flowerpot with the roses. Use the key. Get in and get out."

"You sure about this?"

"Positive," Jimmy declared with a grin. "Piece of cake."

Ted sighed a breath of resignation. "When am I supposed to be burglarizing his home?"

"Freddy said Wednesday nights the daughter takes the old man to the doctor and dinner. Perfect timing."

Not making eye contact, "And the key will be there."

"Of course," said Jimmy, then he placed a hand on Ted's shoulder.

Ted flinched at the pressure. Jimmy didn't say a word.

"OK," Ted said, almost in a whisper. "I'll do it. But no key, and it is off. "Sure. No problem."

"I will go in take the bills. We meet when and where?"

"At Uncle Dan's Pizzeria on fifth, say around ten." Jimmy watched for a sign of recognition.

Ted got up and looked at Jimmy. Jimmy got up. The conversation had ended. They nodded as a sign of agreement.

Ted announced, "My dad is in one of his moods. I need to get in before he gets too drunk."

Neither looked back. Ted listened to Jimmy's footsteps as he was walking away down the street. Jimmy heard Ted enter the house and call for his dad.

The deal was sealed.

CHAPTER 2

TED WAS ALREADY up when the phone rang. The caller ID said JD. Ted was tempted to ignore it. Ted was about to turn 19 and wanted to be on his own.

The phone call was a double-edged sword. It gave Ted a chance to make a clean break from Jimmy and Freddy. It also meant his life could get complicated beyond belief. The phone stopped ringing.

Ten minutes later, the phone came alive again with the same caller ID. Ted answered it with caution.

"Hey, Jimmy"

"Did I get you at a bad time?" he asked. Their voice had an edge.

"Nah, the phone is on vibrate, so I don't wake dad. I was about to call."

"Yah, yah, yah. Listen. Freddie called, and he confirmed old man Kelley will be out tonight with his daughter. They are going to a show. Anyway, tonight's your night. Don't let us down."

"Tonight?" Ted's brain stalled for a moment.

"What, are you deaf or something?" A new sense of urgency entered his voice. "Yes, tonight! Wednesday-remember? Anyway, Freddy said the old man and his daughter are leaving around seven. Eight or nine should be perfect. It shouldn't take more than five or ten minutes. In and out. Use the key, return the key, and nobody will be the wiser."

"OK. Let's get this done. I'll meet you at Uncle Dan's at ten.

"OK, I'll see you at Uncle Dan's."

The phone went dead. Ted stared at it for a few seconds before putting it in his pocket. What had he gotten himself into? Tonight, Ted had agreed to commit a felony. If the old man discovered money missing, the police were not going to sluff it off. There would be an investigation. If he got caught, his future was over. "Do not get caught," he thought.

Mack was up and fixing his breakfast of cereal and milk. "Who was that?"

"Huh?" Ted was still focused on the call and what it meant.

"On the phone. I saw you on the phone." Mack was looked through old mail.

"Oh. Jimmy Dickens," attempting to sound casual.

"What did that piece of crap want?" without stopping or looking at his son.

"We're meeting later tonight at Uncle Dan's for some pizza."

"That is a bad idea. Nothing good can come of meeting. Not with a guy like him." Mack found the newspaper Ted had brought in earlier. Mack sat down with his cereal and a cup of instant coffee, reading the newspaper. Mack was now dead to the world.

Ted fixed a piece of toast. When the toast popped up, Ted grabbed it walked behind his dad. "I'm going to work," Ted yelled. He closed the door. Ted had started working at Taco Bell a couple of months earlier. He enjoyed the work. However, Ted was not scheduled to work the weekend. Saying he was going to the Bell got Ted away from his dad.

The Kelley house was two blocks over. Without thinking,

Ted found himself walking past the house. The old man's shiny red Ford Ranger pickup was in the garage. Mr. Kelley had given up driving a while back. He had a daughter who came once or twice a month. They would go out in his truck. She had a nice-looking C-class Benz, but her dad enjoyed riding in the Ranger. So, that is what they did.

Mr. Kelley and his wife, Jessica, or Jess as she was known, had enjoyed theater and were season ticketholders for the local theater troupe. Unfortunately, Jess lost her two-year bout with breast cancer. After his wife died, Mr. Kelley and his daughter would go to the theater in her car. She enjoyed teasing him, saying, "I think going to the theater calls for a car and not a truck."

Ted stopped at the Taco Bell. He ordered a seven-layer burrito and a Dr. Pepper. Then visited with the on-duty manager and a few employees. An hour later he was home. Mack was asleep on the couch with a movie showing on the television.

The refrigerator was the communication hub when they were apart. Each would leave the other a sticky note with various messages. A new note was there in Mack's chicken-scratch writing. "Call Freddy Wheller." It did not state when Freddy called. As a sign of his independence, Ted purchased an inexpensive smart phone. Ted believed his dad would not keep up with a cell phone. There were few landlines left in town and Ted's family had the same number since Ted was a baby. Freddy, and everyone else in town knew their number. There was only one person with Ted's cellphone number, Jimmy.

Of course, Freddy may have stopped by the house. Either way, Ted did not have Freddy's number and would call Jimmy to get it.

After an hour of playing phone tag, Ted got Freddy's number and called.

"Lo," the voice sounded irritated.

"Freddy? Ted."

"Yo, Teddy. Jimmy wanted to let you know it's a go for tonight."

"I know," Ted said with an air of sarcasm in his voice.

"Yeah, but remember, it is theater night. Don't freak out when you see the truck in the garage. His daughter always drives to the theater in her fancy Benz. I overheard him tell his daughter he would be ready around seven. That means they will be gone maybe three hours."

"Great." There was a pause. "Thanks for the intel," and Ted disconnected.

While he was out running errands and shopping, Ted grabbed a couple of small steaks. Ted had his burrito early and was now hungry. Ted doubted his dad had eaten anything since breakfast. So, he got the steaks and fired up the grill. While waiting on the coals to turn grey, Ted got out two ears of corn and prepared them. The one thing that both he and his dad enjoyed was fresh sweet corn and a good steak grilled on the barbeque.

The house he shared with his dad was small. It was a three-bedroom with a single bath. The wood siding needed a paint job. There was no garage. The original garage was now Ted's bedroom. Ted had no direct access to the house from his bedroom. Ted's access was through the kitchen. On the other hand, Ted and his mother sometimes used his room, seeking refuge from Mack's drunken tirades.

Ted remained outside, away from his dad, while the steaks were on the grill. After bringing in the steaks and corn, Ted set the table and called his dad to eat. The two ate in silence, not even making eye contact.

After dinner, Ted cleaned up, washed the dishes, and took the trash to the city-provided bin. Mack grabbed a beer and settled in front of the television.

"I'm going out," Ted said. He did not wait for an answer.

It was still light at 8:30; he stayed near home. It was time for recon in the neighborhood and Kelley's house. To play his part, Ted was dressed in dark clothes with a hooded sweatshirt. The hood was not pulled up. Some in the neighborhood recognized Ted. They had also seen him with other boys the neighbors suspected of some petty crimes happening in the area.

The first time he passed the house, some neighbors visited, did yard work, and played outside. About 45 minutes later, he made another pass. Everyone had retreated into their homes, and he decided to walk around the block one more time, then make his move. As he rounded the corner on his third pass, red and blue lights came on. Behind him, a squeal from a siren. Ted turned and watched the car pull up and stop. The driver got out. He came to him. Ted read the door of the vehicle. POLICE was emblazoned in all caps, with Traverse, Illinois centered underneath.

Without realizing it, Ted's hands had become clammy, and he found himself wiping them on his jeans.

"Oh, it's you," said the officer with a smile. "You lost?"

"No. Dad's home and carrying on. So, I had to get out. I needed to walk."

"Third time you passed this way, according to a neighbor."

Ted's heartbeat quickened.

"I know. It's far enough away from home, so I don't have to worry about my dad confronting me. So, I figure one or two more times. By then, he'll be asleep. Or at least quieted down."

"Let's make it one more time. Then you either find another block, or you go home."

"Deal."

Still watching Ted, the officer added, "You can't blame people for being a bit nervous with the rash of home invasions."

"Home invasions?" Ted asked, trying to act surprised.

"Yes," the officer went on. "Someone breaks in and looks

around. Often they don't take anything."

"And the rest of the time?"

The officer smiled and shrugged. "It's always junk. Things the homeowners never immediately missed."

"Oh, yes. I've heard about those. I also heard the homes were unlocked, or the location of a spare key was common knowledge." Ted could have kicked himself with that statement. He did not want an extended conversation with a police officer.

"You are right on both counts." The officer looked up at the sky. Then to Ted, "People should feel safe in their homes, locked or not. Don't you agree?"

Ted's stomach did a quick flip, afraid the officer was about to accuse Ted of the burglaries or casing Mr. Kelley's darkened house.

"Agreed," said Ted. "One more round, and I'll head home. Promise."

"Let's hope Mack has calmed down by then. Have a good night."

"You too, officer," Ted repeated as he stood watching the officer for a few minutes.

The officer got back into the car. He turned the lights off, something on his radio, and waved. Then drove out of sight.

Ted let out a sigh of relief and started walking again. His first steps were tentative, and then he froze. Ted was in front of Old Man Kelley's house. He stood there for a few minutes, aware of a noise coming from within the home. Ted could not quite figure it out and walked up the driveway. A dog was barking from within the house.

Ted walked up the walkway to the front door and pounded.

"Mr. Kelley, you alright?" he hollered.

He did this with no response. Ted heard the dog barking. Ted walked around to the back. He repeated his actions. Same results. Ted remembered the key, lifted the pot of roses, and found the key. He unlocked the door and entered the house.

"Mr. Kelley, it's Ted James. Are you OK?" Ted fumbled around in the dark, hunting for, then finding the light switch. The yapping dog kept getting underfoot, and twice Ted almost stepped on him. He did his best to avoid barking mutt.

The dog was Mr. Kelley's black terrier. The tail was wagging, but the dog kept running up to Ted, barking, turning, and running towards the living room. The dog repeated this scenario until Ted followed the dog and found the living room light. Mr. Kelley was on the floor, lying on his back. He wasn't moving. The dog would run and lick the man's hand. He then ran back to Ted and bark.

Ted guessed Mr. Kelley was in his middle to late 50s, possibly early 60s. The old man appeared taller than himself. Mr. Kelley was overweight with a full head of salt-and-pepper hair. He pretended to be a gruff. But everyone in the neighborhood knew it was an act. Rumor was he was one of the state's wealthiest men. But no one knew for sure. His house was modest. His favorite vehicle was a three-year-old red Ford Ranger.

Ted's knee-jerk response was to back away. He could leave and go home. He would call 911 on the way home, mentioning the barking dog. He would not mention seeing Mr. Kelley.

After regaining his composure, Ted realized he could not leave the man. It was not who he was. Ted knelt and began shaking the old man's shoulder.

"Mr. Kelley, wake up!" Ted repeated this while continuing to shake the old man's shoulder. Ted remembered some of his first-aid training in school, and He felt on the man's neck and his wrist. There was a pulse. Then he got down, observing the man's chest rise and fall. The old man was breathing. His breath had a sweetness to it. Ted tried calling and shaking the old man a couple of times, then pulled out his phone and dialed 9-1-1.

"What is your emergency?" asked the 911 operator.

"My name is Ted James, and I am at Mr. Kelley's house. The address is 431 Sycamore. Mr. Kelley appears to be unresponsive."

"What have you tried?" asked the operator.

"I have called his name, and I have shaken him several times. He does not respond. I can feel a pulse in his neck and at his wrist. His chest is rising and falling, so he is breathing. His breath smells sweet."

"Do you know CPR?"

"Yes. I took the course in school."

"Good. Do you see any blood either on or around Mr. Kelley?"

"No, I don't see any blood."

"OK. I have dispatched the EMS and the police. Stay there until they arrive and tell them what you told me. If you see any changes, start CPR compressions if he stops breathing or can no longer find a pulse. Can you do that?"

"Yes, I think I can."

"Good," she said in a calm voice. "I will stay on the line until help arrives. It should be within three minutes now. Let me know if the situation changes."

Then, red, and blue lights came to a stop in front of the house. Ted went over and let them in. It was the same officer that had stopped him earlier.

"You, again?" he looked at Ted with suspicion.

Ted took a deep breath and told his story. "After you left, I started to walk away when I kept hearing this sound. I couldn't figure it out, so I just stood there and listened."

"And you figured it was his dog," the officer said.

"No, not at first. I just knew it came from this house, so I came closer."

"Then you let yourself in. And you found him."

"Well, sort of," Ted said, starting to get irritated.

"I heard the dog barking. I pounded on the front door and called for him, but no answer."

"Oh, let me guess, the dog opened the door?" The officer stared at Ted. He looked skeptically at Ted.

Ted knew the officer was not buying his story. Running with Jimmy and Freddy had not done much for Ted's credibility. Ted took a deep breath and let it out. "Look. The dog was barking, and I knew something was wrong. So, I went to the back. I pounded and called. Everyone knows the old man keeps a key under the rose pot. With the key, I let myself in. I turned on the light, and the dog sort of led me to him. I checked and found that he had a pulse. He was unconscious but breathing. So, I called 9-1-1 and waited for you."

While they were talking, the EMTs arrived and began treating the old man. The chief EMT said, "Lucky you came in when you did. You may have saved this man's life. At least, now he has a fighting chance."

"OK, kid. Good job," the officer said, patting Ted's back.

In a relaxed tone, the officer continued. "I know he has a daughter, Pam."

"There's a name, Pam, with a phone number by the phone." Ted left. He came back and handed the officer the card. The officer pulled out a cell phone and began punching in the number.

Feeling guilty, Ted inquired, "You've been awful suspicious of me tonight. Have I done something wrong?"

"No, son. I'm Tim Kelley. Jack is my uncle, and I can be over-protective sometimes. But seriously, I thank you for your quick thinking. Can you take care of Napper? Maybe for a day or two?"

"Sure. I'll take the dog home with me tonight."

While Officer Kelley talked with his cousin, the EMTs loaded Mr. Kelley on a gurney and put him in the ambulance. Officer Kelley was at the dining table and filling out some paperwork. He asked for Ted's contact information, then gave Ted a business card.

"I'm going to take a quick look around, OK?" Officer Kelley began wandering through the house, a lighted flashlight in hand.

Ted picked up the dog and did his best to calm the dog. Then, satisfied everything was OK, he said, "Hey, Ted. I'm heading to the hospital to check on my uncle. Can lock up when you leave?"

"Sure, no problem." Ted still did not relax. He and the dog were there alone in the house.

Before leaving, Ted picked up the house, put the dishes in the dishwasher. Then, out of curiosity, Ted checked the drawers of Mr. Kelley's dresser. In the chaos, he forgot about the money. Then, wanting to be truthful, he searched. He blew a sigh of relief when there wasn't.

As promised, Ted took Napper home. Ted gave the dog some food and water and took the dog to his bedroom. The dog sat on the floor. It was looking at Ted, head cocked to one side. It didn't bark; it just got excited whenever Ted moved in its direction. Finally, the dog stood and backed up, never taking its eyes off Ted. Ted thought the dog might be scared. It took several attempts before he managed to pick the dog up. Ted petted the dog and talked in a quiet, soothing voice until the dog relaxed. When Ted climbed into bed, the dog watched him. When Ted started snoring, Napper settled down and fell asleep. Curled at Ted's feet.

CHAPTER 3

TED GOT UP and checked on Mack. Napper looked up. He did not move from his spot at the foot of Ted's bed. Ted stood at the doorway for a few minutes, watching his father sleep. Napper did not move but watched Ted in the doorway. Ted was quiet when he got dressed. He grabbed a Dr. Pepper and a banana, then returned to his room. He picked up Napper. The two left Ted's house. They walked leisurely back to Jack's. They entered, and Ted found food for Napper in a cupboard and put fresh water in the water bowl.

Ted examined the house in daylight. Mr. Kelley's bedroom was on the south side of the house. Two bedrooms were on the north side. Kelley's room was a mess. Mr. Kelley's bed was unmade. There was a hamper full of dirty clothes. Ted found a few dirty dishes, on the table and in the sink. It was apparent the house needed a good cleaning. Two bedrooms were on the other side. One appeared to be a guest room with a twin bed, a chest. A small television was on a table. There was dust on the chest, but it was otherwise clean. Ted guessed it had been a while since anyone had slept in the bed. The third bedroom was cluttered with bookshelves, boxes, and a make-shift worktable. Someone was doing scrapbooking and then stopped. It was obvious nothing had been touched in a while. Instead, it appeared someone had shoved everything in the room, closed the door, forgot about it.

◆ ◆ ◆

Ted was aware a car had pulled up outside but ignored the noise. He heard a key inserted into the lock. Then listened to the door open. Ted stepped into the living room. A short woman not much older than Ted with dark hair entered. They both stopped for a second. The woman reached into her pocket and pulled out a can of pepper spray.

With an expression of panic, Ted raised his hands. He said, "Don't shoot. I'm Ted James. I am the one who found Mr. Kelley last night and called the EMTs. I took Napper home with me last night, and I brought him back this morning. I didn't have any dog food at home." Ted was having difficulty controlling his breathing.

Hesitating, she said, "OK." Then, continuing to hold the pepper spray, she asked, "What are you doing now? Are you casing the joint?"

"No, I'm not casing the joint, as you put it. I was looking around. I hoped to see if I could figure out what happened. That's all." He put his right hand up in a Boy Scout salute. "Scout's honor!"

The woman relaxed and put her pepper spray back in her pocket. "I'm Pam Tullus., Mr. Kelley's daughter." She moved toward Ted with her hand out. Ted was hesitant, then put out his hand, and they shook. "I want to thank you for being here for my dad."

"No problem." Ted looked down and did not make eye contact when he spoke.

"Look, I'm on the way to check on dad. Come with me. He will want to thank you. For what you did last night."

"Is he alright?" asked Ted.

"I spoke to his doctor last night, and he said dad should be fine. He said Dad is lucky you found him. Or the outcome might not be positive."

Pam had a new black C-class Mercedes-Benz. Pam pointed

to her key fob and pushed a button. There was a beep, lights flashed, and the car was unlocked. Pam started the car and drove the short ride to Mercy Hospital.

On the way, Ted learned both Pam and her husband were lawyers. They had a small private practice in Woodland, about ten miles away. She comes at least once a month to visit her dad and take him for a ride in his pride and joy, a bright red Ford Ranger. Jack nick-named his truck the Red Ranger. Pam's husband, Eliot, did not come on those trips. If you believe Pam, Eliot was fond of saying, "No man, six-four is going to fit with two others in a little Ford Ranger." So instead, he comes when something needs fixing around the house.

Pam parked her car in the garage, and the two entered the hospital. They stopped at the information desk and were given directions to Mr. Kelley's room.

"Hi, Dad," Pam said with exuberance. She walked over and kissed her dad on the forehead. "How are you feeling this morning?"

"How do you think I feel? I fell and knocked myself out." Touching his head, he said, "There is a knot the size of a walnut." Pointing to Ted, "Who's the kid?"

"He's the one who found you. He saved your life." Pam stood and smiled at her dad.

Jack studied Ted for a moment and then frowned. "I know you. You run with that rotten Jimmy Dickens."

"Dickenson," Ted corrected.

"Whatever. The guy is no good. Anybody hanging with him ain't no good neither."

Ted remained behind Pam, motionless and biting his lower lip. Ted's hands were in his pockets, and he was rocking back and forth.

Pam whirled around, looking first at Ted, then her dad, and

back to Ted. She did her best to hide the surprise her dad's last remark created.

Mr. Kelley broke the spell. "Pam. I'm tired of water and sips of juice. Can you see if you can round up a diet soda for me? I need to thank Ted. For last night."

Pam nodded and left.

◆ ◆ ◆

On the way to the hospital, Pam said her dad turned 61 last month. The old man looked decades older. His hospital gown didn't fit right, and there was an IV in his right arm and a heart monitor beeping. Jack needed a shave and a haircut.

"So, did you find it?"

For a moment, Ted found it challenging to breathe. There was a sour taste in his mouth.

Recovering, "I'm sorry, Mr. Kelley. I don't know what you mean," Ted said.

"You know, the money everyone thinks is hidden in the house." He winked.

"I didn't see any money. But then, I didn't look." Ted's heart was racing as he said this.

"Well, there isn't any. I keep maybe 20 or 30 dollars in my wallet. I pay everything with a credit card Pam gives me."

"Good idea," Ted said, meaning it.

Pam brought a can of Diet Dr. Pepper and a straw. She gave it to her dad and watched him take a few sips.

Changing the topic of discussion with Jack, Ted asked, "What happened anyway?"

"Dad's a stubborn diabetic. Type 2, and he is on medication. Dad did not take his pill yesterday and did not eat according to his doctor's guidelines." Pam took a deep breath. "As a result, his blood sugar dropped, and so did he. Napper sensed something was wrong and kept barking for help. The doctor said he may also have had a small stroke. They are waiting for test results now."

"Dang dog. I did not have a stroke. And I promise I did not pass out. Instead, I tripped over the mutt running circles around my feet. I hit my head, got a concussion, and passed out. If you're telling the story, get it right!"

"I am, Dad. The doctor called when you were admitted. He said, you're lucky Ted came by. Without medical attention, you might not have made it."

Needing to talk to Ted alone, Pam said, "Dad, neither Ted nor I have eaten this morning. Unlike you, living the life of leisure, we have things to do. We are going to the cafeteria. We will be back in an hour. Let the nurses do their job without your harassing them. OK?"

Waving his hand, "Whatever, go!"

Pam got a bagel and coffee. Ted settled for a Dr. Pepper. Pam led them to a table in the corner, pretty much away from everyone else.

After a few minutes of absolute silence, Pam broke the spell. "We need to talk."

"'Bout what?" asked Ted.

"You, my dad, and the whole situation."

"Look," Ted interrupted, "I did not break into the house to rob, steal, or whatever you think I was planning. I heard the dog, I got concerned, and I did what I did."

"Relax," Pam said, looking Ted in the eye. She gave Ted a reassuring smile. "You are not in trouble. Everybody believes you did what you said you did."

After his conversation with Mr. Kelley, Ted knew the last statement was not accurate.

Ted sat watching her. Then, finally, he sat back in his chair. His hands-on the table, and he looked at his shoes.

"I asked Eliot."

Ted looked up in surprise and asked, "Who's Eliot?"

"My husband. I told you he is a lawyer, too."

"But I thought you said."

"Ted, we don't know you, and while our instincts told us you were OK, we are lawyers, and it is in our nature to check people out." Pam took a breath. "You turned out fine. No police record. There is no evidence of trouble. You graduated from high school in the lower quarter of your class, but that is not an indictment."

"Try telling my dad," Ted said, looking down again.

"Anyway, you do hang with a few questionable friends, but we are not judging you by your friends. We, Eliot, and I, believe, deep down, you are a good guy. Your parents split a while back, and you live with your dad, who drinks a lot. Many kids in your shoes may have chosen a different path. You stayed at home. Whether you want to admit it or not, you love your dad, and you are at home to keep him safe."

"Safe from what?" Ted asked with his head still lowered.

Ted studied her for a moment.

"From himself," Pam said, looking at Ted.

"Look," Pam started again, "My dad is old, and truthfully, he has lost some of his spunk. When mom died, part of him died with her. So, dad is stuck at home."

"He's got the truck."

"But no keys." Pam stopped and, dropping her voice, she said, "He has a form of dementia. He might also have had a series of small strokes. Before we took the keys from him, he got lost coming home from the grocery two blocks away."

"I didn't know," Ted said. He was looking at Pam.

"We had two options. But unfortunately, neither was good for dad."

"Had?"

"Yes. We could hire a live-in caregiver or put him in an assisted living facility. Our home is large enough. We can accommodate Dad to come and live with us. But all three options would tell Dad he is approaching the point." There was a pause, "Of losing his independence."

"Bummer," murmured Ted.

"I agree," Pam said in almost a whisper.

Studying Pam, Ted asked, "You now have another option? A third option?"

"Yes. You." Pam paused and observed Ted for a reaction.

"Me?" Ted asked, shaking his head. "I am no caregiver." Ted paused and looked at Pam for a long second. "You don't even know me. Sure, I know Mr. Kelly, but only by name. We speak when we pass each other on the street. However, I have never had a conversation with him."

"I know. Dad disapproves of your choice of friends, but he has also noticed a difference between you and them."

"Difference? What difference?"

"You don't act like them. You," pausing as Pam searched for the right word, "are just different. You seem to have matured–grown up a bit since your mother left."

"He knows my mother?"

"Like you said. He was polite and spoke to her to at the store. Thingd like that."

"I still am not a babysitter. Especially not for a grown man!"

"Dad, Eliot, and I talked on the phone last night, and Dad offered a suggestion."

"I am still to be his babysitter?"

"No one wants that." Then, after a short pause, Pam continued, "Dad has agreed to be YOUR caregiver."

"Now, wait a blessed minute! I'm not nuts, and I don't need anyone taking care of me!"

"You're right, but hear me out, OK?"

Ted clenched his teeth and blankly stared ahead. Finally, he slumped in his chair with his arms folded in defiance.

"I don't care what you cooked up last night." With his hands in a stop motion, he said, "I am not a babysitter."

"Right. No babysitting." Pam waited a few minutes for Ted

to calm down.

"What Eliot and I propose," and paused. She took a deep, calming breath and continued, "We want you to move in with dad. Dad tells me you live at home, so you would be close enough to your own dad to be able to keep tabs on him and let my dad believe his life still has value."

There was silence. Ted watched Pam take a bite of her bagel and a sip of coffee.

"I'm not sure his dog likes me. It keeps nipping at my ankle." This was a lie. Ted and the dog were getting along fine.

"Not a problem. The dog nips at everyone's ankle." Pam's turn to tell a lie. The dog barks and runs around but has never nipped anyone's ankle. "Tell you what, I will take the dog home with me for a while. Once you and dad have adjusted to the new arrangement. I will bring Napper back. Then, the two of you can become best buds."

Ted sat there for several minutes without saying anything. Then, finally, Ted closed his eyes in contemplation.

"If I do this. I am not saying I will. What do I have to do?"

"Simple. Keep dad company. Make sure he stays on his diet. If he needs to go somewhere. If he wants to go for a ride. You load him up in that Ranger of his, and you go."

"I don't know. Sitting around all day and night. Sounds boring."

"You are right. It would be boring. If that is all you did."

Ted interrupted, "I knew there had to be a catch."

"Not a catch. More of an opportunity."

"I'm listening," Ted said, folding his arms.

"First, we're going to pay you. $30 an hour for eight hours a day. You will live with dad, rent-free. We will pay for groceries."

"Gotta be more. This is way too easy."

"You are right. There is one more thing. You must go to school. You need to enroll at Emmerson College and get your associates degree."

"First, I'm no brainiac. As you said, I graduated at the bottom."

"Lower quarter," Pam interrupted.

"Whatever. The point is I don't have the grades. To get into Emmerson. Or any other school. What's more, I can't afford school. So, I work at Taco Bell for minimum wage."

"Dad wants to pay for it. He thinks you are staying with him in exchange for room and board. He wants to give you more."

"Can he afford it?"

"Are you familiar with KBW – Kettering Battery Works?"

"Sure," Ted said with a nod. "They have a process to recycle and recharge those batteries in electric cars. It is supposed to be safe for humans and for the environment. Also, it makes all those electric cars more affordable."

"Well, KBW did not develop the technology on their own."

"No?" Ted was now interested.

"No. The technology was developed by a small company here in town called JK Industries, and KBW bought everything from JK Industries."

"So, they bought everything and are making millions."

"You're right about them making millions, but they did not buy everything. They could not buy the patent. So, they pay a royalty to the patent owner for every battery they recycle and recharge using that technology. They also paid millions for the original factory and exclusive rights to the technology."

"JK – your dad, Jack Kelley?"

Pam smiled and nodded. "He's worth millions, and he wants to spend a few pennies on you and your education."

"And if I can't get in?"

"It's a junior college; there are no admission tests. However, there is a Test of Adult Basic Education that will measure your English and math proficiency. Because of your class ranking, you will have to take the test. I am confident you will do well."

"What happens if I fail the test and can't get in."

"Ted, you can't fail the test. If you meet the minimum proficiency level, you can begin taking courses for your degree."

"And if I don't."

"I have been watching you and listening to you. I am a pretty good judge of character. As a lawyer, it is my job. I don't believe for a moment your grades are indicative either of your intelligence or your abilities. I have every confidence you can and will meet those minimum expectations. But should you fall short, they will put you in remediation classes to bring your skills up to the appropriate level."

"And if they can't."

"They can, but Ted, I am serious. You can do this."

Pam got up and gathered up her purse. She put the remnants of the bagel and coffee in the trash. Then waited for Ted to follow her lead. When he got to the trash can, she said, "You don't give me your answer right now."

"When do I have to give you an answer?"

"When we get to dad's room. Dad will make you the same offer. In his gruff tone, of course. And you will have to give him your answer then. Are you up to it?"

He nodded, and they left the cafeteria. Ted's head was spinning. He considered all that had happened in less than an hour. He was wondering what he should do. More to the point, he was thinking. Thinking about what he wanted to do. Was this his ticket out? Or were there more conditions ahead? As he headed back to Jack's room, Ted considered everything he was told. Ted stood at the door watching Pam going over, took her dad's hand. They had a conversation out of Ted's earshot. Ted had not yet made his decision.

CHAPTER 4

PAM CALLED THAT morning. It was Monday and would be a hectic week indeed. Although she had talked to the doctor and her dad would be ready for discharge at 9:30. Ted was to be at the hospital at least a half-hour earlier. No need to keep Jack waiting. Pam was confident Ted would live up to expectations. However, there was that doubt. She wanted to have the same level of confidence her father demonstrated. It just was not there.

On Sunday afternoon, Ted took the truck for a spin. First, he filled it up with gas, then ran it through the tunnel wash. Next, Ted stopped at Kroeger to pick up groceries for the week. After that, he stripped Jack's bed, washed the bedding, and did a general housecleaning. With the dishwasher was running, he put everything away before hitting the hay for the night.

Jack was up, dressed, and impatiently pacing, waiting for his new caretaker to arrive. Although he exuded confidence in front of Pam, Jack had many of her same misgivings. What Ted did in saving Jack's life was extraordinary. The rest was a mess. His choice of friends and no ambition or goal in life. A year after graduating, Ted's life lacked direction. Then Jack heard Ted coming down the hall and relaxed. Ted found Jack sitting in the room's only chair. Jack tried to hide his smile.

"You need to go to the business office, or they won't let me out," Jack said matter-of-factly. He grunted and dismissed Ted with the wave of a hand.

"Got it. Be right back." Then Ted disappeared down the hall. Jack relaxed when Ted left for the business office. He let out an audible sigh. Jack's grin filled his face, and he chuckled to himself. Jack was confident he had made the right decision.

When he located the business office, Ted entered and signed a few papers. Pam had arranged the bill's payment and authorized Ted to pick Jack up. Ted gathered everything and headed back to Jack's room. When he got off the elevator, Ted saw a nurse with a wheelchair. Jack was in it, but he was not too happy. He wanted to walk out independently.

"It is about time." Jack had a hint of a smile. He raised his hands in victory saying, "Let's get out of here."

"Nice wheels."

"Shut up. This nurse says I can't walk out on my own." Then, pointing to the nurse, "Don't let her good looks fool you; she is a slave driver."

The nurse smiled at Ted and quietly said, "Hospital rules." Then leaning down and patting Jack on the shoulder, "For everybody."

Neither Ted nor Jack said much on the way out. Not for lack of trying on Ted's part. Every statement was met with silence. Occasionally Ted got that stare saying, "Give it up!"

Ted was not sure of what Pam had talked him into doing. Was he taking care of Jack? Or was it the other way around? As for Jack, he had always been a risk-taker. It was more hope than concern about taking Ted on as his new "roomie," as Jack called Ted when discussing the arrangements with Pam. Neither was sure how Ted would react to Jack's stubborn ways. Jack's truck had an extended cab. Ted put the old man's stuff behind the seats. They got in the truck and left.

"You wash the truck?" More of an affirmation than a question.

"I thought you'd like to come home in a clean truck. The gas tank is full if you want to drive a bit before we go home."

"How many miles you put on Ranger while I've been laid up?"

"Whatever was necessary to get things ready for you. You know, getting gas, getting it washed, and picking a few groceries."

"Anything else?" Jack said, eyeing his driver but not looking his way.

Deciding the meet Jack's sarcasm with some of his own, Ted said, "Oh, I did take a trip to Mount Rushmore. Got back in time to get you." They both laughed, and the tension was eased considerably.

During the ride, Ted kept his eyes on the road. He did not look at his passenger.

"I've been couped up a while. I am happy to ride a bit."

"Let's swing by Lakeside Park?" asked Ted.

"Fine with me." Jack was taking in the scenery he knew so well. He found it relaxing to be outside in more than a week.

"The doctor says you need exercise. Lakeside has a path around the park. We'll try one lap; it will do us both good. There are benches along the way if you get winded."

That got a reaction. Jack turned and stared at Ted. "And if I don't want to exercise?"

"Fine, you sit at a picnic table, and I'll jog my five miles while you watch."

"Or?" Jack asked with a raised brow.

"Or we will stroll one lap around the track, more if you feel up to it. I don't want to tire you out."

"I can do laps around you any day," Jack said without enthusiasm.

It was a warm, sunny day. People filled the park enjoying the day. Ted and Jack completed a half lap when a barking golden retriever came up to Jack and stopped. The dog sat and looked at Jack while dusting the path with its tail. It was evident two knew each other. Ted noticed an attractive woman jogging up to them. The woman appeared younger and was shorter than Jack. She was slender and dressed for exercising. Whatever her hair color was when she was younger, the woman now had beautiful, shiny white hair cut short. She came up to them and grabbed the dog's collar.

While smiling at Jack, she said, "Jack's been looking for his namesake. When he saw you, he took off running. Sorry about that." With her attention on the dog, she said, "He's missed you."

Jack smiled and ruffled the hair on the dog's head. "How have you been, old boy? I sure have missed you."

Jack introduced Ted to Ruthie. He explained it has been a while since the two were at the park together.

"And the name?" asked Ted.

"I took Ruthie to a friend who giving away puppies. Ruthie pointed and said, "Jack, look at that one. The pup stopped, looked at her, and ran to her. The dog has been called Jack ever since."

Elbowing Ted and then bending over to pet the dog again, Jack explained, "The trouble is. Elbowing Ted, Jack said, "I am never sure if she is yelling at me or calling her dog."

"I heard about your scare," Ruthie said. "Are you doing alright?"

Still petting the dog, "Ted, here is my new roomie. Pam has got him to get me out exercising today. He says I have to make at least one lap," talking more to the dog than his human friend.

"That'll do you good. Let me know next time. Maybe we can make it a foursome. You, me, Ted, and the four-legged Jack." She laughed when she suggested the walk.

Ruthie and her four-legged Jack retreated to the dog park. Ted and Jack did one more lap and headed home.

"Hungry?" asked Ted.

"I could use a jelly doughnut. We should have stopped at Mary Lou's on the way home." Mary Lou's was the local doughnut shop. Unlike the chains, Mary Lou's did not fill your doughnut until ordered. And you could then request any filling you desired. Chain shops put a single shot of filling in the doughnut. Mary Lou's put in two.

"Why didn't we stop and get that doughnut you were dreaming about?"

Ted did not immediately respond. "Not on your diet. How about a fried egg?"

On the way back, they enjoyed the scenery in silence. Ted pulled into the driveway. Jack went into the house. Ted put the truck in the garage.

"Who created this no doughnut rule?" Jack asked as he surveyed the clean house.

"Your daughter and your doctor set the rules. I'm the hired hand following orders," Ted said as he set about setting the table and getting the eggs from the fridge."

"Warden, am I allowed to have any meat or bread with the egg?"

"Yes," Ted said, giving Jack a mock angry look. "We've got bacon, sausage, and wheat toast. For your sweet tooth, we have sugar-free Smucker's Strawberry." There was a slight pause as Ted got out the fry pan and vegetable oil spray.

"How do you want your eggs?" Ted asked without looking at him.

"Up. Is there any other way? Have to let in the sunshine!"

"OK, bacon or sausage?"

"Sausage." Jack walked over to the coffee table and picked

up his mail.

"One or two?" Ted asked as he lit the stove and started warming the pan.

"Two links and one piece of wheat toast."

"Coming right up, sir," Ted said in his best waiter's imitation.

"Any coffee?" asked Jack as he dumped the junk mail in the trash.

"Get your own. It's fresh decaf. Made it this morning." Ted said while he busied himself with making breakfast.

"I hate decaf!" Jack growled.

"Tell the boss,"

"Pam?"

"Pam!"

"She's not here. She doesn't have to know."

"True, but she has this uncanny sense that detects any attempt to deceive."

"That's my daughter for you. Ever since she passed that blasted bar exam, I haven't been able to pull anything over on her." Jack got a cup from the cupboard and poured himself a cup of coffee. "Good thing I like it black, or we'd be arguing over cream and sugar."

Jack sat down at the table and took a sip of coffee. He then began to open and read the mail. There were a few advertisements and bills. He handed Ted the bills to put in the basket on the counter. Ted put the plate of food down in front of him.

"What? How am I supposed to eat this?"

"Sorry about that," Ted said. He gave Jack a knife and fork, and a paper towel napkin. "Warden was concerned you might get violent." They both laughed. Back at the stove, Ted fixed his own eggs.

"What's on the agenda?"

"I've got to run to my dad's and check on him. I am not aware if he knows where I am now. He was pretty drunk when I last saw him. So anyway, I go over and do a bit of house cleaning. You know, make his bed, run the dishwasher and make sure he has food."

"Does he know you are doing this?"

"Don't know, don't care," said Ted.

"Then why?"

"It is what I did on those days when he worked. Love my dad but can't live there. Too depressing."

Jack and Ted talked for a bit about nothing important. After breakfast, with dishes in the sink, they settled in the living room. Jack turned on *The Price is Right*. After the first spin to determine the final showcase, Ted left. He headed to his dad's house.

It is a fifteen-minute walk from Jack's house to his dad's house. It took Ted a little over an hour doing his usual. His dad's bed was made. Dirty dishes were on the table. Ted put those in the dishwasher and started it.. The trash was full. So, he tied it up and put it in the big trash can. Returning, he replaced the bag. He placed it under the sink. Satisfied everything was done, Ted locked the door and headed back to Jack's house.

Ted returned to find Jack in the living room. The television was on. Jack, however, was asleep in his recliner. Ted quietly went to his room. He glanced at the information he had received from Emmerson College.

Ted checked on the sleeping Jack and then returning to the scrapbook room, as Ted had begun to call the third bedroom, and began re-organizing its contents. It had taken a couple of days. Now the room was presentable. On the one hand, Ted enjoyed glancing through the albums and the loose photos. On the other hand, Ted also felt guilty about invading Jack's privacy.

Ted was a pretty good chef. At least he was pretty good at following recipes. Ted had prepared a meatloaf from his mother's recipe book, new potatoes, and asparagus for dinner. The two sat at the dinner table without saying much.

"Thank you," Jack said out of the blue.

"For what?" a puzzled Ted asked.

"For cleaning up the scrapbook mess. I haven't been able to do since Jess died."

"I wasn't sure how you would react." There was a brief pause, then Ted added, "I didn't do much. I put everything into piles. I put the loose photos in a box. If you want to, we can go through them when you're ready."

"Nah." Jack was quiet for a few minutes as he had his head down, staring at his food. "Scrapbooking was Jessica's thing. She was awesome with it. I'm not ready to do much with it."

Breakfast the following day was coffee, toast, and Cheerios with blueberries.

"I will be at Emmerson most all morning," Ted said in a matter-of-fact tone. "You be alright?"

"Sure. Go do what you have to do. When does school start?"

"I've got to take this TABE test first thing this morning. Then I meet with my academic counselor, a Mrs. Logan, and we'll decide what goes next. Either way, classes start a week from Monday."

"Good luck on the test. I was always a horrible test-taker," teased Jack.

Laughing, Ted said, "Thanks. I think I will need it."

The Slauson Testing Center was on the Emmerson College campus. Because it gave tests for a variety of purposes, entering the actual testing area was restricted. Therefore, when Ted signed in, he was given a lock.

"Take everything out of your pockets and put it in the locker. That includes pens, pencils, your wallet, loose change you can put in here. Don't forget to put your cellphone in the locker." The girl behind the desk gave him a baggie. "When you have everything in the locker, close it and lock it. Pull your pants pockets inside out."

There was a girl behind the desk, presumably a college student. She wore no name tag, but the desk plate said, Check-In. The ritual completed, and the girl satisfied Ted had nothing with him, they entered a large room. Computers were lined along each wall. She guided him to a computer in the middle on the left wall.

"The blue ticket is your test log-on information. You will have two and half hours to complete the test. There are two tests. You choose which test to complete first. If you need to use the restroom, try to do it between tests. Once you have completed the tests, bring me the blue ticket, and I'll give you a key to your lock. There is also paper and pencil if needed." She pointed to a couple of sheets of lined notebook paper and two pencils. "Leave them at the computer when you have finished. Any questions?"

"No, I think I've got it," Ted said.

"Great, your time starts when you log into your first test. Good luck!"

She was shorter than Ted, and he thought she was cute. Ted watched her until she closed the door to the testing room. For the first time, Ted realized he was alone in the testing center. Ted finished in an hour and forty-five minutes and was out the door. Ted had half an hour before his appointment with Mrs. Logan and took the opportunity to stroll around the campus. The campus was large, with a lot of green space and shade trees. There was an open court area in front of the student center. A large fountain in the middle with a fish facing upward, spouting water out of its mouth. The school was between semesters, and Ted had the campus to himself. Inside, Ted found a snack bar and the bookstore, bought a pastry of unknown origin, and a

Coke. He sat at a table enjoying his snack as he contemplated what he was about to do.

Mrs. Logan was a middle-aged woman with long, braided brown hair. She had a friendly smile for him when he entered her office. Mrs. Logan was obviously a runner; given the various running numbers, the kind he had seen on marathon runners, he assumed she was athletically inclined. Mrs. Logan had an engaging smile as she motioned Ted to a chair in front of her desk and took the big green office chair behind the desk. They exchanged pleasantries. Mrs. Logan did a little typing and made some notes. Then, after three excruciating minutes, she got down to business.

"Mr. James, as I told you, the TABE test would determine when you could begin course work. Or if you would need remedial classes."

"I remember. How did I do?" There was a hesitancy in his voice. Ted was unsure he wanted to hear the results.

"I have to say, considering your transcript, I had more than a few reservations. Most students with your academic record generally require at least a semester of remediation. However, I have the results of your tests, and they are excellent. The minimum proficiency level for the reading test is 1320. You scored 1790. For math, the minimum proficiency is 1450. You scored 1430."

"So, what does that mean?"

"It means you do not have to take any remedial classes. Although you did not meet the minimum for math, your reading score was high enough, so the combined scores put you outside the criteria for remediation. Let's see what classes are available."

Before he left, Mrs. Logan stopped him. "Winston," Ted did not correct her, "you graduated near the bottom of your high school class, and yet you can do so much more. Why?"

Ted wanted to ask, "Why what?" But he knew what she meant. "My family situation, I guess. I mean, I just didn't see the point of putting for the effort."

"You have a second chance," Mrs. Logan said and smiled at Ted. "Don't disappoint me. But, more importantly, don't disappoint yourself."

◆ ◆ ◆

An hour later, Ted had his schedule. English and a history class were on Tuesday and Thursday mornings. He had an interpersonal communication class on Monday and Wednesday evenings, which Mrs. Logan said was a speech class. Biology was on Tuesday and Thursday afternoons for a total of twelve hours. Twelve hours is considered a full load. Ted was happy he had three days without classes. He also had three evenings free.

Jack was waiting for Ted when he got home.

Jack met Ted at the door, "We're going out for dinner."

Caught by surprise, Ted took a moment to recover. "But it not even a quarter after."

"I know. Ruthie's brother owns The Lobster Shack in Villa Nueva, about 45 minutes down the road. But plan on an hour's drive. Dinner is at six. Ruthie's daughter is a nursing student at Emmerson. They invited the two of us for dinner. I'm buying!" He stood there with an ear-to-ear smile on his face.

"Well, get going! We've got to be on the road no later than 4:45."

"What time is it?" asked Ted, hustling to get ready.

"You can slow down. We have time. Since it is not even 4:15 by my watch," and then laughed.

"What is the occasion?" Ted wanted to know.

Jack shrugged his shoulders. "How am I supposed to know? I didn't set this up."

"Ever meet her daughter?" Ted wanted to know.

"Maureen? Lots of times. Sweet girl. Has her mother's disposition and looks!"

Ted shook his head. "Matchmaker?"

"Not me, but I can't speak for Ruthie. Now, go get ready!" At 4:40, they were on the road.

◆ ◆ ◆

On the way to the restaurant, Ted kept an eye on his passenger. Jack was sitting there listening to the radio, but not really hearing it. Ted had something on his face. It was somewhere between a smile a grin. Ted wanted desperately to ask Jack what was going on. Instead, he elected to drive in silence. It was nice to be with people. Mostly, they confined themselves to the house.

Ted and Jack rolled into the parking lot at 5:30 on the dot. Ruthie's little red convertible was parked at the end of the row.

"They're here already," Jack announced. "That little red thing," pointing to a red Camaro convertible, "is Ruthie's."

When they entered the restaurant, the hostess expected them and led them to the table where Ruthie and her daughter were seated. There was a long, curved padded bench with several tables. Each table had two chairs opposite the bench. Ruthie and her daughter were sitting on the bench. The guys took the chairs. Jack sat across from Ruthie and, without hesitation, reached out for her hand and mouthed, "Thank you."

Ruthie was a widow, and Jack, a widower. Most did not understand nor appreciated this kind of bond. They liked each other and looked forward to the times they spent together. Each provided the other with the friendship they wanted with the understanding they needed. Instinctively, they knew the other's thoughts. Words were not necessary. Neither passed up the opportunity to be together. These opportunities were mostly unexpected and spontaneous.

Ted sat opposite Maureen. Jack's description did not do her justice. She was shorter than Ted by at least three inches. Her fiery red hair was cut short, like her mother's. Her deep green eyes met Ted's, and her smile was both mischievous and disarming. Her voice, when she introduced herself, was soft and silky. Later, when asked, Ted described Maureen in one word. Gorgeous.

Maureen dominated the conversation between the two of them. If Maureen had a question, she asked it. If she had an opinion, she stated it. Ted was at first taken aback by her directness. He was also hypnotized by her unabashed curiosity.

By the end of the dinner, Ted and Maureen had exchanged phone numbers and agreed it would be nice to have lunch together on campus when their schedules would allow.

"Well?" asked Jack. "What do you think?"

"About Maureen?" Ted asked.

"Of course, about Maureen."

"Gorgeous. And funny. But definitely gorgeous!"

As they strolled through the restaurant, neither Ruthie nor Maureen said a word. Instead, they found the car, got in, and were soon on the road.

On the way home, Ruthie noticed her daughter relaxed, with a hint of a smile on her face and softly humming an unfamiliar tune.

"You and Ted seemed to hit it off," Ruthie said by way of observation.

Not looking at her mother, Maureen sighed heavily. "He is the most interesting guy I've met in a long time. Maybe ever."

Expecting Maureen to continue. Instead, she kept smiling and humming.

"So, you like him?"

"In a word, of course."

"That's two words," corrected Ruthie.

"Oh, Mother!" Maureen exclaimed and turned to her mother.

Ruthie focused on the road ahead. "Like him enough to see him again?"

Then, smiling at her mother, Maureen asked, "Are you and Jack playing matchmaker?"

"Now, would either of us do that? To the two of you?"

"Without a doubt," Maureen said to her mother. She settled back in her seat. The smile returned to her face. The tune could be heard again. Softly Maureen murmured, "Without a doubt."

Ruthie reached over, patted her daughter's arm, and thought to herself, "Without a doubt, indeed!"

CHAPTER 5

THE TWO WEEKS between testing, scheduling, and the first day of class flew by.

Jack decided Ted's bedroom needed a fresh coat of paint, and after three trips to Sherwin-Williams, they agreed on a neutral beige. As Jack and Ted were painting, they talked, joked, and had a good time. The two were clearly enjoying each other's company.

Jack's and Ted's arrangement turned out better than expected. After Jessica had passed, Jack began to withdraw. He saw Ruthie occasionally, but there was still a void in his life. When Jess was alive, they would joke and tease one another, and Ted was beginning to help fill that void. Finally, there was someone to talk with other than Matt Dillon. He was glad he had listened to his instincts.

Ted was Leary of the old man. Sure, they were polite on the street. But people regarded Jack as being rude and grumpy. Ted expected an angry and bitter man. Instead, Ted found a man with a wonderful sense of humor. He both livened up the place and brought Ted out of his own shell. Ted loved his dad, but he could not say they were friends. Through Jack, Ted learned what it was like to have a friend. More importantly, Ted learned how to be a friend.

"You know, I painted this room right before Jessica died. The pastel blue doesn't fit for a single guy, and that's why I decided we need to paint the room."

"I appreciate that. The blue made me feel as if I was sleeping in a fishbowl." Ted opened the paint and added more to his roller pan. As he began painting again, Ted asked, "How long were you married?"

"Jessica and I were soulmates in high school. I joined the Marine Reserves and did a two-year active-duty stint at Cherry Point, North Carolina. I was an aviation mechanic. It's where I learned to do the tinkering I did later on. Jessica and I got married when my active-duty tour was over. Unfortunately, Jess passed away a year and a half ago of pancreatic cancer on our 53rd anniversary, April 5th is both the happiest day in my life. It is also saddest. Happiest because it is when we got married. Saddest because it is also the day I lost her."

They painted in silence for a few minutes. As Ted observed his new friend and caught Jack's lower lip quivering.

Jack picked up the conversation again. "Jess loved scrap-booking. She'd study a picture. She did not see the picture. She saw the story it told. For the hundredth time, Jess would tell me the story. About why, when, and where. There was one good thing, f you can call it that. The cancer was aggressive. She did not suffer long. We had three months from diagnosis to funeral. She would go into the scrapbook room and spend hours. She sat looking at what she started and completed. I would listen and talk to her for hours. I go in there now and then. I talk with her. In some ways, she is still here."

"I'm sorry. I didn't know." Ted dropped his gaze to the floor.

"Don't tell Pam. She'll have me in the looney-bin for sure."

They both laughed. "My lips are sealed," Ted said with a zipping motion across his lips.

Finished, the room had a more masculine vibe. Ted left, and an hour later, began hanging pictures he brought from his house. Photos of his parents and a calendar with scenes of Italy.

"Mom had a bit of Italian blood in her and dreamed of going. She never had the opportunity. I have seen some beautiful pictures of Venice, Florence and Rome. Maybe I can go one day."

Jack looked at the pictures. "You realize, Emmerson has a study abroad program. Ruthie said Maureen is thinking about going next year. So, you might consider it. Know why?"

"Maureen is going, and you are playing match-maker," Ted said with a smile.

"And that would be a bad thing?" Jack asked with a sly grin on his face. Then with a more severe face, "No, you Goofus. They are going to Italy. So, here's your chance to check that trip off your bucket list, and the company won't be too shabby either, eh?" Jack slapped Ted on the back. As they gathered up the painting materials, Jack said, "Let's get cleaned up. I'm famished. If you don't mind Mexican, I'll treat at Gringo's."

"You're on," said Ted with newfound enthusiasm. Ted was smiling while cleaning the brushes and rollers.

Ted liked Jack. He even started to appreciate him.

Ted had a fried avocado stuffed with shredded chicken and a shrimp taco. Jack had his usual Sombrero Plate of three beef enchiladas. The conversation was light and alive as Jack told life with Jessica. It was an enjoyable evening, and Ted felt that he and Jack were bonding and becoming friends.

Nights in Jack's house were often quiet. However, this night was different. Ted awakened to a sound coming from the living room. Ted listened intently but could not identify the sound. Finally, he looked at the alarm clock; it showed 2:30 in the morning. Ted lay still for a few minutes. and then realized it was Jack talking to someone. Ted lay in his bed, listening. He realized Jack was not talking to Ruthie. Still, he had no idea to whom Jack could be talking. Not at this hour.

Ted got up. In the dark, he made his way to the living. He found Jack sitting on the couch with a side table lamp on low. He had one of the old scrapbooks on his lap, and he was talking and laughing as he pointed to various pictures. Jack would occasionally turn and talk as if someone were next to him. He would mention his late wife's name, Jess, and ask, "Do you remember when we got lost on that trip in Michigan?" He was smiling. "We thought we would still be there until December and decorating those beautiful trees. Remember? We sang that old Christmas song. 'Oh, Christmas Tree.'" Jack closed the scrapbook, leaned back, and glancing at the ceiling, Jack blew a kiss, then closed his eyes. Ted noticed a tear on Jack's face. It was barely visible.

Ted was quiet as a mouse as he returned to his room. He continued to listen. Within a few minutes, the talking stopped. Assured the silence was real, he again made his way to the living room. He found the closed scrapbook and Jack asleep on the couch. Unsure what he should do, Ted retrieved an extra blanket from his room. He covered Jack and studied him for several minutes. Ted then moved the scrapbook to the table's center.

Ted observed him for a few minutes. Ted saw Jack was smiling. Satisfied Jack was alright, Ted went back to his room.

At breakfast, Jack said nothing. He said nothing about the night's incident or sleeping on the couch. Ted checked the living room. The blanket had been folded. It was on the sofa. The book was closed. It remained where Ted had left it.

"I see you were looking at one of the scrapbooks."

"Sir?" Ted in surprise and hoped Jack did not notice.

"The scrapbook on the coffee table. You had it out, right?" It was apparent Jack did not remember the night's incident.

"Sorry, I meant to put it back before I hit the hay," Ted lied.

"One of these days, I will tell you about those pictures.

What day is it?"

"Wednesday," Ted answered.

"Oh, yeah. You'll be at your dad's this morning, right?"

"Do you need something? I don't have to go."

"Nah, go on over. I'll be fine for a few hours. James and I have a date." He held up the new James Patterson novel.

Ted cleared the table and put the dishes in the dishwasher. Ted told Jack, "I am going to my dad's house. I will be about an hour."

"Take your time." Then, holding up the book again, Jack said, "James and I will be fine."

Ted enjoyed the walk back to his old house. He realized it was trash day, relieved to see the trash can at the curb when saw dad's house. Ted did not see his dad's car and assumed he was at work. The house was neat and clean when Ted entered. Still, he walked through the house, inspecting each room. This was the cleanest he had seen his house since his mother left, and he moved in with Jack.

Ted filled the dishwasher with the dirty dishes. He added a few on the countertop and the sink. Ted did a second walk-through looking for dirty dishes or glasses. Ted found two glasses: one in his dad's bedroom, another one in the bathroom. Ted grabbed both and added them to those already in the dishwasher. He put a Cascade pod in its place. He closed the door and started the dishwasher.

"Thank you." The voice was quiet, firm, but friendly. Ted did not hear his dad come in. He was startled to see his dad in the doorway.

Ted looked bewildered but recovered quickly and said, "No problem."

Mack was clean-shaven with clean clothes on. Ted noticed the hamper was empty, so he assumed either Mack had mastered the washing machine or sent his laundry out.

"Do you have a minute to talk?" Mack asked, pointing to a dining table chair.

"Sure," said Ted. "I don't have school today." He found a safe place to sit.

"I'm not sure where to begin," started Mack.

"Start wherever you want," Ted said with a chill in his voice. His arms were folded across his chest.

"Look, Winston."

"Ted, I go by Ted now," he said to his father, dropping his crossed arms.

"OK, Ted. I realize I have been a monster. I hurt your mother and ran her off. I never physically hurt you, but I did worse. I made you hate me and hate your home."

"I don't hate you. I don't like you when you are drunk." Ted arched his shoulders with his arms out and palms up.

"Not that you will believe me, but I haven't had a drink since you left." Mack waited for a response and got none. Instead, he was pacing and bit his bottom lip. "I have been working full time, too."

"Today's Wednesday. Why aren't you at work?"

"I have a doctor's appointment in an hour. So, I took the morning off. I did not want to be late. I'll be on the job by one."

"How is the work going?"

"We're framing houses in a new subdivision in Avalon. Three hundred houses will be built there. Your uncle has a contract for 50. We should be busy for at least six months."

"Good for him." Ted always liked his uncle.

"There is more. I am now going to AA every Saturday morning."

"We talked about AA a lot before I left."

"I know. I didn't start out going to AA. I first went to church."

"Which one?" asked Ted, his curiosity piqued.

"The Reach. It's out on Broadway. Randy Gladstone is the

preacher there. He bought one of the houses we are building in the new subdivision. We talked, and I went to church that weekend. We talked a little after church, and he gave me a card. Turns out I am not the only one with a problem in his congregation. He reminded me we all have our crosses to bear."

"The house looks nice," taking the opportunity to change to subject.

◆ ◆ ◆

"Where are you living?"

"Do you know old man Kelley?"

"Yes."

"Well, he had a medical emergency a few nights ago. I found him and got him to the hospital. He and his family believe I saved his life."

"I am proud of you. You were always the thoughtful one in the family."

"Well, his family is paying me to stay with him. Mr. Kelley is a diabetic, The doctor said he may have also had a small stroke. They have also given me a scholarship to attend Emmerson College."

"Glad you can get a good education. I knew you had it in you."

There was a long pause.

"Look, Winston, uh, Ted. I appreciate what you have been doing. You coming over and making sure I was alright."

Ted monotoned, "Like I said, no problem."

"Son, don't."

This startled Ted, and he became angry, which his dad recognized.

"This is your house too, and you are always welcome. You don't have to sneak around. Come when I'm home. I'll be sober, and we won't fight. Promise!"

"I will think about it."

51

"What are you doing Saturday?" asked Mack with hesitancy in his voice.

"Nothing planned."

"And Mr. Kelley?" Mack continued.

"Don't know. I will check, but I don't think Jack has anything planned. Why?" Ted was studying his father for signals.

"I will grill couple stakes and have you over for dinner."

"And what will we be drinking?" Ted with an air of suspicion.

"Look in the fridge. Soft drinks, tea, and water are all I have to offer. Unless you want to drink orange juice with your steak."

"I'll pass on the juice. What time?"

"Sixish. I'll throw the steaks on the grill when you get here. Is Mr. Kelley able to eat steak with, you know, his diabetes?" There was genuine concern in Mack's demeanor.

"Yes, the steak will be fine. What can we bring?"

"Whatever you want to go with your steak."

"Jack makes a mean kale salad. How about we bring the salad?" Ted offered.

Pointing to the counter, "I got one of those new gizmos, and we'll have air-fried fries. Healthier for us all."

Looking at his watch, Ted said, "Dad, I've got to go. I don't like leaving Mr. Kelley alone too long. I will call later and confirm. On Friday, I'm making mom's lasagna. Want to come? We'll watch a Bond movie."

Mack and Ted looked at one another. Unsure what to do. Each wanted to hug. But they unsure how the gesture would be received. In the end, they shook hands, and Mack watched Ted walk up the street and out of sight. Reaching the house, Ted saw Jack was waiting for him at the door.

"Saw you coming up the street. How'd it go?"

"Better than anticipated."

"Come, tell me what happened." They were at the table. Jack brought back a couple of cans of Dr. Pepper and sat down with anticipation.

Ted laid out how the morning passed. The trash at the curb. The clean house and the unexpected encounter. And the invitation to steaks on Saturday. Jack thought it would be fine and agreed to make the salad.

"One more thing. I invited my dad over here for dinner on Friday. I'll make my mom's lasagna, and we can watch the latest Bond flick on Netflix. What do you think?"

"Sounds great. Give your dad a call and let him know it's a green light."

Ted found an unidentified weight had been lifted from his shoulders. He felt lighter and happier, given all that had happened that morning.

The two set up the card table and laid out a thousand-piece jigsaw puzzle picturing Venice's canals. After hearing about his potential trip to Italy, Jack bought the puzzle to get Ted excited about the possibility of traveling to Italy.

Jack had dumped the puzzle piece on the table and turned them face up. Out of the blue, Jack asked, "Ever hear from your friends?"

"What? Who?" Ted asked in a surprised voice.

"You know, Little Jimmie, what's his name."

"Jimmie and Freddie?" Ted asked.

"Yeah. Them two lowlifes." Jack never thought much of the two.

"What brought this trip down memory lane?"

"Had a nightmare, I guess."

"Yeah, right! Can we just work on this puzzle?"

"They're your friends," Jack said sarcastically.

"Jack!" Ted said and gave an exasperated look. "They are not really my friends. We just sort of hung out together. I haven't seen them, and I have not heard from them."

"OK, OK. I'll shut up" and connected three pieces together.

◆ ◆ ◆

The television was on. However, no one was watching. They had worked for a half-hour without saying much. Then, finally, Jack picked up a piece, looked, and studied it.

"I miss Napper," Jack said, not to anyone in particular.

"I hate to admit it, but I miss the mutt myself." Ted was smiling. "Tell you what. Let's go to Pam's Sunday. We'll bring him home."

When Ted hit the hay that evening. It had been awhile since he slept without tossing and turning.

CHAPTER 6

O N Thursday, Pam called Ted to tell him she and Eliot would be bringing Napper home on Saturday morning. She also needed to talk to Ted about a project the two were exploring. They were apprehensive about the impending change.

Ted and Jack got up. They made sure the house was ship-shape. Then, rather than dirtying dishes for breakfast, Ted used the money he was earning to treat both to breakfast at Gringos. Ted had his usual Migas, substituting chorizo for the traditional sausage. Jack had to limit the amount of meat he ate. He decided to experiment with scrambled eggs and cactus.

"So, why name the dog Napper?" Ted asked, looking over his coffee at Jack.

"We didn't. We named the dog George."

"And," Ted said, trying to hide a smile.

"He didn't like the name. Never did. He ignored us when we called him." Jack sipped his coffee. "George liked to sleep on Jessica's lap when she was in the glider reading, knitting, or sleeping. I said, 'look at that little napper.' His head shot up. He looked at me and barked once."

"Does he like the name Napper?"

"Beats me, but he does respond to it. An independent little cuss if you ask me."

They both laughed at the joke.

"So, did you trip over Napper?"

"Nah, did he nip at your ankles?

Ted realized the jig was up. He smiled and said, "Nah"

"Well, there you go!" said Jack. "I am glad he was not under-foot while we got you settled. But I sure miss the thing."

Looking thoughtfully at his plate, Ted said, "I can't say that I missed him, but, still I am glad he is coming home to where he belongs."

When they got back, a yellow Jeep Renegade was parked in the drive.

"Eliot drove today. Pam wouldn't be caught dead driving the Jeep. She enjoys her luxury too much."

Eliot opened the door, took Ted's hand, and introduced himself. "You must be the Ted I've heard about. I'm Pam's husband, Eliot."

"Glad to meet you," responded Ted.

Everyone was seated in the living room. Jack sat in the glider. Napper ran from person to person before hopping into Jack's lap and began to nap.

"How's school been going?" Pam inquired.

"3.75 GPA this mid-term. Biology is proving to be a bit more difficult than anticipated."

"It was for me too, Eliot aid. But hey, that's great."

"What about next term?" asked Pam.

Ted shot a glance at Jack, who winked and motioned him to continue.

"Every other year, those in the international studies group take a trip. This is an off year. So, no trip. I would like to go with them to Europe next year."

"Europe?" Pam responded.

"More specifically, Italy. Through Jack, I met a nursing student who got me into the program. Two years of a foreign language are required, and the school offers Italian. So, if I take

Italian next term, I will qualify to go. That is, if I can afford it."

"And are you taking Italian?"

"Mrs. Logan, my academic advisor, has approved my schedule for next term, and yes, it includes Italian."

"Learning a second language is always good. But Italian? So why not French or Spanish? What do you think, Jack?"

"Well, he did graduate last in his high school class," Jack said with a wink and a smile.

"Bottom quarter," Ted corrected.

"No one is asking, but I consider it is a splendid idea," interjected Eliot.

"When do you go? Before or after mid-term?"

"After."

"Good. Well then, if you maintain a 3.75 minimum GPA after next term, I expect we can extend your scholarship to include the trip."

"Thank you," Ted said, trying to hide his excitement.

"And this nursing student. Is she going also?" Pam asked, drawing out the question.

"Yes, she is planning to go," answered Ted.

"Do you like her? I mean," It was Eliot who was talking now.

"Do I need to draw you a picture? She is his age. She is cute. Heck, yes, he likes her." Jack bellowed, waking up Napper, who politely and barked three times and settled back down in Jack's lap.

"I am not sure what you mean," Ted said, looking at Eliot. "We are friends. Occasionally, we eat lunch together on campus. Maureen is doing her nursing practicum. She is a year ahead." Ted looked at Jack. "We have not gone on a date."

"Ted, you did too! You even had Ruthie and me along to chaperone." Jack said with a loud laugh. Napper sat up and looked at him. If a dog could give someone an evil eye, Jack got it from Napper. Jack looked down, petted the dog, and said, "OK. OK. I get the message. I'll be quiet so you can enjoy your nap."

Pam decided to change the subject. "Jack tells me you reconciled with your dad. Is that true?"

"Yes, mam. My dad and I are getting along much better now."

"You are staying with Jack here; is that problem?"

"No. Jack and I went over to my dad's once or twice. Dad has been here once or twice. So, everything is working out fine." Ted looked at both Pam and Eliot while he was talking.

"Mac, Ted's dad, has quit drinking, and he is working more steadily." said Jack. "But he realizes it is time for Ted to strike out on his own. I am not sure if he is happy with Ted being here. Mack and I had a long talk. Everything is copacetic," pointing to Ted, "as this college kid likes to say."

Ted turned and looked at Jack.

"Last Tuesday. It was raining, and he was home that day. I invited him over for coffee, and we talked. He is proud of you, Ted, and wants you to succeed."

Pam looked pleased and said, "Great. Now, Ted, we need to talk about phase two."

"Phase two? Heck, I didn't know there was a plan, let alone multiple phases."

"Nothing sinister. Is your dad home now?"

Ted thought so, called his dad and invited him over. A half hour later, Mack came in and joined the conversation.

Mack talked about working and his new life. and some things he wanted to do. Somewhere down the line.

Changing the subject again, Pam said, "We, Eliot and me, have decided it is time for dad to become a granddad." This produced a collective gasp from the audience.

"We've talked about it for a while time," announced Eliot. "We bought the house, and things got hectic at work. It is calming down now. We looked at everything, and this is the next logical step. We realize waiting until it is the right time, we will never have kids."

"To be honest," Pam said and stopped to look at her audience. "The family thing has adopted us." Then, she said, "I got suspicious and took a home test. It says I am going to be a mama."

Everyone cheered and asked a million questions-all at one time.

Pam raised her hand to stop the commotion. "I went to the doctor on Thursday, and the ultrasound confirmed. Should be here this summer!"

Jack sat there, beaming from ear to ear. Even Napper sensed something was up. He jumped down and was moving among the feet. "This calls for a celebration. Donavan's for dinner, my treat. I'll spring for the champagne, but you, my dear," looking at Pam, "will have to settle for sparkling white grape juice!"

Everyone laughed; Mack said he would join Pam with the grape juice.

"Make it a threesome," said Ted. "Unfortunately, I am too young to drink champagne."

"You guys continue with the jocularity, but I have to have a serious talk with Ted."

No one heard the comment. Pam touched Ted's arm and motioned him over to the dining table. "Have a seat. We need to talk."

"Am I in trouble?" Ted asked.

"No, not at all. Eliot and I are extremely pleased at how things are going."

"Are you firing me, then?"

"What?" asked a startled Pam. "Of course not, she said, reassuring Ted.

Ted was studying her, trying to determine what was about to come.

"Ted, let's turn back time. You are now a junior in high school."

"Boy, I hope not. I hated my junior year. That is one reason I was near the bottom in my class." Ted said, a smirk on his face.

"Well, when students are planning on attending college, they start the ball rolling in their junior year. They begin thinking what college they want to attend, and maybe what career path they might like to pursue."

"I'm in college now," Ted reminded her.

"I appreciate that, but where are you heading? What are your career goals?"

"This gig sprang up from out of nowhere," Ted reminded her. "To be honest, I haven't given much thought to an actual career."

"OK, that's pretty much what we thought. Listen, we have another proposal, a more permanent solution to everyone's needs."

"I'm listening." Ted had folded his arms and was becoming both nervous and skeptical.

"Southern State University has a branch at Emmerson College. So once you finish your associate's, you can continue and get your bachelor's from Southern State without leaving home."

"Home?"

"What I mean. You won't have to travel to Greendale, the closest Southern State physical campus, and that is an hour's drive each way. We can extend our arrangement until you graduate from State."

"And what do I study?"

Ted was beginning to get defensive, wondering what he had gotten himself into.

"Whatever you want. Want to teach, be an engineer, whatever tickles your fancy. You need a career path and living with Jack is not it. You know it, Jack knows it, and we know it."

"I don't have the money to attend Emmerson, let alone Southern State," Ted said with a note of disappointment and concern in his voice.

"When you graduate from Emmerson, changes will occur."

"I knew there had to be a catch," Ted said, louder than he intended. This caught the others' attention.

Pam waved, letting everyone know all was under control.

"I don't know what you're thinking, Ted. No trap being sprung on you."

Softening, Ted asked, "OK, so what is the catch?"

Pam opened a large envelope she had brought with her. Ted did not notice it when she had him join her at the table. Pam laid out brochures and announcements, and applications.

"First and foremost, Eliot and I like you. What you have done for Dad is more than we had expected."

"I like Jack." Ted smiled and took a quick glance at Jack. He could hear them talking football when Pam brought him back to her proposal.

"And he likes you, Ted." Pam touched Ted's forearm.

"Here is the information you need to be admitted to Southern State upon graduation from Emmerson. It needs to be done as soon as possible." She studied Ted for a long moment as he picked up and began reading the application form. Next, she handed him two other forms. "This first form is a government student-loan form. All state and most private colleges require you to file this for student aid. The next two are scholarship applications. Both Emmerson and Southern State have scholarships for which you qualify. Anything leftover we will cover as we have thus far."

"And what do I owe you once I graduate?" Ted wanted to know.

"Good question. The bottom line is you won't owe us anything."

"But? I hear a but coming down the pike." Ted said, looking at Pam.

"Ted, you have been paid through a charitable foundation we set up when dad got his windfall from his invention and selling the company. We are looking for someone to take it to the next level. Allowing the foundation to have an impact on this community." She stopped and looked at Ted.

"Here is what we are hoping. First, you will go to Southern State and get a marketing degree."

"And second?" Pam had Ted's full attention.

"Second, you come and run the foundation for us. It would be your job to find projects which fit the foundation's mission and goals."

"OK. So far, so good."

"Well," Pam stopped and took a breath, "Once you have graduated from Emmerson and you are enrolled at Southern State, we bring you on as a board member. This will allow you to learn about the foundation and how it works."

"Do I get paid?"

"No, not right away. Board members don't get paid. It is all voluntary."

"I thought, Jack."

Pam interrupted. "Jack is the CEO, and he gets a paycheck. After all, it is his money!"

Ted picked up the Southern State brochures again. "I'm listening."

"For now. Assuming you agree, you will be paid a handsome salary when you come on board. The amount is yet to be determined."

"I replace Jack? What does he think about this deal?"

"No, you won't replace Jack. As I said, he is the CEO. However, we will create a new position, giving you considerable autonomy and authority over the projects we fund."

"And whose bright idea was this?"

"This comes from the top," Pam said.

"Jack's?" Tom turned and looked at Jack, who waved at him.

"Precisely." Pam waved at her father.

"You know I showed up to rob him. Not proud of it, but it's the truth."

"Jack had his suspicions, and he said he even confronted you about it."

"Yes, he did." Ted put the papers on the table.

"Well, he insisted you be given a second chance. He saw something in you. Something we did not see. But, you know, Ted, my dad, can be persuasive. So, we gave in. Jack was right, as usual."

Pam got up, put everything in the envelope, and handed it to Ted.

"Think about it. It is all we ask." Ted said he would. He took the envelope to his room.

◆ ◆ ◆

"Well, Jack, you said something about Donavan's. I'm famished." Looking at her father, she asked, "When do we go?"

"Not so fast, young lady. It's still early. "Come and visit. Ted will get you a Dr. Pepper!"

Everyone was laughing when Ted rejoined the group.

Mac's eyes followed Ted into the room. "Everything alright, Son?"

"Couldn't be better," Ted said, and they sat down. He wasn't hearing anyone. Ted was considering when and how he would share this new path with Maureen. While Ted thought Maureen was beautiful and fun, he was oblivious to their blooming romance. Maureen pegged Ted as the lover of her life. She, too, was a novice in the love department. Maureen was doing everything she could to get Ted to ask her out on an actual date. She thought planning for the future might be the spark to ignite their relationship.

Ted hadn't said anything to Jack about his lunch meetings with Maureen, but Maureen and Ted had been brainstorming ways for Ted to continue his education. Now, Pam has solved that problem. That and more. Ted now had a future. He had plans and a career goal.

CHAPTER 7

AFTER EVERYONE HAD gone, Ted helped Jack clean up. Then Ted lay on his bed and sent a text to Maureen. Three thumbs up with an exclamation point.

"???" was the reply.

"C U 2morrow."

Jack was up and eating breakfast when Ted rolled out of bed.

"Mornin' sunshine." Jack was in a good mood.

"Hey." Ted was not fully awake.

"Hear the phone ring?"

Ted looked at him. "Nah, I was in the shower."

"Maureen. She said she wanted to talk to you."

"Did she say when? She's working 3-11 today."

"Said she'd meet you at the Mack Shack at noon and call if you could not make it."

Ted got out his phone. "Thanks," he said to Jack without looking at him. Then texted a single thumbs up to Maureen.

"You and Napper OK if I go over to my dad's this morning?" Upon hearing his name, the dog ran over to Ted and barked his presence.

"We'll be fine. Take your time. I there are things you need to get off your chest." Jack waited for a reaction from Ted. "Just remember, kiddo, everyone is here for you."

Half-hour later, Ted was at his dad's kitchen table with a cup of coffee. His dad had his second cup and talked about the new subdivision work.

Ted interrupted, "Dad, we must talk."

"OK. If it's about college, Eliot filled me in while you and Pam were at the table. I think it's great."

"Yeah, well, there's more to it." Ted studied his dad for a minute.

"Pam said that I could go to Southern State University through Emmerson."

"Hey, pal. That's great!"

"She said I could go there without having to leave home."

"Even better," Mack said with genuine excitement about the opportunities unfolding for his son.

"Pam meant Jack's house when she said home." Ted watched his dad for a reaction. Seeing none, he took a sip of his coffee and continued. "Dad, this is my home. I want you to understand that. You will always be my dad and my family. And this," sweeping his arm, "will always be my home."

"I know, son. But I also have been a horrible father to you and a rotten husband that drove your mother away. I wish I could change those things, but I can't."

Ted sat there seeing his dad, seeing the true Mack James for the first time.

"Winston, uh, Ted, you are an adult, and it is time you struck out on your own. I am not jealous or hurt that you live a few blocks away with Mr. Kelley. But, hey, I am extremely proud of you. You saved the man's life, and you continue to watch over him."

Ted held his coffee cup in both hands and stared down at the table. "Dad."

"You mean the burglary thing?"

Ted looked up in surprise and almost dropped his coffee cup. "You know?"

"Jack filled me in on that during one of his phone calls last week or so. No, I am not proud of that. I have not been a fantastic father, but neither did I raise a criminal. I cannot imagine what was going through your mind. The important thing, Ted, is you did not follow through. That night, you saved Jack's life. What father could not be proud of his child saving someone else's life?"

Ted made an audible sigh of relief and began to blush with embarrassment.

"Take them up on the college deal, Ted. I'll help whenever and however I can, but they see a lot in you and are offering you a fantastic opportunity."

"No argument, there." Ted got up and refilled their coffee cups.

"And," Mack said, "if it works out that you are a part of their foundation, then they are the richer for it."

"Thanks, Dad," said Ted, and he meant it.

"Oh, one more thing, Maureen sounds like a wonderful girl. I am eager to meet her real soon."

Ted assured his dad he would meet her soon. They talked for another hour about sports, the weather, politics. Then they were quiet. There was no more to say.

"Well, I better get back. Hope Napper hasn't tripped Jack again."

When Ted got to the door, Mack said, "You didn't ask."

Surprised by the question, Ted turned and looked at his father.

"You didn't ask why I was home and not at work."

"I didn't consider it my business." Then, after a brief pause, "So, why are you home?"

"I changed jobs. I now work for Hill-Haven Homes. Or I will tomorrow."

"That's great, dad. But why the change? Why now?" Ted was confused. "You've worked for your brother for a long time. Have a falling out?"

"No, nothing like that. I need the benefits. I'm not getting any younger, and with Triple-H, I get medical, and they offer a matching 401(k) retirement plan." It was clear Mack was proud of himself and his new job.

"That is great, Dad." Ted walked over and hugged his dad. It had been a long time since he hugged his dad. It caught Mack by surprise, who, with hesitation, hugged his son back.

"I am proud of you, dad," remarked Ted as he stepped back.

"Proud of you, too," Mack replied with a quiet voice.

While Ted was making his way back to Jack's, Ted relived the past 24 hours in his head. He thought relived the night he first found Jack. How their lives hanged by that single event. He thought about his dad, no longer a drunk, but his father." He was unaware a smile was growing on his face.

Ted ignored his surroundings until he felt a hard shove from behind. He spun around to find Little Jimmy Dickens and Freddy standing behind him.

"What the?" Ted said in astonishment at their actions.

"Well, if it ain't mister college kid. What do you think, Freddy?"

Freddy stared at Ted but didn't answer.

"We sent you on an errand. We were expecting something in return."

"Yes, but," Ted started.

"But nothing" Freddy cut him off.

Jimmy continued. "Yeah, we know. The old man was there. So, you saved his life. We still want our money."

"Look," Ted said, his eyes moving between the two. "Jack doesn't keep any money lying around. He gets confused, so his daughter manages his money for him."

"So," it was Freddy's turn to talk, "We're supposed to be happy with nothing while you're living it up in his house?"

"Things have been slow around here. I know that," Ted said.

"Tell us about it. But then, you are living large, aren't you, buddy boy?" asked Jimmy.

"Listen, I have a good thing going. And I owe it all to you two."

"Warm fuzzies don't help us," Freddy said with obvious sarcasm.

"You're right," Ted said, looking at Freddy. Then moving his gaze to Jimmy, "Look, a lot has been going on. I know you think I should have reached out to you earlier. And say what?"

Jimmy and Freddy just stood there staring him down.

"Look, if I had ignored Jack, Mr. Kelly, and met you at Uncle Dan's as planned, what would have gotten?"

"Don't care" Freddy said. "You didn't show."

"Well, you would have received precisely what you got. Zilch. Nada, Nothing."

Jimmy asked, "You expect us to be happy with that?"

"Listen, I think there is a way I can make it up to you." Ted studied his friends from his past life.

"We're listening," the two said in unison.

"I've got money. How much do you want? What did you expect?"

"Three-hundred minimum," Jimmy said.

"OK, tell you what. I said I owe you more than you know. Let me give you that $300. We'll call it a finder's fee." Ted waited for an answer, and the two exchanged whispers.

"OK, but we want the money now!" Both boys narrowed their eyes at Ted.

"Look, I don't carry that kind of money on me. I don't carry much money with me. You meet me at Third National, on Dayton Street, at noon tomorrow. I'll go in and get your money. Will that work?"

"We'll be there." The two turned and left. Their conversation was animated.

◆ ◆ ◆

Jack was in his recliner watching a Bonanza re-run when Ted came in. "Maureen called. Said to remind you she would be at the shack at noon. Got a hot date?" He looked at Ted with an approving smile on his face.

"Nah," Ted said in slight embarrassment.

"Well, you're stupider than I thought if you let her get away."

Ted ignored the comment. "I'm taking the truck." He went through the kitchen, got the keys, and headed to the Mac Shack. Maureen was in her scrubs and waiting for him in a booth along the wall.

When he got to the table, Maureen stood up. She took his head in her hands and kissed him on the lips. Hard.

"Wow, what was that for?"

"You don't like it?" Before he could respond, she repeated the gesture, "There, I've taken it back. That way, I'm not so forward, and we haven't kissed." She sat down and smiled. After a moment, the smile evolved into a quiet laugh.

"Sorry. I had to find out."

"Find out what." Ted was thoroughly confused.

A little embarrassed, she said, "If you are gay?"

"And the verdict?" Ted asked, looking at her.

"You may be a dork, but there is no question. You are not a gay dork!" Both were now sitting, and she reached over and grabbed his hands.

"I am almost afraid to ask, but what made you presume I was gay?"

"Simple, you've never asked me out."

Pulling his hands away, Ted said, "Let me get this straight. If a guy does not ask you out, they are assumed to be gay?"

She looked at him. Grabbed his hands again and squeezed

them. "Ted, we have been meeting for the past few months for lunch. Two or three times a week on or near campus. Yet, you have not asked me out."

"I've called you. Doesn't that count?" Ted Asked.

"Not even close. You call to ask a question, a question always related to school. You never asked me over to watch Netflix, or for pizza. Or anything. Don't you like me?"

"Like you? Are you kidding? Who wouldn't like you? You are gorgeous, smart, and funny. I didn't think I would stand a chance with you." Finally, it was Ted's turn to squeeze her hand.

"OK, now that we have established that you are not gay, you are a good kisser, and you think I'm gorgeous and funny. So, when are you taking the leap, and ask me out?"

Stumbling and stuttering, Ted began, "This leap forward in our relationship."

Maureen cut him off. "Do I have to do everything? You are coming over to my apartment tomorrow night. I am off since I am working the weekend. I am a fantastic cook, and I do magic with meatloaf. Seven, sharp! Now, do I need to lead you, or can you find my apartment?"

"No, I am quite capable of finding the way."

"Just to settle things. I think you are awesome, taking care of Jack and going to school. You are my kind of guy. You are tops in my book, even if you do not consider me your girlfriend. So, buddy boy, you are my boyfriend. No dating other girls. Got it?"

"Got it!" They laughed as their mac and cheese arrived.

"I ordered ahead. I hope you don't mind."

"Woah, you must have eaten your Wheaties today," Ted said, smiling at the girl of his dreams.

"Special K."

"Huh?"

Maureen said, "I eat Special K cereal. Not Wheaties."

"Always have to have the last word. So, is this how it is?"

"Now you're starting to understand!"

Maureen had the four-cheese mac with bacon and ordered Ted his favorite, Lobster mac with jalapenos. They talked about school and her current hospital duties, working 3-11 in the emergency room.

"Jack called mom after your get-together with Pam and Eliot, and she called me. So, it seems you have the green light to go to Italy next year." Maureen took a bite of Ted's lobster mac and watched for a reaction. Instead, Ted looked up and stared at her. Maureen just shrugged.

"What?" Then took a second bite.

"Well, that's not all," Taking a bite of Maureen's mac and cheese. "Pam and Eliot created a foundation with Jack's earnings and money from his patent."

"I think mom said something about that."

"The foundation is putting me through college. Pam is helping me get enrolled at Southern State University."

"Hey, that's great. I start there in the fall to get my B.S. in nursing." She took another bite of Ted's mac and cheese. "What are you going to study?"

Watching her chewing his lobster mac. "You want to switch?" using his fork to indicate the two meals.

"Oops," Maureen said. She smiled and took a bite of her own meal.

Ted watched her for a beat and then said, "Pam said it is pretty much up to me. They will cover the costs regardless of my degree plan, but."

"There is always a but," Maureen interjected.

"My thoughts precisely," and Ted took a sip of his Dr. Pepper. "They are encouraging me to consider a business degree and play a major role with the foundation."

"Hey, that's fabulous. I knew I had a genius for a boyfriend."

Ted did not immediately respond. "I would start getting my feet wet with the foundation this summer. I will be more active while working on my degree if all works out. A lot of questions remain."

"Will they pay you?"

"Not at first."

"Bummer," Maureen stated in mock disappointment.

"I would be a non-voting member of the board, and board members don't get paid. But upon graduation from Southern State, I would move from a non-voting board member to a salaried officer of the foundation."

"Think, your burglar skills made all this happen."

Ted dropped his fork and looked at her in astonishment. "You know?"

"We can't get married if I don't know everything. I mean everything."

"Marriage? Where did that come from? I have been your boyfriend, what," looking at his watch, "for all of 13 minutes?"

"Relax." Maureen put her hand on his. "Jack told mom who told me. I have to admit, it was disappointing. The guy I was starting to like a lot was a low-life burglar."

"And now?"

"Let's face facts; it would have been easy to burglarize the house. Jack was unconscious on the floor and not able to stop you. You could have taken anything and everything. But the true revealed itself. You saved Jack's life."

Ted let out a sigh of relief. "Let me assure you I am a retired burglar now." They both laughed.

"So, I don't have to lock up all of my jewelry? You know it's worth a pretty penny. I mean that literally!"

"Your family jewels are safe. As I just said, I am retired." It was Ted's turn to reach out and give his girl's hand a reassuring squeeze.

"Now, about tomorrow night's meatloaf. What kind of wine do you want?"

"With a drunk for a father, I never developed a taste for alcohol. So, tea, water, or a soft drink will be fine. And don't forget I am underage. I am not legally able to indulge in such devilish behavior."

"Then we'll invite the good doctor to join us." She was smiling when she said this.

"The good doctor?" Ted asked.

"Why, the good Dr. Pepper, of course."

"And he is a good doctor!"

Maureen looked at her watch. "Wow, how time flies when you are having fun. I've got to run and finish getting ready for work. I told them I would come in an hour early."

They got up and left the shack. On the sidewalk, Maureen turned and asked, "Since we are now officially an item, can I kiss you goodbye?"

In a stern tone catching Maureen by surprise, Ted said, "No. It is about time you learned who is leading this relationship." He kissed her.

"Yes, sir!" and she gave him a mock salute, "until tomorrow night."

She gave him a quick peck on the cheek and headed off to her apartment. Ted's feet were unable to move. He was frozen in time. A smile filled his face. He could not believe his good fortune.

CHAPTER 8

THAT NIGHT, TED found sleep elusive. First, reliving the meeting with his dad, Jimmy, and Freddy. Lunch with Maureen was out-of-this-world. Next, Ted realized he had a throbbing headache. Nevertheless, he was happy for his dad and the changes in his life. He also hoped the money he would give Jimmy and Freddy would ease their tension. But Maureen? Ted was at a loss when it came to his love life.

Throughout high school, Ted had few friends, and fewer were of the opposite sex. Sure, he had friends who were girls, but none came close to girlfriend status. He had never been on a group date, let alone a solo adventure. In all his life, no girl had ever kissed him. Pecks on the cheek didn't count. Maureen was correct in her assessment of Ted's romantic side. "I am a dork!" Ted said aloud to no one.

Then there was the wine. True, Ted's father was a drunk. Therefore, alcohol was never an enticement for him. Even when hanging out with Jimmy and the gang as they drank beer purchased by older friends, Ted never partook. He did not understand alcoholism, and he read somewhere hereditary figured in. Not want to be like his dad meant turning down beers. That was not a problem.

Alcoholism aside, Ted was a year behind Maureen, who could buy beer and wine. What did she expect him to say? "Hey, Maureen, I'd love to have the wine, but you know, I'm only 20.

I'm not old enough to consume alcohol." He laughed at himself. For the first time, he was happy his dad was an alcoholic. He could use his home life to avoid an awkward situation.

Today is Thursday: classes would occupy his mind until seven. That would be when he would meet Maureen, alone, in her apartment for dinner. There was no denying the physical attraction to her. But is this love or lust? While watching the movie, will sitting next to her be enough? What was he supposed to do? Hold her hand? Put his arm around her? What happens if she kisses him? More to the point, what happens if he kisses her? Ted was headed into uncharted territory, and it scared him.

While sorting things out in his bed, a bang on the door startled him. It brought him back to reality. Jack came in hollered, "Up and at 'em, boy. You got school you know!" And then
    disappeared.

At the table, Jack sat drinking his coffee and reading the paper. Ted was hurrying through a bowl of Wheaties when he stopped. "Oh, crap!" he shouted.

Startled, Jack almost spilled his coffee and eyed Ted. "What?"

"Today is Thursday."

"No surprise there. Yesterday was Wednesday," Jack said with a knowing smile on his face.

"I have biology tonight." Jack happily saw the wheels spinning in Ted's head.

"Been that way since school started. So," drawing the word out, "what's the surprise?"

"I have a date tonight with Maureen at her apartment. She is cooking a meatloaf. I can't break our first date. I just can't!"

"Whoa," Jack said, holding up a hand in Ted's direction. "You said date, not a dinner date. Is this a for-real date?" Jack narrowed his eyes at Ted.

"Nah, it's a date-date. Yesterday Maureen said I was her boyfriend, and she will be cooking dinner for me tonight. Now, what boyfriend breaks their first date?"

In a barely audible whisper, Jack said, "It's a for-real date, buddy-boy." Then Jack chuckled and returned to the paper. Then, in his best state trooper imitation, Jack said, "Boy, you in a heap o' trouble now!"

"Oh, by the way," Jack said, still reading his paper. "Your two buddies stopped by yesterday looking for you."

"Jimmy and Freddy?"

"That would be the two lowlifes. What did they want with you?"

"To talk," Ted said.

"Say, about a sock full of money? Hidden in an old man's dresser drawer?"

"Double crap!" exclaimed Ted, ignoring Jack's last question. "I'm supposed to meet them at the bank at noon. But School's not out until12:10. I can't get there before 12:30."

The state trooper spoke, making another appearance. "Man, you got yourself into a double heap o' trouble." Showing sincere concern, Jack asked, "What are you going to do?"

Ignoring the comment and question, Ted got out his phone. His fingers did the talking, letting his two friends know he would be there at 12:30. He was cryptic in his message but let Jimmy and Freddy know school caused the delay.

"There, one problem is solved."

"I'm assuming your message was to the dynamic-duo. What about the girl?"

"Don't know," responded Ted, still looking at his phone.

As he left, Ted announced, "Well, off to class." A few minutes later, Jack heard the truck leaving.

Jack waited a few minutes. He needed to make sure Ted had not forgotten. Confident

Ted was gone, Jack picked up the phone and dialed Ruthie.

"Hello, Jack," Ruthie said in a friendly voice.

Jess and Ruthie became friends when they met at the dog park. Ruthie was a widow. Ruthie and Jess enjoyed girl time. He rarely intruded. After Jess died, Ruthie would come around and check on him. Now, when the opportunity arose, he was excited to see Ruthie. She had become a very dear friend.

"Did you hear? They got a date tonight." Jack had a difficult time controlling his enthusiasm.

"Maureen texted me when she got off work. They were swamped by a bad accident by the river. She worked until after two this morning. Then she said she'd call me around nine. What time is it?"

"It is a little after eight. Make sure you're sitting when Maureen calls." And hung up.

At half-past ten, there was a light rap at the front door. Jack peaked out and saw it was Ruthie. At the wave of the curtains, she waved. The door opened, and Jack invited her in.

"You know, I did not realize macaroni and cheese could be so romantic. What did Ted say?"

Jack smiled. "Ted said they had a date for dinner. From his actions, though, there is no doubt it is a for-real date. Oh, he said Maureen told him she considered him her boyfriend. How 'bout them apples?" They both laughed.

"Maureen likes Ted a lot, and she is positive he likes her. But Ted has never made any move. He did not show a desire to move the relationship along." Ruthie talked while she prepared two cups of coffee and laid out the cookies she had brought with her.

"What did you say?"

She had Jack's attention.

"First, Maureen thought maybe Ted was gay and not attracted to her. Perhaps he didn't find her attractive. Maureen had dozens of rationales why things were not moving forward. Finally, I told her to take the lead. Find out for herself."

"And?" Jack asked, anxious for more.

"When she called this morning, I didn't have to say anything. She said Ted was definitely not gay. Apparently, they had a wonderful lunch. In fact, she announced to Ted, he was now hers, and she wasn't in the mood for competition. So, she is cooking for him tonight."

"Well, there is a hitch there."

"What? You mean he is gay?"

"What? No! What? He has class on Thursdays, and school conflicts with current matters of the heart."

"Should I call and warn her?"

With a raised his voice, Jack said, "Heck, no! Let them work it out. We've done our part. Let's run a victory lap and sit back watch the fireworks."

They watched *Gunsmoke*. Napper hopped into Ruthie's lap and fell asleep to the glider's gentle rhythm. Ruthie glanced at her watch. "Jack, I better be going. Maureen indicated she may stop by around noon."

Jack followed Ruthie to the door, watching her disappear in the new red convertible. Jack was pleased with getting the two kids together.

Ted arrived at the bank at 12:30. Jimmy and Freddy were nowhere in sight. At first, he thought Jimmy had not gotten the text. Ted went inside and chatted with the teller. She was Jack's neighbor. Ted withdrew three hundred from this savings account. He and the teller exchanged a few more pleasantries, Ted went to meet his friends. Jimmy and Freddy sat on the bus bench across the street and waved when Ted emerged from the bank.

Ted walked over and handed them the money. "Here you go. One day, we laugh at this whole situation." Jimmy and Freddie, confused, nodded in agreement.

"We still friends?" Jimmy was checking on the status of their relationship.

"We were never not friends. Sure, we are still friends."

"Good." Jimmy put out his hand, and they shook.

"Look, I've got to go. I'm late for class now." Then to his friends, "Don't spend it all in one place, OK?"

At 4:30, Jack heard the truck pull in the drive. Ted came in, putting the keys on the counter. After taking his usual seat on the sofa, Ted asked Jack, "So, how was your day. You and Napper do anything exciting?"

"We ran a marathon, served meals at the food kitchen, and re-roofed the house."

"In other words, not a whole lot." This had become their usual banter.

"More to the question, what about you? Solved the girl and the meatloaf problem?"

Ignoring Jack, Ted said, "I have to be there at six. Do you want me to fix you something or bring something in for you?"

"Nah. What about school?"

"Got that covered," Ted said without much emotion or conviction.

Jack paid no attention to Ted's response and said, "Besides, you got your date, and I, too, have a dinner date."

"With whom?" Ted asked, turning the tables on Jack.

"Wouldn't you like to know? I still turn a woman's head. So, again. What about class tonight?"

"I talked with the biology professor. Told a little lie. If anyone asks, your doctor ran some tests run today. He recommended you not be home alone tonight. Besides, the lesson focuses on an online video I can watch before class on Tuesday."

"In other words, your girlfriend is capturing your heart by feeding your face?"

"Something like that."

"Well, go for it!" Remembering what Ruthie said about Maureen's concern.

"You ain't gay, are you?" Jack asked, cocking his head to one side.

"First Maureen, and now you! Enough is enough. First, it is none of your business. And you and Ruthie." Jack raised an eyebrow. "You heard me. You two need to stay out of my love life!"

In a gesture of surrender, "Just wondered."

Ted let out an audible sigh as he raised his eyes to the ceiling and rolled them.

Ted had five minutes to spare. He had stopped by Kroger and picked up a small bouquet and Welch's sparkling grape juice. When She opened the door, Ted handed Maureen the flowers.

"These are for you, your highness," and gave a deep bow. Ted brought out the grape juice and handed it to her. Then, smiled, shrugged his shoulders, "Too young to buy wine."

Maureen took his hand and pulled him into the apartment. Her arms wrapped around his neck, she gave him a long kiss. Maureen took the flowers and juice, patted a chair at the island. She motioned him to sit. Putting the flowers in a vase, she put them on the counter. Two place settings were prepared. They were placed side by side.

The two talked while Maureen finished preparing the dinner. Ted told her about Jimmy and Freddy. He then told her how he got out of class to keep his date with her during the meal. She told him about her night and the accident keeping her working until after 2 am.

Ted got up, patted his stomach, and said, "This was the best meatloaf."

"Is that all?" Maureen asked with a mischievous look in her

eye.

"What?" surprised by her question.

"You said it was the best meatloaf you have had." She stood there with her hands on her hips.

"OK, the best meatloaf ever?!" Ted reached and put his arms around her waist and kissed her.

While pushing him gently away, she admonished, "Let's not get ahead of ourselves. We have to clean up this kitchen." She kissed him on the cheek and started putting the dirty dishes in the dishwasher.

Ted helped her with the clean-up. Maureen opened poured the juice into wine glasses.

"At least you won't get me drunk and take advantage of me!" she giggled.

Maureen turned and looked at Ted. He knew something serious was up.

"Uh, oh. What did I do wrong now? You wanted the red juice?"

"No, stupid. I have been thinking about what you said at lunch."

"You listened? Now, I know I am in trouble."

Ignoring him, she continued, "You might work for the foundation, right?"

"Might–and a mighty big might!"

"Well, consider this. The Southtown Projects and that whole area is without any real access to groceries. What if?" she briefly paused. "What if the foundation were to fund a neighborhood grocery store? Sell fresh fruits and vegetables and dairy. Everyday grocery store items and keeping the prices low enough for the people living there could afford them."

"I hadn't thought about it. It sounds like a good idea. I run it by Pam next week."

"And once a month or so, we could do different health checks. You know, blood pressure and other tests. Joyce, who lives across the hall from me. She works at the daycare across from the hospital. She said the Lions Club came in and did screenings for vision problems. Didn't cost them anything and anyone with eye problems got a free eye exam at the Westlake Eye clinic."

"I think we may be getting ahead of ourselves. First things first. I must get into Southern U. and then graduate. However, as I said, I will share your ideas with Pam. She seems to be in charge at the foundation."

Maureen led Ted to the couch and picked up the remote. "What do you want to watch?" "Anything but a western." Ted chuckled. "It's all Jack watches, and they are old westerns."

She pushed a couple buttons, and the television came to life. "Have you seen *Yesterday*? It's a movie where this guy has an accident. He wakes up, and the Beatles never existed. Yet, he knows all the songs and makes a lot of money pretending to write them."

"Who are The Beatles" Ted asked in mock seriousness.

Maureen punched him hard in the arm and then rubbed it to ease the pain. "I was going to fix popcorn, but with that remark, you get stale trail mix."

"What kind of popcorn?"

"Orville Red-something," she said, bringing up the movie.

"Not the brand, what kind. What type?"

"We're watching a movie, so it has to be movie theater." Maureen focused on the television screen.

"Fresh or nuked?"

"Huh? Oh, microwave. Nobody does fresh anymore."

"Great," he said, getting up; "where is it?"

"Popcorn is on top of the fridge. Microwave is over the stove." In the kitchen, Ted found the popcorn. He popped a bag, found a large bowl, and dumped the popcorn when the microwave bell sounded.

"Told you I could be useful," when he returned with the bowl.

Maureen looked up and smiled at him, then patted the seat next to her, and he sat down. She snuggled up to him with arms entwined. Ten minutes into the movie, he became aware she was quiet. He looked down and found her fast asleep, leaning against his shoulder. When the movie ended, trying to be gentle and not wanting to wake her, Ted laid her down. He then covered her with the blanket folded on the back of the couch. The lights down, the television off; Ted let himself out.

When he got home, Ted found Jack already in bed and asleep. He texted Maureen. "Food was great, movie OK, boyfriend a bore. He put his girl to sleep as soon as he sat down. Sweet dreams."

After he showered, Ted checked his phone. No messages. Maureen was down for the count. Within minutes, he, too, was out like a light.

CHAPTER 9

TED LAY AWAKE, not able to will his body to get up. The chirping of his cellphone filled his consciousness– Maureen was calling.

"You awake?"

"I am now." he said to himself, "She is way too cheerful this early in the morning."

"Get dressed—good clothes. I'll be there in fifteen."

"Where are we going?" His curiosity aroused.

"You'll see." Ted started to talk, then realized the phone was dead. She was gone.

Fourteen minutes later, Maureen and her lime-green Kia Soul arrived. She tapped the horn twice and waited impatiently. Finally, Maureen was relieved, and a bit surprised seeing Ted emerge wearing dark trousers, dark socks, dark shoes, a dark sport coat over a light blue button-down shirt, open at the collar. No tie. She smiled and said, "Perfect."

"Perfect? for what?" asked a mildly confused Ted.

"You're the perfect one for me," Maureen purred and his hand.

They were at The Reach, a non-denominational Christian church, a few minutes later.

"This is my new church. I've always gone to church, but this one has more people our age. Plus, I like their band."

"Band? I thought you said this was church. You know, sleepy sermons, choirs hidden behind long robes, and a pipe organ to keep you awake!"

"No, silly. Those churches are fine for some, but I like modern Christian music, what the music minister here calls praise music."

"You sing? Like in the choir?"

"I sing when in the shower." Ted gave her a big, mischievous smile.

Relax there, big boy. "Don't get any ideas. It will be sometime before you get my shower serenades," Maureen said, looking over her eyebrows.

"The music minister here is the brother of one of my nursing-student friends. So, relax, you'll enjoy it. I promise."

Ted had been to church a couple of times. The ones with the sleepy sermons. This was indeed different, and he found himself enjoying it. A feeling came over him he could not describe. Later, the best Ted could do was say he was moved by the service.

With the band playing, it was not easy to catch her singing. Maureen had a good voice. There were times when the congregation sang. Ted heard Maureen's voice, loud and clear.

The service was over. Ted was aware Maureen was in no hurry to leave. They mingled with other people their age when Maureen caught the eye of Wendy, the music minister's sister.

"Ted, this is Wendy and her boyfriend, Allan McElroy. And this is Ted." They greeted one another. "Wendy and Allan are going out for lunch, and they invited us to join them. I said yes."

Ted looked at her. With mock superiority, Maureen said, "Remember, I am older, and you have to respect me." She gave

Ted one of her alluring smiles. She lowered Ted's chin and said, "And don't you forget it!" She then turned her attention to Wendy.

"In that case, I'd love to join you. I always respect my elders."

"Wendy Miller and I were in high school together," Maureen started as a way of introduction. "We are both working the second shift in the ER. Allan is an insurance agent, and he has his own agency. Allan does quite well. They got engaged about a month ago. Promise to be a good boy, and I'll bring you to the wedding."

"Another date?" he chuckled.

"Sort of. If I let you come, you will be on your own during the ceremony. I am in the wedding party. There will be lots of girls. Lots of gorgeous girls there. Can you be trusted?"

"It depends on what you mean when you say trust."

She slapped his arm. "You know very well what I mean."

"My question to you, my dear. Knowing how charismatic I am, can you trust the girls?" That got Ted another glare from Maureen.

Changing the subject, Ted said, "OK, why the last-minute invite to church? I would have gone had you asked over dinner." Then he smiled, "Or before you so rudely fell asleep during our first date."

She laughed. "That was pretty rude of me, wasn't it?"

They were at Maureen's Soul, and Ted opened the door for her. As she slid behind the wheel, she said nothing. Maureen waited until Ted was in the car. Then, she was on the road before continuing her story.

"Truth was, I didn't invite you during our first date because I wasn't sure how you felt about church and all. I didn't want to scare you off."

"And this morning was safer?"

"Two things. Wendy was insistent on meeting you, and this was the perfect time."

"And the second," raising one eyebrow.

"If you said no, then I would invent some excuse and maybe stay home. You saying no would have been a real bummer."

"But you gave me no chance, one way or another."

"Sure, I did." She studied him for a moment.

"Eyes on the road, please, madam. You said was get up. Get dressed in good clothes. You gave me fifteen minutes. And you even lied about the time."

"I did not! I was there on the dot."

"No," stifling a laugh, "you arrived in fourteen minutes. One full minute ahead. Besides, to what was I agreeing? To get up. To get dressed in good clothes. You never explained why the rush."

"Oh, I guess I didn't. Want to go to church with me? And to brunch with some friends?"

"I'd love to." He paused. "Now, that wasn't so difficult. Was it?"

They laughed as she pulled into the Dead Fish, an upscale seafood restaurant. "I remembered how much you like seafood. Turns out you and Allan prefer the same food fare. Wendy and I want to keep our menfolk happy."

Wendy and Maureen had the chipotle-honey glazed salmon. Allan had crawfish, and Ted had the shrimp trio: broiled, fried, and scampi. Whether indifference to Ted's inability to drink because of his age-or something else altogether, the four had tea. Each couple shared how they met and their plans for the future. Maureen plans to go to Southern State. Wendy and Allan were planning a June wedding. Ted still had another year of school. Allan was expanding, with a second office opening in the next county.

"What company are you with?" Ted asked. "State Farm? Allstate?"

"I am an independent," Allan said. "If you sell for one the big boys, you are limited by what they have to offer. As an independent, I am not tied down to any one company,"

The food arrived, and their attention moved away from the talk of work.

◆ ◆ ◆

As they drove back to Jack's, Maureen brought up church again. "I have always gone to church. It has always been a big part of my life. One of the reasons I chose The Reach is its commitment to giving back to the community. The church operates a weekly food pantry. It also has a game day for seniors every Wednesday. They sponsor three summer mission trips: Junior high students have a week of doing projects in town. There is a week-long mission trip for high school students somewhere in this or an adjoining state. Adults have out-of-the-country mission trips. This past year, they traveled to Nuevo Laredo and installed pews in a church there. It was struck by lightning the year before and burned. This year, they are returning to Nuevo Laredo. That little church has grown five-fold, and miraculous things have happened. They will be taking more church pews to be installed in a recently completed addition."

"Which one are you doing?" Ted was sincere in his question.

"None. I can't take time off. I need the money I make over the summer to help pay my expenses. I have gone with the high school students a couple of times. At some point, I plan to go with the adults. But nursing is a time-consuming career. I don't want to use my vacation time working. I need time to de-stress and wind down."

"Are you suggesting I go on the adult trip? I mean, I don't know anyone. And I have no clue what Pam and Eliot have in store for me. And let's not forget Jack. He always has something up his sleeve."

"Then there is the fourth mission. It is ongoing. Several of the men-and women participate in Habitat Community. It is a local charity building new houses for a selected family."

"I'm aware of Habitat Community. They do good work."

"I thought, since it would be local, you might like to help. It is not limited to church members. In fact, most workers are not members of our church. It might give you an insight. May be give you an idea how Jack's foundation might do the most good."

"I'll think about it. But, of course, I will have to run it by Pam, Eliot, and Jack."

"Of course."

Pulling into the drive, Maureen saw Jack come out. He looked at the car and smiled when he saw Maureen and Ted. Ted leaned over and kissed Maureen's cheek as he got out. The two of them watched as Maureen backed out and was gone.

"Ever think I might be worried? About where you were?"

"Sorry. Boss called and demanded I go. Gave me a whole thirteen-minute notice!"

"Women!" Jack said as he shook his head. "Can't live with them."

"Can't live without them," Ted finished. They both laughed as they took their usual positions in the living room. *Maverick* with James Garner was on. Jack sat in his recliner with Napper secure in his lap. Ted picked up the paper and read the latest news when he heard the familiar snore. Jack was out, but Ted never attempted to change the channel. He did once, and only once.

"What are you doing?" Jack barked. "I was watching that show."

Ted argued snoring was a signal the show was not being watched. "I will have you know that I was just resting my eyes. I heard every word they said," Jack bellowed. "Besides, I have never snored a day in my life."

The week had been a whirlwind. Ted was in desperate need of activity not requiring brainpower. Ted got up, walked to the window, and looked toward the street. The lawn was green but also getting tall. Ted walked through the house and looked through the kitchen window in the backyard. Like the front, it was getting high. The decision was made. He needed to mow the yard.

Ted changed clothes. Jeans, a t-shirt featuring an album cover by one of his favorite bands, Imagine Dragons. He wore his oldest pair of sneakers and an Emmerson College ball cap. Ted returned to the shed, pulled out the mower, and checked the oil; it was full. Ted checked the gas and added some. Ted pushed the mower down the drive and onto the corner of the front lawn. Two strong yanks and the engine roared. It took over half an hour to get the front and side yard mowed. He then tackled the back. More than an hour later, Ted pushed the mower back into the shed. He grabbed the weed-wacker and rake.

Ted trimmed the grass around the fencing, shed, garage, and patio using the weed-wacker. Ted then moved to the front, where he did the same, tilted the device, edged along the drive and sidewalk. That done, he raked and bagged the clippings. Ted could never understand how two small lawns would fill four thirty-gallon trash bags. He tied them and put them next to the garage. To be taken out on trash day.

The heading back to the shed, he got the leaf blower. Most of the neighbors blew the clippings onto the street. Ted believed the raking was good for the grass, so he bagged the clipping. That way, the street did not look. He blew a few clippings and grit on the lawn.

Ted went in a checked on Jack. He was awake now and doing a crossword puzzle listening to the Beach Boys having *Fun, Fun, Fun*. Ted grabbed a Dr. Pepper and collapsed in the glider. Napper noticed there was now a lap he could use and leaped up. With soulful eyes, he looked at Ted. In return, Ted petted him. Then, knowing he was welcome, Napper curled and watched Jack with his pencil and book. Finally, Ted leaned back and closed his eyes.

Before drifting off, Ted was aware of a commotion to his left. It was Jack in the kitchen.

"Hey, sleepyhead! I'm getting hungry. What are we doing for dinner?"

"Don't have a clue. What do you feel like?"

"I feel like steak, and I don't want to go out. We don't have any to grill. So, what do you feel like?" He sat there watching for a reaction.

Ted never opened his eyes. "Wing Stop?"

"Nah, I had chicken salad for lunch."

"Where'd you get that? We used the last of that for lunch yesterday."

"Wouldn't you like to know?" Jack said and filled in a word in his puzzle.

"OK, no steak and no chicken. Pasta then?"

"Gambino's has a lasagna special today. Two dinners for ten bucks. I'll buy if you fly." Jack looked for a reaction.

Ted sat up, and Napper jumped to the floor. "Works for me. I'll go change shirts and grab us two dinners. Dessert?"

"I don't know. I'm trying to watch my waistline."

Assessing Jack, Ted said, "It's doing just fine." Ted left to change shirts.

"Here's twenty," Jack said to Ted, handing Ted two tens. "Get tiramisu; it is large enough for two."

Ted took the money. "Got it. Two lasagna dinners, extra breadsticks, and one tiramisu. That's enough for me; what can I get for you?" Ted pointed his finger and pretended to shoot Jack. Ted was out and in the truck. Jack stood there, watching in silence.

Twenty minutes later, he pulled back into the drive and

brought the food inside.

"What took so long? You and Maureen decide to have dinner on me?"

"How d'ya know?" Ted set the food on the table. Then Ted set a place for them. "Drive-thru was busy, and it took a little longer than expected. I'm sure you are not on the verge of passing out from starvation. So, I splurged and got us a salad. Need some fiber in our diets, don't you think? "

Jack frowned but nodded in agreement.

"What do you want to drink?"

"I want a beer but will settle for tea." Jack sat down and opened his to-go container. There was a large slice of lasagna with two breadsticks on top. Jack set the breadsticks aside, opened the crushed red peppers' packet, and applied a liberal amount. Jack repeated the action with the parmesan cheese. He waited as Ted came back with the drinks. Before Ted could doctor his lasagna, Jack began saying grace. "Finished," Jack said, "Jess and I did this before every meal. It has fallen by the wayside after her death. You're going to church this morning brought back that memory. Mind if we resume the tradition?"

Ted said, "A good tradition to continue."

"How was church this morning?" Jack asked as he put some lasagna in his mouth.

"It was OK." After that, it was Ted's turn to put food into his mouth.

"Jess and I used to go every Sunday. Never missed one unless we were sick or on the road somewhere. What about you? Did you go to church when you were a kid?"

Ted stopped eating and thought for a few minutes before responding. "I think we went a few times, but when dad started drinking, we stopped. And mom, you know, did not have a traditional job. I don't think many church-folk approved."

"Can't say that it's a profession I would encourage my wife or daughter to pursue. I've learned to accept people for who they are and not their job. But, of course, if you're a murderer, it is hard to distinguish between the two."

Ted nodded in agreement. "Guess so."

"Your mother was a sweet lady."

"You knew her?" Ted with a voice laced with surprise.

"Knew her?" Jack paused. "No, not really. But I would see her at Kroger or Handy Dan's, and we would talk as neighbors talk. As I recall, she had a quiet voice. She saw the good in all people. I think she did what she had to do." He stopped in mid-sentence. "No. Without walking their shoes, no one can say why anyone does what they do. Not with any certainty. I did not grow up or live in an abusive situation. It was not my place to judge."

"I always wondered. What would it be like having a typical family?"

"Ha! What is typical?"

"You know," Ted protested.

"Look at you. Your dad was an alcoholic. Your mother had a job of which most people disapproved. Yet here you are. An old man's savior. You're going to school and have a wonderful girl and a promising future."

He paused and looked at Ted. When they made eye contact, he continued.

"The Grisman's were a church-going family. He was an accountant, and she was a schoolteacher. They were the envy of most people. They had a lovely home. They had everything going for them. But then their only child, Harry, got into the wrong crowd. He got hooked on drugs and wound up killing a store clerk during an armed robbery. Now he is locked up in prison for murder. It devastated his parents to the point they moved away. The last I heard, they wound up getting a divorce. So, which one of you had what you call a typical childhood?"

The two sat there without talking. Finally, Jack broke the silence when he said, "You know, Ted. It's not what you are given, but what you make of what God gives you. Don't forget that. Not ever!"

"Yes, sir." They ate the rest of the meal in silence.

CHAPTER 10

Pam was coming to pick up Jack for two doctor's appointments, Ted was up before his alarm sounded.

Jack's first appointment was with his neurologist. The second was with his personal physician for his annual physical. "Plan on most of the day. We'll catch lunch after the doctors." Then Pam promised to have Jack home for dinner.

Jack rolled out of bed and got dressed. He came into the kitchen and made himself a cup of coffee. Ted made them scrambled eggs with an egg substitute along with two plant-based sausage patties.

"I do believe I am getting used to these substitute food things. But I sure do miss my eggs fried in butter, my English muffin with jelly, and four strips of crispy bacon."

"The doctor suggested this for breakfast. Since you will be seeing him this morning, I thought you should at least eat the healthy stuff today." Ted doctored his eggs with hot sauce, but nothing was to be done with the sausage.

The front door opened. Pam came in and was radiant. Prospective motherhood looked good on her, and her baby bump was visible.

Jack walked over and gave her a hug and a kiss on the cheek. As he bent down touching the baby bump he asked, "How's it hanging in there?"

"Like you," Pam said, "it likes to keep on the move. Keeps

me up most nights." She turned to Ted. "Hi, Ted. Are you keeping my old man out of trouble?"

"Can't say. As you are aware, Jack is a little sneaky." The comment garnered a one-eyed stare from Jack.

"Come on, dad. We have to go. Can't be late. You know how your doctor gets when you are late."

"Yeah, I heard you," he said with a wink. "See you this afternoon if I'm lucky!" And the two were out the door.

Ted put the dirty dishes in the dishwasher, closed the door, and pushed the start button. Monday was laundry day. Ted stripped the sheets from both beds, putting them in the washer. Ted then poured in Tide and started the machine. With the washing doing its thing, Ted finished a few more chores.

He got out the paperwork for Southern State and began reading it. He began to fill out the forms for admission, student aid, and JUCO transfer scholarships. In addition, there were a few government forms for grants and student loans. He called his dad, and they talked about the process. Maureen called while he was talking to his dad. "Gotta go, dad, the new boss lady on the line."

"Maureen?" he asked with a smile in his voice.

"You guessed it," and clicked over.

"Good morning," she said.

"And top of the morning to you. What are you doing up at the crack of dawn?"

" I will be busy the rest of the week, and today is the one day I can squeeze in lunch. Are you up for tacos at Gringos?" There was a pause. "Don't go getting all worked up; mom is coming. And she is buying. I tried to talk her out of it, but she insisted I invite you. Truthfully, it was more of a demand than a suggestion." There was a laugh in her voice.

"I am in the middle of laundry. What time?"

"Well, aren't you the little homemaker? Can you tear yourself away from housework, say around 11:30?"

"Needs to be casual. No clean good stuff."

"Fine, see you at 11:30. Remember, mom doesn't like it when you are late!" Maureen disconnected before Ted could respond.

The washer buzzed, signaling it had finished with the cycle. Ted moved the sheets to the dryer. He reloaded the washer and started both. He grabbed a Dr. Pepper from the fridge when his phone rang.

Not looking at the number, Ted said, "I promise I'll be on time."

A woman's voice said, "I'm glad to hear that, Winston. But I have no idea what you are talking about."

"Who is this?" The voice was vaguely familiar. There was a pause. "Hello?" Ted said, thinking maybe they had a wrong number and had disconnected.

After a pause, the voice said, "It's your mother."

"Mable?"

"No, Winston, I now go by first name, Marie."

Ted heard from his mother with a note or card delivered by Lois. However, this caught him by surprise. It had been over two years since hearing her voice.

"Winston, are you still there?" asked Marie.

"Yes, I'm here. You just caught me by surprise. And I go by Ted, now."

"I'm sorry. Ted, did I call at a bad time?"

"No. this is fine. I have a few minutes."

"Good. As I was saying, Marie was also my mother's name, so I went by Mable when I was young to avoid confusion. But my given name is Marie."

She had a sweet, quiet voice. Ted missed hearing that voice, and it brought back memories. He was remembering when he saw her last.

"But everyone called you Mable." He spoke quietly.

"Your dad introduced me to everyone as Mable. For whatever reason, Mack enjoyed calling me Able Mable. Mable is a name I would prefer to forget. Marie is what I go by now."

"Sorry, Mom. Where are my manners? How are you? Where are you?"

"It's OK. I'm fine, and I am in Florida."

"I sort of guessed that with the last card you sent. So, what are you doing now?"

Marie interrupted, "Before I met your dad, I was certified as a bookkeeper. I took courses at Sinclair College of Business. I work at the Third National Bank here in Tallahassee. I am a teller."

"Great, mom." Ted searched his brain for something to keep the conversation going.

Aware of the awkwardness, Marie said, "I met a man. He runs a shoe store. He has asked me to marry him." There was caution with every word she uttered.

"When?" is all Ted could get out.

"When what? When did he ask me, or when will we get married?"

"Well, I guess both." Ted was mentally kicking himself for his juvenile responses.

"He asked me a few weeks ago, and we haven't set a date. While we were dating, I did not tell him I was divorced. Or had a grown son."

"Ashamed or embarrassed?" Ted could feel some anger welling up inside and fought to control it. After all, she left his dad, not him. He was just collateral damage.

"Oh, Winston."

"Ted," he corrected.

"Of course. Ted, I could never be ashamed of you, and you could never embarrass me.

The topic never came up. Neither of us set out to be where we are today. Hank is also divorced with three grown children, if it makes you feel any better. He did not mention them to me until I told him about you."

"OK." Ted was unsure where this conversation was heading. There was a pause. Ted closed his eyes, wishing the call to be over.

After waiting for Ted to say something, Marie continued. "We are driving up. We are going to start with meeting Hank's kids. They all live in and around New Orleans. Then we'll drive up and see you. At some point, we would like our children to meet one another. He wants his kids, twin girls and a boy, to meet me. His kids are in their late 20s. And of course, I want you to meet him."

"A trial run?" Ted did not intend to sound angry, but it was there.

Taken aback by Ted's tone, his mother said, "We are grown adults, and we are going to get married. We don't need your permission." Then softer, "However. We would like your blessings. He's a good guy. I hope you will like him." Marie assured Ted he was still important to her. However, this was her life and her decision.

"When will you be here?" Ted softened his tone.

"We should be there on Saturday. Is the LaQuinta still standing?"

"Saturday? Great," and meaning it. There was something inside of him. He wanted to see his mother again. "Now it is a Super 8. There is a new Holiday Inn Express. It is on the south end of town. It opened about two years ago."

"How's your dad?" she asked with a tinge of reluctance.

The question took him by surprise. "Great. Dad is sober, goes to AA, and works for Triple H manufactured housing. We get together a few times a week."

"Lois said you are taking care of Mr. Kelley. Something about a stroke or something. Are you still with him?"

"Yeah. It's been a good. For both of us." The dryer buzzed.

Ted looked at his watch. Time was running out. He could not be late for Maureen and Ruthie. "Mom, look, I am looking forward to seeing you and your new boyfriend. But I have an important date, and if I don't leave, now I'll be late."

"School?"

"No, mom," speaking while getting ready for his lunch date.

"A girl?" Marie asked.

"Mom, a lot is going on. I will tell you all about it on Saturday, but I gotta go. Bye."

Ted shut his phone and opened the dryer door. Ted grabbed the keys to the truck, ran out, started the truck, and left. He had 13 minutes to get to Gringos, 15 minutes away. He prayed silently, "Please, let the lights be green," as he made his way to the cantina.

He walked into Gringos sixteen minutes after he had been summoned. Maureen and Ruthie sat in a booth at the back. She leaned over and waved to get his attention. Ted slid next to Maureen. She rewarded his promptness with a kiss on the cheek and squeezed his hand.

"Ladies." Ted studied Ruthie and then Maureen for a clue. "To what do I owe the pleasure?"

A giggle came from his left. He turned to look at Maureen. She shrugged and smiled.

"Mr. James." It was apparent that Ruthie called this meeting, and she would start things off. However, it was hard to take the meeting seriously. Especially with Ruthie trying to stifle a laugh.

"Ruthie?" Ted asked.

"Mrs. Rittenhouse" staying with the formality she had established. "What are your intentions concerning my naïve daughter?"

Taken aback by the question, his hands raised in surrender asked. "Whoa, where did that come from?"

While managing to maintain composure, Ruthie said, "It's a simple question, don't you think?"

"I cannot imagine what you believe has been going on. Or what your daughter has told you. But I have been nothing but a complete gentleman."

Maureen squeezed his arm and leaned into him. Then she purred, "Isn't he adorable?"

Ruthie smiled, "Relax, Ted. I was blackmailed. I have no worries about your relationship with my devious daughter."

Maureen reached up and turned Ted's head and kissed him on the lips. "Better?"

"Seriously, have I done something wrong? Am I in trouble?"

"Relax, silly," Maureen said with a soft laugh. "She needs to talk to you about something. It has nothing to do with our flirtatious relationship."

"OK." Now he was curious. "Before you start, I need both of you to understand. I do love, and I am in love with your daughter. With that being said, I believe we are essentially in high school. I am living with Mr. Kelley and have responsibilities there. I do not have much money, nor am I employed. She is living in an apartment for which I believe you are paying the rent. She is about to graduate and enter the workforce. However, it has not yet happened. I assure you, I will aggressively pursue this wickedly devious woman you fondly refer to as your daughter when my situation is appropriate. OK?"

"I will be watching and keeping my guard up," Maureen said, raising her fists in a boxing gesture.

"Relax, Ted. When you are ready to take it to the next level. I promise you will be welcomed into the family. Assuming she hasn't started using your picture as a dartboard," Ruthie shot a stern glance at her daughter. "It is hard for me to imagine how she could improve on you as a catch."

"Oh, I'm a catch, now, am I?"

Maureen grinned and pretended to be reeling in a fish.

Everyone relaxed, munched on chips and salsa. Finally, the waiter came and took their order. Maureen and her mother shared chicken quesadillas, and Ted had two shark tacos. After ordering, Ruthie was ready to resume.

"Ted, I noticed you signed up with Habitat Community at The Reach."

"Yeah, I thought it would be a good project for someone with my limited skills."

"That is hogwash. And we both know it!" She waited for a retort, but nothing came. "Everyone knows you have worked construction with your dad." Finally, Ruthie stopped, bit into a chip dipped in queso, and continued. "I have been working with Habitat Community for the past four or five years. The next project doesn't start for another six weeks, but I would love to have you on my crew. What do you say?"

"First, let us get things straight. My dad is the home builder. So, yes, I know the business end of a hammer. I also have learned to keep my fingers away from the saw blade. Still, I am no carpenter."

"That is OK. We have professionals doing the important stuff. What we need is manual labor. People willing to drive a nail home or cut a piece of lumber. You may also be asked to get materials to the right crewmember. It will take most of the summer. One crew will prep the site, lay the plumbing, and pour the slab. Then, my team and I will take care of what goes on top. You are looking at eight, maybe ten-hour days. Are you up to it?"

Without waiting for an answer, Ruthie said, "I have talked to both Pam and Jack, and they are behind you. Of course, you will lose a little care-taking money. The Habitat project is voluntary. Some will work the entire time. Others work a day here and there. We are flexible. We understand you may need time off. To tend to other business. I want you to consider being on my team?"

The food arrived when Ted agreed to the proposal. Everybody ate, and the lunch conversation was of no consequence. Once the plates were gone, Ruthie saw it as her opportunity to leave the two love birds alone.

◆ ◆ ◆

"Wait," Ted said, reaching out and touching Ruthie's hand. "I need to talk. To both of you."

"You sound serious. Are you sick?"

"What? No! I do need a favor. Can you keep Saturday open and be flexible to meet me on short notice?" Then, turning to Maureen, "You know, as you do with me." Ted was smiling.

Both agreed and expressed curiosity.

"My mom is coming to town on Saturday."

"Mable?" asked Ruthie.

"It's Marie now." He studied them for a moment. "We will leave that for another day." He paused and then continued. "I don't know if she knows about us," alternatingly pointing at Maureen and himself, "and I want her to meet my girl and her mom."

"My mother has a new boyfriend, Henry Karl, and they are serious. They are going to meet his kids in New Orleans. Then be here on Friday so I can meet him."

"Does your dad know?" Maureen was studying him.

"As far as I am aware, he doesn't. But I got the impression Mom will spring it on him. Probably when they are here. So I may warn him ahead of time."

"When did you find out?" Ruthie's curiosity was aroused.

"This morning. That is why I was late." Looking at Maureen, "The phone rang right after I had hung up with you. I thought you had forgotten something, and I answered, expecting your voice. Instead, it was Mom's. We talked until I had to leave."

Everyone was quiet. Ruthie broke the silence, "Of course, Ted. We're here for you." Then, laughing, she said, "However, don't follow Maureen's lead. Do not wait until the last moment. Girls need more time to prepare. After all, we don't want to scare anybody."

"I will learn more when I meet them Saturday morning. I will give Maureen a heads up. I will give her the day's activities when I know. OK?"

They all agreed to the plan, and Ruthie picked up the bill. She smiled at the two lovebirds. She then the left to pay. Ted and Maureen stayed and finished their drinks and the chips. They talked about their budding romance, the upcoming graduation, and what lay ahead over the summer. Finally, he walked her to her car and watched her drive off.

Pam and Jack were back. Jack received a clean bill of health from his primary care physician, and the neurologist said things appeared steady. However, the doctor needs to see him again. In two or three months. Ted shared with them his with Maureen and her mother, and he agreed to be on her Habitat Community crew.

Without warning, Ted blurted out, "Mom's coming this weekend."

"Old Able Mable?" Jack asked with a laugh.

"It's Marie, now." Jack shot him a glance. "Long story for another day."

Pam wanted the details. Jack repeated what he had told Ruthie and Maureen.

"Well, we will be here," Pam said. "We would love to meet them. I want them to know how you are doing here with dad. Does Mack know?"

"I don't think so. I may tell him Wednesday or Thursday.

I don't want it to be a complete surprise." And with that, she headed home.

"Doc said I could have a steak. So, I bought two rib-eyes. Just tell me when you want me to fire up the grill."

"Will do." Ted sat in the glider, and Napper jumped into his lap. Finally, Ted was exhausted, and the two fell asleep.

CHAPTER 11

AT A LITTLE after nine on Friday night, Hank Karl and Marie James arrived at the Holiday Inn Express. They checked in and put their things in their room. Then walked across the street to the Waffle House. There they had a light breakfast-dinner. Both had a two-egg breakfast with crispy bacon. Marie opted for plain hash browns and wheat toast, while Hank added smothered and covered with a side of buttermilk pancakes. Over Hank's decaf and Marie's water, they rehearsed the next day.

Hank got a newspaper from the machine when they returned to the motel. While he was glancing through it, Marie called Ted.

"Hi, Ted," she said when her son answered the phone.

"Hi, Mom. Which motel did you elect?"

"We're at the Holiday Inn Express, room 115. We ate at the Waffle House. Hank is reading the paper, so I thought I would give you a call."

"Great. How was the trip?"

"Long and exhausting. I need a long bath."

"Relax tonight and call me when you get up. I'll come and take you to breakfast. I know a much nicer place than the Waffle House. Elmer's is a new place. Not too far from the hotel."

"You don't have to do that. The hotel has a free breakfast here."

"I know, and I have had their imitation food before. Can we plan on eight or eight-thirty? We three need to talk. Before the day unfolds."

"We'll be in the lobby by eight-fifteen."

"You will need to follow me to Elmer's. I don't think we can all fit in Jack's little Ford Ranger. Besides, you may want to make a hasty escape." Ted's voice cracked when talking and ended with a forced laugh.

"We'll be ready." The usual pleasantries were exchanged before they ended the call.

The next call was to Maureen, and Ted told her about the phone call with his mother. It was planned to be a quick call. But an hour later, Ted hung up.

Sleep did not come easily for anyone. Marie and Hank talked well past midnight. Trying to figure how the next day would play out. Maureen lay awake worrying about Ted and how best to help and support him. He had to be an emotional wreck. Ted tried to figure out the best way to explain his role with Jack and introduce his new girlfriend. Ted considered how to bring his parents together without an all-out war. Somehow, Ted also needed to throw Pam and Eliot into the mix. Finally, after 3:00 am Saturday morning, all participants in the upcoming drama fell asleep.

Ted was up and dressed before seven. Despite having little sleep, he was full of energy and expectations. Ted tiptoed around the house. He did not want to wake Jack. After dressing, Ted made his bed and tidied his room. He did not figure anyone would be inspecting his room, but he needed to do something to reduce his anxiety. At seven-forty-five, he called Maureen. She answered on the first ring. Maureen had been up since seven. Like Ted, Maureen was not feeling the effects of so little sleep.

"You ready?" he asked.

"Ready as I'll ever be. You?" There was excitement in their voices.

The original plan called for Ted to meet his mother and Hank alone. However, Maureen convinced him that her presence would be a buffer and reduce tensions. Much of the previous night's call was spent debating. Maureen wanted to go with Ted. Ted suggested she stay home. Ted was hesitant, but Maureen won out. She would accompany Ted to meet his mother. And his mother's new love interest.

"I will meet you out front." Closing his eyes, Ted hung up, took a deep breath, and prayed. Ted began to count how many ways this could go wrong.

Ted was quiet when he picked up the keys. He went out and started the truck. He backed and waited at the end of the drive. A few minutes later, he spotted the lime-green Soul heading toward him. It stopped in front of the house, and Maureen got out, beeped the car locked, and slid into the truck. They smiled at one another, and she squeezed his hand three times. This gesture had become the silent "I love you." Both used this gesture when they wanted to be discreet. Finally, Ted put the truck in gear, and they were on their way.

At eight-ten, he pulled the red Ranger into the hotel's parking lot and noticed the slots were full. He dropped Maureen at the door. He found a spot at the end of the parking lot. Ted hurried back to the lobby. They entered as an older couple rounded the corner.

The woman was slim, attractive, with blonde hair hanging straight, touching her shoulders. The man was six inches taller. He was 225-250, red hair cut military-style, wire-rimmed glasses, and a goatee. They moved with confidence toward Ted and Maureen.

"Oh, Winston," the woman exclaimed, and embraced her son. "Let me look at you." She gave him a hug, then, still holding his hands, she stepped back. She gazed approvingly at the transformation her son was undergoing. The man stepped forward. He put out his hand to Ted.

"Hank. Hank Karl. I've heard a lot about you, Winston. Your mother is proud of you."

"Thank you, sir." Ted stood there looking at them. "I go by Ted now. Can we leave Winston where he belongs? Back among the ruins." It was a miserable attempt at humor that failed. Ted's mother and Hank looked at him with a quizzical look. They noticed a beautiful young woman hanging back.

Stepping forward, "Hi, I'm Maureen." Maureen held out her hand. Marie brushed it aside and gave her a hug. "Lois was right. You are beautiful. Ted may not realize it yet. But he is lucky to have you in his life."

"Oh, I know it," said a beaming Ted and put his arm around Maureen. "She reminds me every chance she gets." Maureen turned and popped Ted one on his arm and then shook hands with Hank.

"Where's your car?" Ted asked.

Hank pointed in the opposite direction from where Ted parked. "At the end of the lot."

Hank said, "You girls wait here. We'll go get the wheels and pick you up." The girls nodded in agreement.

"How is Ted?" Marie asked Maureen after an awkward moment. "He has been a little vague in his conversations. I can't read him."

"I guess you and Mack separated on less than amicable terms. Ted is aware you will be seeing each other. For the first time since you left. So, he is understandably nervous. Ted is great. He is the best thing to happen to me."

When Hank and Ted pulled up, Marie turned and whispered, "Tell him to relax. It will be fine. I promise." Then Hank followed Ted out. Ten minutes later, they were seated at Elmer's.

The waitress introduced herself and took their drink orders. All had coffee and water. "Make it hazelnut. All around." Ted turned and said to Marie and Hank, "The hazelnut coffee is one reason we like coming here. Trust me, you'll love it."

They picked up menus and began scanning. While scanning the menu, Hank asked, "What in blazes is a German pancake?"

"Hank. Imagine a pizza-sized crepe with the edges turned up a quarter inch. It is served with butter, lemon juice, and powdered sugar." Hank made a gesture with his hands. He studied what he created. Then shook his head. "Son, this may not be Texas. But this has got to be one Texas-sized pancake." As he put his hands down, Hank said, "Ted, my boy. I have to be honest with you. I have never associated lemon juice with a pancake. Butter and powdered sugar, maybe. But never lemon juice."

"Trust me, you'll love it. That will be our appetizer. So, if you don't like it, you won't have to eat much." Then, looking at his mother, he said, "Mom always told me, if you don't try it, you'll never know what you've missed." Everyone relaxed with that comment. The conversation was turned to the usual chit-chat. Old friends catching up. After a long absence.

"Mom, why don't you take time and show Hank around our wonderful town and relax. When you go by the old house, you won't recognize it. Dad has it fixed up."

Marie lowered her head and mumbled, "I don't know." She was biting her lower lip.

"Relax. Dad is at Triple-H until two, so you won't run into him. Promise. I checked with him last night. He's been clean and sober for months now. Dad looks and acts differently. You'll see that for yourself at dinner tonight."

"Come on, hon," Hank said, and he gave Marie a side-hug and a quick kiss. "I'm dying to see this little burg you once called home."

"Good, here's the plan. First, we will meet at Jack's for lunch. Mom, you know where he lives, right?"

"Still on Sycamore?"

"Still there," assured Ted.

"Then, no problem."

"Good, noon a good time for you?" Ted said as confirmation.

"Works for me," Hank boomed.

"It will be a light lunch. Ruthie, Maureen's mom, is fixing finger food. You'll reconnect with Ruthie and Jack. I've told them you changed your name warned Jack to not embarrass anyone. You will also meet Pam and Eliot, Jack's daughter and her husband. She is expecting their first child in a few months. Pam, Eliot, and I will fill you in with what I've been doing. And what the future may hold."

"And," turning to Maureen. Marie asked, "What is with you two? Are you engaged? Are you living together?"

"Mom!" Ted protested. "For the record, we are boy-friend-girlfriend. End of story."

"For now," chuckled Maureen. Ted whipped his head around and looked at her. "Don't be so surprised. I have got you in my grasp, and I am not letting you go. I see a bright future with eight children for us."

"Eight?" Ted asked.

"After all, I am a passionate girl."

Ted blushed. "You need to warn me when springing information like that in front of my mom."

Talking to Marie, Maureen began, "We are what my mom likes to call an item. A lot is happening in our lives right now that complicates an already complicated relationship. I told Ted that I love to sing in the shower and assured him it would be quite a while before I would serenade him." Ted blushed again, and everyone laughed. "However, I assure you we are moving toward a more romantic relationship. Marie, may I call you Maire?" Marie nodded in affirmation, "I hope you won't mind having me as a daughter-in-law."

Everyone laughed again, and Marie assured Maureen nothing would make her happier than having Maureen in the family.

Maureen turned to Hank. "Hank, we've been so busy talking about ourselves. Tell us more about you."

Ted was impressed with Maureen's hostess skills.

"Not much to tell. Got married right out of high school. Then drafted. I gave two years to the Army. Spent the time at Ft. Hood in Texas. Met Dedra, my first wife, and lived in Katy, Texas, outside Houston." Taking a breath, "I started a shoe store there, and it grew to about 30 stores across the southeast. Had three kids; twin girls, Tammi and Traci, and Lance, our son." Hank paused and took a breath. "All three live around New Orleans. The girls are teachers. Tami is an elementary teacher, and Traci teaches English and Theatre Arts at LaMont High School, a few miles outside New Orleans. Lance is an architect for NOLA Engineering, a construction company. Three grandkids, all girls, one from each."

No one noticed the waitress had returned. She stood there with her pad and pen in hand, ready to take their orders. There were a few questions, and then everyone ordered their meal. Ted added the German pancake as an appetizer.

"So, what's the story? How did you get hooked up?" Maureen's inquiring mind was on a roll.

"I have a shoe store-she needed shoes. That's about it."

"Ah, there's gotta be more," pleaded Maureen.

"Nope! I happened to be at the store one day. A beautiful lady who had come in. I took advantage of the situation. The store was dark. The light behind her formed a halo."

It was Hank's turn to take a punch.

"Ouch," Hank said in mock protest. "I complimented her on her feet and choice of shoes. After that, we saw one another. Here and there. Nothing planned. Each time we would talk. I decided to take a chance. I asked her out for dinner. The rest, as they say, is history."

The food arrived, and the conversation moved to the weather, the trip from Florida, and other mundane topics. Maureen was finished first and continued the previous discussion.

"So, you are engaged? When is the wedding? Are we invited?"

Marie said, "We haven't set a date yet. We wanted to see how our children reacted to the news. So, we'll talk when we get back home and let you know. And yes, you are most welcome. Consider yourself invited. We'll formalize it after the date is set, and we'll send you an invitation. But, please, do plan on coming."

Curiosity settled; Maureen returned to her quiet but observing self. Finally, the check arrived, and before Ted had time to react, Hank scooped up the bill. "No need for two college lovebirds paying for two old farts' breakfast." He was laughing, leaning back in his chair and patting his stomach. Ted, that pancake was better than I expected. We may come back before we leave."

"When are you planning to head back?" Ted asked.

"Oh, no set time," said Hank while getting up from the table. "It is a boss's perk. I choose my own routine." Then glancing at Marie, who was looking up at him. "Except you-know-who," throwing a thumb at Marie, "makes an executive decision."

Everyone agreed it was a good breakfast, and they enjoyed the others' company. Marie confirmed Jack's address on the way out. Marie said they would arrive before noon. Maybe a bit before. Then the two couples went their separate ways.

CHAPTER 12

AFTER ARRIVING AT Jack's, Ted and Maureen sat in the truck reviewing what had happened. They sat, considering what lay in store for the rest of the day.

"I like your mother," Maureen said, squeezing Ted's hand. "She is sweet."

Ted did not respond.

"Hank seems like the perfect guy for your mom. I can tell your mother adores him."

"Huh?" Ted said.

"Winston Thibodeau James, are you listening to me?" A smile was on her face.

"I am now. Yes, Hank seems good for Mom. I am glad you like her. So it is, I have had." He left the thought unfinished. "I'm just worried about this afternoon. So many things could go wrong. You are aware this could be a total disaster," Ted said quietly. He was not looking at Maureen.

"I know," then Maureen put her arm through his. "You have had this tremendous stress. Wondering how this morning would go. Now, relax. The morning was fine. In fact, I can't imagine it going any better. So, take it as a sign. A sign of good things happening afternoon."

After a few more minutes of relative silence, Maureen leaned in and whispered, "Relax. Everything will be just fine. You'll see," then kissed Ted on the cheek. Whispering, she said, "I have to go." She slipped out the door. Ted stayed in the truck and watched Maureen drive off.

"About time you came in," Jack said. He had been standing at the window watching them. "That bad, eh?"

Confused, Ted asked, "What's that bad?"

"Your meeting with Mable and Henry."

"Come on, Jack. I told you it's Marie and Hank."

Jack smiled. "Had to wake you up." He paused and watched Ted for a second or two. "Well, spill the beans. How did the meeting go? I see you were smart enough to take reinforcements."

"It was life and death. Maureen said she would murder me if I did not take her along." Ted smiled and sat down in the glider. Jack took his spot in his recliner. After running between the two, Napper settled on Jack. The dog jumped into his lap, curled up, and closed its eyes.

"We ate at Elmer's for breakfast."

"That's a good start," interrupted Jack.

"In the beginning, everyone tip-toed around everything until the fearless one."

"Maureen?" Jack said, more of a statement than a question.

"Of course. Maureen asked the direct questions, and everyone loosened up. Hank is a nice guy. He and mom fit well together. Better than my dad and her, anyway. I told mom to take Hank around town. To show the place off to him. I assured her she would not run into Dad if they drove by the old house. He's working at Triple-H until two."

"Oh, your dad said he would be here around three. OK with you?"

"Sure. I don't see a problem, do you?"

"No. I am praying for a positive outcome this afternoon." Ted was looking at the ceiling.

Jack raised an eyebrow. "And what would be a positive out-come?"

Keeping his eyes on the ceiling, Ted said, "Not having officer Tim come and break up a fight."

Jack laughed. "Ever consider that might be fun?"

"Not in a million years would I consider that fun." Ted was not convincing with his retort. He did not say anything. He was worried the stress might cause a relapse for his dad. Or the two would have one of their infamously loud arguments.

Bypassing her apartment, Maureen drove to her mother's. Ruthie met Maureen at the door.

"Well?" was all Ruthie said. Maureen came in, put her purse down, and seated herself at the dining table.

"Surprisingly, everything was fine. We met Marie and Hank as they got to the lobby. We had breakfast at Elmer's. It was a perfect time. I like Hank, and I like Marie a lot. Mom, why does everyone want to call her Mable?"

"When she was married to Ted's father, he always introduced her as 'Able Mable,' and we assumed her name was Mable."

"Didn't she say anything?" wondered Maureen aloud.

"It was not a good marriage. Not for anyone. Ted was affect-ed by his parent's relationship and his dad's drinking. Her job didn't help either."

"Why, what did she do?"

"In polite terms, she was an exotic dancer."

"A stripper?" asked Maureen.

"Let's just go with an exotic dancer. What I understand is one night, Mack got violent. He was always a loud drunk, but he never got physical." Ruthie paused. "Then one night, he said it was an accident. Any way Ted's dad hit his mother. Marie fell to the floor with absolute terror on her face. She put her hand up to block another slap. Mack did not hit her again." Ruthie watched for a reaction from her daughter. "He walked out the back door. Marie was bruised. She decided enough was enough. That night, Marie left the family. And never looked back."

"Good for her!"

"I would not bring this up. At least not right now. He is under enough pressure. I am not sure how Ted would handle that discussion."

"I love him, mom, and I would not do anything to hurt him."

"I know," Ruthie said, putting her hand on her daughter's hand.

"My, look at the time. It's almost ten already. I've got to get the food for this afternoon. I need to do a little cleaning. You know. In case someone decides to drop by."

"You mean Jack?"

"I mean anyone. You might bring Ted by. I cannot have him see what a lousy housekeeper I am."

"Oh, mom!" Maureen protested, rolling her eyes.

Maureen suggested they use her car to get the groceries. Ruthie did not object. After a quick dusting and picking up around the house, they headed to Kroger's. "I've ordered two trays. One with finger sandwiches and one with fruit and cheese. Do you think it will be enough?"

"We're going to Gringos for dinner, right?"

"Either that or pizza at Uncle Dan's. I guess it depends on how things go. If it is tense, we'll be at Gringo's for sure." Ruthie was surveying the house. She looked at her list. Satisfied, she said, "Let's go."

At eleven, Maureen pulled in and stopped behind Jack's red truck. Maureen and her mother got the food trays from the back of the Soul. Ted came out and gathered up the food trays. He took them into the house. Ruthie grabbed two bags of 2-liter drinks, and Maureen picked up two gallons of tea: one sweet and one unsweet.

Maureen and Ruthie began setting the dining table up for an informal buffet. First, there were the two food trays. Next to the trays were plastic cups, faux silver plastic ware, and napkins. Next, Jack brought out a large bowl and a plastic ladle. "Here," he said, putting the items on the table. "We can use these for ice. People can get however much they want."

Pam and Eliot arrived. They came in as Jack was putting the bowl and ladle on the table.

"Hi, everyone!" Pam said with enthusiasm. "We got a later start than anticipated, I," Pam stopped mid-sentence. "Oh, I see we are actually early."

Jack shook Eliot's hand and gave his daughter a kiss. "Perfect timing. The guests have not yet arrived. We were putting everything out on the table. So have a seat in wild expectation. And relax. Need anything?"

"I could use a Jack and Coke," Eliot said with a smile.

Pam slapped his arm, "I told you, no booze!"

"So you said," in a mock protest. Pointing to Jack, he said, "Jack did ask what I wanted."

Maureen jumped up. At the window, she announced, "They're here," watching a sliver Escalade pull in front and park behind Eliot's Jeep. Maureen waited until the couple reached the door. She opened it before they could ring the bell. "Good morning, again. And welcome. Come in." Marie gave Maureen a quick hug, and Hank nodded her way.

Maureen elected herself hostess and made the introductions. She then invited them to join the conversation circle. At first, it was awkward, and Maureen decided to break the ice.

"Well, Marie, mom, and Jack here, and even Ted on occasion call you Mable. How come?"

"Maureen!" Ruthie scolded her daughter and shot her a killer look. Maureen ignored the look. She did not take her eyes off Marie. Marie had a smile on her face.

At Ruthie, she said, "It's OK, Ruthie." Then, turning to Hank, "He knows the whole story, and we don't want this girl. my future daughter-in-law, to be wondering about her mother-in-law."

At that, Ted took his turn, giving his best stern expression to his girlfriend. But, again, with her penetrating green eyes fixed on Marie, Maureen never saw his attempt at being stern.

"My full name is Marie Mable Merriweather, a mouthful, to be sure. I was named after my mother, also named Marie. To distinguish between us two, my family called me Mable. When Mack and I met, we were young, naïve, and in love. We gave each other pet names. Mack, like his namesake, was a trucker, and I called him Big Truck. He took to calling me Able Mable. When he changed jobs, his nickname was no longer appropriate and disappeared. However, my name stuck. When I moved to Florida and began to establish new roots, people called me by my given name, Marie. It also gave me a reason for the name change and a real chance at a new beginning."

"What about the exotic dancing?"

This time, both Ruthie and Ted chastised her with a stern, "Maureen!"

"What?" she asked. She looked at them both. "I want to know my future mother-in-law."

"Marie was laughing out loud. Hank knows that story as well."

"So, you were really an exotic dancer?" asked Maureen demurely.

"In a word, no. I worked at a club where girls would remove clothing while dancing. However, it was nothing like Smiley's, where nothing is left to the imagination. I was the bookkeeper, assistant manager, and bar tender. Mack liked to shock the neighbors and say I was an exotic dancer. Finally, I got tired of correcting him. He was having so much fun. I gave up. I let people think whatever."

Ted looked at his mother and said, "You left because dad hit you, right?"

"Well, Ted, that was partly true. The girls were encouraging me to leave your father because of his yelling and drinking. Or was it his drinking and yelling? I really don't remember. Anyway, if I had gone to work. I would have had difficulty explaining why I was still with him. So, I talked to Lois, and she helped me get out of town. I closed my savings account and withdrew a bit from our checking account. I got a bus ticket. I wound up in Tallahassee."

"Why Tallahassee?" This was from Jack. He was now fully involved in the story.

"Lois has a brother, a chiropractor. He agreed to help get me to get settled. I found a job as a bank teller. He also found a studio apartment. This was all I could afford. With my first paycheck, paid back Lois's brother. I also bought a few clothes and groceries. The second check went for luxuries, for instance, new shoes. That's how I met Hank, and you know the rest."

"OK, young lady," Marie said, looking directly at Maureen. "Spill the beans. How did you get hooked up with my handsome son? And may I ask what are your intentions?"

"Turnabout is fair play," Ted said, almost laughing out loud.

"Simple. Ted crashed a lunch I had with my mother and Mr. Kelley. He grabbed my arm and pulled me to his side of the table and told me I was his girl and I had better get used to it."

Maureen turned to Ted and stuck out her tongue.

Everyone broke out laughing.

Ruthie interrupted the laughter. "Outlandish as it seems, the story does have an element of truth to it. Jack invited me to lunch and asked if I minded if Ted came along. I said no problem. Maureen needed to get out of the house, so I brought her. After lunch and we got home, Maureen told me she had met her dreamboat."

More laughter.

"Sorry, Teddy. That's what she called you. Your goose was cooked from there."

Marie quizzed, "So, are you engaged?"

"No, he's too chicken."

"I am not!" Ted blurted in his defense. "I told your mother I don't want to rush it."

"But you do have a job. You take care of Mr. Kelley."

"It's Jack," the old man inserted.

"Yeah, I get paid for taking care of Mr. Kelly," shooting Jack a knowing glance and a smile. "And this is not my apartment. So, you know, I can't bring you over here. Not on a date or anything."

"Sure, you can." Jack was smiling. "It would be nice having a feminine touch around here again. Besides, you keep telling me I sleep more than I am awake, so I'd never know!" He smiled and winked at Maureen.

"Oh, he'd know," Ted responded, looking at Jack. "And if we got married and moved into your apartment, then I would lose my income from Jack. Besides, we are both in school."

"That's my son, always the logical one. But Maureen. Tell me, has he kissed you yet?"

"Now, mom!" Ted protested loudly.

"Yeah, inquiring minds want to know," chimed Jack.

"I kissed him first, but he got upset, so I took it back."

Jack wondered aloud, "And, pray tell, how does one take a kiss back?"

"Simple," smiled Maureen, "With another kiss."

"I kissed him. I took the kiss back. Then he kissed me. And yes, Marie, he is a terrific kisser."

"I've had enough. I need a Dr. Pepper," Ted said and went to the kitchen. He came back with two and handed one to Maureen. "Drink this, and maybe we can survive the evening without everyone becoming involved in our relationship."

"Oh," Maureen said, looking at Ted, "So you finally admit we are in a relationship."

"Aw, I give up!"

"Smart move," Hank said with a smile.

There was laughter when the doorbell rang. For a second, everyone was so engrossed with the stories they momentarily froze. The doorbell rang a second time before Ted answered it.

CHAPTER 13

Ted reached the door when his dad raised his hand to knock.

"Hi, Dad. Glad you could come."

"Well," he said, "I wasn't convinced I would be welcomed." Mack stood on the porch looking in, unsure what he should do next.

"Nonsense. This is a family meeting, and all family members are welcome. Come on in."

Mack wiped his feet three or four times before entering the house. He did not make eye contact with anyone. He stayed close to Ted as they made their way to where everyone was seated.

"Dad," he said, pointing to various people, "You remember Jack, Maureen, and Ruthie. I am not sure you ever met Jack's daughter and her husband. This is Pam and Eliot. And this is Hank, Marie's fiancé."

It was an awkward moment, and Ted felt embarrassed. He pointed to a chair next to his for Mack and sat down; Mack made only fleeting eye contact with Marie and kept his gaze downward. Maureen eased his nervousness. Maureen squeezed his hand and whispered, "You did good."

Pointing to Jack's daughter, "Pam and Eliot are both lawyers, and Pam is expecting their first child. Either they are unaware or won't tell whether it is a boy or a girl." There was a little laughter. "Hank, there is a shoe salesman. So, if you need a new pair. I'm sure he could help you out."

Hank gave a slight nod at Mack.

◆ ◆ ◆

Jack coughed then began, "Well, we've heard Hank's story and how Maureen lassoed your son. I understand you are now with Hill-Haven Homes, the Triple-H. How is that going?"

"It's going OK. I'm a framer, the same job I had with Jason, my brother. The main difference is the homes are a bit smaller."

Maureen asked, "Are you indoors or out in the elements?"

"We build the homes and trailers indoors, but we are not immune to the elements. The building is neither heated in the winter nor cooled in the summer. So, it is still hot and cold. You don't feel the direct rays of the sun or the chill of the wind."

"How long have you been there?" Marie asked.

"Going on six months. At first, I worked on the small trailers, but now I am working on the manufactured housing. What we called trailer homes when we were kids."

"What does Jason think of your switch?" she continued.

"I am sober, and I am working steadily. Jason said that's all he needed."

"How did you kick the habit?" Hank seemed interested. "There is an employee or two. Plus a friend that is struggling. You know, with alcohol."

"Church and A.A.," Mack said with a sheepish grin. After Ted moved out, I decided I was the problem. So, I found an A.A. meeting. It was at The Reach, a non-denominational church. One of the members was also a church member, and they got me involved. I won't kid you. It has been a struggle. I will be sober twenty-seven weeks tomorrow."

Ted reached over and put his hand on Mack's shoulder. "Proud of you, Dad."

◆ ◆ ◆

"Well, Maureen." Jack started. "Now that you successfully roped this scrawny excuse of man. What is your plan for him?"

In protest. Ted asked,"Is that all you care about? Any of you?"

"It's all I think about," chimed in Maureen.

"I can't win for losing. Mom, can I move in with you and Hank?"

Maureen wrapped her arms around him. "Listen, buddy. You ain't going nowhere without your woman. And I am your woman!"

Ted got up and cleared his throat. "OK, here's the skinny. We are a couple, and we will get married at some point. When that happens, everyone will be given plenty of notice. We will invite all of you to our wedding. Presently, neither of us has a job since we are still going to school. When we are out of school. And have jobs. Then we may consider marriage. Not a day before."

There was applause from around the room.

Ted nodded, sat down, and then rose again. "And for the record, I snared her. Not the other way around. I knew from the first time I met her she liked to be in charge, so I let her think she snared me."

He sat down. Maureen punched him in the arm. "Liar!"

"To that end." Eliot was speaking now. "And so Maureen won't need to wait for eternity, We do have plans for Ted. We operate a charitable foundation and need a young face to go with it. We have been talking to Ted about heading up the foundation."

Maureen looked at Ted and smiled.

"Now, it is at least a year before he we can add him to our payroll. After that. He must agree to work with us. I am confident the foundation and Ted are a good fit."

"What does the foundation do?" asked Hank. "I may want

to make a donation. It is a 50(c)(3) foundation, right?"

"Hank, we are new. We don't do much of anything. We do provide a few scholarships, and Ted is one recipient. But we do have big plans. Plans we want to impact the community in a positive way. And yes, we are a 50(c)(3)."

Mack looked at Ted. "You are considering this, right?"

"The foundation has approached me, and it sounds intriguing. However, we agreed I need to finish up at Emmerson. Before any meaningful discussion can take place."

"That's part of the deal," said Pam.

"So, when can I become Mrs. Winston Thibodeau James?" teased Maureen.

"I can't say for sure, but it won't be today!" They laughed.

"Anybody hungry?" Ruthie had slipped out unnoticed and fixed the table. Everyone was in the living room. Because lunch was casual, that is where they would eat. Unfortunately, though large by most standards, the dining room table could not accommodate everyone. So instead, a buffet-style lunch was spread out, allowing everyone to move around and select what they wanted.

"We have pimento cheese and ham and cheese sandwiches, fruit, and different cheeses. There are soft drinks, tea, and water. Everybody is on their own, except Pam." Then, looking at Pam, "Relax, hon, I'll bring you something. What do you want to drink?"

"Thank you. Water will be fine." She remained seated with her hands on the baby bump.

It was musical chairs for the meal, and Hank sat next to Eliot. "Tell me more about your foundation. I can always use another deduction."

"The city has experienced an economic boom. The neighborhoods south of the tracks have not benefited from the boom."

"Every city has at least one of those neighborhoods," observed Hank.

"Well, there is a city block that has three unused sections along Monrovia and empty fields behind them. In the good times, these were unpaved parking areas. Now, it is looking bad."

"What are your plans?" Hank was beginning to get interested.

"We want to provide a food store for those having trouble getting to Kroger. There are a few gas stations selling grocery items. Even though the stores are accessible, the costs are often prohibitive for the residents. So, we will convert the largest of the three sections into a food mart. The end one is the smallest and would be a medical clinic. The middle one would be for the neighborhood youth. A place to watch television, play games, and get help with schoolwork."

"Sounds ambitious."

"It is," confirmed Eliot with a sigh. "Our goal is to make community gardens out of the parking areas. One large garden would provide fresh produce for the food mart. In addition, there would be other gardens for community use. We hope to partner with churches and other organizations to get the community involved and grow their produce. It is our plan, anyway."

"What are the hang-ups? What's keeping you from moving ahead?" Hank asked.

"Three things. We are negotiating with the city to buy, but we prefer a low-cost, long-term lease of the building. Second, gardens don't magically appear, so we need guidance from the county's master gardeners. Then, the project will need a face. We see Ted there." Eliot took a couple of bites of a sandwich.

"How much of this does Ted know?"

"He knows the basics, but not the particulars," Eliot said between bites.

"Sound expensive," Mack said between sips of tea. "What is

your budget?"

"Not much, as these projects go. We've set aside about a million," Eliot said, taking a sip of water. "It is ambitious, and we will proceed with caution. At least in the beginning. We need Ted to be comfortable in his new position." Eliot looked at Mack for direction.

"Ted, what is your hesitancy with the foundation?" asked his dad. "It seems like an ideal opportunity for you. Who knows? You can figure this out. How to make it work, I mean."

"I need to get through the next couple of months. Next month, Maureen graduates from nursing school, and I will be working with Habitat Community building houses. Ruthie is the volunteer foreman/coordinator."

"Hey, that's wonderful. Let me know if you need anything. However, you haven't answered my question."

"Would you believe me if I said I was scared to death?" Ted watched his dad for a reaction. "I have never been Mr. Dependable. But, hey, I barely graduated high school."

"That's on me, son," Mack said, apologizing. "I did not provide an environment conducive to academic excellence. But don't doubt your abilities. Look at your college grades. I know it's not Harvard or Yale. But you have been on the Dean's List twice. You need to take the initiative and learn what they expect from you. Trust me, it will pay big dividends in the long run."

Maureen, Marie, Pam, and Ruthie were in their own conversation circle.

"Well, Maureen. Next month is the big day. After that, you'll be a full-fledged member of the working class," said Marie, smiling and holding Maureen's hand.

"Well, you are part right, anyway. I am going for my B.S.N. at Southwestern State. Most major hospitals and larger specialty clinics are looking for a bachelor's degree. Not a simple certificate. Oh, and don't forget, I have to pass my boards."

Ruthie joined in and assured Maureen she would have no problem passing your exam. "You have a 4.0 GPA for the nursing program. Your classmates would die to be in your position."

"I guess," Maureen conceded.

"Have you and Ted talked about the future?" asked Marie.

"You kidding? You heard him. He is, 'mister overly cautious.' But I love him, and I am not going anywhere anytime soon. I can wait, and I have a feeling, big things are going to happen real soon."

Ruthie and Marie asked, "What big things?"

"The last time they were here, I talked with Pam. When she first told us she was pregnant. She said the pregnancy may require her to limit her time with the foundation. She would not tell me more. But I have an inkling they may want Ted more active in the foundation. And sooner rather than later."

"Have you shared with Ted?" Ruthie asked.

"No. I want to graduate first. Maybe Pam will tell Ted by then. If not, I may talk to Ted. Or I may ask Pam for more information and direction. She was cryptic, but I know they want a medical facility south of the track. I hope I can play an active role in the project. I don't know. Anyway, Ted is always saying, let's take it one step at a time. I would like to see him take a giant leap. Just one time. But then he would not be the Ted I admire, would he?"

When everyone finished eating, Pam and Eliot announced they had to leave.

"We need to talk pretty soon, Ted. I would like to speak with you before the baby comes. But we need to talk." They left and set a tentative appointment in two weeks.

Ted was getting nervous about what Eliot was saying. Was his scholarship coming to an end? Was he going to have to move? Ted could think of nothing positive, requiring such urgency.

Eliot and Pam were first to leave. Ted and Maureen did the clean-up, allowing Ruthie and Jack could relax and talk. Maureen was aware Ted's attitude had changed. He was reticent and distracted.

"Was it something Eliot said?" She looked for a response.

"What?" He saw her look. "A lot has happened this week, that's all. I am wondering what could happen next?" He kissed her. "Let's go and check on the elderly couple."

They had a general review of the evening. Everyone believed the afternoon went well.

Ruthie stood and said, "Well, young lady. It's time we head home and give these gentlemen their house back."

Jack watched as Ted walked the two women to their car from the door. He gave Ruthie a hug and closed the door once she was in. Maureen remained by Ted during this routine. She put her arms around his neck and gave him a kiss. Ruthie reached over and honked the horn to interrupt the couple's rapture. Maureen ran to the other side. She waved at Jack, then got in the car. It was gone in minutes.

Hank and Marie were the next to leave. Hank stood up, stomped his feet as if to wake them up, and brushed invisible wrinkles out of his trousers. Marie stood next to him, and they looked at each other.

"Well, it has been a long day. Marie and I are bushed, so we'll be heading back to the motel." Marie and Hank offered to help clean up, but Ted insisted it was no big deal. Then, holding his hand out to Mack, "Nice to have met you, Mack. Good luck with everything."

Marie stood next to Mack and quietly said to him, "Take care."

Marie then went over and gave Jack a quick hug, "Thanks for the hospitality, Jack." Next, she hugged Ted and whispered something in his ear. Then they were gone.

Mack stood and watched as Hank and Marie left. Mack waited until their car was out of sight. Then announced it was time. For him to go. Then, after being assured, his help was appreciated. But not needed, Mack left.

"Well, Teddy, my boy. What motherly advice did you get from Marie?" Jack asked.

"I don't know what you mean?" Ted deflected the inquiry.

"Come on. I saw your mother whisper in your ear."

"Well, Jack, let me ask you a question."

"OK," Jack said curiously.

"Can you keep a secret?" asked Ted.

"You bet your britches I can!" assured Jack.

"Well, so can I," and Ted began cleaning the table.

"All I know is this. I am glad this day is finally over," said an exhausted Jack.

"What are you talking about? You looked like you were enjoying the festivities."

"Yes, but I was scared to death everyone would hang out until I sprang for dinner at Gringos!"

They had a good laugh. They made quick work cleaning up.

CHAPTER 14

THE FINAL MONTH of school arrived, and Maureen was busier than ever. Maureen was on her last hospital rotation, psychology, and was also trying to find a job. Her mother let Maureen understand with a job came the responsibility for living expenses. Maureen's mother said she would continue to help with school expenses at Southern State. However, Maureen realized it was time for her to start testing the waters. She was an independent woman and was more than ready to spread her wings.

Although Maureen's and Ted's paths crossed from time to time, they had little time to spend together. Maureen was in class, writing case studies, working on the psych ward at the hospital, and job hunting. Ted finished his second semester, took final exams, and prepared to volunteer with Ruthie at Habitat Community.

Maureen could sense the distance between them growing. She hoped that it was the pressures of school and work. Maureen hoped and prayed her relationship with Ted had not peaked. And it was now spiraling down. They texted each other, but neither was quick to respond.

While not looking forward to fending for himself, Ted was also busy. Pam would take Jack shopping or to the doctors. Sometimes simply getting him out for an hour or so. With the baby coming, Pam reduced the time she spent with her dad and her time at work. Now that their two-man practice was becoming a single practitioner, Eliot picked up the slack. He spent the majority of his time with their clients.

After the family meeting, Ted had begun spending more time with his dad. He felt guilty spending less time with Jack. Ted was not sure he was providing what Jack needed. However, Ted enjoyed spending time with his dad. He was also anxious to be on his own.

There were nights when Ted still hated his life. He had not left home. He was not on his own. Not like some classmates had done. As he intended to do following the burglary of Jack's house. Ted merely changed addresses. He sometimes it was as if he had switched fathers as well. Ted enjoyed being with Jack but longed for the privacy to bring Maureen over. Without Jack always in the room.

And what was with Maureen? Try as Ted did, Ted was unable to spend time with her; it wasn't working out. Maureen seemed too busy to talk to him or grab a quick lunch. Ted suggested a Coke break, and she refused. Then the unthinkable happened. Maureen found a new man.

Ted was walking by Jenkins Hall. He saw Maureen talking to a man he did not recognize. Ted knew that Jenkins Hall was where she had her psychology classes. And he understood guys were in her classes as well. Not all nurses were women. This is the twenty-first century. But who was this guy? There appeared more to their conversation. More than two students talking about school.

Ted was sure Maureen had not seen him hiding behind the bushes. Then, acting like a jealous teenager, Ted found a brush to conceal his presence. He could see them and Ted was confident he could not be seen. At least not with ease. Ted watched as the conversation came to an end, and then it happened. The couple hugged. Without thinking, Ted gasped, and he clutched his chest. He almost tripped over a rise on the sidewalk.

It was evident Maureen was happy. Ted watched her hug him tightly. Too tightly. In Ted's mind, they were more than casual friends. He watched and shook his head in disbelief. Ted was sure he was so loud that everyone heard him. Either Ted was not as loud as he thought. Or they were oblivious to him. When the embrace ended, Maureen looked at Ted. He almost fainted. Ted was sure she saw him hiding.

Maureen smiled, and she appeared happy. Instead of walking toward Ted, she turned and entered the building. The new guy waved at Maureen as he came walking in Ted's direction. Ted held his breath, kept his eyes down at a book he had opened. The guy walked by without saying anything.

With dilated pupils, Ted couldn't focus on anything. When he recovered from the close encounter, Ted said to himself, "I wonder if he noticed I was looking at the book upside down." After he was sure he could not be seen, Ted stood up. He closed the book, looked in the direction of Jenkins Hall, and said one word. "Stupid!"

Ted was in class when his phone buzzed. "Where are you?" was the text. It was from Maureen.

"Class," he texted back. He put the phone in the backpack's side pocket. He ignored the phone the following four times a message came through. Finally, when Maureen called, Ted chose to ignore the call. He was not in a dumping mood. At least, not tonight. Possibly tomorrow. Tomorrow would be less humiliating. But not tonight.

Before going to bed, he saw Maureen had called two more times. He had had his phone on silent. He did not want to hear the phone ring. And he was not ready to explain things to Jack. Ted plugged his phone in for charging. "Good night," he said. He stood looking at the phone. "Or is it goodbye?" He put the phone aside. As he turned the lights out, he climbed into bed. Sleep was elusive and short-lived. Ted found himself awake several times during the night. And several times, he lay there, staring into the darkness.

◆ ◆ ◆

Maureen tried to reach Ted two more times, then she called her mother. "Mom, I'm worried," Maureen said. Obviously distraught. "It's Ted. He seems to be ignoring me."

"Did you have a fight?"

"No. I cannot remember ever having a fight." Maureen sat, looking at her phone with a puzzled look.

"I texted him yesterday and asked where he was. I was hoping we could meet up this afternoon."

"Did he respond?" asked Ruthie, studying her daughter.

"Yes," Maureen said without enthusiasm.

"What did he say?"

"Class. That's all. Just one word. Class."

"So, he was in class; what's the problem."

"He has never texted me a one-word answer before. He would always tell me what class he was in. He told me how it was going. But this time. Only one word. Class."

"Hmm," Ruthie pondered the situation.

"What about later? Did you text Ted again? Did you try calling him?"

"Dozens of times. No answer. Ted never texted me back, and he won't answer my call."

"Sleep on it tonight, OK? You want to sleep in your old bed tonight? The sheets are clean."

"Yeah," Maureen said, heaving a sigh. "I don't want to be alone." Maureen replayed the events over and over in her mind. Trying desperately to figure out what happened. Finally, when she got to her mother's house, Maureen went and hugged her mother. They hugged for several moments as Maureen shook, trying to hold it all together. When they broke their embrace and Maureen stepped back, tears were rolling down her cheeks.

"I have never had a boyfriend. Not a real boyfriend, anyway. I have never had one who makes me feel the way he does. I am not sure how to describe how I feel when we are together. It's even worse when we are apart."

"I know. I know." Ruthie said, hugging Maureen and kissing the top of her daughter's head. "Give it a little more time. Ted has a lot on his plate. Sleep on it, and we'll talk more in the morning."

◆ ◆ ◆

When Maureen was in the shower, Ruthie called Jack.

"Yo, Ruthie, you are disturbing my beauty rest," Jack said with a laugh.

"Jack, is Ted there?"

"Sure is. Do you want to talk to him? I'll go get." Jack offered.

Ruthie interrupted. "No, don't do that. Is Ted alright? Is he his usual self?" Ruthie asked.

"Since you mentioned it, he has been silent tonight. I am sure his phone chimed, but he never answered it." Jack shared.

"Did he say anything about Maureen?"

"Not a word, which is quite unusual. On a normal day, the kid won't stop talking about her."

"Maureen is worried. Without rhyme or reason, Ted quit talking to her. She asked him where he was. and he answered with one word. Maureen said this was not like him. And to top it off, he hasn't spoken to her since. He won't text her back or answer his phone when she calls."

"What's Maureen doing now?"

"She's in the shower."

After a pause to make sure Maureen wasn't within earshot, she said, "Maureen is staying here tonight. Says she doesn't want to be alone. I feel it in my bones; those two were made for each other. Should we meddle?"

"You bet your bottom dollar we are going to meddle. Heck, Maureen's the best thing to happen to that idiot. I am going to make sure he knows it."

"Jack, don't go overboard and get into a fight with him. We want things to get better. Not make things worse."

"What do you mean?" Jack asked.

Laughing, "Jack, remember who you are talking to. I know you!"

The two agreed to check back after the morning routines, they hung up. For a while, both sat in silence. Wondering what might have happened. Unsure what could be done to fix it.

Before going to bed, Jack called and told Eliot about Ruthie's phone call and Ted's uncharacteristic quiet behavior. Eliot agreed to talk to Pam and get back to him the next day.

Ted was surprised to find Jack up already. In the kitchen, Jack had breakfast ready for them on the table.

"You are up. And you fixed breakfast. What's the occasion? It isn't my birthday."

"How observant. You wouldn't be Mr. Holmes, would you?" Jack said with heavy sarcasm.

"But you never fix breakfast," Ted said as he followed Jack's instructions and sat down.

"Not true, my boy."

"My boy? Now, for sure, something is wrong."

"As I was saying before, you interrupted me. I have never fixed breakfast for you, but I was the breakfast champ at the local breakfast cookoff five years running."

"Breakfast cookoff? There's no such thing. Is there?" Ted was getting nervous. Ted found his blood pressure rising, and cotton filled his mouth. It was difficult to speak.

"No, but I bet I would have won it for at least five consecutive years. Probably more. Now we: you and me. We need to talk." Jack glared at Ted.

Ted asked, taking a bite of egg. "About what?" doing his best nonchalant imitation.

Taking the bate, Jack replied, "You, for now. Could include Maureen, as well. Then we can talk about the important stuff. For instance, is it going to snow in Hell today?"

"You don't believe in Hell," Ted said, moving the target away from him.

"I don't. I was asking whether it was going to snow in Hell, California today, smarty-pants!"

"Don't think so." Ted kept his eyes on his breakfast.

"Don't think so?" repeated Jack.

"No, no snow in Hell, California. To be around 90. The desert southwest in the '90s, today."

"Then we'll talk about you."

"Nope, nothing to talk about."

"Topic number two, Maureen."

"Nope, nothing there either. So, I guess we're all talked out." Ted was looking down at his breakfast. He was smiling.

"Listen, numbskull. You came in yesterday and didn't say two words all evening. You didn't say a word about your favorite topic, Maureen. You didn't even talk about your second favorite topic-me and how much I annoy you."

"You don't annoy me," Ted countered. He refused to make eye contact.

"Well, buddy, that's about to change. Right here! Right now!" Jack was not amused. "And I am not finished with yesterday. I heard your phone go off at least twice. You always answer your phone. Yesterday, you didn't. Don't need a rocket scientist to figure out something is eating at you."

"Didn't feel like talking. Anything else?" Ted looked at Jack.

"OK. Topic number two, Maureen. You two have your first fight?"

"Not really."

"Come on, Ted." Jack's patience was beginning to wear thin. "Not really? Either you had a fight, or you didn't. Which is it?"

"OK, we did not have a fight. Are you satisfied?" There was irritation in Ted's tone. His face reddened, and veins became visible in his neck.

Jack studied Ted for a moment. "No! Not even close."

Ted did not respond. He sat there with both hands around his coffee cup and stared at it.

"How is Maureen?"

"Don't know, don't care. Why don't you ask her?" Jack noticed Ted was struggling to control both his temper and his emotions.

"I'm asking you. You are Maureen's boyfriend."

"Are you sure about that?" Ted was hurt and angry. It was in his voice. It showed on his face as well. Jack was sure Ted was struggling to hold back tears.

"OK, OK, I'll drop it for now. But whatever this is between you two. You need to work it out. And work it out now."

"Or what?"

Jack was getting exasperated. "Or you will regret it the rest of your miserable life." Jack took a breath and watched for a reaction. There wasn't one. Then, in a softer tone, Jack said, "Look, Ted. I don't know what you think you saw, heard, or whatever. Been around the block, buddy boy. At least a time or two. I believe you two were meant for each other."

"Yeah? Well, tell that to her." Unable to control his emotions, Ted got up from the table and took his dirty dishes to the sink.

"No. You need to tell Maureen. If you still love her, then you need to tell her."

"It is not anything she said."

"Something you saw?" pressed Jack.

"More like someone. Maureen has a new man. And they were not shaking hands," an angry Ted roared. Tears were welling up in his eyes.

"Perhaps you're mistaken. Maybe your imagination got in the way. Who knows?"

Before Jack could finish, Ted spun around with tears in his eyes, "You think I imagined what I saw? You think I made this up? You think I would be this miserable if I didn't care for her?"

Jack stood beside Ted and softened his voice. "This is the point, Ted. Whatever is doing this to you, you need to resolve it. If you don't, and you let Maureen getaway. You will be miserable. For a long, long time."

Jack put his arm around Ted's shoulder, "Besides, I have it on good authority; Maureen is as miserable as you."

Ted's anger flared up again. Then, stepping away from Jack, spun and yelled, "How do you know? How could you possibly know?"

In a quiet and calming voice, Jack reassured Ted, "You're right. Maybe I don't know. I do know her mother. Ruthie would not raise a daughter who would flip that switch off. She wouldn't. Next time she calls, talk to her. Alright?"

"I'll think about it." It is all Jack could get. Then in a quieter voice, Ted repeated, "I'll think about it."

Ted went to his room. In a few minutes he was back. Then, in a controlled tone, Ted announced, "I've got an appointment with my counselor, Mrs. Logan. I shouldn't be too long. You be OK?"

Jack studied Ted for a long minute. Then, finally, he turned and walked into the living room. He gave Ted a thumbs-up as he left the kitchen.

With that, Ted was out the door.

Jack was tempted to call Ruthie. He wanted a status report on her end. He picked up the phone and put it down without dialing. Jack remembered Maureen spent the night at her mother's. He elected to pour another cup of coffee while waiting for Ruthie's call.

CHAPTER 15

RUTHIE WAS AT the table when Maureen came in. "Rough night?" she asked.

"That would be an understatement. Any coffee?" answered Maureen.

"On the counter. Help yourself. I brewed full bore. You can use the caffeine." Ruthie said, smiling at her daughter.

As she stood at the sink, Maureen poured herself a cup. She looked out to the backyard. "Birds are hungry," her voice devoid of enthusiasm.

"Have a seat. We need to have a good ole mother-daughter talk."

"Don't know if it will help." Maureen was even more depressed.

"Any word from Ted?"

"Worse." Unable to hold back her tears, she said, "Ted has his phone off. Everything goes directly to voice mail. Mom, I don't know what to do. I don't want to lose him." Maureen paused and took some sips of coffee. Then giving her mother a pleading look, "I have no idea what I have done or said. To make him," she paused, hunting for the right words. "To make him so angry with me." Then, looking to her mother for help, "Honestly, I have no idea what I have done." Finally, she stopped, examined the cup between her hands, and sipped more coffee.

Ruthie remained silently watching her daughter.

"Boy, is this coffee strong or what?" She said, coughing and unable to stifle a small laugh.

"Works every time. Now, when you are ready – and able, I am here for you." She motioned for Maureen to sit. "Whatever it is between you two, don't let it fester. Don't let it ruin your relationship. But, more importantly, don't let it ruin your friendship." Ruthie was watching her daughter's face. "If you don't work this out, you may regret the outcome for a very, very long time."

"I know, but."

Ruthie cut her off. "Drink your coffee. Then we will talk."

She got up and put her cup in the sink. "I'm going to take a shower and get dressed. I'm glad I left emergency clothes over here. And, believe me, this is an emergency!"

Ruthie had a bowl of Special K cereal, orange juice, and fresh coffee on the table when Maureen came it rubbing her hair dry. She was dressed in jeans, slip-on deck shoes, and an old Emmerson Sweatshirt Ruthie wore when she attended the school. Maureen stopped at the doorway and surveyed the breakfast.

"Boy, am I ever in for it."

Laughing, Ruthie asked, "What makes you say that?"

"Simple, the last time you prepared a full breakfast for me without me begging was when you, in great detail, told me about the birds and the bees." They both laughed.

"Listen, honey. I won't pretend to know what is going on with you and Ted. What I do know is how you each feel about each other. I am utterly dumbfounded. If you don't resolve this and resolve it now, you may wind up regretting it."

"What do you mean?" Ruthie had her daughter's attention.

"Your graduation. You do want Ted to come, right?" Ruthie was carefully watching her daughter.

Maureen dropped her eyes. "Maybe he doesn't want to

come."

"Do you know for sure?" Ruthie said. "Maybe he does, or maybe he doesn't. Maybe you want him to come, or maybe you've changed your mind and don't want him to come."

"I haven't changed my mind," Maureen said in a voice barely audible.

"Great, but let the decision be about graduation and not this argument. If you let this tiff be the deciding factor and Ted doesn't come, what will you do if it is all a big misunderstanding? How will you feel knowing Ted wasn't there to celebrate your big day with you because you had a silly?"

"It is not silly," Maureen interrupted.

"Because you had a silly misunderstanding." Ruthie waited for a reaction. Any reaction. There was none.

Maureen had trouble focusing on her mother, and her chest had tightness in it. "Look, mom. I have had many friends who were boys. But nobody, and I mean nobody, does to me what Ted does. When I am not with him, I am not worth crap!"

"When was the last time you told him how you feel?"

"You mean word-for-word?"

"Yes. Using those exact words."

Maureen was quiet for a minute while she pondered the question. "I guess never. At that first lunch, we sort of clicked on the same wavelength. I thought Ted felt the same way."

"Has he ever said he misses you when you're not with him?"

"Yes. Once in a while, Ted will say something, not in those exact words, but with the same meaning."

"Then, the second thing you will have to do is tell him how you feel."

"I keep throwing the idea of marriage out in the open."

"But are you being facetious or serious? And does he know which?"

"OK, that will be the second thing I do. What is the first thing?"

"We have to figure out how this snowball got rolling in the

first place. Do you have any idea what could have made Ted feel distant? Maybe Ted wasn't the one for you. What might have given him the idea maybe you didn't want to be his girlfriend anymore?"

"Mom, don't you think I've been racking my brain. I have no clue what happened. We were inseparable at the party, and today he won't take my call or answer my text. So, what do I do?" Tears began rolling down her cheeks, and her lips began to quiver.

"Go home. Go to work. Do what you have to do today. Let me put my mother's cap on and see what I can come up with. Call me if you have any sudden flashes of wisdom. OK?"

"OK." Maureen used a tissue to wipe her tears away then finished her breakfast in silence. She put the dishes in the sink and grabbed her stuff. She kissed her mother on her head on the way out. Ruthie watched from the living room window as her daughter drove off.

"I've got to call Jack," Ruthie said to herself. She returned to the kitchen. Ruthie put the dishes in the dishwasher. She went over to the coffee pot and poured herself another cup. Ruthie sat pondering the situation, clueless to its source. Or a remedy.

Jack picked up on the third ring. "Jack? Ruthie. Any luck?"

"Absolute zero. You?"

"Same. I have an idea, but I want Pam's expertise. I am bringing my computer over, and we'll give her a call."

"I have a computer here. Why bring yours?" Jack wondered.

"Do you ever call Pam on your computer?"

"No, I use my phone," Jack said, somewhat confused.

"Well, Pam put a program on my computer called TEAMS. I can open it up and click on the phone next to her name, and it will call her. It is face-to-face, just like she is in the room with us. Anyway, we can be on my computer. We don't have to put the phone on speaker. If she needs to bring Eliot in on the call, with a click, she can have him join the conversation."

"Sounds like Buck Rogers and science fiction. But, whatever, I am game, come on over." Jack's comment garnered a chuckle from Ruthie, "Be there in ten," and hung up.

Before heading over to Jack's, she texted Pam to make sure she would be available. When Ruthie pulled in front of Jack's, her phone buzzed. She pulled it out and looked at the screen. It was a text from Pam. No words, only a thumbs-up emoji. Pam would be waiting for the call. She brought in her laptop and set it up on the dining table.

"Give me a few minutes," Ruthie said to Jack. Then she finished getting everything set up and logged in to TEAMS. She clicked on Pam's name, and Pam answered right away.

"Hey, guys. What's the emergency?" Pam was on the couch, feet up and the laptop resting in her lap.

Ruthie started the conversation. "The kids are not speaking to one another. And we don't know if Ted did something to upset Maureen or vice versa?"

Jack added, "Neither one is saying anything. Maureen's graduation is in about three weeks, and we hope to help them resolve this situation before it becomes a regret."

"What have you done?" asked Pam.

Ruthie and Jack took turns telling their story. Jack shared his breakfast experience with Ted, and Ruthie told Pam about her breakfast with Maureen.

Eliot joined the conversation, and each took turns bringing him up to speed.

"Listen, let's go back to the beginning. You introduced the two over a meal. Use a meal as a conduit to the resolution."

Jack added, "Can you use simple English with this old man?"

"Pick a restaurant where you four can meet. Ruthie and Maureen agree to go to dinner without mentioning Ted or Jack. Jack and Ted do the same thing. Make it an upscale restaurant like Frenchy's. That way, they are less likely to make a scene.

Once everyone is seated, you lay the ground rules. Everyone is civil, and the meal isn't over until the air is cleared."

"Consider it done," Jack and Ruthie said, looking at each other and nodding in agreement.

"The upside," Eliot continued, "is the lovebirds find their path again."

"And the downside?" asked Jack.

"The differences are beyond repair. But everyone will know what is what? I have seen they are in love. This spat has to be a misunderstanding. You have the most difficult job in this."

"What is that?" asked Ruthie.

"First, you have to be neutral. You need to encourage the dialogue, but you cannot appear to be taking sides or attempting to force a resolution. Whatever the problem is, they must work it out on their own terms. Call us back with the results. And I would do this soon. Preferably tonight or tomorrow night."

"Thanks," and everyone disconnected.

"Ted can always get away, so it will be up to Maureen's schedule. You let me know when and what time to have Ted at Frenchy's. Who should arrive first?" Jack asked.

Both sat there contemplating the situation in silence. Ruthie finally spoke up.

"I agree with Eliot and think it would be easier if you two arrived first. However, I think I can get Maureen to join you two. She thinks I am in love with you and won't want to spoil our chance to be together."

"You mean you're not in love with me?" Jack asked teasingly.

"Jack, one problem at a time," Ruthie said, gathering her computer and kissing Jack on the cheek, then she was out the door.

"Don't forget to let me know."

Ruthie waved her hand, and within a minute or two, she

was gone.

◆ ◆ ◆

Jack and Ted arrived at Frenchy's precisely at six two nights later. Jack even sprang for valet service. Ten minutes later, a bright red Camaro pulled up. The valet service parked the car. Ruthie announced their arrival to the hostess, who directed them to the table where Jack and Ted were waiting.

"What is he doing here?" asked Maureen with a chill in her voice, her eyes focused on Ted.

"Well, I enjoy Jack's company and would not pass on the opportunity to have a wonderful dinner with him. As for Ted, well, what can I say?"

Seeing Maureen enter with her mother, Ted turned and said, "Jack, I'm not so sure this is a good idea. I think I'll head home," Ted began scooting his chair away from the table.

"Sit your butt back down." First, whatever has got you two in a twit will end, and I mean, it ends tonight. Second, I have the valet ticket in my pocket, and I am not giving it up without a fight." The voice was firm but not harsh.

When the two arrived at the table, Maureen said, "Mom, I don't think this is a good idea," and turned to leave.

"Young lady, did you hear what Jack said to Ted?" Ruthie never took her eyes off Maureen.

"Yes," Maureen said quietly.

"I'm sorry, I did not hear you."

"Well, then. Yes, I heard what Jack said to Ted," Maureen said in a voice harsher and more loudly than intended.

"Well, ditto his remarks. Now, let's get the formalities of ordering a wonderful meal out of the way, then we can talk. But make no mistake, missy, we will talk. We will resolve this twit, as Jack called it. I don't much care if you take it as a promise or a threat. Now, sit down!" Ruthie gave Maureen and Ted a stern look, then relaxed and smiled. She reached over and touched

Jack's hand.

Turning to Jack, "How did I do?" she asked with a smile on her face.

Jack stood as the ladies were being seated.

"Perfect, my lady," and did a mock bow.

Throughout the meal, Maureen and Ted's conversation started barely civil and softened as the meal continued. After the dinner, four coffees were brought.

"Showtime, kiddos. Let's have it. A few weeks ago, one could get diabetes from the sugary nature of your relationship. Today, one would die of thirst. What changed?"

"Ask her," Ted said, nodding to Maureen. After that, Ted felt a tightness in his voice and refused to make eye contact with anyone.

"What do you mean to ask me?" Tears were welling up in Maureen's eyes. She sat staring at Ted and biting her bottom lip. "You're the one who has their nose bent out of shape," She pounded the table, adding emphasis to her statement.

"OK," Ruthie said, "take a breath and let's take a different approach. Ted, let's start with you. Why are you upset with Maureen?"

"For the past few weeks, I have heard nothing from her. My phone calls go unanswered, and my texts go without a response. What am I supposed to think?" Ted's voice was shaking. He was also biting his bottom lip and still not looking at anyone.

"I told you," Shouted Maureen. Ruthie put a hand on Maureen's arm. Then, in a forced calm, she added, "I told you I would be swamped as the year ended. I have my final rotation, final exams, nursing board study, and finding a job. I did not have time for socializing."

"That didn't stop you from snuggling up with Barry," an angry and hurt Ted exclaimed in a raised voice.

147

"Ted," Jack said, wanting to calm him down.

"Barry? Barry who?" Maureen looked at her mother and pleaded, "Honest, mom, I have no idea who he is talking about."

"So, you did you or did you not hug Barry outside Jenkin's hall last week? Lovingly, I might add," Ted's voice was filled with hurt. For the first time, his eyes moved to look at Maureen.

"That? You saw that" she asked in total surprise.

"Aha!" The truth finally surfaces."

Maureen started laughing. "This is ridiculous."

"I fail to see the humor in this," snapped Ted. Jack again had to calm Ted down.

"Barry Smith is Italian, and he had landed his dream job."

"Smith doesn't sound Italian to me."

"No, but Baldacci is. Baldacci is his mother's maiden name, and she has family all over Italy. Barry is fluid in Italian, even taking advanced Italian at Emmerson. Royal Caribbean Cruises hired Barry for ships ported in the Mediterranean."

"And the embrace?" Tod started to feel embarrassed, and his face turned red.

"Spontaneous. Barry has been a good friend. I've known him most of my life. He got his dream job, and I shared in his excitement. That's it. Besides, Barry is engaged!" Maureen slumped back in her chair and folded her arms across her chest in defiance.

"Maureen," Jack asked, "do you have anything you want to ask or say to Mr. Knucklehead here?"

With her lips quivering and her voice shaky, she replied, "Only that I love him, and these past few weeks have been the worst few weeks of my life. But then, mom reminded me, I have not expressed my true feelings, at least not often enough."

Maureen shared with Ted what she shared with her mother the previous night. The two reached across the table and held hands. Ted reciprocated and shared his feelings for her.

"Alright, alright!" Jack said. "Take your lovey-dovey apology show elsewhere."

Jack reached into his pocket and brought out the valet ticket. "Here, you to love-birds

need to go somewhere away from us old coots. Meanwhile, I want to finish my coffee with this beautiful lady here who promised to make sure I get home safe and sound."

Ted shook Jack's hand, smiled at Ruthie, and then kissed her on the cheek. Maureen kissed both Ruthie and Jack on the cheek. The two left, arm in arm. The bounce in their step returned.

Ruthie leaned over and kissed a surprised Jack on the lips. "Mission accomplished."

Returning the kiss, he said, "You bet your bottom dollar, missy. Mission accomplished."

CHAPTER 16

THE DINNER OVER, and the misunderstanding cleared up, Ted and Maureen agreed to talk. Daily, either in person or on the phone. They realized the importance of knowing the other was there for them.

Ruthie had everyone over for dinner. This was Ruthie's longtime wish. Then Jack reciprocated a few weeks later.

The final weeks of school flew by quickly. Once again, Ted finished the term with a perfect 4.0 GPA. He considered summer school then, remembered his obligation to Ruthie and Habitat Community. He decided against it.

Maureen continued to be swamped right up to graduation day. There was the obligatory sending out announcements and graduation pictures, plus the fitting for the cap and gown. Maureen would take her Nursing Board Exam the week after graduation. She felt confident she would pass. Maureen also landed a job with a local surgical clinic. Until Maureen had passed her boards and received her RN license, she would help in the office by answering the phone, filing, and doing other mundane chores. She used this time to observe. And to learn about her new job.

Graduation day arrived and was filled with pomp and circumstance. Unfortunately, Maureen was needed at the convention center two hours before the ceremony and left without eating breakfast.

For the umpteenth time, her mother asked. "Honey, do you have everything?"

"Yes, mom," Maureen answered. Also, for the umpteenth time.

Ted sent a text. "It's your day. Shine like the superstar you are." He started to call, then chose to not add to her stress. The previous night, they talked for over an hour.

There was a Kay's Jewelers bag on the floor. Ted picked it up and pulled the rectangular black box out. He opened it and examined the necklace inside—a gold heart with a solitaire diamond in the center. On the back was engraved MR+TJ. Satisfied everything was perfect, he put the box in a graduation gift bag with blue and gold tissue, the colors of Emmerson College.

"Ted, shake a leg in there. We don't have all day." Jack bellowed from his bedroom.

Ted picked up the phone and dialed the number.

"Yes, Ted, I'll be there." The voice was kind, but it had answered the question so often it was becoming annoying.

"Thanks, Dad. But it is not why I am calling," Ted said. "Ruthie is having a reception at the country club. and asked me to verify would be able to attend."

"Yes, I got the invitation yesterday. I sent Ruthie a text last night. However, I will call and confirm when we're done. Just to make sure. OK, son?"

"Love you, dad. Talk to you later." Ted said and hung up. Since moving out and taking care of Jack, he and his dad had grown closer. The important people to Ted were with him, His girlfriend and his dad. Nothing could be better. Well, almost nothing could be better. He never said it aloud, but secretly wished his mother could be there as well.

The three-Jack, Ruthie, and Ted could not fit in one car. Jack and Ted arrived at Ruthie's in the Ranger. The Ranger could not hold three people. Ruthie pointed out the Camaro had a back seat in name only. So, when it came time to leave, Jack rode with Ruthie, and Ted drove himself to the convention center.

Mack greeted them at the convention center. He gave Ruthie a hug and shook Jack's and Ted's hands. Ruthie handed them each a ticket, allowing them inside the convention center's main hall. They found seats. Ruthie and Jack were together. Ted sat next to Jack. Mack was on the other side. Ruthie and Ted kept fiddling with their phones to ensure they were charged and working.

Ruthie was sworn to secrecy about Maureen being valedictorian. She would be one of two student speakers at the commencement. The three men were surprised watching Maureen and Barry Smith took their seats on the stage. Rather than with the other graduates.

Ted leaned over and looked at Ruthie, who held up her index finger.

"Well, I'll be," Ted said, almost to himself.

"What's going on?" Mack asked.

Ted turned to his dad and had a broad smile on his face. "My girlfriend is number one in her class!" They did a high five and settled back in their seats. Ted could not hide his pride for Maureen, or Mack, his happiness for his son.

Maureen always had a strong, clear voice, and she delivered her address with enthusiasm and confidence. "Nursing is a calling," she said, "and we have answered that call. Around the nation." Then glancing at Barry, "and the world."

There were the usual formalities as the graduates were confirmed and names were called. The graduates shook a few hands and received their diplomas. Their pictures were taken. When the Provost read "Maureen Kathleen Rittenhouse." The four jumped up and applauded, ignoring a request to hold the applause until the end. Ted put his camera mode on video and captured the moment for posterity.

With the ceremony over, families and graduates found one another. They moved through the melee on the floor. Ted was the first to find Maureen. He gave her a long kiss and a hug. Ted was hesitant to let her go. But her family won out. Maureen got hugs and kisses from her mom, Jack. Even from Mack. Ted's dad had always been polite, but reserved around her. So this sudden show of emotion surprised her. When Mack had finished hugging her and stepped back, she hugged him and whispered in his ear, "Just so there is no confusion, I am in love with your son." She then stepped back, and Mack mouthed, "I know," and they both grinned.

Maureen arrived an hour after everyone else. There were signs and balloons outside announcing her accomplishment. Inside, the house was filled with neighbors and friends. The aromas reminded her of a funeral home. There were Five large bouquets. One was from her mother, and Jack, Mack, and Marie each sent a bouquet. The largest was from Ted. Overwhelmed, Maureen made the rounds, hugging and thanking everyone, fighting back the tears of joy.

Eventually, there were the five. Ruthie, Jack, Mack, Ted, and Maureen. Mack sensed the time was appropriate, and said, "I need to hit the road. Working morning shift tomorrow."

"Wait, dad."

Ted's request caught Mack by surprise.

"Can you stay a little longer?"

"Sure," he said with some hesitancy. He studied his watch. Then with enthusiasm said, "No problem," Mack assured his son.

Ted went to the food table. First, he reached for the graduation gift bag hidden under the table. He went to Maureen, bag in hand.

"I said we could not be engaged until I had a job allowing me to support a family."

"No," Maureen interrupted, "you said, and I quote. 'We cannot get engaged until one of us has a job capable of supporting a family.' Well, buddy boy. I've got that job. So, what's the hold-up?"

Blushing, "Old fashioned," he said. "I need to be able to support you before we commit to marriage."

"So, what do we have here?" Maureen said, grabbing at the bag.

Ted kept the bag out of sight and said, "I am not prepared to propose to you right now. But I am committed to you. Check with my dad and Jack, and they will tell you. That Barry thing."

Cutting Ted off, "Oh. So, it's now that Barry thing?" She was teasing Ted.

Jack said, "Your dad and I are old men. We don't have forever for you to give her whatever is in the bag." Everyone relaxed and laughed.

Handing her the bag, Ted said, "I can't give you a ring right now, but I can give you my heart."

Maureen removed the tissue and pulled out the black box. She opened it and starred at the necklace. "Oh, it's beautiful!" Then she turned and showed everyone the heart. She pointed to the solitaire diamond in the middle.

"Look on the back."

"MR plus TJ," she read. "I believe the MR is me, but TJ? I love with a guy with this weird name. Winston."

"When we get married, the license may say you are marrying Winston. But your husband will be known as Ted-Ted James!"

Maureen walked over, pushed him into a chair, and sat on his lap. She put her arms around his neck and looked straight into his eyes. "I love it! I love you! Whatever you choose to call yourself!" And gave him a long kiss.

"You understand," she said, "I can melt this down and forged into a ring."

"You wouldn't," he said, with raised eyebrows, "Would you?"

"Winston Thibodeau James, aka Ted, you seem to be the only one who is unaware we are engaged. With or without a ring."

"Oh, I am fully aware. I have been told by everyone." Then looking at Ruthie, "except your mother."

"Oh, you are so engaged to my daughter!" Ruthie said with a laugh and leaning on Jack.

"Well, like the song goes. 'When will my little finger get a ring?'" She gave him another hug.

"Soon." Ted said, "Soon, I promise."

"You've made a promise in front of family and friends. They are my witnesses, and we are all going to hold you to it." She kissed him one more time, then she got up.

With everyone gone, Ruthie and Maureen sat and talked about that day. Maureen kept touching the necklace Ted had given her.

"Well, mom, I think I'll be heading home. There are things to finish up at Emmerson before starting at Southern State next month."

"Sweetheart, sit down. We need to have a talk."

"Can't this wait until tomorrow?"

"No, it can't. And it is not something I could bring up earlier. Not with everyone here."

"Mom, you have me worried. Are you OK?"

"Never better," she said. She reached for an envelope on the table. Maureen had not noticed it before.

"Your dad and I had always planned to have a college fund for you. But the accident took him from us. Way too soon. We never had that opportunity." Tears welled up in Ruthie's eyes.

"I got some money from insurance and a settlement over the accident."

"I seem to remember that."

"Well, with Pam and Eliot's help, we set up a trust account for you. We decided to keep it a secret until the time was right."

Ruthie's hands were now trembling. Tears were in her eyes, and one rolled down her cheek.

"I would give everything I have. For your dad to be here. Right now. But this. This is the best I can do. He would be so proud of you."

Maureen put her hands on her mother's hand to settle their shaking. "Mom, you have me worried."

"OK! Here it is, from your dad and me. This is your graduation present from us. From both of us," and handed the envelope to Maureen.

Almost afraid to open it, Maureen was quiet and sat staring at it. Then, with hesitation, Maureen opened the envelope. She gasped when she saw a check made out to her. It was for $25,000. She looked at her mother in disbelief, then back to the check.

"Mom!" and Maureen started to cry. Maureen and Ruthie freely cried as they clung to each other. Finally, Ruthie broke the embrace, but continued to hold her hand.

"There's more," Ruthie said. Afraid to make eye contact. She continued looking at their hands.

"More?" Maureen asked.

"Pam and Eliot put safeguards on the trust. Tomorrow, Eliot will be here and explain everything. But, dear, you are a wealthy young woman." Ruthie paused and continued, "The $25,000 came from the trust. And there is more. More money in the trust. I can't say how much more. I did not want to know. There are conditions to be met before you have full access to the money. Eliot will explain everything tomorrow."

"Wait until I tell Ted, she exclaimed. We can get married now!"

"No, Maureen. You can tell him about the check but keep quiet about the trust. Not yet. You need to meet with Eliot first. There is no provision that it remain a secret once you are aware it exists. But please. Talk to Eliot before saying anything to Ted. OK?"

Maureen kept her eyes on the check and was only half-listening to her mother and nodded in agreement.

"With money comes responsibility. Before you make any decisions, listen to what Eliot has to say."

"Does Mr. Kelley know?" Maureen asked.

"Yes and no. Jack knows there is a trust set up for you. He is unaware of the particulars." Ruthie studied her daughter. "I received this money and knew your dad would want you to have it. I checked with the bank, and they suggested I talk to a lawyer. Jack told me his daughter was a lawyer. So, I called Pam."

Maureen was doing her best to take it all in.

"I talked with Pam and Eliot, and we set up the trust. We haven't talked about the trust since then."

"Do you know how much is there?" Maureen asked anxiously.

"No. As I said, we haven't talked about it since it was set up."

"Whew." Maureen let out a breath and sank back in her chair. She kept looking at the check. "Change of plans. Mind if I spend the night?"

Ruthie leaned toward her daughter, squeezed her hands, and smiled up at her. "Honey, this is your house, too. Rich lady or not. You are always welcome here."

"Mom, what about you?"

"Maureen, dear. Do not worry about me. Pam set up a trust for me, as well. It pays me a monthly income, and I have access to money whenever I need it. It covers my expenses should I need to be put in a home. So, no, don't let me hold you back on your dreams. Talk to Eliot tomorrow. He will be able to answer your questions and help you plan your future."

Exhausted, Maureen said good night, showered, and fell into bed. Ruthie debated for a few minutes, then called Jack.

Jack answered on the second ring. "I told her"

"Does she know how much is there?" Jack asked.

"No. I told Maureen you know about the trust but not the particulars."

Jack said, "Good, I don't want the particulars." Then asked, "What happens next?"

"She meets with Eliot tomorrow. Any word on Pam and the baby?"

"Nope. Baby watch is in full swing," he chuckled. "Hope it waits until after Eliot and Maureen have a chance to meet."

Ruthie asked, "Does Ted know? About the trust?"

"Doesn't need to know, so unless someone else has spilled the beans. Ted is in the dark."

"Good." Ruthie sighed a sigh of relief. "I told Maureen not to tell him tonight. Not sure she bought my argument, but let's hope she waits until she talks to Eliot."

They talked for a few minutes more and hung up.

Jack lay on his back in bed, studying the ceiling. "Well, Jess," he said to his deceased wife. "You missed one humdinger of a day. You would have enjoyed it. Good night, my love."

CHAPTER 17

ELIOT MET WITH Ruthie and Maureen at Ruthie's house. The meeting was casual, low-key, and lasted an hour. Maureen learned she was now a millionaire. While she could pull money out whenever she wanted. Eliot suggested before she got married, a pre-nuptial agreement should be drawn up. At first, Maureen objected, but saw the wisdom and agreed.

"One more thing," Eliot said, putting the papers back in his briefcase. "Do not say anything to Ted. Not about the trust. Not about the pre-nuptial. At least not until you are engaged. I have gotten to know Ted since he began taking care of Jack. I believe he is an honest and honorable man. I don't foresee a problem. But then why tempt fate."

After saying their goodbyes, Maureen and Ruthie sat at the table. Maureen held a copy of the trust, glancing over it.

"Gee, mom, this is a lot for your little girl to take in. It is a game-changer, for sure!"

"Maureen, don't let it be." Ruthie studied her daughter. "Ted loves you-not your money. I believe your relationship can withstand anything the world throws at you." Ruthie paused and looked out the window. Returning her gaze to her daughter, Ruthie said, "Honey. Tell him about the graduation money. Save it, spend it, burn it. It is all up to you. However, when he pops the question."

"If he pops the question," interrupted Maureen.

"When he pops the question," Ruthie continued, "and there is no question he will. Then sit down with him. Lay all your cards on the table and ask him to do the same. I don't think he has a million bucks buried in the backyard. But you never know." Maureen laughed. "The last thing a married couple needs are secrets. In the beginning, discovering those secrets makes romance possible. Don't hide anything from each other."

"Am I not deceiving him now?" Maureen asked.

"I said secrets, not lies. The secrets are about who you are. Not about what you have. You don't know everything about Ted. Nor does Ted know everything about you. In fact, you may never learn everything about each other. The important stuff you will learn over time."

Ruthie took a deep breath and watched her daughter. Reassuring her daughter, she said, "That day is not today. And it won't be tomorrow. It won't even be the day you get married. The path to a happy marriage is learning little things about your soul mate."

Not convinced, Maureen let out a breath of air and said, "OK, I guess."

"When you are engaged, Pam and Eliot will guide you through the process."

"At least I won't need to worry about paying for the wedding."

"Whoa! Maureen, I know I said you could spend or save that money. It would be wise to put half of what you received today away for your wedding. Let that be your budget. Keep your feet on the ground and your head out of the clouds. Ted needs to feel needed in this relationship. The truth is everybody needs to feel needed. If Ted sees money as no object, it may raise more than a few red flags. Think about all the singers and movie stars who flaunt their money. They can't keep a relationship going. Those who keep their wealth to themselves tend to enjoy long-lasting relationships."

Maureen thought about it and nodded in agreement.

"You have no idea what lies ahead. If you view this windfall as easy money to spend, it will be gone in a flash. Down the road, you may need this nest egg, and it won't be there." Ruthie never took her eyes off her daughter.

Maureen smiled and gave her mother a hug. "You are the best mom a girl could ever have," she whispered in her mother's ear.

A week after the graduation ceremony, Ted got a call from his dad.

"Son, can you and Maureen come over for dinner on Friday?"

"I think so," Ted said. "I will have to check her schedule. She is busy at her new job and has started Southern State classes."

"Great. Call me after you talk with her."

This piqued his curiosity, and Ted asked, "Is everything OK? Is there something I should?"

Mack cut his son off. "There are many things you should know. For instance, how lucky you are with Maureen in your life. No, no, there is nothing going on. I am fine. However, there are things we need to discuss."

"OK," Not convinced, Ted played several scenarios in his head.

Mack brought his son back to reality. "Ted, don't go getting paranoid on me. Everything is fine. As Maureen's future father-in-law, I want to make sure she knows how welcome she is in our family."

"OK. I'll call Maureen and call or text you back."

With Ted's curiosity on high alert, he texted Maureen to call when she got a chance.

A hurried voice asked, "What's up?" Then Ted heard the noise of a busy clinic in the background.

"Dad wants us over for dinner on Friday."

"Great, what time?"

"When you get off."

Maureen was quiet a minute, and Ted could hear papers shuffling. "OK, no surgeries on Friday, so the office will close early. Text tell me when I call you this evening."

"I'll tell him six. OK with you?" Ted heard more papers shuffling.

"Six is great. Gotta go. Love you," and she was gone.

Ted assumed his dad was getting ready for work, or maybe even at work, so he texted him. "6 pm, OK?" A few seconds later, a thumbs up appeared on his phone. Ted smiled. He was surprised at how tech-savvy his dad had become.

Ted spent most of the day with Ruthie learning his Habitat Community crew duties. At first, Ted would be the gopher. Go for this and go for that. Then, he would have an opportunity to show what he knows about various tools. As the project progresses, he will be given more responsibilities.

Maureen called her mom and told her about the dinner with Ted and Mack on Friday. Maureen suggested they move their dinner to Saturday. "Hope you understand, Mom." Maureen gave her a quick update of her responsibilities at work and starting classes, then hung up.

Ted and Maureen arrived at a quarter to six on Friday. Ted always had stressed punctuality, and he liked to arrive a few minutes early. He hated being late, whether for a dinner date or a job interview. Ted was dressed in jeans and a polo shirt.

Maureen wore an Emmerson sweatshirt. Mack greeted them and welcomed them into the house.

"You said casual; are we too casual?" Ted said.

"Nope, you are perfect." He gave Ted a hug and then hugged Maureen.

"Is it them?" A woman came from the kitchen.

"Yes, it's them," Mack hollered back. "Come and meet them."

A tall woman about Mack's age came in, smiling and wiping her hands. She went and stood next to Mack. The woman had jet black hair with brown eyes, and she was dressed in distressed jeans and a sweatshirt advertising tool company Ted did not recognize.

Pointing to Ted, "This is number-one son, Ted."

"I am his only son," Ted said, reaching to shake her hand. She had a warm, friendly smile.

"And this is my son's million-dollar catch, Maureen."

Maureen gasped and then recovered. "Hi." is all she could get out.

"This is Melinda Rich," Mack said by way of introduction. "She works at Triple-H with me. And she is recovering like me."

Together, Ted and Maureen relaxed and said, "What a nice surprise."

Mack said, "We've been quasi-dating for a couple of months. I did not bring Melinda with me when your mom was in town." He said, "I was aware it was going to be tough enough. No need to add to the tension. I am sorry," he said to Maureen. "But Melinda's schedule meant working the day of your graduation," he said, "or I would have brought her with me."

"Enough chit-chat; we can talk over dinner."

"Oh," said Mack. Then, with a smile, he added, "I kind of lied. I am not cooking; Melinda is in charge of the meal tonight."

Waving her hand at Ted and Maureen, she asked, "We are having steaks. How do you want yours?" After getting their orders, Melinda returned to the grill.

They all complimented Melinda on the meal.

"Mack and I trade off cooking duties. Been this way from the get-go. We decided the guest will prepare the menu and cook the meal."

"That explains why dad was not on grill duty tonight."

"So, tell me, how you met?" Maureen asked with keen curiosity.

His thumb aimed at Maureen, Ted said, "She is the definition if inquisitiveness,"

"Well. You will never learn anything if you don't ask," Maureen said with a smile.

"At AA. The meetings are at The Reach. Mack had already been attending church there when I attended the first meeting. I came before I went to work and had my Triple-H shirt on. If I had known what a magnet that shirt was, I would have worn it sooner."

Laughter filled the room.

"During the break, Mack comes up and introduces himself. That is when I learned he, too, works at Triple-H. A little more chit-chat, and he asked me on a date."

"Way to go, Dad," Ted said, slapping his dad's back.

"Wait. It gets better. The date was for nine-thirty on a Sunday morning. Yup. Our first date was attending a church service at The Reach."

"Does that rate an amen?" teased Maureen. Everyone said, "Amen!"

"After service, we ate at ye old Waffle House where I learned to love smothered and covered hash browns."

"You mean, you never had them before?" asked Ted.

"Before you can have them, you must know they exist. And to do that, you must physically go inside a Waffle House. Until

I met Mack, I had driven by the joint but never brave enough to venture inside."

"Well, Dad does set a high culinary bar," winking at his dad.

"Not to be outdone, I told him I would cook a real breakfast at his place after church the following Sunday."

Maureen's curiosity was getting the best of her. "And did you? Did you cook him a real breakfast?"

"Eggs over easy, small sirloin steak, country potatoes, and my special breakfast blend coffee."

"What is your special coffee?" Ted asked.

"Can't tell. If I did, it wouldn't be special anymore, now, would it?"

"Fair enough," Ted said and took a sip of water.

"Anyway, that started the cooking thing. Mack said he would do me one better. He had everything needed to cook fried chicken and invited himself over. I hate to admit it, but it was the best fried chicken ever!"

"I am confident Melinda doesn't own a string of shoe stores," Mack started.

"But one drawer full of shoestrings!" she teased, and everyone laughed.

"But she is easy on the eye and has a wonderful sense of humor. And we keep each other honest in the booze department. Our days and shifts are flexible. So, we must take advantage of those opportunities to share a home-cooked meal."

"I think that's the sweetest story ever." Turning to Ted, "When do I get the now-famous James' treatment. Like being wooed with your home-cooking?"

"I wouldn't get my hopes up if I were you," Mack said with a grin. Maureen turned to look at him, "If it doesn't say micro-wavable, he doesn't cook it!" More laughter.

"Actually, learning to take care of Mr. Kelley has meant learning how to cook. He has some special dietary needs. So." Ted paused a beat before continuing. "Like my dad enjoys pointing out. The one positive thing about my cooking."

Maureen looked at him questioningly, "I haven't killed the old coot—yet!"

Turning to Maureen, Melinda asked, "What about you? Do you do much cooking?"

"Used to," Maureen responded. "I am on my own while attending Emmerson. I've pretty much relied on the Ted James school of cooking—take out or microwave. Once we are married, I plan to fatten him up with my fantastic culinary skills."

"Mack," Melinda said, "you didn't tell me they are engaged."

Ted interrupted. "We're not"

"Not officially," corrected Maureen. "Once he realizes it," pointing a thumb in Ted's direction, "it will be official. Then you absolutely, positively must be there." It was not a suggestion.

"Not to change the subject. Have you talked to your mom lately?" asked Mack?

"Not me. Maureen, on the other hand."

Embarrassed, "Marie called, and we had a long conversation a few days before graduation."

"That's great. So, have they set a date yet?"

Both Maureen and Ted shook their head no.

Ted asked, "Mom know about you two?"

"Not yet. We are talking more, mostly about the two of you. I will tell your mother about Melinda soon."

"Tonight was the happiest I've seen my dad in a long time," Ted said, driving Maureen back to her apartment.

"I like Melinda. She is good for your dad." In the truck, Maureen sat next to Ted, her head leaning on his shoulder.

"So, master chef. When are you going to cook something? Meaning not ready-made or microwavable?" asked Maureen.

"What do you mean me? You're the one with all the fantastic culinary skills," Ted said, mocking her voice.

"When you admit I am the only girl for you, then maybe," Maureen said.

"Haven't I already done that?" Ted asked, showing a little confusion.

"Oh yeah, the heart thingy." She reached up and touched the heart necklace.

"It's a heart thingy, now?"

"Oh, you know what I mean." Maureen sat us and turned to face Ted. "Tell you what, you invite your dad and Melinda to mom's house on Sunday after service, and I will prepare a brunch extraordinaire."

"Do I get to pick the menu?"

"Absolutely not. If I am cooking, I select the menu. Then, when you get brave enough to cook, you can set the menu. Just be prepared to be blown away."

After Ted had left, Maureen called her mother.

"How did it go?" Her mother asked.

"It was wonderful. Mack has a girlfriend, Melinda Rich."

"I know her," said Ruthie. "Her parents owned a restaurant for a while."

"Well, that explains that. Malinda cooked us fabulous steaks."

"I am glad you enjoyed yourself. How is Ted handling it?"

"Ted is thrilled for his dad."

"Me, however. I may have gotten myself in over my head. I have invited Mack, Melinda, and Ted over for brunch on Sunday. At your house. I am cooking."

"Oh, dear. Is Ted aware of how bad you are in the kitchen?"

"Well, I kind of sort of let it slip that I was a fantastic cook."

"And you don't want to disappoint?" Ruthie said with her mind racing. "OK, I'll help you out with a simple menu. But, and this a major but. You, young lady, will have to do the cooking. Melinda can tell if you faked it. Are you still coming to-morrow?"

"Yes, mom, I'm coming." She said with a hint of reluctance.

"Good, we'll waste some food, but that happens when you are learning to cook. We'll have you cook the menu tomorrow, so you will be prepared for Sunday."

With that, the call ended. Ruthie started to plan out a simple brunch her daughter could pull off and impress Ted and his dad and his dad's new girlfriend.

CHAPTER 18

RUTHIE GOT UP, armed with her trusty cookbook, found a simple breakfast she felt her daughter could handle, given her limited culinary skills. They would do a dry run and Ruthie would run it over to Ruby Pugh. If it came out respectably. Ruby was an elderly woman in her 90s. She always appreciative of a free meal. The best part was her eyes and taste buds. Both were such even a marginal breakfast was gourmet quality.

Maureen arrived as promised. Over a cup of coffee, they agreed Quiche Lorraine would be an ideal breakfast. The best part-Ruthie had many ingredients on hand. The Cheese Cavern should have the preferred Gruyere cheese. If not, they were known to have the best Swiss cheese around. Next, they need to pick up freshly grated Parmesan, bacon, heavy cream, and a ready-made pie crust.

Ruthie and Maureen were the first customers as The Cheese Cavern opened. They bought the Gruyere and freshly grated Parmesan cheeses. Ruthie suggested a trip to Kroger, where they got the rest of the ingredients. Maureen checked the items off the shopping list. Then added fresh orange juice and 18 large eggs.

Ruthie and Maureen returned and laid out the ingredients. There were enough ingredients to make three quiches. She hoped one would be good enough for Miss Ruby, as Maureen had always called her neighbor.

There was an easel on the windowsill. While preparing

meals, Ruthie used it to hold cookbooks and recipes. Ruthie put the recipe on the easel and set the easel on the counter.

"You are all set," Ruthie said with satisfaction. She took a seat behind her daughter.

Turning to look at her mother, "Aren't you helping?"

"No way am I getting involved. You got yourself into this pickle. You get yourself out. Besides, I can make Quiche Lorraine in my sleep. You, on the other hand."

"OK, OK. I get it. You are free for consultation, right?"

"I'm right behind you," Ruthie.

An hour later, Maureen was taking her masterpiece out of the oven. They did the knife test. It passed. Ruthie called Miss Ruby and told her what Maureen was up to. "Feel like quiche."

"Bring it on over. Diane and Tim are coming for lunch. Now I have something to serve them. Won't they be surprised? I bet I can convince them I made it myself." The two had a good laugh at that.

"Just be forewarned. Don't be surprised a small sliver is missing. This is Maureen's first quiche, and we don't want to kill anyone!"

"So? That is where I tested my latest creation," Miss Rubie said with a laugh and hung up.

Ruthie had her head buried in the paper when she advised her daughter, "You better call Ted and tell him you won't be in church tomorrow."

"Why?" Maureen asked her mother.

"Well, it takes almost an hour to cook the quiche. But suppose you wait until everyone is here when you start cooking. In that scenario, everyone starves to death before tasting your culinary masterpiece," said Ruthie, never lifting her head up from the paper.

"Ted. You, Mack, and Melinda go on to church without me.

I will be slaving over the stove to impress my future in-laws." She was laughing.

"And what about impressing your boyfriend?" questioned Ted.

"No need. I've already got him hooked. He thinks I'm gorgeous and funny. He is not about to give up a prize like me. Besides, the number one rule in pre-nuptial relationships. Impress the future in-laws. Win them over, and you got it made," Maureen said, trying to sound authoritative.

"And how do I impress my future mother-in-law?" Ted asked.

"Well, that will take some educating. But not today."

"OK, back to the matter-at-hand. Church is over at eleven. We will be there no later than eleven-twenty. Is that enough time for you to create your culinary masterpiece?"

"Perfect-have to go, bye," and Maureen was gone.

Ted, Mack, and Melinda arrived as the oven buzzed. The quiche was, in theory, ready. While Maureen took the quiche out of the oven, Ruthie welcomed the guests. Maureen did the knife test. The knife came out clean, and Maureen did a fist pump! Ted handled the introductions as the group made their way to the living room. They found a comfortable seat, and everyone relaxed. They had no more gotten settled when Maureen's voice rang out.

"Hi, everyone," she was in good spirits. "Mom. Sit them at the table. I'll serve up brunch in a minute." The refrigerator door opened and closed. There was banging. Then all was quiet.

Maureen was standing at the doorway to the kitchen with her masterpiece in hand. She winked at Ted. She put the quiche on the trivet in front of Mac. Everyone had a cup of hot coffee and a small glass of orange juice. "Anyone need anything else?" she asked. With everyone holding their thumbs-up, Maureen took her spot next to Ted.

"Mack, would you be so kind as to say grace?" Ruthie asked. They joined hands, and Mack thanked The Lord for the meal and friendship. While Mack was praying aloud, Maureen was praying silently that no one would get sick.

After grace, everyone passed their plate to Mack for a piece of quiche

Maureen began, "Brunch, this morning, consists of Quiche Lorraine, made from my mother's secret recipe. There is fresh fruit, orange juice, and hot coffee."

The Brunch was casual and cheerful. Stories were told with the singular intent of embarrassing Maureen, Ted, or both. Mack and Melina praised Maureen on her masterpiece.

Ruthie grabbed scooped the last bit of quiche into a container. She put the fruit in a second container. "I am taking this over to Jack. Be back soon, but don't wait for me. You two can clean the kitchen before getting into any mischief." Then she was out the door.

"Well, nobody got sick. I guess that is something."

"What do you mean? You were a culinary genius. It was fantastic."

"I have only made quiche twice." Maureen was blushing.

"OK, I'll bite. When was the first time?" Ted asked as he put his arms around her waist.

"About 24 hours ago. I more or less exaggerated when I implied that I was a great cook."

"You mean, you lied," Ted said, and he squeezed her a little.

She broke his hold on her and turned to face him. She put her hands on his chest and gently created a little distance. "I never lie. I may exaggerate a little, but I never lie," she said, batting her eyes.

"Whatever." Ted gave her a quick kiss. "You impressed both

your boyfriend and your future in-laws."

Settled on the sofa, they turned on Netflix. "Ooh, I love *You've Got Mail.*" She snuggled closer to Ted as he put his arm around her. The movie barely began when he heard a strange sound. He looked down at Maureen. Her eyes closed and breathing steadily. She made a sound somewhere between a whimper and a snore.

The movie finished as Ruthie came in. She took one look at her daughter and said, "She looks comfortable."

The door's closing woke up Maureen. She was surprised to see her mother standing there looking at her.

"Don't worry, nothing happened," Maureen said as she rubbed the sleep out of her eyes.

"That is obvious. Ted is too much of a gentleman to take advantage of his sleeping princess."

"I was not sleeping, was I Ted?" Maureen pleaded.

"No, you were not asleep. But you were sort of snoring," Ted said with a smile.

Maureen punched Ted in the chest and stood up. Looking down at him, hands on hips, she announced, "I do not snore!"

"Gourmet cooking does wear you out," she said as she stretched and yawned.

Ted got up and excused himself. "I need to go by Dad's. I want to pick up a tool belt and some hand tools. Tomorrow is my first day. I need to be prepared."

Maureen tried to stifle another yawn and gave Ted a quick kiss. Then she disappeared down the hall.

Ruthie said, "I'll take care of our new Rachel Rae. Meet me at the office at seven tomorrow. You can follow me to the worksite."

"Gotcha! See you at seven." Ted gave Ruthie a hug and left.

Melinda was still with Mack when Ted walked in. They were

173

sitting on the couch, watching a movie on Netflix. Each had a brown bottle. Mack saw Ted's face. He knew that look.

"Relax," he said and held up the bottle with the label showing. "Root Beer."

"Wasn't going to say a word," Ted assured the couple. "I start with Habitat Community this week and may need a few tools. I need a tool belt and a few tools?"

"Your belt is on the table. Take whatever tools you think you might need." They returned to the movie.

Ted left and found the belt. Next, he grabbed a hammer and a flashlight, though he wasn't sure why. Ted also added folding and metal retractable tape measures. Then he added a carpenter's pencil. "I guess this will get me through the first day anyway" Although it wasn't necessary, he retraced his steps through the house.

"Got everything?" Mack asked.

"Think so," Ted answered. As he stopped at the door. To Mack and Melinda. he said, "Try to stay out of trouble." He was laughing as he shut the door.

After the door closed, Melinda yelled, "Killjoy!" Then took a swig of Mug Root Beer.

Jack was watching *Gunsmoke* when Ted returned. "Well, how was the gourmet brunch?"

"You should know, Ruthie brought leftovers."

"Yeah, but it is more fun to hear it from you. Ruthie doesn't blush!" And he broke out laughing.

"It went well. At least no one got sick. I came from Dad's, and he and Melinda were watching a movie. They did not seem to be suffering from quiche poisoning." Ted left, returning with a Dr. Pepper.

"Miss Ruby called Ruthie. Said the quiche was also a hit with her family."

"Good. Maybe your girl will be able to fatten you up." Jack let out a loud laugh and woke up Napper.

"Yeah, whatever," Ted said dismissively. "Tomorrow, I will be on the job. Are you going to be alright?" Ted was genuinely concerned. Ted had left Jack alone in the past; he was always a phone call away. Ted was not sure how easily he could leave if needed.

"Sure, I'll be fine." Jack, not taking his eyes off the television, said, "Eliot is coming over tomorrow. He is giving me one of those things I can use to call for help if I fall. It even has a button if I need help."

"That's a good idea. You'll be on your own again while I am building houses. You can call but can't promise when I can stop and come over. I feel more comfortable you having one of those emergency things."

Jack turned and studied his caretaker. "Don't worry, I'll be fine," he said. "I will have that device. I have your number. Besides, Ruthie checks in from time to time."

"Those Rittenhouse gals sure take care of us." Ted took a sip of his drink and watched Jack for a reaction

"That they do. You know, you better hurry up, or Ruthie may beat her daughter down the aisle!"

"You two are serious, then?" Ted wondered.

"Jess is the love of my life. Always will be. But I do like Ruthie. A lot. And the way she keeps finding ways for us to be together, I think she feels the same." Jack was quiet, then sighed. "Is it love? At our age, who knows. Then there is the fact I am a bit older." Jack looked at Ted and offered a wink.

"At your point in life, age is just a number." Ted said. "And a meaningless number at that."

Jack waved his hand, turned back to the television, and said, "Whatever."

"Off to bed. I will try not to wake you in the morning," Ted said as he disappeared down the hall.

Ted heard Jack holler, "Better not. You know I need my

beauty rest!"

This was followed by a short laugh. Then a gunshot from the set. Ted thought, "Marshall Dillon has taken care of one more bad guy."

CHAPTER 19

I T WAS A bright, sunny day. Ted hopped out of bed, got dressed, and then had a bite to eat.

"You don't want to be late. Not on your first day," Jack said, sipping his coffee and reading the morning paper. "Hope you don't mind Cheerios. No time for anything more. You are on your own for coffee,"

"Cheerios is fine for me," Ted said, pouring milk on the cereal. He grabbed a mug and poured himself a cup. Ted picked up a section of the paper and glanced at it while eating.

"You sure you are alright with me working? You'll be home alone all day."

"Not the first time. Won't be the last," Jack said with a note of sarcasm. "But you keep that phone handy. The baby is due any time. I don't want to miss the arrival."

Ted finished his cereal and took a large gulp of coffee. "I have it all cleared with Ruthie. Once you get the call, I will be here lickity split. We'll head down so you can welcome your first grandchild." Ted was gone before Jack could respond.

Ted called Ruthie. "I'm on my way," he said, starting the truck.

"Listen, Ted. I have a last-minute meeting. Go on to the job site. OK? You know where it is, right?"

"Sure, no problem." Ted headed to the project site.

When he arrived, two men greeted Ted. John "Buck" Rogers was tall and muscular. He was two inches taller than Ted and more than fifty pounds heavier. He had thick blond hair, piercing blue eyes, and a goatee. The second was William Davidson, affectionally known as "Will." Three or four inches shorter than Buck and a bit heavier. Ted guessed those brown eyes didn't miss much. Will had a shaved head and sported a four-inch beard. Both had smiles on their faces, and they shook hands with Ted.

"You must be that kid Ruthie is bringing on board." Buck said jokingly to Will.

"Nah, he can't be. Too scrawny!" Will responded, nudging Buck in the arm.

"Hi. I'm Ted Roberts," and shook their hands.

"Glad to see you are being greeted properly." Ruthie had come up behind Ted. "Will, here is our electrical foreman, and Buck is our general contractor. Together, they are one big pain in the, well, you know where. But you will get used to them. That's the plan, anyway." Ruthie had a clipboard in her hand. "Hi, boys!" The last remark was directed to Buck and Will.

"What we need," Buck said, pulling Ted aside, "is to get the framing done. We will get the exterior walls done today and then lay out the base plates for the interior rooms. Our goal is to get the bones of this house put together. Quickly. This has to be done before Billy-boy there can string his electrical conduit."

"To avoid any unnecessary disruptions," Ruthie interrupted. "He is Mack James' son. Ted here has helped his dad and Jason James frame houses before," Ruthie cutting off any pranks for which the two were famous. "He knows there are no left-handed pipe wrenches. And he is not going to the hardware store searching for one. Understood?"

All three laughed.

Buck was the first to respond. "Well, kiddo. Let's see what you're made of."

Will chimed in, "Don't worry, kid. His bark is a lot worse than his bite." Then, laughing, he added, "has to be-he ain't got no teeth. They're all dentures. And wooden at that!" Will slapped his thigh.

Ruthie followed behind, shaking her head. "Children!" She had a smile on her face and a twinkle in her eye.

The four surveyed the worksite as a few other workers and volunteers arrived. Ted recognized a few from church, but not anyone's name. After surveying the site, Buck pulled everyone together and handed out work assignments. As Ted manned the table saw, he cut 2x4s to the appropriate length. With everyone busy, the day flew by.

At home, Ted showered and had a quiet dinner with Jack. They talked about Ted's first day on the job. Then the day Jack had.

"Anything from Eliot?"

"Phone's been deader than a doornail."

Ted cleared the table and loaded the dishwasher. He put in a Cascade pod, closed the door, and set the timer. The idea started by Jack's late wife, Jessica, was to run the dishwasher while everyone was in bed. That way, it did not disturb the socializing after dinner. And clean dishes were always available in the morning.

Ted retreated to his room, lay propped up on his bed, and got out his phone. Maureen answered on the first ring. He was always thrilled when he heard her voice.

"Well, he-man. Survive your first day of honest work?" She giggled.

"Met Buck and Will. Both like to joke. But when it comes to work, there is none finer. I worked a summer with my Uncle Jason doing the same thing. I thought they were pros, but they got nothing on Buck and his crew." Ted said, thinking back on his day.

"You are aware they're related, right?"

"How? They can't be brothers. They have different last names, and they sure don't look alike. Could be cousins, I guess." Ted left the sentence hanging.

After a brief silence. "Tell me about the wonderful world of a surgical nurse."

Maureen was excited about her new position. She began to relate stories of procedures with names Ted could not pronounce. Maureen described it as nothing short of miraculous.

An hour later, they said their good nights. Ted lay there listening to Have *Gun-Will Travel* on the television. "I'll give you an hour," Richard Boone was talking to the bad guys.

Ted decided to go out and watch television with Jack. He wanted to give Jack some company, and he wasn't ready to hit the hay.

"Popcorn?" Jack asked without looking at Ted.

"Sure." Ted went to the kitchen. "What kind? Movie Theatre or Kettle."

"Kettle. Other is too greasy."

"Kettle it is." Ted busied himself. He returned with two popcorn-filled bowls and a glass of water five minutes later. Ted stayed and watched the end of one show, and then a second Have Gun came on.

As the credits rolled after the second episode, Ted got up, gathered up the empty bowls and his glass of water. "More water?" Ted asked Jack.

"Nah, I'm fine. I think I'm going to bed. Ruthie is coming over at noon."

"Tomorrow? We start on the house tomorrow." Ted said, a little confused.

"Don't know about that. Guess when you're the boss, your time is your time." Jack said, looking at Ted. "Hey, tomorrow is Tuesday. She brings me casseroles for lunch. She doesn't want me to go hungry while you are working."

"Yeah. You look like you're starving." Then, each went their separate ways.

"In the morning, keep the noise down. You know me and my beauty rest." Jack hollered from his bedroom and then closed the door.

At the end of the second day, the interior wall framing was done. The roof trusses started to take shape. Ted was still manning the saw, cutting the lengths. He then used the miter saw to cut the angles Buck needed.

"Kid, you're doing a great job. I have had other saw-savvy carpenters. Or so they said. Not one could read a carpenter's square. Keep up the good work."

Ted looked up but kept working. "Thank you," is all he said.

Jack was in a festive mood when Ted got home. He had on dress slacks, regular shoes, and a button-down, long-sleeved shirt. "Get cleaned up. We're going out."

"Going out?" They did not often eat out during the week.

"Melinda has a reputation for cooking a mean rack of baby-backs. So, she and Mack have invited us over to her place for dinner."

Melinda lived across town in a small, three-bedroom, craftsman-style house. She had a custom-built grill on a covered patio. It was a warm evening, and they would be eating on the deck. A picnic-style wood table was covered with a red and white checkered tablecloth. Mack was finishing setting the table when Jack and Ted arrived.

"Come on in. We're out here on the patio," Mack yelled when he heard them arrive, and the doorbell chimed.

Ted was not a connoisseur of baby-back ribs. That was Jack's thing. Even he understood these ribs were fantastic.

"Melinda, my dear," Jack started, "these ribs beat anything I've had so far. And, I have eaten more than my share."

"Thank you, kind sir," she said and then did a little curtsey. "Let me get the dessert." She left and returned with four pieces of pie.

"I don't know," said Jack, eyeing the pie.

"Don't worry. It is an ancient family recipe. Sugar-free peach pie with a gluten-free crust."

"Thanks, mam. But as I was about to say. I can't say what everyone else is having for dessert. If those are anything like the ribs. They are all mine." There was laughter all around.

"Hey, dad. I thought. You were supposed to be cooking?"

"Exception to every rule," and he gave his son a side hug.

The evening was enjoyable. Jack and Mack spent the evening talking with each other about various professional sports teams. The only one thing on which they could agree; pro-athletes were paid way too much.

"How does Maureen like her new job?" Melinda asked Ted.

The floodgates opened, with Ted smiling and talking about his girlfriend.

"And how is the Habitat work coming?"

"It's coming. Working with John Rogers and Bill Davidson. They are great to work with. And a lot of fun.

They exchanged essential information and Melinda took a sip of tea. She asked, "So, Ted, when are you going to pop the question?"

"Huh? What question?" Surprised by Melinda's question.

"When are you going to ask that gorgeous girl to marry you?"

A little embarrassed, Ted said. "We agreed not to cross that bridge until I finish my coursework at Emmerson."

"You know, Ted, you can ask her before you graduate. Then afterward, you can get married."

"She has made me abundantly aware of that," Ted said, still a little embarrassed. "As Willie Nelson said. 'Always on my mind.' I am glad I have the construction job. It keeps my mind occupied, and I don't go bonkers."

"So, you do plan to marry her?" Melinda asked.

"If she'll have me," Ted said with a wide grin.

"Oh, you have no problems in that department," Melinda assured him.

"You think?"

"Women sense these things." She grinned and patted Ted's hand. "I am sure she would jump at the chance to be Mrs. Ted James today. Even if it meant calling home a cardboard box."

"Come on, bud," Jack bellowed. "I need to get home. You have to keep building that house you've started. Besides, these two have got to compare notes." He slapped Mack on the back.

"Notes? About what?" Ted asked, teasing Jack.

As for Jack, he just bowed, looked at Ted, and shook his head.

◆ ◆ ◆

Ted lay on his bed talking to Maureen when he asked, "What do you think of living in a cardboard shack?"

"What?" she asked in astonishment. "Where did that come from?"

"Melinda. Jack and I had dinner with her and my dad tonight."

"Melinda?" Maureen asked, "and how did a cardboard shack enter into the conversation."

"She said you would marry me tonight, even if it meant living in a cardboard shack."

"Is that a proposal?" Maureen asked teasingly.

"No, I've got to get the shack first," Ted teased back.

"Well, I'm not living in a cardboard shack, that's for sure."

"That's what I thought." Ted agreed.

"It's got to be at least scrap plywood. It's more waterproof," Maureen said with a laugh.

"Funny, very funny!" They ended the call for the evening.

The following two days flew by, and the house was taking shape. All exterior walls were wrapped in Tyvek. The interior sheetrock was going up; the roof decking was going up. Buck announced his admiration for the workers and told they were ahead of schedule. "Don't get too excited. Rain is in the forecast. For the beginning of the week. No working in the rain."

When Ted got home Thursday, he found Maureen and Ruthie there. Jack was again gussied up. "Mack and Melinda are coming over for dinner. Ruthie made her world-renowned meatloaf, potatoes au gratin, and a spinach salad. Too bad you won't be staying."

Ted looked at Maureen. "We're meeting Wendy and Allan at Uncle Dan's for pizza," she said. "Now get changed. I want to be gone before Melinda arrives and talks me into that beautifully decorated cardboard shack!"

Jack and Ruthie looked with raised eyebrows at Maureen. "Inside joke"

Ruthie finished setting the table.

As they about to leave, Ted looked back and yelled, "Hey, Ruthie."

"Yes?"

"In-laws. Bill and John are in-laws."

"In-laws?" Ruthie asked in total confusion.

"Maureen said you knew they were related but didn't know how."

"OK," she said. She was unsure where this was going.

"They're brothers-in-law. They married the Braun twins,

Brynley and Bailey."

Ruthie and Jack looked at each other, shook their heads, and continued preparing for their dinner guests.

CHAPTER 20

F RIDAY! TED HAD reached the end of his first week building a house with Habitat Community. He was pleased he was more than a "gopher," as Ruthie had indicated when she brought him on board. He enjoyed working with Buck and Will, and he was learning a lot from them. About construction, and teamwork.

Ted spent much of his youth alone. He had a few friends in high school. But they were not the kind of friends most parents wanted for their kids. Let's face it, his family is not not one he would have chosen.

For the first time, he envisioned a future for himself. He could provide for himself and a family doing construction. Ted was surprised by what he learned from his uncle, and his dad stayed with him. Buck and Will were also amazed at how quickly he picked things up. One thing impressing the two supervisors is how little supervision Ted required. Ted anticipated the needs. Rarely was he asked to re-cut a piece of lumber. This was expected on a professional crew. However, this was not true of a volunteer crew.

◆ ◆ ◆

The pizza party with Maureen, Wendy, and Allan was fun. It allowed everyone to let off a little steam. With time to spare, the four hit the bowling alley. They were all respectable bowlers, but Ted took the prize with a top score of 225. Ted had few opportunities to relax and enjoy himself. What with worrying about home, or what others may be thinking.

The night's joke came while playing the arcade games, Ted won a ring with an expandible band. With the ring in hand, Ted got down on one knee, taking Maureen's left hand in his, and with mock seriousness, he said, "Will you be my best friend." They all had a good laugh. When he stood up, Maureen lightly slapped Ted's face, and she quickly kissed his cheek, where she hit him.

It was close to midnight when Ted rolled in. Jack was already snoring in his bedroom. Quietly, Ted showered and put on his PJs, and climbed into bed. He had a smile on his face when he fell asleep.

Six-thirty came early, and Ted jumped up at the sound of the alarm. He turned it off. He did not want to wake Jack. Too late. Jack was already at the table.

"Out kinda late for a work-night, eh?" Jack spoke without looking at Ted.

"Tell me about it. A party animal I am not!" Ted grabbed a piece of bread and put it in the toaster and, poured himself a cup of coffee, and buttered the toast. Next, Ted sat down and grabbed a section of the newspaper. The clock on the stove read seven. Time to head off to work. "Catch you later, alligator," and headed out the door.

Ted was engrossed in work when his cell phone rang. He looked at the caller ID. It was Jack.

"Baby is here" is all Jack snapped when Ted answered.

"OK. I'll be right there. Gotta talk to Ruthie first." Ruthie agreed Ted could leave as soon as possible when Pam delivered her baby. It would be Jack's first grandchild, and Jack was beside himself in anticipation.

"Go, Go. We got this covered here," Ruthie said, making

a shooing motion with her hand. "Have Jack call me with the good news."

"Of course." In 20 minutes, they were heading to the hospital to see his new grandchild.

"Hope it's a boy," Jack grunted. "Too many women in my life now."

Ted looked over at his passenger. They both had a good laugh.

Jack called Eliot to alert him they were pulling into the parking structure. "OK, we'll meet you in the lobby." After hanging up, Jack turned to Ted and gave him a thumbs up.

Eliot met them in the lobby. "Jack, I need to prepare you before you see Pam."

"Why, what's wrong? Is she all right?" Jack's face showed concern.

"She's fine. The babies are fine," Eliot reassured.

Ted picked up on "the babies" part long before Jack did.

Eliot put both hands on Jack's shoulders. "I know you are excited to meet your first grandchild. And I know you wanted a boy."

"So, it's a girl. Just so she's healthy," Jack was trying to get around Eliot.

Eliot stopped Jack with a hand on Jack's chest. He then held up two fingers.

Jack was frozen for a minute, looking at the two raised fingers. Then it hit him. "Two babies?" Eliot Nodded. "Two babies?" Jack said again. "I have two grandchildren?"

"Two granddaughters!" Eliot beamed with pride as he led the two to Pam's room.

Pam was resting in bed. There were two bassinets. Each with a pink bundle of joy.

Jack went over. He examined one and then the other. Then

back to the first. Finally, he looked up at Eliot and beamed. "They are gorgeous. Absolutely gorgeous."

"With twins on the way, we decided to learn the gender. Were they identical or paternal twins? We've known, for a while, we were having twin girls."

"And you didn't say a word?"

"Nope. We had already convinced everyone we would learn what God had given us, along with everyone else. So, why spoil the fun?"

"And the yellow nursery?" Ted asked.

"It's been pink since we learned we were having twins. We were not prepared for two! We were concerned enough with one. And now we are blessed with two." Eliot was touching one and then the other as he was speaking.

"Meet Jessica and Jennifer," Pam said, waking to find visitors in her room. "Jessica Kathleen is on the left."

"Jessica Kathleen?" Asked Jack.

"Yes, dad. I named her after mom and her mom. I thought she would approve."

"Yes, she would," said a proud grandpa. Tears of joy welling up in his eyes.

"So," Ted said to Eliot, "your mother must be Jennifer."

"Nope," Eliot said, moving over to be next to Pam. "My mother's name is Eva Marie, after the actress. My grandmother's name was Jennifer. So, in keeping with the scheme of things, meet Jennifer Marie."

The babies started making some noise. "Jack, why don't you take a seat over there?" pointing to a rocker. Eliot then picked up Jessica Kathrine and handed Jack his granddaughter.

Pointing to another rocker, "Have a seat." Ted followed directions and was handed Jennifer Marie. "Meet your uncle Ted," said Eliot.

Ted looked up. "Uncle?"

"Ted, you are a part of this family, like it or not. Since you are way too young to be a grandpa, so Uncle Ted, you are." Ted looked up and mouthed, "Thank You."

Eliot was sitting on the bed next to his wife. Both were looking at their daughters meeting their extended family. Eliot looked at his wife, bent down, and gave her a quick kiss.

"We are so blessed," Pam said softly to her husband.

"Yes, we are, and we have been," Eliot back, barely audible.

Ted took pictures of everyone and several of Jack holding Jessica and then holding Jennifer. Then he looked at his watch. "Getting late, he said."

Eliot and Ted walked down to the Ranger and got Jack's suitcase. "I know Jack wants to spend time with his new granddaughters, so we'll keep him here for a couple of days. My parents are coming later tonight."

"OK if Ruthie and Maureen come over the weekend?" Ted said, handing Jack's suitcase to Eliot. "We don't want to wear anyone out. How long before Pam goes home?"

Eliot thought, "Today is Friday. Sunday, I guess. Monday at the latest."

"Great," said Ted. "Call me if the old coot becomes a problem. If so, I will come. Crowbar in hand, and pry him away." They both laughed at the image.

Ted went with Eliot to the Jeep. Eliot put the case behind the passenger seat and locked the car.

"What about going home? Won't Jack be in the way?" a concerned Ted asked.

"Nope. We'll take the girls home in Pam's car. My parents will bring Jack over to the house. Everything should be OK. At least, that is the plan." They walked in silence back to the hospital.

Once inside, Eliot stopped Ted. "Ted, the babies were both planned and unplanned. We wanted to start a family. But this sort of snuck upon us." Eliot was examining his shoes. The looking at Ted. "This changes things. We need to talk."

"About me, Jack and the foundation?" Ted asked.

"Yes."

"I realize I am probably not ready to do what you want." Ted stopped. He waited for a signal. "If you want me to move out, cut my pay, whatever. I appreciate what you have done for me. I really do." Ted was sincere.

"Relax. Nothing is happening to change the current arrangement. At least for the time being."

"For the time being? What does that mean?" Ted was concerned.

"It means things are moving faster than we anticipated. Are you still getting your ABA in the spring?"

"That's the plan. Do you know something I don't?"

"Have you made up your mind? You know, about coming on board with the foundation?"

"We haven't talked in a while," Ted said. He paused and said, "Yes, it is my goal to become a part of the foundation. I like what you have shared with me thus far."

"Good. Then we need to talk about possibly bringing you on board sooner than later?"

Ted gasped.

"Relax, we can talk after we get the twins settled at home. We can teleconference it or do it in person at our offices here." Elliot gave Ted a pat on the back.

"I will tell you more later. We better get back up there now. Or Pam may think we ran away."

They arrived back in the room. Pam did not appear to have missed them.

"I've got to go. There is a Southern State deadline on Monday. I must make sure I have my paperwork in order." Then, turning to Jack, "I am counting on you, old man. Behave yourself. Don't make me come back because you are causing a stir."

Ted kissed two fingers and touched Jessica, then did the same for Jennifer. Finally, he squeezed Pam's hand and said,

"They are too beautiful for words."

Smiling up at him, Pam said, "Thank you, Uncle Ted."

He shook Jack's hand and then shook Elliot's hand. "I look forward to our conversation. And congratulations, proud dad."

With that, he was out the door.

He called Maureen before he left the hospital. Said he had pictures and a surprise.

"You mean the twins?" Maureen asked.

"You knew?" Ted was shocked.

"Mom and I were convinced Pam was too big for only one baby. So, yes, we speculated."

"Well, I'll meet you at your mom's house. Want me to pick up something?"

"Family pack from Colonel Sanders should tide us over," Maureen suggested.

"Then the colonel will be joining us for supper," Ted said as he disconnected.

The women were waiting for him when Ted walked in the door. "Forget the food. I want to see pictures!" Maureen said as she grabbed Ted's phone.

Ruthie watched as she asked, "You know his password?"

"Mom!" an exasperated Maureen said.

The two women looked at the pictures. Then, still looking, Ted said, "Food's over here, and it's getting cold," Ted failed at his attempt to wrestle his phone from Maureen and her mother.

"I like cold fried chicken," Ruthie said, still looking at the pictures.

"What mom said," Maureen added.

After having their fill of the pictures, they reluctantly let Ted have his phone. Then they settled down to eat, and Ted explained the exciting news.

"Jessica Katherine is named after Pam's mother and grandmother. Jennifer Marie is named after Elliot's grandmother and mother."

"Bookends," Maureen said between bites.

"Oh, I am now an uncle!" Ted announced.

"How? You don't have any brothers or sisters," observed Maureen.

"Pam said they considered me part of the family, and the girls will call me Uncle Ted."

"Then I am Aunt Maureen," she said, sitting straighter in her chair.

"That has not been determined yet," teased Ted.

"You two can fight over that later. Aunt Ruthie wants to know when she can see the newest members of the Tullus household."

"I have gotten appointments for you two tomorrow afternoon."

"How nice of you, kind sir. And what do we owe you?" Maureen asked sarcastically.

"This one is on the house," he said, looking over his eyebrows at her. "I will be staying home. Elliot's parents will be there; the room is small. So, you two go and fill me in when you get home."

After dinner, Maureen and Ted were sitting on the couch, seeing but not watching the Hallmark movie. "Uncle Ted and Aunt Maureen. I like the sound of that."

"I do too," Ted admitted.

"Proposal?" Maureen asked.

"No," Ted said, and gave her a hug. "Soon." It's all he would say.

"Elliot says there is a development regarding the foundation and me," Ted said

"Good or bad?" Maureen quizzed.

"Can't say. We really did not discuss particulars. Eliot asked if I was planning on working for the foundation."

"And what did you say?" Maureen said, with her head still on his shoulder.

"I said yes."

"Good," Maureen murmured. Ted knew she was headed to la-la land,

"Hey," he said, moving his shoulder. "Wake up."

"I am awake," Maureen said while she stretched and yawned.

"I've got last-minute paperwork for Southern State to complete and get into the mail. So you two go tomorrow. And have fun with Jennifer and Jessica. We'll talk when you get back, and I'll pick you up for church on Sunday." Ted said, standing up, checking to see if he had the truck's keys and his phone.

"Night, Ruthie," he said down the hall. Ruthie had retreated to another room to give them a little privacy.

She appeared at the hall's entrance. "Thanks for the pictures and the report. And thanks for dinner. Keep us posted on your discussions with Elliot," Ruthie said, and brushed a loose piece of hair out of her face.

"You heard?"

"A mother's ears hear everything. You need to remember that!" Ruthie grinned as she waved him off. Once again, Ruthie disappeared down the hall.

Maureen put her arms around his neck and kissed him. "Good night, Uncle Ted."

CHAPTER 21

THE EXCITEMENT CONTINUED through the completion of the Habitat Community house. "Uncle Ted" made several trips to visit Pam, Eliot, and the two newborns. He went by himself sometimes, and others were with Maureen. Pam and Eliot were great parents. They fixed up the nursery in a beautiful Princess motif. Two cribs were identical except for the wording on the ends. One had Jennifer and the other Jessica. Pam could not stop smiling as she talked about the additions to their family.

"How's it going?" Maureen asked on one visit.

"Not too badly. Jessica often wakes up first, so I get up, change her and give her a bottle. No sooner do I get back to bed, and Jennifer awakens. Eliot helps a lot. With Jenny, he gets up and follows the same routine."

"Jenny?" a bemused Maureen asked?

"Well, Jennifer sounds too formal. We must be formal at work. We are more relaxed at home. So, Jenny is what we call her."

"And Jess?" asked Ted.

"No. We are going with the rhyming thing. Jessie is what we've been calling her."

"Makes sense," Ted and Maureen in unison.

Ted gave a status on the home front. "Jack's shirt buttons are always about to pop. Everyone noticed Jack always had a smile on his face and more bounce in his step. Even Napper has seen a change but has not figured it out. All Napper knows is Jack's lap is in constant movement. So, Napper has taken to sleeping in his doggie bed when Ted's lap is not around."

"Ted?" It was Eliot.

"If you have a moment, can we meet next week?"

"Virtual or in-person?"

"Pam and I have talked about it," Eliot began, "and we believe an in-person meeting is more appropriate."

"So, Pam will be there, too?"

"No," Eliot said. "We may teleconference with her. However, there are things you must see. This cannot be done remotely. I want to show you the proposal. You need to see the physical aspect. If needed, we can bring Pam in on TEAMS."

"OK," Ted said with a bit of hesitation.

"How about Tuesday morning? Say, about 10?" Eliot waited for a response.

Ted thought about calling Maureen or talking with Jack before committing to the meeting. In the end, he agreed, saying, "Great, I'll be there. Do I need to bring anything?"

"Only your enthusiasm and ideas," Eliot said. "Look forward to seeing you then."

That evening, Ted decided to check with his dad. He had never asked his dad for anything, career or personal. But since Mack quit drinking, Ted thought he could use a little advice.

"Hello?" Melinda said after the fourth ring.

"Hi, I am looking for my dad. I called his phone, but no answer. I drove by the house, and it was dark. Do you know where he is?"

"Yes and no," Melinda said with caution.

"What kind of answer is that?" Ted was getting irritated.

"Here is what he told me. He had to go out of town. It would only be a few days."

"And where did he go?" Ted asked.

"He wouldn't tell me. He said he had business to take care of. He said he had to keep it on the down-low, in case should it fall through. I realized it was important to him, so I didn't ask anymore."

Ted took a few minutes to ponder this new information.

"Ted," Melinda asked, fearing Ted had hung up.

"I'm here. Do you?" Ted paused. "Is Dad is sick?"

"I asked the same question. But, again, Mack assured me it had nothing to do with his health."

"OK," Ted drew out the response. "When will he be back?"

"He said he would be gone two nights. He left yesterday, so he will be home sometime tomorrow. He drove himself to the airport—part of his secrecy plan, I guess. He said he would call once he landed." There was silence on the line. "Ted, is everything alright with you?"

There was not an immediate response.

"Ted?"

"Sorry, just thinking. No. Everything is fine with me."

"And Maureen?" Melinda asked.

"Everything is fine. I have a meeting with Eliot next week. I wanted to talk to Dad about it. When he calls, tell him I would like to talk to him."

"Sure, Ted. No problem. And relax. I am sure whatever your dad's secret adventure turns out to be, it will be fine. He is a good man, your dad. I have grown fond of him. I hope you don't mind if I keep him occupied."

"No. You know Dad doesn't say much, but he also likes you. I retain no illusions of my parents reconciling. However, I do not see you as a threat to that happening. I'm glad he got himself together, and he has you to help him. Maureen and I also like you."

"Thank you."

"No," Ted protested. "I am not simply saying it. I mean it. You are good for my dad."

"OK. I will tell Mack when he calls and tell him you need to talk with him. Bye,"

Maureen noticed Ted was concerned. She suggested a quick meal at The Mac Shack. They looked over the menu; Ted got his usual Lobster-Mac. However, Maureen didn't have a favorite and ordered Bacon-Mac. While waiting for their food, they talked little. Not wanting to force the issue, she remained patient, allowing Ted to initiate the conversation.

The food made them livelier. Maureen talked about her mom, Wendy, and work. Ted avoided talking about what was bothering him. With the meal over, Ted became quiet again. Maureen became concerned there was a problem in their relationship.

"Ted, what is going on? You haven't said a dozen words all evening. Maureen showed her concern to Ted. In her voice and on her face.

"Huh? Oh, I am sorry to be poor company. I have a lot on my mind."

"Ted, you have me worried. Are we having a problem?"

"We?" Ted asked, surprised by the question.

"Yes. We. As in you and me. Are we," Maureen said, waving her left index finger between Ted and her, "having a problem?"

"Oh, no. I am not mad, upset, or anything."

"Then what?" asked Maureen more forcefully.

I have a meeting with Eliot next week and wanted to talk with my dad. Melinda says he took a mysterious trip. She didn't know where or why."

"He didn't tell Melinda?"

"Not a word. Dad would not let her drive him to the airport. That is all I know. He has personal," making quotation marks with his hands, "business somewhere requiring an airplane to get there. He wouldn't tell her anything more other than it is not health-related."

"A new job?"

"No. I don't think so. Dad would tell her if it was job-related. At least I believe he would."

"Pray tell. What did she say to you?"

In a matter-of-fact voice, Ted said she asked if I was cool with her seeing my dad.

"I know I'm cool, but are you? Do you see Melinda as a threat?"

"She asked the same question. I assured Dad liked her, and I have no illusions of my parents reconciling."

"OK. Take a deep breath and look at me."

Ted took a breath and held it. Letting his air out, he looked at her.

Then, looking at him, "I love you," Maureen said. "Whatever this deal with Eliot is, we'll get through it together. Whatever it is with your dad, we'll get through it. We will do this together."

"I love you, too. I am thankful you are behind me on this." Ted kept his eyes on her.

Playfully letting go and pushing Ted's hands away, Maureen said, "Listen, buddy. I am never behind you. We are a couple, and I am at your side. Always! Got that?"

With a mock salute, "Got it, ma'am. Got it loud and clear!" They held hands and squeezed three times. This had become their discrete way of saying, I love you. Then the waiter came and handed the bill to Ted.

Maureen grabbed the bill. "I am a working woman. Thank you very much, sir. And, if I want to treat my boyfriend to dinner? I am going to do just that!" She handed the waiter a credit card, and they laughed over the absurdity of the exchange.

When the waiter returned, she added the tip and signed the slip. Then, putting her card back in her purse, she said, "Oh, buster. I have a busy day tomorrow, and I need my energy. Now get me home. Like five minutes ago!" The two laughed and kissed a quick kiss, getting up and holding hands.

Following Melinda's instructions, Mack called Ted and suggested Ted come to Mack's house for dinner on Monday. Ted asked several times, but Mack revealed nothing of his trip.

All Mack would say was, "In due time, son. In due time." Then, realizing he wasn't getting anywhere, Ted let the matter drop.

The two had an enjoyable dinner. Ted was still curious to know about his dad's secret adventure. It was clear his dad didn't want to talk about it. Ted chose not to raise the subject. Instead, the two talked amiably of sports and weather. Finally, Ted brought up his meeting with Eliot.

"Listen, Ted. If Eliot says there is nothing to worry about, you should take him at his word. Jack and I have talked about you and your potential role at the foundation. Believe me, it is all good."

"You have? You and Jack talked? About me?"

"Don't be surprised. You are my son, and I want you to succeed. Jack is fond of you. He saw the value you have to offer before I did. So, whatever happens, it will be a good deal. Count on it."

Ted still was unsure about the meeting Tuesday morning. However, he was confident knowing Jack and his dad were supportive. Ted chuckled to himself. Happy, Maureen said she wouldn't be anywhere but by his side. In bed and in the dark, sleep was elusive. But Ted knew whatever happened could be a life-changing event."

A warm, hospitable young woman announced Ted's arrival to Eliot.

"Bring him back to the conference room,"

After introducing herself as Eliot's assistant, she said, "Eliot said to meet him in the conference room. This way, please."

The room was large, with a long, eight-sided table. The table resembled an over-sized coffin. It was wider in the middle than at the ends. There were ten oversized office chairs placed strategically around the table. Four chairs on each side. On chair on each end. One chair at the end was different from the others. It appeared to signify authority and was probably Jack's chair.

"Have a seat. Mr. Tullus will be with you shortly," and she was gone.

Nerves were getting the best of Ted. He stood and walked around the room. It was a law library. Most books had letters and numbers. Ted assumed they were legal records.

On the table was a long tube. What appeared to be blueprints were inside. Ted read the hand-written label. "Tullus & Tullus Foundation Project." Ted did not touch anything. He assumed whatever was in the tube could be why they were meeting.

Eliot briskly entered and shook Ted's hand. Eliot put a bottle of water on the table.

"Water?" Eliot asked and moved toward a dorm-sized brown refrigerator.

"Sure," Ted said.

Eliot sat in the authoritative chair and indicated a chair for Ted. Ted's throat was cotton. He drank more water. Eliot smiled and said, "Relax, Ted. This is not an inquisition. I promise you are not going to be beheaded!"

Ted gave a half-hearted laugh, which eased the tension.

"OK, Ted, here's the deal."

Ted's mind filled will all sorts of negative images.

"The foundation wants to improve the neighborhood in the south of town, known as Southtown. We have made an offer to acquire a building with three storefronts. And the adjacent lots behind them. What we need is a project manager. Someone to be the project's face and help us get this project moving. Interested??

"In what? The project? The project manager? I am not sure. What you are asking?" Ted said.

"OK, let me back up. About a year ago, Jack came to us with an idea and said Southtown needed a grocery store, a safe place for kids, and access to quality health care."

"OK," indicating he was listening.

"Pam and I got on board and decided to use the foundation to fund the project. Then you came along. Jack convinced Pam and me," Eliot paused and then said, "that you would be perfect for heading the project."

"He did?" Ted said in amazement. "He barely knows me."

"Maybe not, but he has a knack for recognizing talent when he sees it."

"And he saw talent in me?"

"In spades."

"So, Pam started putting the pieces together. Our goal was you getting a bachelor's degree. Preferably in business administration or a related field. The foundation would cover your education expenses along the way in exchange for your watching over Jack."

"I like Jack. He's a hoot."

"He says the same about you. Only in a more colorful way." They both laughed, and Eliot took another drink of water.

"Jack helped us find the property. We tried to work out a minimal-cost lease, but the city planners said no. In the end, we put an option on it. It means while we have not yet purchased the properties. We have the right to first refusal. If someone comes along and wants the property. The city will give us the opportunity to match or beat the offer. In other words, we are the preferred buyer."

"And someone wants to buy the property?"

"We were notified the day before Pam went into labor. This is why I needed to know your intentions. Are you coming to work for us once you graduate?"

"But graduation is what? Three years away," Ted pointed out.

"Yes, but you will have your ABA in June, right?"

"Hopefully."

"A caveat, a condition of the purchase, is we have one year to begin implementing our plan."

"And what happens if you don't?" Ted asked.

Eliot ignored Ted's question. "It gets complicated, Ted. We have essentially purchased the property contingent on providing the services we proposed: a grocery store, a youth center, and a health clinic. The sale of the building is not completed until we uphold our end. If we don't deliver as promised, we could lose everything."

"But you could make another offer."

"Maybe. The current project comes with a few perks from the city. They would probably disappear if we had to renegotiate."

"OK," Ted said, then questioning his situation, he asked. "Where do I fit in?"

"The board has agreed, in principle, to hire you as the project manager with two conditions. The first is you continue and get your bachelor's from Southern State."

"And the other,"

"You sign a contract. Once you complete your Associate's in Business Administration, you will be employed at a small salary. We will determine your salary when the time comes. You will continue your studies, and when you receive your bachelor's degree, you will get a significant bump in your pay. You would receive your full salary."

"Anything else?"

"Two things." Eliot was watching Ted for reactions. "If you fail to get your degree. Or, in some way, be incapable of fulfilling your duties; you will need to reimburse the foundation. You will repay the money spent on your education."

"Graduating is not a problem. The second condition?"

"There is a non-compete form you will sign today saying you won't jump ship and work for another foundation doing the same thing we are doing. This applies from this day forward. Plus five years after leaving the foundation."

"So, that's it?"

"For now, anyway. Let's take it one step at a time, OK?" Eliot took another drink of water.

"Can I see the project? Ted asked, pointing to the tube on the table.

"Not yet. The usual legal things need working out. Once done, we will bring you back for a full board meeting. Then you will be hired as a consultant for a nominal fee. Once you graduate, you'll sign the contracts, and we're off and running. Is something you might want to do? Want to sign the non-compete contract now? It becomes effective immediately. OK?"

"Whew, what a relief. I know you said to relax. But I have been on pins and needles waiting for this meeting. So, yes. Everything is a go with me. OK if I let my dad know? I want his advice. You know, a father-son type thing."

"Sure, no problem. Talk with Maureen as well. As we move forward, assuming you two get married, this will affect her as well."

Pam joined via video conference, and Eliot brought her up to speed. Everyone agreed this meeting was productive. While Pam was on TEAMS, Eliot walked through the non-compete contract. There were two copies. Pam and Ted each would sign both. One would be kept by the foundation. The other was for Ted.

With the formalities completed, everyone relaxed. When Ted left, he had difficulty containing his excitement. He could not wait to share the news with his dad. And with Maureen.

CHAPTER 22

WORK CONTINUED SMOOTHLY, with the house nearing completion. Buck and Will agreed to quit early on Friday, giving everyone a long weekend.

When Ted arrived home, he found Jack asleep in his chair with Napper on his lap. *Gunsmoke* was on with Festus and Marshall Dillon, sitting around a campfire. Jack woke up as Ted shut the door.

"Mack called," Jack said, calling over his shoulder.

"What did he want?" Ted asked and got a Dr. Pepper from the fridge.

"Put the doctor back. Mack said he needed to meet with you as soon as you got home."

"Is Melinda going to be there?"

Ted considered what Malinda had said. That possibly their friendship was growing.

Maybe that's what he wanted.

"Didn't say. Didn't ask. Believe it is the two of you."

"OK. I'm on my way. Later!" Jack waved a hand of recognition as Ted left.

Mack was on the back deck when Ted arrived. He was in slacks wearing a polo shirt, drinking a glass of iced tea. "Back here," he hollered, hearing the Ranger pull up and the door slam shut.

Mack stood and greeted his son.

"Dad. What's so important that you needed to meet so quickly."

Mack raised his hands up in surrender. He had a smile on his face. "Relax." Mac sat down and pointed to a seat for Ted. "Boy, you seem on edge lately. You must cut back on those Dr. Peppers." Sipping his tea, Mack watched Ted sit down.

"Well. Everyone is springing surprises. I never know what to expect. One of us is going to wind up with a heart attack. And I am afraid it maybe me."

Mack laughed. "Winston, you gotta relax. Learn to roll with the punches."

As he raked his fingers through his hair, Ted responded, "Winston might have learned how. But Ted is a nervous wreck."

"OK, here's the skinny. Your mom and I have been talking about you and."

As he leaned forward, Ted asked, "Is everything OK? She still getting married? Are you getting married?"

"Back up and slow down. Everything is fine. Your mother and I are better friends today than when we were married. And yes, Hank and your mom are still planning a wedding in early December. And no, Melinda and I. are not getting married. Any more useless questions?"

Ted audibly sighed, "I guess not," Ted said, his face flushed with embarrassment.

Mack said, "You know I took a secret trip."

Ted nodded in acknowledgment.

"I went to see your mother."

"That's great. Why didn't you say so?"

"She set the rules. Anyway, when I proposed to your mother, I was doing well financially. I gave her an engagement ring with a rather large stone."

"I remember it. I've been looking at a similar ring. Actually, Maureen has been showing me similar rings."

Mack laughed and took another sip of tea. "Women!" And he shook his head.

"When we got divorced, I agreed she should keep the ring. It was the only decent thing I ever gave her."

"OK." Ted said slowly. His curiosity was rising.

"While she was unattached, so to speak. I didn't think about the ring."

"And now, you want to give Melinda the ring."

"What? What? No, whatever gave you that idea? Besides, I just told you Melinda and I have not talked about getting married." Mack bowed his head and shook it. Then looking up. "You know your mother would never part with that ring. Not for the Queen of England. Let alone Melinda. No, the ring is hers."

"So, what, then?"

"As I said, I had to keep everything secret at your mother's request. We both agreed on what we wanted done with the ring. At the same time. We needed to keep each other honest."

"So, what is up with this ring?"

"Your mother and I know you and Maureen are both in love. We know you are a perfect match."

"Tell me something that either I don't know. Or that everybody and their sister haven't already told me." Ted looked around the deck.

"Dr. Pepper is in the cooler," Mack said, pointing to a green ice chest. Ted walked to the chest and lifted the lid. "I think I'll take water tonight." and settled back in his chair. Mack continued. "Your mother has a new engagement ring from Hank. I must admit, it is a doozie. Makes the one I gave her look like a toy."

"The ring, dad. The ring," Ted prodded.

"Right. There are no daughters in our family. So we decided the ring should do something besides collect dust."

"There is always the pawnshop," Ted stoically.

"True, but your mother suggested another option, and I

agreed." Mack studied Ted and sipped his iced tea.

"So," Mack continued. "When, not if, but when you pop the question to Maureen, we would be honored if you would give her your mother's ring. Unless, that is, you've already bought a ring or don't want to give her your mother's."

"I think it would be great. I think-no, I know Maureen would love it." Ted finished off the water and tossed the bottle in the trash. "I still don't understand the secrecy."

"I told you, we had to keep one another honest."

"Right," Ted said, nodding his head.

"Well, we had Eliot draw up a contract. I flew to Florida and have her sign it. We had it notarized. Then, I brought the ring home with me."

"Great, dad. That's exciting. Where is it? Can I see now?"

"The ring is with Pam and Eliot. The deal is simple. You get the ring when you are ready to propose to Maureen. There is no time limit. However, if you two decide to call the whole thing off. Well, it goes back to your mom."

"She wants to make sure you don't give it to Melinda."

"Or any other woman of my choosing."

"She doesn't trust you, does she, dad?"

"Do you blame her?"

Ted did not respond. He spent some time examining his fingernails, then looked at his father. "Maureen is the best thing to happened to me. I am madly in love with her and fully intend to make her Mrs. Winston James. I even have a plan."

"Finally, the boy has a plan." They both laughed.

"In the Spring, we go to Italy."

"Ah, Rome and that famous fountain."

"Close. The class is going to Florence. I read up on the city. There is this huge. And I mean a humongous cathedral called El Duomo. We will be going inside this beautiful church. When she is mesmerized by the beauty of this church. That is when I will propose. What do you think?"

"I think you're crazy!" Mack said with a laugh.

"Gee, thanks, Dad," Ted stood and said with the wind deflating sails.

"Seriously, Ted. It is Perfect!" Mack stood and gave his son a hug. "In my opinion, it is a brilliant plan. I wish your mother and I could be there to witness it all. As far as Maureen saying no. Well, that is not possible. You can trust your mother and me on that!"

"Well, you will. I talked to Ms. Logan, my Emmerson counselor. I told her what I want to do, and she'll have my phone and record everything. We both figure Maureen will be oblivious to just about everything else and won't see Mrs. Logan filming the engagement."

"Well, it seems you have it all planned out."

"Can I show her the ring? Or at least tell her about it?" Ted asked.

"Here's the deal. Maureen can't see the ring or know if its origin until you propose. Once it is on her finger, you can tell her anything you like. I will make sure you have the ring before you leave."

"Does Jack or Ruthie know?"

"No. And you can't tell them anything you can't tell Maureen. Basically, you can say you have a ring. You must decide whether you tell them what you shared with me. I'd be careful because you don't want to ruin the surprise."

Despite having a restless night, Ted woke well before the alarm went off. He silenced the alarm, showered, shaved, and dressed for work. He was about to pick up the phone when Maureen made her morning call.

"Good Morning. Did I wake you up?"

"No, not even close. I'm up, dressed, and my bed is made."

"Well, aren't you the early bird? I wanted to hear your voice. Before you left for work." There was a smile in her voice.

209

"A busy day ahead," Ted said. "I won't be able to meet you for lunch as we planned. How about dinner?"

"Dinner is fine so long as it does not involve me cooking for you," Maureen's voice was laced with sarcasm.

"Promise. No cooking duties for my private nurse." They both laughed and hung up.

A million things were running through Ted's mind when he got a call. He felt his phone vibrate but did not answer. He was busy cutting lumber for the house. When he looked at his phone, he noticed a call from Ruthie.

"Hi, Ted. I am grilling pork chops for Jack and insist you and Maureen join us for dinner. Not coming is not an option. Besides, my daughter all but guaranteed your presence." Ted smiled and said to himself, "Those Rittenhouse women can be demanding."

"You're just figuring that out?" Ruthie asked with a laugh.

"Actually, this works out great. These past few days have been chaotic. I need to share some of this with you before I explode."

Melinda had nothing on Ruthie when it came to cooking. The meal and everything was fabulous. Maureen and Ted cleared the dishes and rejoined Jack and Ruthie.

"OK, Ted. Spill the beans." Jack was direct, if nothing else.

Turning to Ruthie. "I am in love with your daughter. But I am not sure how she feels about me."

"Liar!" Maureen said, punching his arm.

"I told your somewhat pushy daughter I had a couple of conditions I need to meet before we get engaged, let alone married."

"And how did she take the news?" Ruthie asked.

"She's your daughter. How do you think she took it?"

"That's what I thought," Ruthie said, giving a stern glance at her daughter.

Looking at Maureen. "I have good news, and I have bad news, sort of." Ted watched for a reaction. "The good news is I have the engagement ring."

Maureen's eyes lit up, and the chatterbox began. "Can I see it? Where did you get it? When did you get it?"

Putting up a single palm as if he were directing traffic. "Slow down," Ted said. He took her hand. "That's part of the bad news. You can't see it. Not until I propose. Unfortunately, I am still not ready."

"Killjoy!" Maureen said, then she folded her arms and pretended to sulk.

"Love,"

"Don't you be calling me love and try to sweet-talk me! I want to see the ring!"

"Love, the ring is a very special ring. I have been sworn to secrecy. Actually, I can't say anything until I place it on your finger."

"And whose stupid idea was that?"

"All I can tell you is it wasn't mine. I wanted to show you the ring tonight. Short of that, I wanted to tell your mom about it. But the secrecy bit extends to both Ruthie and Jack. Sorry." He gave her a tentative smile.

Upset and starting to cry. Maureen stormed to the bathroom.

"Hormones," said Ruthie, and looked toward her daughter's room.

"I had to promise to keep it secret. Rest assured, you will see it before she does. I told Dad my plans, and he approved. If I tell you, can you keep it a secret?"

Both Ruthie and Jack nodded.

"I will propose to her while in Italy. I have a specific spot where I am going to propose. Mrs. Logan will film the whole thing on my phone. You will be see the moment."

They heard the bathroom door open, and they broke their huddle. Ruthie gave a thumbs up, as did Jack. Maureen came out with several jewelry store flyers. "I am going to take you at your word, buster. That I don't need these." She threw the brochures in Ted's direction. They landed on the table, in Ted's lap, and on the floor.

"I promise you two things. You don't need those to entice me to buy a ring. And you will be blown when your little finger gets a ring." He raised his right hand with the three middle fingers raised. "Scout's honor." He gave her another smile.

"Bet you weren't even a Boy Scout."

"I was too. I made it to Tenderfoot."

"That's the first rank."

"Yeah. But it makes me a Boy Scout and bound by the oath,"

"Mom, what do you think. Should I trust this scoundrel?"

"Unless you've got a millionaire tucked away somewhere that is also movie-star handsome, he seems trustworthy enough to me." Ruthie said, aiming a smile at Ted.

"OK, mister, big shot Boy Scout. I want a deadline for this super-secret proposal of marriage you've got up your sleeve." She sat down and moving her chair to face him directly. There was nothing between them. Although Maureen was fighting the emotion, there was a smile breaking through her façade.

"Short sleeves," Ted said, pointing to his bare arms. "nothing to hide."

Then in a more serious tone, He said, "On or before graduation day from Emmerson College, I will ask your mother's permission to put the ring on your finger."

"Mother," she said in a stern voice. This was hard, since her smile had broken through. "You better not say no!"

"You can count on my blessings," Ruthie said, reaching for her daughter's hands.

"And you," Maureen said. She paused, pointing a finger at Jack, "You better not mess this up! No fair putting doubts or fears in his little head."

"Not me," said Jack, holding his hands up in a sign of surrender.

"Finally," turning to Ted. "This better not be a ploy to shut me up. About a ring."

Ted never answered her. He gently grabbed her face with both hands and kissed her. The kiss lasted a long time, and the others at the table began clearing their throats. Ted and Jack were gone; Maureen was at the door. She turned to mother, winked, and said, "Operation Mrs. James is in full throttle."

Ruthie kissed her daughter on her cheek, and whispered, "Whatever do you mean?" then smiled and ushered her daughter out the door.

CHAPTER 23

ELIOT ARRIVED IN his yellow Jeep. He carried the tube from the conference room and his briefcase.

Addressing Jack, "Mind if we use your table?"

"Have at it," Jack said, watching Eliot.

Eliot began laying everything out.

"Ruthie and her dog Jack are on their way over. So, Ruthie, me, and the dogs will spend quality time at the park. At least that were my instructions."

"Have fun. I appreciate it is hard. But try to behave yourself," Ted chided.

With everything laid out, Ted and Eliot took a seat at the table. Eliot began the conversation. They heard a car drive up and honk.

"Ruthie's here," Jack announced. "We're off to the park," and picked up Napper. Then they were on their way.

"Ted, the board met last week and approved everything we discussed," Eliot said. "Here is the paperwork I told you about." Eliot gave Ted a set of papers. "Please sign where I have marked. There are two sets. You need to sign both. One is for you, and one for us.

Ted took a few minutes to read each document, then sign where a yellow 'sign here' arrow indicated. Once signed, the papers were placed in two stacks. Ted gave one stack to Eliot and set the other aside.

"Now that is done. Let's get started." Said Eliot. He put the documents in his briefcase and took out more papers. Eliot glanced at them and then handed the documents to Ted.

"These are photographs and artist renderings of the project. We will close on the property next week. We received concessions from the city and county. There is a provision we are up and running within a year."

"What happens if we miss the deadline?" wondered Ted.

"Depends on a lot of things. The worst-case scenario is we lose the concessions moving forward, and everything becomes more expensive."

"Bummer."

"Before that could happen. We would have caused the delay. With a project of this magnitude, there are myriad inspections involved. It is not unusual for deadlines to be missed. In that case, we would file for and most likely be granted an extension."

"OK." Ted looked at everything on the table.

Eliot began, "Let's start with the photographs." Ted picked up several photographs. "These are the three storefronts. The largest of the three was an old NAPA auto parts store. I think the middle one was last used as a barbershop or hair salon. The last one was Acree's Insurance before Mr. Acree retired."

As they were looking at the photographs and asking questions. A car drove up and came to a quick stop. They looked up as they heard the car arrive. When the front door swung open, they looked up. A distraught Maureen standing there. Ted was shocked by her appearance. Tears were in her eyes, and she was struggling to breathe normally.

"There you are. Why haven't you answered your phone?" She said with exasperation.

Pointing to the coffee table, "It's on the table. I turned it off for our meeting. Why? What's wrong?"

"You need to come!" Neither one moved. "Now! We need to

get to the hospital."

They stood and went over to console his girlfriend. "What's the matter? Is it your mother? Is it Jack? Did they have an accident? Are they alright?" Ted kept asking questions without allowing her to answer.

With tears rolling down her cheek, she put her hand on his mouth. "It's your dad," she began in a soft tone. "He had a heart attack" When he started to speak, she put her hand on his mouth again. "Melinda was there and got him to the hospital quickly. We need to go! Now!"

"Go, go!" As Eliot shooed them out, he said, "I'll clean this up and meet you there. What about Ruthie and Jack?" Eliot asked.

"I called mom, and the dogs are going to be with Miss Ruby. Her grandkids are there, and they love to look after them. So mom and Jack will meet us at the hospital."

The two rode in silence for several minutes. "Have you seen my dad?" Ted asked.

"No." Maureen said. She kept her hands on the wheel. She never took eyes off the road. "When she could not reach you, she called me."

Ted reached over and placed a hand on her arm. "I'm sorry. I hardly ever turn my phone off. I can't explain why I did it this morning."

"You have to keep it on. You never know what may happen." Maureen was not harsh, but she was abrupt in her response.

They drove the rest of the way in silence. Finally arriving at the hospital, Maureen said, "You go up and see your dad. I'll park and come up."

"No, we'll."

"No, Winston," she said. After that, she never called him by his given name unless she was upset. "He needs you. Now!"

Ted agreed and went into the hospital. He was informed that his dad was being prepped for surgery and was directed to the waiting room cardio-vascular surgery room. When he rounded the corner, he saw Ruthie and Jack. A nurse with a clipboard was talking to Melinda. She handed the clipboard to Melinda, and she signed something.

"How's my dad?" he asked Melinda. "Is he OK? I was told something about surgery."

"He's going to be fine," Melinda said. "Let's go to the conference room. Over there," pointing to an opened door. "We can talk."

"What did you sign?" Ted blurted out.

"It was a surgical consent form," Melinda explained.

"But."

"I'll explain later. Let's talk about Mack first, OK?" Melinda said in a soothing voice.

"OK," Ted said, and they all took a seat. Melinda sat close to Ted, holding his hand in hers.

"Your dad was on the phone this morning. I can't say for sure. But I think he was talking with Marie. He made a strange sound. I looked up. He clutched his chest and collapsed."

"Heart attack?" asked Maureen, who had silently joined Melinda and Ted.

"Yes," Melinda said, nodding her head. "I called 9-1-1 and checked Mack. He did not have a pulse, so I did CPR until the EMTs arrived. Thankfully, Mack had a pulse when they arrived. They attached an AED and transported him here."

"I am grateful you were there," Ted said with tears in his eyes.

"I kept calling you, but no answer. So finally, after the third or fourth try, I called Maureen, and you know the rest."

"Sorry. I was in a meeting. I did not want to be disturbed."

"So, what's the surgery?"

"He needs a triple by-pass. They said because he got immediate assistance and was in the hospital literally within minutes of the attack, the prognosis is excellent."

There was silence in the room.

"Ted," Melinda said, "Mack is strong and stubborn."

Everyone smiled at the stubborn remark.

"He will pull through. But it will be a few hours. Maybe all day until we learn anything."

"Who is his doctor?" Maureen asked.

"A Dr. Barkemeyer. Know him?" Melinda asked Maureen.

"He's in good hands," Maureen assured everyone. "He is the best heart surgeon in the county."

"Let's go out and join everyone else," suggested Melinda.

Ted grabbed Melinda's elbow. "Tell me about the consent form."

"Ted, I promise you before the day is over, I will answer all of your questions. Right now. A man I care very much for. Is in there," pointing down the hall to closed double doors. "Fighting for his life. I understand you are worried as well. Let's get him through this surgery first, OK?"

"Melinda. Mack may be someone you care very much for. But he is my father. You are holding something back. I feel it in my bones."

"Ted. the only thing I am holding. I am holding back." she wiped a tear away, "tears. Understand he died in front of me. I brought him back, but he was, for a few moments," Melinda paused to regain her composure, "he was dead. I can't handle any more drama. Not until I." She took a breath. "Until I am sure he will be alright."

Ted softened his stance and put his arm around her. It was the first time he had shown any affection to Melinda. She reached up and patted his hand. "When he is out of danger, we will talk. I am sure it is what he also wants. Oh, have you called Marie?"

"No, why?"

"I think he was talking to her when he had his heart attack. You need to give Marie a call and let her know what is happening."

◆ ◆ ◆

Ted walked away from the group. Maureen followed when Ted held up his hand and halted her progress. He then turned his back on everyone and called his mother.

"Mom?" he asked when she answered the phone.

"Winston? How are you?"

"Not so great, to be honest. Were you talking with Dad earlier today?"

"Yes. I don't know what I said, but I must have upset your dad. I heard something. I could not make it out. And then he hung up. I tried calling, but all I got was voice mail."

"Mom, before hanging up, he didn't say anything to you. But, then, he had a heart attack and collapsed."

"Oh, my! Is Mack alright?" Marie gasped.

"Melinda was with him. His heart stopped beating. Melinda saved his life. After he collapsed, she called 9-1-1 and then did CPR. The doctor told her that he was cautiously optimistic because of her quick action. The next few hours are critical, but I am confident he will make a full recovery."

"Where is he?" Marie asked. "Let me talk to him."

"He is in surgery. He is undergoing triple-bypass surgery. He was in surgery when I arrived. I didn't have a chance to talk with the doctor. It is my understanding the prognosis is good. We should know something soon. Hopefully, in a few hours."

"OK. I'll pray for Mack. Hank and I will pray for him. Call me as soon as you learn anything. I don't care what time it is. Call me." There was a brief pause. "Oh, Ted, I forgot all about you. How are you doing? Sorry for calling you Winston earlier, a nervous habit, I guess."

"I am fine. Maureen is with me. So are Melinda, Jack, and Ruthie. Eliot and I were in a meeting when this happened. Eliot has just arrived. I'll keep you posted."

They exchanged a few more comments. Finally, Ted hung up and rejoined the group. "I called Mom. She thought she had upset him when he abruptly hung up. This idea was reinforced when she was unable to reach him. I told her about the heart attack. She sends her prayers and well-wishes."

"How is he doing?" a voice asked from behind Ted. He turned around and saw Pastor Randy Gladstone. "Melinda called me and filled me in. I came right away. If it is OK, I'd like to remain. To be with each of you. During this vigil. May I say a prayer for Mack and for all of you?"

Everyone stood in a circle and joined hands, and Pastor Gladstone offered a brief prayer. He took a chair by the window. "I will be here, praying for your dad, Ted. And for each of you. If you need to talk. I am here." He sat down and opened a prayer book. He was a part of the group. And yet he wasn't. He was close enough to show his support for the family. He was also distant enough to allow them their time together.

Melinda was the first. She walked over and sat next to Pastor Gladstone. They talked in hushed whispers, and then facing each other. He took Melinda's hand, and with heads bowed, Pastor Gladstone said a brief prayer for her and for Mack.

A few minutes later, Ted and Maureen sat with him. Again, Pastor Gladstone listened, made a few comments, and prayed with them. Throughout the long, arduous ordeal, everyone visited with the minister. At the end of each conversation, he offered a brief comment and a prayer.

Five hours later, the double doors opened, and a tall older man in blue scrubs and wearing a long, flowing lab coat came over to them. "I am Dr. Barkemeyer. Who is family?"

Without hesitation, Ted stepped forward and announced, "I'm Ted James. I am Mack's son."

Melinda started to join Ted but held back.

"He had three arteries severely clogged, and one more than 50% obstructed. So we did a quadruple by-pass. Despite the circumstances of his admittance, Mack is a strong man. He endured the surgery well." He paused for a second or two. "His prognosis is good, and he should make a full recovery. Right now, Mack is heavily sedated and in recovery. None of you will be able to see him until tomorrow. I suggest you go home and get some much-needed rest. And then, only immediate family members may see him. One at a time. For the next day or two. Do any of you have questions?"

Everyone looked at each other, and Melinda stepped forward. "Thank you, doctor. Mr. James is a special person to all of us. We appreciate what you and your team have done."

The doctor disappeared behind the double doors. Everyone pretty much just stood there. There were smiles and silent prayers.

"Before we go home, can you all please take a seat? There is something I need to tell. Tell all of you." Then, looking at Ted, "Especially you, Ted."

"I don't think it has escaped anyone's attention that Mack and I have grown close these past few months. He would sometimes spend the night at my place, and I was a frequent overnight visitor at his." Everyone nodded, confirming they were aware of this fact. "Ted, your dad is old-fashioned and felt the over-nights were wrong. So, rather the make us both miserable by ending the stays, we got married."

"What?" Everyone said at the same time.

"We are too old. We did not want the circus of a formal wedding. One afternoon, we drove to the courthouse and got married."

"Why not share the good news? Why the secrecy? Ted wanted to know.

"First there was Maureen's graduation, and then Pam's twins," turning to Ted, "And there was your work with Habitat Community. We thought if we shared our secret, it would somehow take away the importance of the other events."

"Does my mom know?"

"You remember the conversation you had with Mack when he got back from his mysterious trip?

"Yes." Ted was very quiet. He did not make eye contact with anyone. He was afraid the secret would be revealed.

"This wedding made that discussion possible."

"What discussion/" Maureen demanded.

"When Dad disappeared, he had gone to talk to Mom about the pending marriage with Melinda."

"You knew they were getting married? And you didn't tell me?"

"No. The marriage part I did not learn about until today. Dad only said it was personal business, and he would explain it all to me very soon."

"Ted, we were going to tell everyone at a barbeque. At my place this weekend. I am sorry. Sorry it came out this way."

"And the surgical authorization?"

"You weren't here, and he needed the operation. I hoped you would be here and could sign the consent."

"I have one question. What do I call you?"

Melinda walked over and gave Ted a hug. "No one can replace Marie. You can call me what you've been calling me."

"What? I have to call you dad's girlfriend?"

Melinda laughed. "No. you may call me Melinda. Like you've always done."

Pastor Gladstone said. "If you want a do-over. I'd be happy to officiate."

"Thanks, Randy." Melinda smiled.

Ted was momentarily surprised by the familiarity of calling the minister by his first name. But then Ted remembered how they first met.

"Mack and I will talk it over and get back to you, OK?"

The pastor nodded, and everyone Surrounded Melinda and congratulated her. Ted, Maureen, and Melinda stayed behind when everyone left. The three knew there was more. More to be said. But without an audience. They talked for another half-hour, then walked out of the hospital together.

As they were about to walk outside, Ted turned and gave Melinda one more hug. "Thank you for being there and saving my dad's life." The hug lasted several seconds, then Melinda kissed Ted's cheek. "You are most welcome. Thank you for your understanding. And for welcoming me into the family. It means a lot to me. It will mean even more to Mack." They stood in silence for a few seconds. Then departed, going their separate ways.

CHAPTER 24

MELINDA WAS IN Mack's room when Ted arrived the following day.

"Hi, Dad. How are you feeling?" Ted nodded acknowledgment to Melinda.

"Feel like a Mack truck hit me. Then parked on my chest." Mack found it hard to breathe and talk. He was heavily bandaged, with an IV in his left arm. A blood pressure cuff was on his right arm. "I guess I owe you an apology." The words did not come easy.

"What for?" Ted asked. "The wedding? I'm not your dad. You certainly don't need my permission." There was a pause. Ted continued, "Sorry. That came out more harshly than intended."

In a soothing voice, Melinda said, "No apology is needed." Then Melinda touched Ted's arm. Ted recoiled slightly.

In quick breaths, Mack said, using one or two words at a time, "Ted, don't be mad at Melinda. She did nothing but cave in when I said we needed to get married." Mack closed his eyes and rested a minute before continuing. "We were not hiding anything. You and Maureen were filled with so much excitement. And her graduation. Then Ruthie got you involved in Habitat."

Melinda finished the explanation. "There was no convenient time. Not without taking away from you."

"When?"

"When?" Melinda repeated.

"You know what I mean. When did you get hitched? Married. Or whatever?" Ted asked.

Melinda relaxed and smiled. "Shortly after, you came and got your tool belt," Melinda started. "I wanted to tell you right away. But Mack," Melinda paused, looking at the sleeping patient, "said it could wait. So, we simply delayed the announcement. Had we known." Melinda never finished the sentence.

After a few awkward minutes, Melinda suggested they go into the hall, finish the conversation. She did not want to disturb Mack, who needed rest. And calm.

"What did you mean you were the reason Dad and I talked after his Florida trip?"

"Marie did not trust your dad. And for a good reason. It was her idea to offer you the ring for Maureen. However, she wanted assurances. Actually, she wanted a guarantee that it would not wind up on my finger." Melinda stopped and watched for a reaction from Ted. A smile appeared on her face. She continued, "So Mack flew to Florida to pick up the ring. He also took our marriage license with him. If we were married, he would not need an engagement ring."

"So, you got married, allowing me to give Maureen mom's engagement ring," Ted said with resignation.

"No. We got married because we love each other." Melinda continued to study Ted.

"So, where is your engagement ring?"

"He never gave me one. Things just snowballed from friend to girlfriend to wife. There was no time. Like I said yesterday. At our age, we went for the gold. We skipped right to being married."

"So, what happens now?" Ted wondered.

"Why, nothing? Nothing has changed. Not between you and your dad. And I hope nothing has changed between you and me. At Mack's and my age, love does not have all the giddiness of couples your age. Mack and I have gone through what you and Maureen are experiencing. Not with each other, of course. Mack with Marie and me with my late husband, Bill. Now. It is enough just being with someone. No obligations or expectations. Being together is enough."

"And you want to be with my dad?" asked Ted.

"More than you can imagine. I want to grow old with Mack. I want to take care of him. I want to share a life together. To share his excitement and enthusiasm as he watches you and Maureen start a new life together. I simply can't imagine not being with him."

"How long will Dad be here?" Ted asked, changing the subject.

"Dr. Barkemeyer will be by this afternoon. So, we'll know more then."

"What about you and your work?" Ted was curious.

"I am working the second shift for the time being. That means I can be with Mack in the morning. He will need his rest. It is easier working in the afternoon and evening."

"When can I be with him?" Ted asked.

"He's your dad. You can come whenever you want. Stay as long as you want. You and Maureen may want to spend some time with him. Perhaps early tomorrow afternoon."

"What about rehab? Will he have to go?"

"He will start rehab here in the hospital. Neither of us can go with him. Once he gets home, yes, he will have to go to rehab. Can get him out and home first?" Melinda's voice was calming and compassionate. "Then we can wear him out with rehab."

Ted looked at his watch. "Please tell Dad I was here. I must leave. Tell him I will be back. Probably this evening. I know you love him, and you will take good care of him." Ted started to leave, then turned. He ran back and gave Melinda a hug.

"I am happy for you both. But mostly, I am thankful Dad had you when he needed someone the most. Thank you for saving his life." Ted Melinda on the cheek.

Before Melinda could respond, Ted was gone. He did not turn around. It would not have mattered. The tears in his eyes meant he would not have seen anything.

Jack was watching a western on the television when Ted walked in. Jack muted the sound, stood, and turned and greeted Ted.

"How is Mack?" Jack asked with genuine concern.

"Sleeping, mostly. Apparently, the surgery went well. The doctor is pleased with Dad's progress."

"And Melinda?" Jack continued.

"She's fine. It was a shock, to say the least, when Melinda dropped the bombshell. But I'm over it. We're fine."

"Are You?" Jack asked, not sure he believed what Ted was saying.

"OK, I feel like crap. I feel betrayed. I know it's not my place to judge. But it's like when Dad was drinking a lot. He would hide things from Mom and me. Little things, you know."

"Ted, marriage is not a little thing. You feel hurt and betrayed. You will get over it. I am sure everything will work out. Eventually. However, that doesn't mean it won't be painless."

"I hope so," said Ted, not too convincingly.

"Oh, your girl called."

"Maureen? What did she want?" Ted asked with renewed excitement.

"Don't know. Maureen said you are to call her at work when you got home. Be prepared for the same from her. Only worse." Jack laughed. "Get used to it, Teddy, old boy. Women need to know everything. No, that's not true," he said as he shook his head. "They merely want you to confirm what they already suspect!" And laughed.

"How's your dad?" were the first words out of her mouth. "After the surgery, I saw Dr. Barkemeyer. He couldn't say much. But gave me a thumbs up when I asked."

Without enthusiasm or emotion, Ted said, "As well as can be expected, I guess.

"Was Melinda there?"

"Yes, and we talked a little." Ted gave Maureen a brief recap of his talk with Melinda.

Maureen consoled Ted, saying, "I think it's wonderful your dad has someone in his life. I really like Melinda. I think she is good for him." And after a brief pause added, "and for you, too."

Ted and Maureen talked for a few more minutes when Ted's phone alerted him he had received another call. It was from Emmerson College.

"Mrs. Logan from Emmerson is calling so, I gotta go. We'll talk tonight. Love you," and disconnected.

"Mrs. Logan?" asked in confirmation.

"Good morning, Mr. James." She was always formal when it came to school.

"What can I do for you?"

"I am not sure what you remember of our initial conversation. As part of our ABA program, you need to spend a semester working on a practicum. Real-life experience in the business world. Do you have a company willing to work with you? Or would you prefer me to locate one for you? We have several companies that welcome our students."

"I am involved with the JK Foundation." Ted began.

"I vaguely remember something about that."

"Do you know Eliot Tullus?" Ted asked.

"I've known Eliot and Pam a long time."

"How about I have Mr. Tullus," Ted thought it prudent to

be professional in this discussion, "call you?"

"Let me call him. The practicum is not a set course. The companies will provide the direction. I'll check back with you after I talk with Mr. Tullus."

Ted and Mrs. Logan continued to talk. They covered personal things: Ted's dad, Maureen, and Ted's career plans.

Eliot called Ted an hour later.

"Good morning, Ted. How is your dad? Have you seen him today?" Eliot asked.

"I was with him and Melinda this morning. Dr. Barkemeyer is pleased with the surgery and said Dad will start physical therapy later this week."

"Did the doctor say anything? Like when Mack might come home?"

"No. Maybe by the end of the week. The doctor said we will play that by ear." Ted took a breath. Then asked, "Did Mrs. Logan from Emmerson talk to you?"

"Yes. I said the foundation would be pleased to take you on your practicum. Are you busy this afternoon? Can you stop by, say, around two?"

Ted confirmed the appointment and hung up.

"Aren't you the busy beaver today?" Jack asked with a soft laugh. "How about you go get us one of them impossible things from Burger King? I'll even pay."

"OK," Ted replied.

Jack added, "No French fries."

"Got it, no fries. Need to make one more call. Then I'm off to the King."

"Fine with me," Jack hollered after Ted as he left the room.

Ted and Eliot were in the conference room with a large monitor. This allowed Pam to join the meeting via TEAMS. The table was littered with blueprint plans, photos of three ugly storefronts, and architectural renderings. Ted listened while Pam and Eliot talked over one another. They occasionally asked Ted questions.

Eliot moved everything around so Ted could focus on a series of color photographs of three connected storefronts' exteriors and interiors. They took up one block. They had been home to various businesses over the years.

Pointing to the first one, Eliot said, "Most recently was a NAPA auto parts store," pointing to a faded logo. "The building itself is in sound condition. Obviously it has been neglected."

"Not by the graffiti artists," Ted said, pointing to parts of the building.

"Nope. The spray-can artists have had fun."

Pointing to the middle storefront, "The last tenant for the middle section, I believe, was a barbershop or hair salon. An insurance agent for State Farm was in the last storefront." Ted noticed the familiar logo still on the store's large window.

"What happened to the good neighbor? Give up and leave?"

Eliot gave Ted a one-eyed look and said, "Really?"

"Yeah, yeah, bad joke," Ted said with a smile.

Moving the exterior shots aside, Eliot placed the interior photographs. "The interiors are in pretty good shape. We may put new flooring down. This one." Eliot said, pointing to the former auto parts store, "will be a grocery store. Right now, Southtown is a food desert. Lots of places to buy booze but not many places to buy bread, milk, and such."

"Like in none?" Ted asked.

"Oh, there are a few convenience stores. As you might expect, prices are high. Higher than this neighborhood can afford." Then, holding a picture of the store's interior, "We'll take up the existing floor, repair the cement foundation and polish it. It will be less expensive than putting down new tile."

"Hmm," was the only comment from Ted.

"The architect has suggested vinyl plank that is almost as durable as sealed cement. In addition, he says it is more inviting. We're still considering our options. It all comes down to our budget."

"Dad put a floating vinyl plank in his living room and dining room in his house. He says he really likes it."

"If we go with the vinyl plank, we will probably go with glued down. The vinyl itself is waterproof. Not necessarily true for the sub-flooring."

"Sounds interesting–and ambitious. What about the backs of the buildings?" Ted asked, picking up aerial photos of the block-long building.

"Gardens. The garden area behind the grocery store will provide fresh seasonal produce for the store. Hopefully, this will keep our produce costs low."

"And the other areas?"

"Have you heard of community gardens?" Ted indicated he had. "At least half of the area will be devoted to a community garden concept. We want churches, service organizations, and neighborhoods to farm the smaller garden plots. They can give some or all of what they grow to the grocery store. They may also take it for their own use. Our mission is community involvement."

Ted studied all he had been shown and then asked, "OK. So, where do I fit in?"

"For your practicum, you will oversee the exterior renovation of the three buildings. The two street-sides," picking up the street-side views of both the former auto parts store and insurance agency, "would love a mural. We want to use local talent to create these murals."

"Local talent?" Ted asked.

"A local paint contractor, Consolidated Paint. I know little about them, but Jack's nephew, Tim, knows them. Oh, and Ruthie says she highly recommends them. I will get back to you after checking them out." Eliot got out a notebook and scribbled a note.

"The grocery store and the medical clinic," picking up pictures of the auto parts store and the insurance agency again, "need to be neutral. It should also reflect their purpose."

Ted picked up the middle picture and asked, "What about this one?" He showed Eliot the picture.

"With this one, the painters are free to be creative."

"A youth center?" asked Ted in surprise.

"Kids need a place to chill. And to hang out. A place to play video games, watch television, get tutoring and do homework. Computers with internet access will be available."

"You do know some of these guys. How shall we say? Push the limits?"

"Honor system. However, they will be monitored. We will be able to track where they go. There will be firewalls. Let's be honest; knowing firewalls will be incentive enough for some to try to breakthrough. If we find anyone visiting a no-no site, goodbye computer access."

"But still allowed in the center?"

"Sex, booze, and drugs. Those will get a youth barred in a heartbeat."

"Smoking?"

"This will be a smoke-free center. No smoking. No vaping. For everyone's health in the center. It is also a fire hazard issue. They won't be barred for smoking, but we will need to either put away whatever they are using or leave the premises."

"And I will be the boss."

"The foundation is funding the project. You work for the foundation, and the board will provide guidance when needed. You will share your progress with me right now, but you will be the on-site contact unless you go entirely off-grid. So, yes, you will be the boss."

"When do I start?"

"Soon. Soon." Eliot began packing everything up, signaling the meeting was over.

CHAPTER 25

TED AND ELIOT arrived at Elmer's at the same time. They took a large booth in the back, allowing them to talk business.

"What did you learn about Consolidated Painting?" Ted asked. He took a sip of coffee.

"Consolidated Painting is a small outfit. They worked some for Habitat Community. Both new construction and in rehabilitating existing homes."

"Never heard of them," Ted said.

"According to Ruthie, Consolidated Painting has been around perhaps twenty years. It is a family business and the current owner is young, but excellent." Eliot looked up when the door open. Two young men in jeans and matching green shirts came in. He waved, and they acknowledged him.

The two caught Ted by surprise. Ted recognized them immediately and saw something had changed. The shorter one was definitely in charge and had "Fred" emblazoned on his shirt. The other one had "Jim" on his shirt.

"Ted, this is Fred Wheller and Jim Dickenson of Consolidated Painting. Fred, here, is the new owner I was telling you about."

"Hey, Ted," as Fred reached out and shook Ted's hand.

"Ted," was all Jim said, taking his turn shaking Ted's hands.

Ignoring Ted, Eliot began, "Mrs. Rittenhouse has recommended you highly. She said you did excellent work with Habitat Community."

"Yeah," said Fred, "We've done a little work for Ruthie. She's good people."

"How did you get started?" asked Ted. He was curious how his former delinquent friends had become successful business owners.

"Dennis Perry was my uncle. Uncle Dennis started the business about twenty-five years ago. I got to work with him when he was short of help. Uncle Dennis taught me how to paint a house. I got Jim involved when we were doing a Habitat house."

"What about what we did growing up?" Ted asked with trepidation.

"An idle mind is the devil's playground." Then he continued. "Uncle Dennis fell off scaffolding. He broke his back. He was in the middle of one job. And had two more lined up. None of Uncle Dennis' kids wanted to follow in his footsteps. So, he reached out to me. Then I talked to Jim. With my uncle's blessing, we decided to take over the business."

Eliot asked, "What did his clients say about the change in ownership?"

"Not a lot," said Fred. "Jim and I were already working on the projects, so we were not totally unknown."

"Well, Ted," Eliot asked, "What about our new paint contractors?"

"If Ruthie says they're OK, that is good enough for me." Ted said, nodding at the two.

The waitress refilled Ted and Eliot's coffee cups during the exchange and brought the newcomers their coffee. Eliot emptied a folder, and everyone moved their coffee cups.

Eliot brought out a manilla folder with several photographs. "This is the project. The foundation has purchased the entire block. This includes building along the street and the vacant lots behind them." In addition, there were photos of each individual storefront.

"This one," Eliot said, laying the first photo on the table.

"Ah, the old NAPA store," said Jim.

"Yes, the old NAPA store," Eliot continued. "It is the largest of the three. We want to turn it into a grocery store." Eliot waited while the painters looked at the photo. Then, finally, he placed a picture showing the building's side. "We visualize a mural on this side representing the purpose of the building. The exact design is up to you."

"Jim's the artistic one," Fred said with his thumb pointing at his friend. "He can come up with an idea."

"Great," Eliot said, and laid down the middle storefront. "This, I understand, was last used as a beauty shop. We want to make it a teen center of sorts."

"Of sorts?" Fred echoed.

"All three of you." Eliot pointed Ted, Fred, and Jim in a sweeping motion. "You know these kids. They need someplace to go after school and on weekends. We are looking to put in a large screen television, game stations, and computers." Eliot paused to look at the others. "We hope to work with other groups and provide tutoring and homework assistance. At least three days a week. The kids in this area are underserved."

"You can say that again," Jim said. He was looking at the NAPA store photo.

"I think we can agree education is the single most important tool," Eliot said, "in becoming a successful and productive adult."

Jim continued examining the photo.

Fred was nodding his head as he listened to Eliot. "I know kids who have dropped out of school. Too many. They are either deadbeat hooked on drugs and alcohol. Or they are locked up." Deep in thought, Fred picked up a photo of the proposed youth center.

"This place must be fun and safe. Where they may come and relax. Free from violence, drugs, alcohol, and porn." Eliot said this slowly and deliberately.

"Amen to that," said Ted. His first words during this part of the meeting.

Jim, holding up the last picture and pointed. "And what? The old insurance office is no longer a good neighbor?"

Eliot grinned, put his head down, and shook it.

"Yeah, yeah," said Jim with a laugh. "Bad joke. But it was an old State Farm agency. The logo is still visible on the window," pointing to the photo.

"This will be our clinic. There will be a dental office. There are two other rooms. One for examinations and one for general use. The offices are not open every day. But there will be a schedule. For instance, if it Wednesday, then the dentist is in."

"Finally," said Eliot, holding up a picture of the insurance store's side. "We want a mural on this wall with scenes and landmarks of Southtown."

"No problem," said Jim with confidence.

"Well, what do you think? Are you interested in working with us?"

"We have jobs already lined up, and we can't afford to drop them. You understand. Not good for business." Fred continued, still looking at the photographs.

Eliot assured them, "Not a problem. We are pretty flexible and don't want you to cancel any business already on the books. Any idea when we can see sketches for the murals?"

"Give me a week," Jim said, looking at the two. "When I have an idea, do I contact Ruthie?"

"No, Ted, here is the project manager. He works for the foundation. You can call him and give him your ideas. He has the authority to approve, reject, or request modifications to your suggestions. Acceptable?"

"Sure, no problem," said Fred. "Give us a week."

Ted took the lead. "Once approved. How long to get the wall outlined?"

"Maybe a week for both walls. Why?"

"I talked with the art teachers at Bruno Malone High School and Emmerson. If you lay it out on the wall and give me a color picture, their art students will do the work. The students at both schools have service project hours to complete. I've seen this done successfully in communities elsewhere. No reason it can't work here."

"Hmm, good idea," Fred and Jim said together.

"As far as the paint goes, you can either purchase it, and we will reimburse you. Or you can give us a list of what you want, and we'll provide it."

"It is probably best for us to get the paint." Fred was saying. "That way. We will have what we need."

"I agree," Eliot confirmed.

"Are we doing the murals only?" Fred inquired.

"No. The whole project is yours if you want it. Both interior and exterior," assured Eliot.

"We're open to ideas there as well," said Ted. "Especially with the middle building. It needs to be inviting - inside and out."

"And the other two?" asked Fred.

"Inviting, but more subdued than the youth portion," Ted said. "Think about it. We can talk more when we review the plans for the murals. You are the paint experts."

"I don't know," mused Fred. "Normally, the customer says you paint this wall mauve, and that's what we do."

"Mauve?" chuckled Eliot.

"Yeah, we get all kinds of weird requests. This is new territory for us. We rarely get to pick the colors,"

"We can give you our suggestions if you want," Ted offered.

"No. I think it will be fun putting our mark on a project like this." Fred was doing the talking while he and Jim huddled over the pictures.

"Can we take these?" Jim asked.

"By all means. They are your copies," Ted said this and then quickly looked at Eliot, who nodded his approval. "The wall dimensions are on the back."

Fred and Jim gathered up the photos and put them in Eliot's manilla folder. The conversation became relaxed as each told personal stories. Eliot wound up doing a lot of sharing as he pulled out his phone and shared pictures of his new twin girls, Jennifer and Jessica. Finally, with business concluded, Fred and Jim stood, shook hands. Ted gave them his phone number. All promised to be in touch. The painters were the first to leave.

"Take a seat," Eliot said as they watched the painters make their exit. "I am aware there is history with you, Fred, and Jim. A history, shall we say, not always pleasant. Are you OK with them on this project?" Eliot wanted to know. "It is precisely your history, Ruthie considered when she suggested them to us. This whole project is about rehabilitation. It is about rehabilitating buildings-and people."

"No, no. I'm fine. I never knew Fed and Jim were part-time painters. I thought we were all, more or less, delinquents. I am happy for them and welcome them on the project." Ted was sincere.

"Good. Once you approve the mural designs."

"Wait. You are seriously giving me that power? That responsibility?"

"Ted, remember how you came into our lives."

Ted looked down. Ashamed of his initial entry into the lives of the Kelley family.

"You started out to burglarize my father-in-law's home. Instead, you found a man in need. You took the appropriate action and stayed behind. You did not to burglarize the home. You also returned to clean up and make sure Napper was safe. What you did says a lot about who you are. A lot more than your attempt at being a criminal." Eliot was talking in a quiet tone.

"Look at you now. My father-in-law depends on you. Pam and I depend on you. And Ruthie depends on you, and her daughter has fallen in love with you. You are doing well in school, excelling far beyond what others might have expected."

"It hasn't been easy," Ted said sheepishly.

"No, but you've done it. You have matured far beyond your years. You have helped build a house for a family in need, and you have accepted the responsibilities demanded of you."

"And the point is?" Ted questioned.

"I think one reason you have not proposed to Maureen,"

"You, too?" Ted interrupted. "You're trying to convince me to propose?"

"No, I'm on your side. I think you recognized you were not mature enough when the notion of marriage popped up." Eliot paused. "We are proud of you and your decision. A weaker man might have caved and gotten married." "I had not considered that. But you are right." Ted smiled at the compliment.

"Not a member of your family. or those that have seen you and Maureen together. We are convinced you make a perfect couple. No! You make THE perfect couple."

"That scares me," Ted admitted.

"That ought to. Marriage is not to be taken lightly. Unfortunately, today's media has made a mockery of marriage. Of the commitment between two people. They believe love and lust are one and the same. They are not. And you recognize that."

"I can't stand to watch those shows."

"One thing we all admire is your understanding marriage is more than an exchange of vows. It goes far beyond those words. With maybe the exception of Maureen," Eliot said with a short chuckle, "

"But the physical part is hard to ignore." Said Ted. And both laughed.

"Ted, if you propose to Maureen today, tomorrow, or whenever. You must know. You have our blessings and support. From all of us." Eliot took a last sip of coffee. "Pam, Ruthie, Jack, and even your dad. They all ganged up on me. They pestered me to make sure I told you this. And to make sure you believe it!"

Ted smiled. "I'm surprised Maureen didn't make you get the date when I will propose."

Eliot rubbed his left bicep. "Let's just say it wasn't for lack of trying." They both laughed again.

"Mr. Tullus, Eliot, I cannot begin to tell you how much I appreciate what you and your family have done for me. I am definitely not the same person today I was when I discovered Jack on the floor that fateful evening." Ted paused and gave Eliot an opening to respond. There was none. "I believe I am ready for this next challenge. I know with you and Ruthie behind me." Ted paused, searching for the right words. "I have what I need to succeed."

"Great. Let's leave before Elmer's decides to charge us rent. Let me know when Consolidated Paint gets back with you."

"Will do," assured Ted. The two shook hands and went their separate ways.

◆ ◆ ◆

Sitting in the Ranger, Ted got out his phone. He dialed the number, and it was picked up on the second ring.

"Hi, Ted. How did the meeting go?" Ruthie asked.

"Thank you," Ted said.

"You're welcome." There was a pause. "Ted, I don't mean to be short. But I have got another." Ruthie paused mid-sentence, then said, "I have been waiting all day for this call."

"No problem. I had to call and say thank you." The call ended, and Ted headed over to Emmerson to complete the paperwork for his practicum.

CHAPTER 26

TWO WEEKS AFTER the meeting, Fred called Ted. "Jim has the drawings. Where do we bring them?"

Ted invited them to Jack's house. They would review everything and get the wheels rolling.

When Fred and Jim arrived, Ted introduced them to Jack.

"Well, well, well." said Jack sarcastically. He got up and shook their hands. "Glad things worked out for you."

Ted flinched at Jack's tone. Neither man showed a reaction.

"Mr. Kelley. It looks like the outside could use a little sprucing up," Fred then handed Jack a business card. "We'll even give you a hardship discount." Then, pointing at Ted, "For having to live with Teddy." They all laughed.

"Over here," Ted said, standing at the dining room table. "Have a seat. Need anything to drink? Coffee? Dr. Pepper? Water?"

"Nah, we're fine," Jim said and pulled out some drawings. "Let's start with the old NAPA store." He then laid out three colored pictures. "Each of these is a variation of other murals I've seen. They depict farms, farming, and farmers. I would recommend this one." He picked up one picture and handed it to Ted. "The main focal point is the inside of the supermarket. The four corners show food moving from farm to market. The faces represent people in the neighborhood."

"Looks Good." Ted studied the recommended picture and then picked up the other two renderings. Ted reviewed each image carefully. He said, "You know Jim. We would be pleased having these on the wall. First, however, I must agree with you. I do like the one you suggested, and that's the one we'll go with."

"Great. Now, the other wall. Again, I have three options," handing Ted one of the drawings. "This is the one I would suggest. It depicts life in Southtown. Not life as it is now. But a more positive view of the future." Jim waited for Ted to comment. Ted silently reviewed the pictures. Jim continued, "Here is the AME church, and this is the Baptist church. Here is the Southtown library and Errol White Middle School. MLK Park is in the center with friends and neighbors getting together."

"You sold me. I want to scan all six pictures for Eliot tonight and let him know our selections."

"Works for us," Fed said, nodding in agreement.

"Go ahead and get your paint. Then give me the bill. We pay invoices at the end of the month. But we require a three-day minimum advance notice. Friday is our last work day. I can rush it if you get me the invoice by Wednesday."

Fred handed Ted an itemized invoice showing each paint color and quantity purchased, along with standard painting supplies. "Here is our invoice. This should be sufficient for the murals. The renderings are on us. No charge for those."

"You sure?"

"You haven't done much contracting, have you?"

"No, I haven't. This is new territory for me." Ted admitted.

"Drawings are part of the total project bill, not a separate line item. This is our bill for labor," handing Ted another invoice. "Your only cost is outlining the murals. We will be available for consult and will help paint when we can."

"How long to get the outlining done?" Ted asked.

"A week to ten days. I think that is sufficient," Jim said, looking at Fred for support.

The three talked for a few minutes. After his friends left, Ted stayed behind. He mentally walked through the three buildings again, trying to imagine the transformations about to begin. He was abruptly brought back to the present with the ringing of his phone. He looked at the caller ID.

"Good morning, Eliot. Fred and Jim just left. I have approved the two murals."

"Great news," said Eliot. "However, that's not why I called. Do you think you can swing by the office this afternoon? Say around two?"

"Don't see why not. What's up?"

"I want you to meet our architect. He has a couple of options for creating the interior spaces. Take an hour or two."

"I'll be there. I will also bring what Fred and Jim left with me. I think you'll be pleased with what they have created."

Closing his phone and gathering up the pictures, Ted stood studying Jack. Finally, Ted said, "I worry about you, Jack. You are alone all day. What if something happens to you? After all, I AM supposed to be looking after you."

"Don't worry about me. I'm fine. You have a lot on your plate. Simply knowing you are around is a big comfort. Speaking of comfort."

"Yeah," Ted said with trepidation.

"That girl of yours said you are to meet her at noon at the Mac Shack."

Ted looked at his watch. "Good, that gives me a few minutes to relax." Ted sat down and closed his eyes.

"Ever notice how she asks everyone else but simply tells you?" Jack said, never taking his eyes off Maverick.

"That's my girl. She's got it in her pretty little head that I am her servant."

"Well, we know who will wear the pants in that household,"

Jack said, laughingly.

"Once we get married, that will change. You'll see," Ted affirmed.

"Don't count on it, buddy-boy. Your girl has got a ring in your nose. And she is not letting go. Not any time soon, anyway." Jack looked at Ted.

"She is quite a catch. So, I guess things might be worse."

They sat in silence while the *Maverick* episode played out and a Ford commercial came on.

"Hey, wake up!" Jack was kicking Ted's foot.

Ted sat up with a start. "What? What's the matter?" Ted asked, rubbing his eyes.

"The rope through the ring in your nose is getting taught. It's a quarter till, and you better get going. You don't want to keep the little lady waiting."

Maureen was already at the Mac Shack when Ted arrived. He saw her immediately and walked to the booth. She stood up, gave him a quick but firm kiss, and waited for Ted to sit down.

"Scoot over," Maureen said, pushing on his shoulder.

"What? Why?" Ted asked in a teasing manner.

"I want to sit next to my future husband," she said in an equally teasing manner.

"Do you know what the fifth is?"

"Yeh, it was last week. Nothing happened. A Very dull day."

Maureen nudged his arm. "Next month, you dork. What happens on the fifth?"

"Just another day. As far as I am aware." Ted worked hard, stifling a laugh.

"Alright, dummy. It's your birthday. You turn twenty-one, the big two-one."

"Oh, yeah. I forgot. It's no biggie," Ted said, still not looking at her.

"OK, let me spell it out. You said we could not get married until you finished, Emmerson."

"Still not done," Ted deadpanned.

"Yes. But you do have a job. And that was a second condition."

"Correction. I am working, but I still don't have a job. This is a practicum. I get the honor of paying Emmerson a lot of money for the privilege of working. For no pay, may I remind you? The only money I am making is what I get taking care of Jack. We can't survive on what I make."

"The big hurdle, and those are your words, buddy, is age. You will turn twenty-one next month. After that, I want to start planning our wedding."

"It is clear you would get married today if I asked," Ted said. He still hadn't looked at her.

"Are you asking?" Maureen asked with enthusiasm.

Looking directly at Maureen with a furrowed brow, Ted said, "No. And I don't know how to make you understand. Too many of our friends got married before they were ready. More than half are divorced. Of those still married, they appear heading to divorce court."

"That won't be us," Maureen said with quiet reassurance.

Ted took Maureen's hands in his and turned to face her. "I want to marry you. More than anything else in the world." Ted said with a quiet calm.

"Well," she interrupted, "It's a start. You actually said the words."

"What words?" Ted asked.

"You want to marry me." Maureen smiled. She turned and leaned into him.

"Since the first time I saw you, I knew. I knew you were the girl for me. But I don't want to end up like my parents."

"I promise you. I won't let that happen."

"Easy to say, but Dad told me that one problem he and Mom had," Ted paused, "was they were too young when they got married." Then, looking Maureen in the eyes, "They weren't ready for marriage requires."

Maureen and Ted sat there in silence. They were eating the fries Maureen ordered before Ted arrived.

"My practicum is up in December. If they offer me a job with a living wage, then we can plan the wedding. OK?" Ted put his arm around Maureen and gave her a hug.

"And what if they don't? What if the foundation decides you aren't it? You are not right for the job."

"Simple. I will look for a new job. Eliot, however, has given me every indication they want me to be director of public relations. Or something similar. They see me as the foundation's face. To help in raising grant money. So, if and when they offer me the job, I will pop the question. OK?" Ted pulled her more tightly into him, kissed the top of her head, and laid his head against hers.

They sat in the booth without talking when Ted's phone alarm went off.

"I have a meeting with Eliot and an architect. Want to go out for dinner?"

"How about pizza at Mom's?"

"Sounds great. I'll bring Jack. I don't want him to starve.

Maureen let Ted out and they kissed. Ted picked up the bill and paid on his way out.

◆ ◆ ◆

Ted arrived at Tullus & Tullus and was directed to the conference room. As he approached, Ted heard two men in friendly conversation.

"Ah, there you are, Ted. Come on in. I want you to meet a good friend of mine." Eliot waved Ted over to the two men standing at a window. "Ted, this is Michael Everett of Everett and Earl." The two shook hands, nodding in acknowledgment. "He is our resident architect, and I want him to share with you the ideas he has for the Southtown project."

"Ted James, right?"

Ted nodded in affirmation.

"Any relation to Mack James?"

"I'm his son," Ted said.

"Mack and I go way back. We played high school football together. Tell the old coot to give me a call. We need to get caught up."

"I'll tell him."

Ted and Eliot sat down as Michael moved to a three-dimensional model on the table.

Michael handed a set of drawings to both Ted and Eliot. "This is an exciting project, and," looking at Eliot, "I am glad you brought us in. It is the type of thing Southtown needs. If it is to be revitalized."

Michael reviewed what he understood to be our needs for the next hour and provided three different ways to configure the building. Michael then selected one option. He explained why this option would be optimum. Next, he moved the three-dimensional model closer to Ted and Eliot and went through the information again.

"Mike, you have done your usual outstanding job. I know which one I would pick, but the selection is up to Ted here," he said, putting his hand on Ted's shoulder.

"My decision?" Ted asked with surprise.

"Ted is new at this." Then turning to Ted, "You are the project manager. Just as you selected the wall murals, you select—or reject—the options presented. You can't go wrong, and you don't have to select the one he suggested."

Ted was looking at the three options. Then studied the model. "At first glance, I was leaning toward this one," Ted said, holding up a rendering. "However, your recommendation makes more sense. Let's go with the one you recommended."

Eliot looked at Ted. "No time for equivocation here, Ted. Either it is your recommendation, or it isn't."

Ted stood, offering his hand to the architect. "Then we have a plan. We will go with the model you created. It will be awesome." The two shook hands.

The architect left. Ted and Eliot reviewed the renderings. Then they examined the model more closely.

"There is a color scheme for the interior but not the exterior," Ted observed.

"I told Mike, Consolidated Paint were the creative forces for the exterior. However, what we do need is an architectural sketch. A sketch of the finished project. This will help us get more community involvement and support. It is also a goal to be obtained."

As he looked at the drawings, Ted said, "I see."

"Can Jim do it?"

"I'll get them started. Then, if Fred and Jim are not comfortable, I call Mr. Everett. I can give him what the two developed. And let him do the drawing. OK with you?" Ted asked.

"You're the project manager," Eliot said with a smile.

Ted put Fred and Jim on speakerphone and explained the foundation's needs. "We can do that," assured Jim. "Give us a day or two. Then, I'll call Ted."

"Good," said Eliot.

"And if it isn't what you want or need, you won't hurt my feelings if you have your architect guy re-do the drawing," said Jim.

"I think whatever we get from you will be fine." Eliot gave Jim the specs for the drawing.

The call ended and a mild commotion could be heard. "Uh, oh," Eliot said, laughing. "The two Js are here. Want to see them?" Eliot was gone Ted could answer.

Eliot picked up one carrier and pointed to the other one.

"That one is yours."

"But, I." Ted stammered.

Pam said, "Relax, they won't break. You need to learn the art of fatherhood. I have a sneaky suspicion. Maureen is not waiting long for you to have your own kids."

"I think you are right," said Ted, and he studied the bundle in his arms.

Eliot and Ted kept Jennifer and Jessica occupied while Pam took care of business in her office. She was gone. Pam worked for an hour. But it seemed only minutes to Ted.

"You know, Pam. You have gotten me into a whole lot of trouble," Ted said.

"How's that?"

"Maureen can smell baby a mile away, and I'm having dinner with her tonight. There will be an inquisition. No way am I going to escape." They laughed as he handed his bundle back to Pam. Then he was on the way home.

CHAPTER 27

THE SOUTHTOWN PROJECT made the evening news. A local television station showed a video of students painting murals as a backdrop.

"The law office of Tullus & Tullus has scheduled a press conference for Monday. Eliot Tullus has promised to unveil an aggressive plan to revitalize this Southtown neighborhood. All we know at this time is art students from Bruno Malone High School and Emmerson College are painting murals on the sides of this block-long building."

Pam, Eliot, and Ted were at the dining table in Jack's house. They were preparing for the next day's press conference. They agreed what each would say.

"I will introduce the project in general terms," Pam was saying. "I will stress the need for our project."

"I will then lay out our budget,"

"What is the budget?" Ted asked.

"We have committed $1.1 million." Answered Eliot. "I will mention the partnership with Consolidated Painting, Everett and Earl architects, and C&C Construction."

"Then I will describe the three facilities," finished Ted, his eyes darting between the two lawyers. It was a question, not a statement.

"Yes. You will describe the four elements of the project. How the three buildings will be used. You will end laying out the community gardens in the rear."

"Who will answer the questions? You do know there will be questions. Lots of questions!"

Eliot looked at Pam, who nodded to Eliot. "We all will. But I think most will be directed at you, Ted. You are the project manager. You will lay out our vision and what community support is needed."

There was to be a watch party at Jack's. Ruthie was bringing two-foot-long subs from Subway. Jack was providing the drinks. Mack and Melinda would be there, along with Maureen. The press conference would be at City Hall. They agreed the room was primarily a media space. The meant Ted's fan club would watch from home.

At twelve, Eliot drove everyone to City Hall. They had two large architectural renderings. They showed the front of the project. The brochures, prepared by Everett and Earl with help from Jim, included floor plans. They laid out how the projected gardens would be utilized.

The media arrived a few minutes later and staked out their territory. Two local television stations were represented and a third station from the capital. Radio stations made up the next most prominent section of the media. Few people get their news from newspapers. However, the three papers serving the community were there.

"Welcome. I want to thank you for coming," the speaker announced, and the audience began taking their seats. "We are here to share some exciting news for a neighborhood. A neighborhood in need of good news." It was mayor Paul Powell. He was obviously excited to share a significant influx of money into his city. "At am pleased to introduce Mrs. Pamela Tullus of the law firm of Tullus & Tullus. She will take over from here."

"Good afternoon." Pam started. She was dressed in a dark-blue, pin-striped pantsuit with subdued jewelry. This was her closing argument suit and wanted to command the full attention of the media. "My firm, Tullus & Tullus, is working with the J.K. Foundation to revitalize one block of the Southtown neighborhood."

Pam identified the numerous locations available for purchasing alcohol. Pam said, "Except for two convenience stores. People are unable to purchase basic groceries." She waited a beat. "And no place to buy fresh vegetables." Pam surveyed the audience. Then, finishing, she said, "The foundation believes this neighborhood needs this project. Not just to survive. But to grow into the vibrant community. A community we know it can be."

Eliot introduced himself and began with the financial commitment. "We have pledged $1.1 million. We invite others in the community to participate. We welcome their help to maximize this investment."

Next, he introduced the architects, the construction firm, and Consolidated Painting. A few hands shot up. "I am going to ask our project manager, Ted James, to go into greater detail. I believe he will answer most of your questions. When he is finished, we will answer your questions."

Ted had a PowerPoint presentation with his remarks. Most of the slides we also in the brochures. Ted showed each storefront. He then explained how the storefronts would be used.

As he addressed the community gardens. Ted began, "We anticipate having eight raised gardens. Four providing produce for the grocery store." Ted relaxed and began to smile as he talked. "The remaining four gardens would be for the community. We hope to partner with churches and civic groups to develop these gardens. Whatever is grown is theirs. While they may donate some of what they harvest to the new grocery, that is neither required nor expected." He paused as more slides depicting the gardens in various stages appeared on the screen. When the slide showing key-hole gardens came up, Ted continued his presentation. As he spoke, his voice became more robust and more authoritative.

"These are key-hole gardens. Our goal is at least three of them. These gardens are especially needed. They allow folks to participate without bending over or kneeling on the ground. We want the gardens to be just that, community gardens."

The actual press conference lasted three-quarters of an hour. Another half-hour was devoted to answering questions. The various media outlets interviewed each of the participants individually. As expected, most questions were directed to Ted. Pam and Eliot took the opportunity to mingle with the audience and ensure each media outlet had brochures.

It was after four when the trio rolled into Jack's house. They were greeted with a standing ovation.

"Awesome job, Pam," her dad said. He walked over and kissed her cheek. Then, turning to Eliot, "And you weren't half-bad yourself."

"Thanks," Eliot said while pumping Jack's hand.

"The camera loved you," said Maureen told Ted and kissed him.

"He is a natural." Said Eliot.

"We have the perfect face for the project," affirmed Pam.

"Yeah, right? I was about fainted with every question. I had to ask reporters to repeat some questions. I could not hear what they were saying because of the noise of my shaking knees," Ted said, and laughed.

"You looked cool as a cucumber," Ruthie said in support of Ted. "I agree with Pam and Eliot. You are the perfect person to head this campaign."

"What's next?" Jack wanted to know.

"We made a brief presentation last week to the City Council," Pam said.

"Yes, and they want a more formal presentation next week,"

Eliot.

"I will make sure each receives a brochure," Ted said. "And I will present my PowerPoint for them. And I get all the questions."

Looking at the brochure, Ruthie said, "I am impressed with the community garden idea. How will this work?"

Pam said, "We are scheduling Ted in front of civic organizations and church groups over the next few months. He will hopefully sell them on participating. Each will be responsible for one of the public-raised gardens. Or one of the key-hole gardens."

Jack chimed in, "Why not get the Vo-Ag classes at the high school involved?"

"Good idea," said Ted. "I will call them next week and feel them out."

The next few months, Ted met with the service organizations. As well as the churches. While there was broad support for what Ted proposed, only the high school Vo-Ag department signed on to manage one of the gardens. The following week, he was in front of the school board and pitching his ambitious plan.

"What we would like," Ted began addressing the school board. "Actually, what we need is to have the high school Vo-Ag department commit to maintaining at least two of the gardens. These are the gardens intended to supply the supermarket." Ted surveyed his audience. "This way, we have those with expertise in gardening helping the community. The goal is providing fresh produce to the community. And assistance to the other gardening groups."

Ted made a similar presentation to Emmerson College and Southern State. It was not long before students from the high school, Emmerson and Southern State, began to prepare the gardens for planting. This was done during the week. Timber and cinder blocks were used to designate eight gardens. Emmerson, Southern State students, helped establish the gardens. Boy Scouts supporting an Eagle Scout project provided an irrigation system to ensure crops would be irrigated with minimum water lost to evaporation.

The key-hole gardens were placed at the back, between the traditional gardens. Three neighborhoods signed on for these.

Paramount Fencing donated materials and labor to enclose the area with a four-foot, chain-link fence. A gate was behind the grocery store, a second behind the clinic. A third gate was at the back.

Ted said, "Not to keep people out. But to keep dogs and rabbits out. Unfortunately, we can't do much about the squirrels." Ted said with a smile.

The First Methodist, St. Francis Catholic, St. Michaels AME, and St. Paul's United Church of Christ each adopted one of the four public gardens.

"What about birds?" asked Mrs. Maze, the First Methodist organist?

"And butterflies," asked her junior-high daughter.

After several minutes of discussion, it was decided sunflowers would be planted along the fence line, receiving the most sunlight. There would also be a flower garden designed to attract butterflies.

The ABA candidates met with the three practicum supervisors. They met in the lecture hall and presented an overview of the work they had done during the semester. There were eleven students. Ted was the fourth of eleven candidates to present. It took three hours for all students to present their work to the professors. This was, in essence, their final exam for the semester. The committee would collectively assign the grade for the job accomplished. It was a formality. In five years. Most students received an A. This class followed the norm. Everyone received an A.

◆ ◆ ◆

Ted met with Eliot and Pam on the following Monday. Ted was asked to bring Jack with him. Upon arrival, the two of them were ushered into the conference room. Eliot and Pam came in a few minutes later.

"Well, how did your practicum presentation go?" Pam asked.

"Got my A," Ted said matter-of-factly.

Eliot congratulated Ted. After the congratulatory remarks, it was time to move onto the business at hand.

"Ted, it has been eighteen months since you entered my father-in-law's house to burglarize it."

"Yes, sir," Ted said quietly. Ted was braced for the worst.

"Since then, I must admit we have been impressed with your accomplishments. You have taken care of both Jack and your dad. You have spruced up the place; inside and out. And you have spearheaded the Southtown Project. All for pocket change."

"And a place to live. And wheels to get around," added Ted.

"Yes. Well, all that is changing."

Ted tensed. His new world was about to implode.

"Jack's house," Eliot said, "will become the new headquarters of the J.K. Foundation. Your bedroom and the scrapbook room. And the office space you created is now needed for foundation business."

"I knew it. I am being evicted," Ted said with apprehension.

"Yes. And no," said Pam.

"I'm confused. It is a three-bedroom house. You are taking over two of them. even the one use. So, I can no longer liver them. From my point of view, I am being evicted," explained Ted. "Am I also being fired?" Ted asked. Ted's voice was a mixture of anger, confusion, and fear.

"Heaven's no!" exclaimed a laughing Jack. "But it is time you stepped out on your own two feet. Of course. We expect you to continue doing what you have done so well. Now, Ted, you will get paid for it. You will earn a living wage. And you will need your own place."

"What about you?" Ted asked.

Pam explained they talked with his doctors, and they believe Jack is capable of living on his own again. He will get one of those alert devices able to detect a fall. It also has a button to push if he needs help.

"Anyway, how can I make a move on Ruthie with you always underfoot?" Jack was smiling at Ted.

"Dad," Pam protested.

"Well, it's true. Every time I invite Ruthie over, there is Ted. Always meddling," Jack winked at Ted.

"Children!" Eliot waited until everyone had stopped talking. Then, finally, everyone got serious and agreed to move forward.

"You will start on January 1 with a salary of $45,000. You also become a voting member of the foundation's board."

"Whew," signed Ted. "I just knew. Knew I was going to be fired."

"You will need your own apartment. And you will need your own set of wheels."

"Bye, bye Ranger," Ted said in a sing-song fashion.

"The foundation considered buying the car for you to use. However, our accountant says it is better if you obtained your own wheels. We will pay you mileage for the business of the foundation. But the car will be yours."

"Fine, but I don't have enough saved to buy a new car. I've never bought anything on credit, so with no credit score. I don't have the ability to finance the purchase of a car."

Pam looked at Ted, smiled. "As Eliot said, no problem. You pick out the car and work out the payment plan. The foundation will co-sign the note. If you default on the car, you will lose the car, your job, and your income. Incentive enough?"

"Yes, ma'am," Ted said in his formal voice and gave a short nod.

It was Jack's turn to speak. "With all of this, you are losing your rationale for not putting a ring on her majesty's finger. Got a plan to keep your wild horse at bey?"

"Not yet, but I will. Once Maureen gets wind, I am gainfully employed, a steady income, an apartment. And, my own set of wheels," Ted enumerated, "she'll come at me with all she's got. Any suggestions?"

"That's your problem," Eliot, Pam and Jack said in unison, and they held up their hands in surrender.

"Thanks a lot. Thrown to the wolves without any protection," Ted grinned.

"A few more things. Before ending this confab."

Eliot pulled out a manilla folder and handed identical sets of documents to Jack and Ted. "The first document is your contract. It is for six months, a traditional probationary contract. If you meet our requirements, it will automatically be renewed annually."

Ted and Jack looked at the document.

Eliot said, "There is a 401 (k) option and, once you are past the probationary period, the foundation will match your personal contribution up to 5% of your annual salary. You are also covered by health insurance. If you get married and decide to add your wife and children, that will be your expense. Understood?" Eliot waited for comments or questions. There were none.

"The second document," Eliot waited for Jack and Ted to pull it out, "deals with your moving out. It says you will be out no later than December 31 of this year. There are other legally required provisions."

Ted read the second document. He looked up and said, "As I understand it. I will not rob you blind, right? And you don't want me to destroy the house." There was an uneasy tone in

Ted's voice.

Eliot nodded. "As I said, it is purely a legal formality. We do not, in any way, question your integrity. We do not believe you will rob us blind, as you put it. Or you do anything to the house."

Ted Said, "Good." Then he turned to Jack. "I don't need another meeting with Officer Tim." There were a few muffled laughs.

Ted was quiet for a long while as he studied both documents. "OK, where do I sign?" Ted asked.

"Before you sign. Do you need another lawyer to advise you? We are prepared to give you a list of lawyers specializing in these things. The last thing we want. Is for you to feel pressured."

"No. You have been nothing but kind and professional to me. I have trusted you for the past year and a half. I don't see a reason to doubt you now."

"Turn to the document's last page. You will find a yellow arrow. It says, sign here. The top one is where you sign, and the bottom one is where Jack will sign. Please sign both. One will stay with the foundation and the other is your copy, Ted."

"Does anyone outside this room know?" asked Ted.

"If you mean Ruthie, Maureen, or your dad? No. It is confidential. Unless or until you tell them. We won't say a word."

"Good. I have a couple more weeks of freedom. And time to develop a plan to stave off Maureen."

Pam asked, "Well, Ted. Have a plan in mind?"

"For what? Staving her off or proposing to her under duress?" Ted laughed.

"Both," answered Pam. She stood there with a silly grin on her face.

"Sort of. But first, I must get organized. I plan to propose to her when in Italy. I have it all worked out. I know when and where, and I have someone to record it for posterity. And satisfy your curiosities. The rest is called flying by the seat of your pants! That is assuming, of course, I don't get raked over the coals in the process."

They shook hands. Pam gave a large envelope for Ted to put his paperwork in.

On the drive home, Ted and Jack were in a good mood. During the quiet time, Ted began developing a strategy to deal with Maureen.

CHAPTER 28

IT TOOK TED time to digest it all. A lot happened over the past ten weeks. He aced his practicum and, again, had a 4.0 average for the semester. Now December was here. It was proving to be an incredibly stressful month.

Marie and Hank elected to have a small, intimate wedding. There were his kids and their families. Ted, Maureen, Ruthie, and Jack were there and sat on the bride's side of aisle. Brynlee, Bailey, Lance, and their families sat on the groom's side. The wedding party consisted of just Hank and Marie. Hank was in a black suit and Marie in a white dress. The whole thing was elegant. Understated, but elegant.

The kids learned they had more in common than they first thought. Each enjoyed sharing stories of each other, but especially about their parents. What started off as an awkward moment ended with a casual party at an upscale restaurant. Then back to the real world for everyone.

Returning from the wedding, Ted was desperate to find an apartment. At one point, Mack suggested Ted move back home. However, that was before Mack and Melinda got married. Ted no longer considered that a viable option. Maureen suggested they move in together. It was clear moving in together created more problems than it solved. Time was running out. Ted needed a place to live. Or be homeless. Being homeless was not a positive image. Not for the leader of a million-dollar project. Another issue was transportation. At the end of the month, Ted was losing his housing and access to Big Red, Jack's beloved Ford Ranger. In the past eighteen months. Ted has not looked at a car, let alone priced one. He was unsure what he wanted. A sedan? A truck? A SUV? New or used? Time is running out, and Ted must decide what he wants and determine what his budget could handle.

Ted could not hide things from Maureen. He understood Maureen had to be included without adding more pressure on him. He was not ready to propose to her. Ted wanted to ask Maureen to marry him. But now is not the right time. Ted had her convinced waiting until he graduated was still the best option. The big question was her reaction, learning Ted has the big three. A place of his own, a car, and a job? Could he convince her to wait until they got back from Italy? After all, he was on probationary status with the foundation. The meant the job was temporary. At least, technically. During this time, they could terminate him. At any time and for any reason. While no one considered the possibility of Ted being released. Ted had to stress to Maureen the possibility was real.

Then, there is the Southtown project itself. It was his project. On January first, he would be paid to deliver. The murals were finished. They were the talk of the town. Good Morning America learned what was going on and sent a crew. Soon, Ted, Consolidated Paint, and the murals would be on GMA. In addition, the local television station show-cased the progress of the gardens.

Paramount delivered on the fence. And the gardening partners had created and planted the gardens.

Phase one of the building renovation was the grocery store. The morning DJ ran a contest to name the store to get community input. The contestants had to live in Southtown, and the winner would receive a $100 gift certificate from the store funded by the radio station. More than a hundred suggestions were placed in boxes at the two convenience stores. The grocery store was on target to open in late February or early March.

One benefit to the whole project was a new sense of pride in Southtown. Houses and yards within two or three blocks of the project were cleaned up. Several were extensive, with fresh paint or siding. Yards were fertilized and turned from brown to green. One was even featured on a cable renovation show. Everything was progressing better than anticipated. In every case, the litter dotting the landscape when the project began was gone. Neighborhood Watch signs suddenly appeared. At the corner of Webster and Monrovia, a block west of the project, the city had erected a permanent sign welcoming visitors to the neighborhood.

James Baldwin, the owner of Baldwin Signs, had committed appropriate signage for the three buildings. They would be the newer, LED-lit signs with the venue's name in bright, vibrant colors. Again, this affirmed the changes happening in the neighborhood.

For most of his life, Ted enjoyed being invisible. Today, Ted cannot walk down the street without being stopped. Then, he was congratulated for the foundation's work. Suggestions for future projects were now commonplace.

Ruthie and Jack joined Maureen and Ted for church. Ted suggested a brunch at Chiu's, a new Korean restaurant, as they were leaving. Maureen and Ted opted for a spicy variation of Tteok-Bobbi while Ruthie and Jack settled for the milder version, and each added a side of Kimchi and hot tea. Ruthie had read up on the restaurant. She described, in familiar terms, the various menu items.

"I need to talk to you," pointing at Maureen and Ruthie. To Maureen, he said, "And especially you." The women looked curiously at one another. Knowing what was about to unfold, Jack was unphased with the drama. However, he was not successful in hiding his smile.

"I am being evicted and restricted." The girls gasped and wanted more information. Both almost choked on the sip of water they had just taken.

Ruthie turned to Jack said inquisitively, "Jack?"

Ted said, "Jack's house is the new physical home for the foundation." Ted nodded toward Jack. "Jack will still live there. The two bedrooms will become offices. My bedroom will become my office. It will be unsuitable for slumbering." Ted showed a smile when he said this. "Therefore, I need an apartment. Do I have a volunteer to help with that task?"

Maureen looked at no one and quietly said, "You could move in with me." Again, she refused to look at anyone and was biting her lip. Watching her demeanor, Ted was silently relieved to have that option off the table.

Neither Jack nor Ruthie said anything. Jack was quiet because it was not his place to comment. Ruthie said nothing, recognizing her daughter was an adult, and Maureen's decisions were just that, Maureen's decisions. "Thought about that." Maureen looked up. She blushed with a hint of a smile was on her face. "However, I think moving in together complicates matters. No. I need my own space. Unlike you, I have never lived on my own. I first lived at home and then with Jack. To be a good husband." Ted turned to Ruthie, "and a good son-in-law. I have to know who I am. I can't do that unless I spend time living on my own."

Maureen lowered her head again. She was both relieved and disappointed. "I understand." Maureen's head and neck had stiffened. Her whole body had become rigid.

"You know, Maureen," It was an effort for Maureen to look at her mother, "living alone does not mean living in different time zones." Then Ruthie said, looking at Ted, "Not a much will change." Ted nodded in agreement.

Still lacking genuine enthusiasm, Maureen asked, "What do you think you will need?"

"Two bedrooms. One for schoolwork. And space for working on Southtown. When away from the office."

"Great. Maureen, your complex has two-bedroom apartments, right?" Ruthie asked. Maureen nodded without cautious enthusiasm. Ruthie continued, "Why don't you introduce Ted to your manager. See what's available."

Hearing her mother talk, Maureen perked up and asked, "Wait! You said restricted. Are you in trouble or something? The only time I was restricted, I did something wrong."

"He is losing access to Red Ranger," Jack explained.

"So, I need some wheels. Any suggestions?"

"Ted, I understand Eliot has a lot of business clients. Maybe he can help you. Then you and Maureen can select your new set of wheels together."

"I want a convertible," chimed Maureen, flashing Ted an excited and broad smile.

"Remember, this is my car," Maureen gave an exaggerated frown. "And I hate convertibles," Ted said in a teasing tone.

After a pause, Maureen looked at Ted. She said slowly and methodically, looking over her eyebrows. "Everything you said requires money. Do you have millions stashed away somewhere? My love."

Jack cleared his voice, and the girls looked at him.

"I am sorry to have to tell you this," and Ted stopped.

"Tell me what?" demanded Maureen.

"I have a job."

"Great!" Maureen almost screamed. "You will have an apartment, a car, and a job. Ask mom for my hand in marriage. Now, before she has second thoughts!" She was suddenly excited and speaking rapid-fire.

"Slow down, my love."

Maureen scowled at him.

"At this point, it is a temporary job. At least it is for the next

265

six months. After that, who knows. Right now, I have a probationary period to complete. During which my new employer may fire me at any time. And for any reason. Or, for no reason at all."

"OK, big shot. Who are you working for?"

"The JK Foundation," Ted admitted, trying to remain calm and neutral. Yet, he could not hide his smile.

Jack interjected, "Ted is on probation as the project manager. He will do what he has been doing, only now he gets paid."

"Why probation?" Maureen asked.

"This is a million-dollar project. While Ted has exceeded our expectations." Jack's tone was serious and business-like.

"Yes, he has," Maureen agreed, "so why probation?"

"He has operated with a set of instructions," Jack continued. "Although he could make certain decisions, they had to be approved by Eliot and Pam. And then by the entire board." Jack paused for effect. "In January, Ted will continue as he has. But now has more autonomy. We are his employer, so Ted will still answer to the board. But he will no longer need approval for his decisions. Ted will be the number one decision-maker. If he performs as expected, there is no reason to think otherwise. He will be our full-time project manager. With full benefits."

Congratulations were offered around the table.

Then, talking to Maureen, Jack said, "Ted loves you, and he wants to marry you. You can trust me on that. You are all he talks about around the house." Then to Ted, "and it is starting to become annoying." Jack grinned, and Maureen blushed. "Ted is also one of the smartest businessmen I know. I can tell you. I wish more men had Ted's work ethic. It would make a much better world. I appreciate patience is not your strong suit. But I can guarantee it will be worth the wait." Jack and Ruthie reached over. Then touched Maureen's hands.

"I know," Maureen said. "It is just so hard to waiting. Waiting for something you want so badly."

"I know," is all Ruthie could say.

Ted put his arm around Maureen. "It is just as hard for me. Waiting is not fun."

It was quiet around the table for a few seconds.

"Anybody up for a movie?" asked Ted with enthusiasm.

"Theater or Netflix?" asked Maureen.

"Gotta be Netflix. I am not a working stiff for another month," Ted said.

Maureen got in Red Ranger while her mother and Jack got in Maureen's Soul. They headed to Ruthie's, a short ten-minute drive. Maureen sat shoulder-to-shoulder to Ted. Neither spoke. They avoided looking at each other. Instead, they were each digesting the events of the afternoon.

Eliot, Pam, and Ted were at the conference table in the law office conference room.

"Well. How did it go Sunday?" Eliot asked.

Everyone was looking at Ted. "About what you'd expect," Ted said. "Tomorrow, Maureen and I are looking at an apartment. It is in her complex." Ted said.

"For the two of you?" asked Pam.

"No. Just for me. I told Maureen-and her mother. I need time alone. I have never lived on my own. And I need to find myself. The real me. Not the would-be burglar. Not Jack's caretaker."

"You do know, Ted," Pam said, "If you don't propose to that girl soon, she's going to die of anticipation. I can promise you that. And that won't be a pretty sight."

"I know," said Ted. "It would not surprise me if she has the wedding all planned. She will have me at the church. Tying the knot, the day after I put the ring on her finger."

Eliot chided, "Propose late in the day. If you propose in the morning, she'll have you at the church before suppertime!"

They all laughed.

There was a slight pause, and everyone became more serious.

"OK, to the business at hand," said Ted. "Let's name our grocery store. Here are the top three vote-getters. Southtown, Jubilee, and Oasis."

Pam and Eliot studied them and asked where Ted was heading with them.

"We have always said Southtown is a fresh-food desert. So with that in mind, I am leaning toward Oasis. You know, a respite in the arid landscape." Ted waited for a response.

Ted was on one side. Pam and Eliot on the other. They had a whispered conversation. They looked at each other and nodded. Then, finally, they turned to Ted. They put the cards on the table. Face down.

"Ted," Eliot said, "you are the project manager. It is your call. We are more than satisfied. We are fine with any of these. This is your call."

"Then, Oasis it is. I will get with Jim to design a logo. That done, Ted said he would call Baldwin Sign. To have the sign created and installed. I will give you a cost estimate once I have talked with everyone." Then, picking up the card, "I will call the radio station. They can let Juliet Garza know she is the winner."

"Sounds good to us," said Pam. "I was kind of leaning toward Oasis for the name myself."

Ted changed the subject and asked, "Ruthie said you have contacts with car dealerships. Is that true?"

Eliot confirmed. They discussed a budget and model.

"What do you envision?" asked Eliot.

"Something along the lines of a Tahoe or Explorer," Ted replied.

Pam suggested a KIA Sportage. "Harry Caruso down at H. J. Caruso has a low-mileage Sportage they have used as a courtesy car. I think it will work. Should I give him a call?"

"If you don't mind. Does he know you will be co-signing?"

Eliot said he and Caruso played high school football together. They were good friends. "He knows your situation. He assured me he would finance the car with reasonable payments. We talked about you, and he is waving the need for a co-signer." Eliot rummaged through a stack of business cards and handed a card to Ted. "Make sure you talk to Harry personally. I will give him a call. He will be expecting you."

Maureen picked Ted up at Jack's and drove him to the KIA dealership. "I almost bought a Sportage myself. But this has been a fun car. I think you'll like the Sportage."

They waited fifteen minutes in the showroom. They were lookig at cars on the showroom floor, when heavy footsteps we heard behind them.

"Mr. James?" a voice boomed from behind. "Harry Caruso," the man said, extending his hand. Harry was 6-5, and Ted estimated the man's weight somewhere north of 300. He had thinning brown hair, an unlit cigar in his mouth, and a twinkle in his eye. The man was a stereotypical car salesman.

"Elliot called. He told me what you wanted." They walked out to a line of cars. A sign on the window proclaimed the vehicle to be low-mileage and super clean. "We recently took this car out of service. We use our courtesy cars for no more than six months. And never more than 10,000 miles. What do you think?"

The Sportage was the top model, with its silver paint sparkling in the sun. Harry reached into his pocket and pulled out a key. "Here. Take her for a spin. Tell me what you think. I've got my finance guy working on the numbers now. I will have everything waiting when you get back."

Ted took the keys and opened the passenger door for Maureen. Ted climbed in and examined the cabin and dashboard. Then, confident he knew where everything was, he buckled up, started the engine, and drove off the lot. They drove around town and on the highway. Ted needed to see how it handled in various settings.

True to his word, Harry had the paperwork ready for him when they returned.

"Well, what do you think? A real beaut, right?"

It took most of an hour to sign the paperwork. The finance manager confirmed Tullus & Tullus had wired the down payment. Finally, the car, freshly washed, was brought to the side of the showroom. The paper buyer plates were already on. Harry shook both Ted and Maureen's hands and disappeared into the dealership.

◆ ◆ ◆

"Well, I'll follow you to your apartment, then I'll take my girlfriend for a ride in my new wheels."

Maureen was smiling as she got in her Soul. The two drove in tandem to her apartment. She and Ted drove to her mother's house. Ruthie got in the back. Then off to Jack's. Ted was proud of his new car. Jack climbed in the back with Ruthie. Ted pulled into a Sonic for a celebratory cherry limeade. Ted dropped Ruthie and Jack at her home. Ted and Maureen spent some time at Maureen's apartment. Before heading home, Ted drove by Ruthie's and picked up Jack.

"Pretty snazzy ride," Jack said when they got home.

"I like it," Ted admitted.

"Today the car, tomorrow the apartment?" Asked Jack.

"That's the plan," Ted said, nodding his head.

"Oh, I almost forgot. A package came for you today. I put it in your room. Is that OK?"

"Thanks, Jack. No problem."

◆ ◆ ◆

The package was an Italian language course from Babel. Maureen did not take Italian at Emmerson. Although Ted was in his second year studying Italian, he was not fluent. He wanted to learn more colloquial terms before their foreign studies trip in March. Ted also figured the language course would help

Maureen. Secretly, he also hoped the course would keep Maureen's mind off marriage. At least for a little while.

Ted watched an episode of *Maverick* with Jack. He told Jack about naming the grocery store, the car buying experience and ended the conversation about the language course.

Ted went to bed that night with feelings of excitement and concern. He was excited about the new direction his life was taking. However, he was also concerned he might be pushing away the best thing in his life. Part of him wanted to propose to Maureen now. Another part said wait. He prayed he was doing the right thing. He needs to be patient. He fell asleep without resolving his quandary.

CHAPTER 29

T ED WAS NOT in a good mood. Sitting at the dining table in Jack's house. His world was crumbling around him. The Oasis Market was set to open in six weeks, and they still had not hired the managers. It was Ted's decision to focus on the talent pool in Southtown to manage the store, and he pushed the idea hard. He convinced Eliot, Pam, and the entire board he had two promising candidates. Now, unable to pass the mandatory drug test, they were back to square one. Ted was convinced the success or failure of the market hinged on who ran the store. To be a compassionate ministry, they needed people. People the neighborhood knew and respected. They had to be visible.

In less than two weeks, Ted needed out of Jack's spare bedroom. Maureen had helped him find an apartment, but Ted was unprepared for everything moving out entailed. He had an attractive, two-bedroom apartment with appliances. Appliances but no furniture. Knowing Ted needed a car and a place to live, they advanced him a month's salary to be repaid over the next six. Ted still had to buy furniture and cookware. And a myriad of mundane items found in every home.

Jack gave Ted the bedroom suite he had been using. At least Ted had a bed, dresser, and two sets of sheets. Pam found him a used table and two chairs. This was his dining room table and a work-at-home desk. Ted was thankful utilities were included in the rent. Cable television wiring was provided, but the hook-up and monthly fees were not. Since he did not have a television, cable tv was not an issue. However, Ted needed the internet and was told it would be late January before he would be online.

Ted went to Goodwill. He found a sofa and chair. He also found two small lamps he could use. One for the living room and one for his bedroom. Ted remembered seeing wood crates that could be used for end tables. While paying for the furniture, he saw a small television. It was an impulse purchase, but the TV fit on his dresser. Not in the living room.

Maureen's attempt to help Ted furnish his apartment was not without its own set of problems. Ted got mad and accused her of spending his money before earning it. She wasn't, of course. Maureen encouraged Ted to spend a more on the kitchen items than he was willing. Maureen pointed out the pans Ted selected would have to be replaced within a year.

For the first time, they raised their voices, and Maureen stormed out. She stood outside Ted's door sobbing, and he could hear her. Throughout his relationship with Maureen, they had had their disagreements. However, they never had a real fight. There was that incident with Barry. When they did not speak for a short period. However, they have never raised their voices. Nor were they harsh with one another. Ted blamed himself for the current situation.

When he called her, she would not answer. Ted called her mother. Ruthie told Ted it was not a good time to talk to her daughter.

Then there was the weather. The weatherman was calling for rain almost every day available to move. It meant possibly moving in during a rainstorm. Ted was hesitant to do that. Any precipitation made using Red Ranger to move the furniture impractical. More importantly, it meant an additional expense to rent a box truck or trailer.

◆ ◆ ◆

"I am not sure, Dad. I may have blown everything." Mack and Melinda listened to Ted explain what had been going on. The problem was furnishing the apartment, finding a manager for Oasis, and fighting Maureen. When Ted finished and had collected himself a bit, Mack pulled a chair in front of his son. Ted examined the ceiling, fighting back the tears of frustration, and bit his lip.

"Look, Ted, you may feel this may be the end of the world. Trust me, it isn't. Take one thing at a time. Let Melinda and me help you. You and Maureen. I will rent a U-Haul truck and move the furniture. We have more everything. Certainly more than we can ever use. Let us help you with what you need, OK?"

Ted did not say anything and nodded.

"Have your feelings changed for Maureen?"

"What? No! I can't imagine being with anyone else. That is why this fight so hard. That is why I hurt so much when she doesn't talk to me. Not a call or a text."

Melinda reminded Ted of their first fight when he would not talk to her. "You wouldn't take her call or answer her text. Remember?"

Ted nodded.

"Well, you two got over Barry. And you will get over this. But, of course, you will always encounter those times when you disagree. It's called life."

"So. What should do?" Ted asked sullenly.

"Give her time to calm down. Then your dad and I will get you settled in your apartment. You need to let us help you with furniture and stuff. You are Mack's only son, and you need to let him be your dad. OK?" Melinda watched Ted for a reaction.

Melinda thought for a second. "Monday morning. As soon as the florist opens up, you need to send six red roses to her at work."

"Why not a dozen?" Ted wanted to know.

"Six will do the trick. First, it will be an unexpected gesture. Maureen won't expect it. Second, the girls in the clinic will fuss over her. They will let her know how lucky she is to have you."

"OK," Ted said. "Then what?"

"Go over to her apartment. Knock on the door. Don't stop knocking until Maureen lets you in. If for no other reason than to get you to stop making a scene."

"OK, she lets me in."

"Then you give her the other six roses and beg her for her forgiveness. It was all your fault. Don't let her take any blame."

"After all. It is always our fault!" Mack said, smiling, looking at Melinda.

"After that. If you don't know? Well, let's just say you are way beyond my help. But don't worry. Five to ten, Maureen and Ruthie are talking right now. About getting you back into the picture."

"You think?" asked a slightly embarrassed Ted.

"Trust me." Mack and Melinda said in unison.

Ted loaded and started the dishwasher. He heard a noise at his door. It wasn't a single rap. It wasn't a knock where you rap with your knuckles a few times. Where you knock and wait for someone to open the door. No. It was a constant pounding. Clearly. Whoever was on the other side. They were not going away.

Maureen pushed him inside and against the wall when Ted opened the door. She kissed him long and hard. She was crying and kept saying, "I'm sorry. I'm sorry."

Ted took Maureen by her shoulders and pushed her gently back. Holding her, he asked, "Mind if I come up for air?"

Maureen nodded and continued leaning against him. When she calmed down, Ted showed off his new digs. The things Mack and Melinda had given him. In the kitchen were a microwave, coffee maker, and a toaster. Next, Ted led Maureen into the living room and showed off his new, used furniture. A coffee table was against the wall opposite the couch, and a new, large screen, smart television.

"No cable for another week, but when it comes."

They looked at the new additions.

"It's beautiful she said and leaned into him."

"What brought all this on?" Ted asked.

"Hormones."

"Hormones?" Ted asked in bewilderment.

"Hormones. Get used to them. They are what make women, women."

On Monday, Ted decided to go full out. He sent the full dozen roses to Maureen at the clinic. Melinda had correctly predicted. The other girls in the office fussed over her and the flowers. Maureen texted back all sorts of smiley faces, happy couples, and hearts emojis.

Ted texted Melinda and Jack about what happened Sunday and about the flowers on Monday.

Ruthie sent a simple text. It read, "Thank you." Ted sent a simple thumbs-up emoji.

The Oasis Grocery sign was installed on Tuesday. Ted stopped by Jack's and picked up the sign company's paperwork. When he was about to leave, Ted's phone rang. Ted looked at the caller ID but did not recognize it. He answered it anyway.

"JK Foundation," Ted said when he answered the phone.

"Mr. James?" The caller's voice was familiar, but Ted could not place it.

"Yes, how may I help you?"

"Jacob Roberts," the voice said. "Pastor of St. Michaels AME."

"Oh, yes," Ted said with enthusiasm when he placed the

name with the voice. "What can I do for you?"

"At the last ecumenical meeting, you mentioned you needed two people to run the grocery store. Have you hired anybody yet?"

"I thought I had. However, they did not work out." Ted was not about to reveal the positive drug tests. "So, no, we haven't filled those positions yet. Why? Do you have a candidate?"

"As a matter of fac. I have two young men you should meet."

"Can we meet at the church?" Ted asked. "I am out and about. I can be there around one. If it would be convenient."

"That would be fine," the reverend said. "The two men are members of my congregation, Malachi Bronson and Jamal Wilson."

"Anything special I should know about them?" Ted wanted to know.

"When you do your background check, you will find both had dealings with the police, but nothing violent and nothing recent." Jacob waited for a response. "Is that a problem?" He wanted to know.

"It depends on what I find. Don't worry. It is not an automatic deal-breaker. What about substance abuse?"

"Not a problem," Reverend Roberts assured him. "I have talked to both men. At length. Both assured me they do not drink or use drugs. I let them know about the testing. I told them hiding it would not be advisable." The pastor gave additional information and assured Ted both would be available for the meeting.

Ted's spirits were lifted, and Pam called before he could put his phone away.

"How is it going?" she asked in a cheerful tone.

"Thought we had the positions filled. But there was a problem."

"Drugs?" she asked.

Ted affirmed the problem and then told her about his conversation with Jacob Roberts. He promised to call her after the meeting.

"What's the latest with you and Maureen? Dad said you patched it up."

"Yes," Ted said with a short laugh. "She came over and beat down my door, literally beat it down." They both laughed at the image. "Anyway, all is good. We have been stressed-out. Maureen at work. Me with the move. I guess it got the best of us. We're good now."

"Great, that's good to hear. Now, I do not want to add to your stress. So, please don't freak out on me. OK?" Pam said in a cautionary tone.

"OK?" Ted was starting to get worried. Ted rolled his eyes in exasperation.

"I heard from the Today show. They want to do a story on Oasis and the Southtown project. Sounds similar to what GMA did. You up to it?" Pam waited when Ted did not immediately respond.

"Kind of goes with the territory, right?" Ted finally said. "Try to give me a little heads up so I can be prepared. But I am good with it."

"Great. You will know more when I do. Have a good day." Pam was gone.

It was 1:15 before Ted got to St. Michael's AME church. The church secretary led Ted to the fellowship hall, where three men were seated. Each had an open bottle of water in front of them. Reverend Roberts handed Ted handed two files. Both candidates were shorter than Ted, and he wondered how either would be able to stock the top shelves. Both were clean and neatly dressed. They smiled at Ted when he arrived. One was quite heavy, while the other was considerably thinner. Reverend Roberts introduced the first one as Malachi and the other as Jamal. Ted was introduced to them as the person hiring for the

Oasis Market.

Ted asked, "Is there was a place where I meet with them? In private. Reverend Roberts ushered Ted and Malachi to a Sunday school room. "This will be fine." Ted said as they sat on opposite sides of a table. The door closed, and the interview began.

"I'm Ted, and you are Malachi, right?" Ted said, confirming who he was interviewing. "Tell me a little about yourself."

"Not much to tell. I graduated from high school, worked for NAPA until they went out of business. I have been doing odd jobs through Manpower. I don't have a car, and the bus service is not the greatest.

"What about your skirmish with the law?" Ted asked.

"DUI. Got drunk when I was a teen and got ticketed. Lost my license for six months. Did some community service. No problem since then."

"Drugs?" asked Ted.

"No, sir. Never did, never will. My cousin OD'd. But I never did try drugs. So don't drink no more, neither."

"Marijuana is a drug. So, I have to ask if you use marijuana?" Ted was scanning the balance of the application.

"No, sir. Don't smoke neither." Malachi was smiling throughout the entire interview. There was something about Malachi Ted liked. He hoped everything would work out.

"Well, that's all I have. Do you have any questions?" asked Ted.

"No, sir. Reverend Roberts told us both a lot about the job. I am excited and do hope you will give me a chance."

"I will set up a time for your drug screen. OK with that?"

Malachi assured Ted it would be fine. He left the room. Ted made a few notes. Jamal knocked, then took the seat previously occupied by Malachi.

The second interview a carbon of the first one. The one potential problem with Jamal, as he was technically homeless.

"My managers must be easily reached in case of an emergency. If you don't have a home address, how do I find you?"

"Pastor Jacob said the church would help me find a home. If I can find a job. He told me to use his address until I got my own. Will that be a problem?" Jamal had a look of concern.

"Let's call it more of a challenge than a problem. OK?" Ted said, trying to relax Jamal. "Let me talk to Reverend Roberts. I will get back to you soon." They shook hands. Then Pastor Roberts entered and took a seat.

"I am impressed with both men. Thank you so much for recommending them. We may have a problem with Jamal, however."

Reverend Roberts explained the situation in detail and assured Ted the church would help him get on his feet once he got a job. "We can afford a month or two of rent, but nothing long-term. I allow those in need to use the parsonage address. When applying for a job. Then, if they get the job, we set them up until they get their first paycheck. We don't ask for repayment. It is not a loan. We do, however, encourage them to support the church financially once they are working."

Ted explained the hiring process and said all candidates undergo a drug screen. "The foundation will arrange for the drug test," and then they shook hands. Next, Ted called Pam and filled her in on the interview results.

Ted asked Malachi and Jamal to meet him at Oasis Grocery the following week. He offered them the jobs they sought and gave them a tour of the facility. Although they both said they were familiar with the project, Ted gave them the $5 tour of all three buildings and the gardens. They would start on Monday with orientation and help with the stocking shelves. "Grand opening" would be in February.

Ted and Maureen celebrated a productive week with a pizza delivered by Uncle Dan's. They also spent an hour with Babel. Maureen was picking up Italian quickly. Ted's study of Italian paid off, and he realized he knew more than he gave himself credit. They excited about the trip to Italy.

CHAPTER 30

OASIS WAS UP and running by the end of February. The dynamic duo of Malachi and Jamal proved to be one of the best decisions Ted made. Not only were they from Southtown. But the two also embodied the spirit of the neighborhood. Many residents knew the two. They immediately felt comfortable in the new surroundings. The one bottleneck was scheduling deliveries. Parking was scarce in the area. With his creative thinking and scheduling, Malachi had devised a plan to keep the store stocked and the streets clear.

Along with being a food desert, Southtown was also a financial desert. There were a few small chain loan companies known for their exorbitant rates. However, with the opening of Oasis Grocery, more businesses were coming to the area. Mae's was a small sandwich shop. It was the area's first food shop to open in more than a decade. According to the local paper's business section, other businesses were looking to come. Southtown was becoming a vibrant hub of activity. However, the big news was Third National Bank. They decided to open a branch office across the street from Oasis. It has been decades since a bank was in the neighborhood.

The Today Show was on hand for Oasis's grand opening, which coincided with Black History Month. Malachi and Jamal were interviewed. The new TNB branch manager, Damon Gabbard, was included in the segment. It was a big boost for the J.K. Foundation. And for Ted. As Eliot put it, "Ted has not only met our expectations, but he has also exceeded all expectations for moving this project ahead."

"We got a problem," Eliot began as Ted answered his phone.

"Slow down, what problem?" Ted responded. Ted's heartbeat increased with the news.

"C&C was to begin construction on the medical clinic next week. But unfortunately, they had a setback on one of their biggest projects. Charlie Harrison just told me. It will be two weeks or more. Before work can begin on the clinic."

"OK, so we move everything back. And maybe look at the youth center."

"No can do. The furniture and equipment on the way. Should arrive before the clinic is ready, and we have no plans for storage. As for the youth project, we don't yet have final plans from Everette and Earl. Nor have we secured the necessary permits needed to begin working. Any ideas?"

"Possibly. Let me talk to my dad and see what he recommends. If Dad I come with an idea, we will meet. We'll meet with the two Charlies and get their approval." Ted disconnected and called his dad.

"Hi, Dad. Got a sec?" Ted asked as soon as Mack answered. Ted explained the situation. Ted asked his dad for any suggestions. Anything off the top of his head. They talked back and forth, and Mack said he might have a plan.

Mack said, "Get your ecumenical council together and see if they can organize a pool of men willing to provide the manual labor."

The following Friday, everyone met at the proposed clinic. Before the meeting, Ted met with Eliot, C&C Construction, and Jacob Roberts of St. Michaels. He shared what he and Mack came up with. They received the green light to proceed.

Once they were all settled, Ted explained the situation, allowing each to provide their part of the solution. C&C would provide the blueprints and a construction supervisor. Triple H provided two employees. One would be the construction foreman. The other would be the electrical foreman. Reverend Roberts had lined up a dozen men who would provide the labor.

The meeting was breaking up. A middle-aged woman walked in on the discussion. She was tall, thin, and had an authoritative presence when she arrived. Everyone turned and eyed the new addition to the group. She introduced herself as Lydia Jenkins, the owner of Mae's, who wanted to participate and agreed to provide food for the volunteers. There was a round of applause approving of her offer. Ted got her a chair and welcomed her to the group. Michael Glaser from C&C would serve as the general contractor. He would ensure all needed materials would be on hand.

"I'll do a quick review of the materials on hand. I believe everything is here. But I want to make sure."

"What about tools? Most of my workers don't own many personal tools."

Mack said, "Don't worry about tools, pastor. I think Triple-H can provide hammers and other hand tools."

Michael, his checklist in hand, reviewed what was in the building. "We have it all. C&C will bring a power miter saw over the weekend. Work can start on Monday. It is not a big project, and we should be done by Friday. Consolidated Paint can come in the following week and get the painting done before furniture and equipment arrive."

"Any questions?" Ted asked, surveying the crowd. There were none. "OK. Thanks for coming, and we'll see everyone here on Monday. Reverend, tell your workers to be here no later than nine. Then, turning to his dad, Ted asked, "Mack, you and your buddy from Triple-H. Can you be here at eight? Kind of get things laid out"

"No problem," Mack said. The meeting was adjourned.

Maureen and Uncle Dan's Pizza delivery arrived at the same time. Maureen paid the driver and, without knocking, used her key to let herself in. After the last fight, Maureen and Ted exchanged keys. Now. They could access each other's apartment.

"Pizza's here!" Maureen announced as she entered the apartment and put her purse on the floor and the pizza on the table. She grabbed paper plates, napkins, and two Dr. Peppers. Ted came out of his office and joined her at the table.

Ted started the conversation asking, "How was your day?" Then he gave her a peck on her cheek.

"Not too bad," Maureen said. "Three new consults, four follow-ups, and a couple of minor procedures in the office. You?"

"I told you about the snag in the project. Well, Dad saved the day. Then, Mae's, the new restaurant in Southtown, wants to feed the volunteers keeping the project on schedule. Talked to the new bank manager. He seems to be a really nice guy. A bank is certainly needed in that part of town."

Ted went to his office. When he returned, he had two large envelopes. Their names were on the envelopes. "Picked these up from Mrs. Logan today. She called and told she had them. These are our work assignments for next month's trip to Italy." Ted handed Maureen her envelope and watched her open it. He then sat down and opened his.

It was a general information brochure with a day-by-day itinerary. Ted looked at the checklist. He detailed what needed done before departing. There were also suggestions for clothing and scheduling sightseeing trips.

"Wow!" Ted said. "I can't believe this." His voice was filled with excitement.

"Why? Where are you working?" Maureen asked, still looking at her paperwork.

"I will be at the Accademia Gallery. It is the largest art gallery in Florence, and it is where Michelangelo's David is housed. I am working with one of the curators, Marco Fancelli. It should be fun. And you?"

I will spend two days at the oldest working hospital in Florence. It is the Ospedale Santa Maria Nuova. I don't have a specific person to contact, but I will be in the surgical suite if my Italian is correct. It will be interesting seeing how they do things."

"Do you have your passport?" wondered Ted.

"Yes. I got it last year when I went to Canada. What about yours?"

"Not yet. Based on the post office's time frame, it should be here Friday or Saturday. I guess we really ARE going!"

Both were excited. Maureen had been to Canada once. Ted had never left the state, let alone the country. Neither had been on another continent.

"Look," Maureen said, pointing to the brochure. "We get three whole days in Rome." She looked at Ted, blinking her eyelids several times. "The city of romance!" The sugar flowed from her voice.

"I know. I know," Ted said, rolling his eyes.

"Who knows?" Maureen said teasingly. "Maybe I will find me a handsome, rich Italian guy not afraid of commitment." Ted didn't take the bait.

"We tour the Vatican on the second day. I've seen pictures. Were you aware there is a mummified Pope on display?" Maureen said with excitement!

"Just one?" deadpanned Ted.

Ignoring Ted's sarcasm, Maureen continued, "For a Pope to become a saint, they have to perform a miracle or something. I understand, people line up, touch the glass case, and say a prayer. If their prayer is answered, it may be reviewed to see if it qualifies as a miracle."

"I think it's a miracle we are still together, Pope or no Pope," Ted teased.

"I don't know. I touched a dead Pope's picture before I came over. It made you apologize to me." Maureen winked at Ted when she said this.

Ted made sure Maureen was at work. The last thing he wanted was Maureen dropping in on her mother. Ted arranged to come before noon. Ted had gotten the ring from Pam and took it to show Ruthie.

Ted sat at the table with a blue box in his hand. He said, "You absolutely, positively cannot let Maureen find out what is going on. This is the ring Dad gave Mom when they got engaged. It is a two karat solitaire." Ted opened the box and showed the ring to Ruthie. "Dad said it was the only decent thing he did for Mom. Mom did not want to see it collecting dust, so she wanted me to give Maureen the ring. What do you think?"

"You got waders? You're going to need them. Her tears of joy are going to roll! It is a beautiful ring. She will love it."

Ted told Ruthie the details of his plan. When, where, and how. And who was filming the whole thing.

"Ted, I must hand it to you. You have been a tough catch for my daughter: a good catch, but a tough one. However, when you do something, you do it up big. I think it will be wonderful and perfect. And I promise. Not a word to you-know-who. And not a word to Maureen either."

"Good idea. Jack is the absolute worst at keeping a secret."

"So, do I have your permission to ask for your daughter's hand in marriage."

Ruthie pulled Ted in and gave him a hug. "By all means."

"Oh, the permission part is super-secret," Ted said, putting the ring back in his pocket.

"Of course. If Maureen knew I had given my permission, she'd have you two engaged going through the airport security checkpoint." Ruthie stood back and smiled. She had a single tear running down her cheek. "Maureen is so lucky to have you."

"No, mam," said Ted. "I'm the lucky one. I am beyond lucky to have found her."

Ted checked progress at the clinic. Mack and Charles Harrison strolled through the building. They laid out the walls. And discussed what each room needed. The slab had been dug up in certain places to install new plumbing. They needed water for the examination rooms, and while a single bathroom suited a one-man insurance agency, it would not suffice for a medical clinic.

The new plumbing was simultaneously done for all three areas. The construction was being done in phases; completion of the plumbing had been included. It would not be an issue. It would not adversely affect the established deadline.

Ted joined the conversation, but mostly listened. He was the outsider. Mack amazed his son at how with his knowledge of construction. Ted always considered his dad a mere worker, the guy with the hammer and nails. But clearly, his dad knew a lot more. As Mack and Charlie reviewed the plans, Mack would occasionally suggest that Charlie had not previously considered. Judging by Charlie's response, the proposed change made sense.

Everyone understood preliminaries needed to be completed first. It was decided workers would not arrive until around nine. The volunteers began filtering in before Mack and Charlie finished laying out the walls. Then Charlie announced his work was done and turned the site over to Mack.

Ted left and headed over to Jack's to meet with Pam and Eliot. Time to finish the third space had arrived. Although smaller than the grocery store. It larger than the clinic. It could also see the heaviest use.

The youth space would require three distinct sections—a television room with a 70-inch television and comfortable seating. There would also be a half-dozen carrels for computers. Kids could come in and play games, surf the internet, type up papers and do schoolwork. The third area was a quiet area with tables, chairs, beanbags, and other seating options. This would be for reading and doing homework, not requiring a computer. This is where the mentoring takes place. A couple times a week, Volunteers will be here. They will help students with homework. Sometimes, they will simply listen. In addition, volunteers will socially interact with the kids: playing games and putting together jigsaw puzzles.

Wednesday is church night. Each member church of the Southtown Ecumenical Council would sponsor a church night. It would be open to all youth. Not limited to members of the sponsoring congregation.

"It looks like you have given this a lot of thought," said Eliot, looking over Ted's proposal. "It has grown since we first started looking at this facility."

"It has," acknowledged Ted. "I worked closely with Jacob Roberts and his ecumenical council, and they want to be more than tenants." Ted waited for a reaction and did not get one. "They believe if the kids help purchase what is in the center, they are more apt to respect it."

"As opposed to?" Pam asked.

"As opposed to its magically appearing. There are kids. Not all kids, by any measure. But some kids don't see the value of gifts. Things appearing out of nowhere don't belong to anyone. Those things don't matter."

Pam and Eliot looked at one another. "I can see that," Pam said. "What do they propose?"

"The churches comprising the council are now raising money. They have purchased three or four large beanbag chairs. A few schools have large balls students use as seats, and they bought a couple. And they purchased five refurbished Dell desktop computers with 14-inch monitors."

"That's great," confirmed Pam and Eliot.

"I also gave them permission to decorate one wall. I've talked with Fred, and he will provide the paint. The kids will come in and paint one wall in whatever color they choose. They can then add whatever they want. The drawings are submitted to me for approval. I must admit, it amazes me what they want."

"Why?" asked Pam. "Are the designs provocative?"

"Not at all," said Ted and handed them copies of two approved drawings. "One is the periodic table. Another is PM-DAS is the math order of operations."

"Did you make any recommendations?" asked Elliot.

"None what-so-ever," Ted said. "They want a few basic art supplies available and somewhere in the room where original art may be displayed. I have been really impressed," Ted said, concluding his presentation.

"When are they wanting to start?" asked Pam.

"They are ready to go. They are eager to paint the walls now. They know other walls are going up. They want to paint those as well. The pastors indicate the kids appear truly excited to have this new space." Ted paused.

"Have you talked to Charlie about this?"

"Yes, and he is on board, along with Fred and Consolidated paint."

"And you head off to Italy when?" Elliot was showing signs of concern.

"Ten days. I know what you're thinking, and I have it covered. Pastor Roberts said he would personally supervise the students while they paint in my absence. The ministers' involvement was in the proposal, anyway. They would supervise the kids as they make the space their own."

Pam and Elliot stood up. Pam said, "We have a hearing to-morrow morning, still needing a bit of TLC before we go to court. It looks like you've got everything in hand." Turning to Elliot, "What do you say, Hon? Let the kid run with it?"

"You won't hear any complaints from me," Elliot said, showing his pride in what Ted had put together. "I knew you were the right person for this job."

They talked for a few more minutes. Pam showed Ted more pictures of the twins, asking about Maureen. Five minutes later, Pam and Elliot were gone. Ted was cleaning up the workspace. He smiled and quietly sang "What a Day for a Daydream" to himself while he worked. There was a twinkle in his eye.

CHAPTER 31

THE MEETING HELD at the city library was scheduled for seven. Ted and Maureen drove up in his new Sportage and noticed others were arriving early. A sign taped to the library doors directing them to a conference room. There they found a half-dozen current and former Emmerson College students. The school counselor, Mrs. Logan, was fiddling with a computer while Mr. Taylor Craig, the Dean of Student Affairs, was at the podium. He did a couple of mic checks and shuffled papers at the rostrum.

Although the meeting started at seven, it was half-past seven when Mr. Craig welcomed everyone. Mr. Craig informed the group that Mr. Logan could not make the trip this year. He was unable to reschedule a prior commitment. Mr. Craig began calling the names of those invited to attend. Everyone was there except two. It was explained they would be making the trip, and he met them privately. Mr. Craig explained the purpose of the meeting and introduced Mrs. Logan. Mr. Craig opened the meeting. However, it was Mrs. Logan who was in charge.

Mrs. Logan had a slide and video presentation giving the Associated Junior College Program's history. She explained AJCP cooperates with various hospitals, charities, and museums in Florence. Mrs. Logan shared students would have ample time to visit Rome's and Florence's cultural and historical sites. Each student would be paired with a facility closely associated with their studies at Emmerson.

Mrs. Logan covered the contents of the envelope each student had previously received. Ted and Maureen grew more excited about the trip with each new revelation. They would spend almost twelve hours flying to Rome. Their hotel was in west Rome, and they would have two days to tour the ancient city. Various tour options were provided. Everyone would be part of an exclusive tour of the Vatican.

"This does not mean we have the Vatican to ourselves," Mrs. Logan pointed out. "It means we will skip the hours-long lines to get in. Instead, we will have a tour guide assigned to the fourteen of us." Next, Mrs. Logan showed a short video with highlights of the tour company's tour.

"Two trains link Rome and Florence," Mr. Taylor began. "We will take the milk-run train from Rome to Florence. This is about a four-hour ride, providing ample time to view the countryside. To avoid problems getting to the airport on the return trip, we will take the high-speed train, reducing the trip to Rome to about 90 minutes. We will spend another 10–12 hours in the air returning home."

Ted and Maureen spent an hour after the meeting mingling with the other travelers. Each student was required to bring certain documents with them to the meeting. Students met individually with Mr. Taylor and Mrs. Logan. One task was to change U.S. dollars to euros. Each student exchanged $200 for the equivalent of euros. As explained, there will be additional opportunities to convert dollars into euros. This was the minimum needed to take care of tips, food, and other incidentals.

On the way to her mother's house, Ted and Maureen talked excitedly. Ruthie, Jack, Mack, and Melinda eagerly awaited the soon-to-be world travelers. Ted and Maureen were so excited that their audience continually asked them to slow down. They also had to repeat a detail or two.

Ted, Pam, and Eliot were at the new JK Foundation head-quarters at the conference table. They were reviewing the progress of the Southtown project, and the impact Ted's trip to Italy had on the project.

"So, when do you leave for Italy?" Pam asked, looking at Ted's brochure.

"We meet at the library at noon." Ted said. "We are taking a small bus to the airport. We should be in Rome on Monday afternoon," Ted said. "We will spend Monday and Tuesday nights in Rome, and precisely at 9:00 am, we board the train for Florence."

Eliot asked, "And when do you arrive in Florence?"

"We'll eat lunch in Florence. Thursday and Friday working. We work on Thursday afternoon and Friday morning. We have time on Saturday for sightseeing. After that, we ride the bullet train to Rome. That ride takes 90 minutes. We arrive back here before ten on Sunday night." Ted was figuring times and time zones. "Florence is eight hours ahead of us."

"And what about work on Monday?" Eliot asked in a half-teasing tone.

"Hey, it's Monday. As the movie says, everyone works on Monday. So, I'll be in the office Monday morning and ready to hit the ground running." Ted said with a slight shrug of his shoulders.

"You'll be under Miss Maureen's spell," Pam said with a note of sarcasm. Then, giving Ted a broad smile, she asked, "Will you have to clear your work plans with her?" Not allowing Ted to answer, Pam said, "After all, she'll be coming back as the future Mrs. Winston James. Her claws will be firmly implanted in your skin."

"She may be the future, Mrs. TED James, but I am still in charge of my life."

"Yeah," chuckled Eliot, "tell me that after a year of marriage. But, hey, tell me that after the first month you're married. Then, Buddy-boy. Your life will be turned upside down-big time!"

Pam threw a napkin at Eliot.

"Not to change the subject, are you sure you are alright with me going? When I signed up for this trip, I was not knee deep in the Southtown Project."

"Nah, go on. It is a trip and an experience of a lifetime. It's not like you'll be gone a month," said Elliot.

"Besides," Pam said. "Mack and Pastor Roberts seem to have everything well in hand. Go and enjoy yourself. Just don't do anything Eliot wouldn't do," and Pam laughed.

"Oh," said Ted. "I have that much freedom, eh?" and joined in the laughter.

They spent several minutes reviewing the Oasis Market's progress and the construction of the medical clinic and youth center. Convinced all would survive without his butting in for a week, Ted headed home to his apartment.

Disappointingly, the flight to Rome was crowded. Most of the group found themselves sitting with strangers. Ted was three rows behind Maureen. Off to the right. She sat closest to the window, while Ted was in the second seat in the center row.

Mrs. Logan and Mr. Craig moved about the cabin, talking to each foreign studies group. "We know the adrenaline rush is on. But do try to get some sleep."

Maureen turned and blew Ted a kiss. Then faced forward, put a sleep mask on, and fell asleep. Ted put his seat back a bit, slumped down. Then, as uncomfortable as he was, he fell asleep.

The plane had a tailwind and arrived twenty minutes early. The trip through customs was uneventful, and three vans carried the group to their hotel.

Ted asked the driver, in his best Italian, "Why three vans. Why not use two?"

The driver responded in perfect English, albeit with an Italian accent. "You can put people in the van. Or you put luggage in the van. But you can't do both. That's why three vans. That way, you and your luggage don't get separated."

Ted responded in Italian-deciding he needed the practice using the language, "Yes, but my luggage is in the van behind us."

"You're in Italy. We have excellent ideas." Then, turning his head toward Ted, he smiled and said, "We just don't use them very often."

They both laughed.

They checked into the hotel and received their room keys. Ted was on the fourth floor at the southeast corner. Maureen was on the sixth floor, in the northwest corner. In their mind, they were in different time zones!

There was a sign on the mini refrigerator filled with an assortment of alcoholic and non-alcoholic drinks. The card required the room's occupant to leave their credit card information with the concierge. Before removing anything from the refrigerator.

Ted and Maureen walked up to the concierge's desk, credit cards in hand.

"May I help you?" It was apparent everyone spoke better English than either of them spoke Italian.

"The mini fridge in our rooms says we need to give you our credit card information before we take anything out."

"Yes, it is what the signs say."

"Well," a bit confused by the concierge's response. Then, holding out the cards, Ted said, "here are our credit cards."

"Are you going to pay your bill when you check out?" the man asked.

"Yes, of course," Ted and Maureen said in unison.

"In full?" the man asked, still smiling politely at them.

"Of course. We will pay our bill in full when we check out."

"Then I don't see a problem. Do you?" The man stood there for a second.

"I guess not," Ted said, and Maureen echoed his response.

"Then, go. Enjoy our wonderful city. It was built for you two."

"Like us?" They asked and looked at each other.

"Yes, people like you. People who are obviously in love." Then the man turned and walked away.

"Who knew?" Ted said as he and Maureen were leaving the desk.

"Silly. Everyone knows. It's Rome. The most romantic city in Europe."

"I thought that was Paris," Ted teased.

"Nah, that's a myth." Then, spreading her arms out and slowly twirling, "This is the most romantic city on earth. Know why?"

"That man just said you loved me. So, you have to propose to me. Here. In the most romantic city on earth." Maureen turned and batted her eyes.

"Not on your life, young lady. If I propose to you here, you won't let me live until we find a jewelry store and a preacher, and then we'll need only one room. No, I'm not risking your mother's rath for nothing. Besides, I have to ask her permission before I can ask you to marry me."

Her head drooped. Then, in a sullen voice, Maureen said, "A girl can dream, can't she?"

Ted lifted her chin and kissed her. "For the record, I do like your dream," and Maureen immediately perked up.

Mr. Craig and Mrs. Logan gathered the group in the hotel's lobby. They gave the group additional information and instructions.

Parts of Rome were overcrowded. Guys were to put nothing in their back pockets. Purses were discouraged. "Take what is absolutely essential," Mr. Craig admonished. "And avoid large crowds at all costs."

"Is it dangerous?" asked one of the travelers.

"Dangerous, meaning you might get hurt? No," Mrs. Logan

said. "Risky in that pick-pockets target large groups. And they are very good at stealing from your pockets and belly-packs. Guys, keep your money and identification in your front pocket. Girls, keep your valuables close to your heart." There were a few puzzled looks. "Girls, put them in your bra!"

Mr. Craig gave each a lanyard with a large, thin pouch on end. Holding the pouch for all to see. "I keep my valuables in this pouch. And then it is inside my shirt."

"I keep mine inside my blouse," said Mrs. Logan.

Mr. Craig said, "Nothing is irreplaceable, not even your passport. It is just a hassle, and it will, without a doubt, ruin your trip. As the saying goes. Been there–done that."

Everyone made a mad dash to their rooms, transferred their essentials to the pouch, and locked everything else in the small safe room.

The group loaded a tour bus and set out to see Rome. They would make three stops. For you to get out and "experience Rome," the tour guide said. The first stop was the famous Treva Fountain.

Maureen and Ted melted into the crowd. They weaved their way to the fountain. Maureen had six quarters in her hand, and when they reached the fountain, she gave Ted three.

"This," she said, pointing, "is the most famous fountain in Rome. Not only Rome. The most famous in the world. It is famous for movies and songs. You turn your back to the fountain and toss the three coins over your right shoulder while making a wish. If you do it right, your wish will come true." They did as Maureen instructed and threw the coins.

Back on the bus, Ted asked Maureen, "How do you know if you tossed the coins correctly?"

"Simple," Maureen said, looking out the window. "If your wish doesn't come true, you messed up."

"What was your wish?" Ted asked.

"Can't tell you; otherwise, it positively will not come true. We did it the right way, though." To herself, she said, "I hope!"

The group stopped at the famous Spanish Steps and climbed the 135 steps to the top. They had some breathtaking views of the city. Ted bought Maureen a small bouquet from one of the flower vendors at the top.

The final stop was the Coliseum. The bus let the group off at the Coliseum's base. Ted and Maureen climbed the steps to the top. This was no easy feat since these steps were two or three times taller than typical staircase steps. Almost 18 inches tall. From the top, they could see where the gladiators lived and trained. In the days of gladiators, this was hidden below the arena's floor.

Dinner that night was pizza at an open café. "Pizza in Italy is not like your pizza back home," began Mr. Craig. "In areas where American tourists frequent, pizzas have the familiar pie-cut slices. In other regions, pizzas are served whole with a knife and fork." Mrs. Logan held up the utensils mentioned. "In those areas, it is considered bad manners to share a pizza. Relax. These pizzas will be cut. No one will be offended if shared."

Ted ordered a traditional sausage, mushroom, and olive pizza. When the pizza arrived, it was not what either Ted or Maureen had anticipated. The toppings were added after the pizza was cooked. The mushrooms were the largest he had ever seen on a pizza. The sausage was not the ground meat found on American pizza, but Vienna Sausage halves set on end. There were a dozen black olives. Ted knew because he could count on them. They were whole olives, including pits.

It was only nine. And unthinkable for young adults to be calling it a night. But. The group had had a long day. They had had a trans-Atlantic flight and a tour of the city. The only one thing was scheduled for the next day. The Vatican. Tomorrow night, they will be in Florence.

Maureen kissed Ted goodnight as he got off the elevator. "Sleep tight," she said as he headed down the hall to his time zone. Maureen rode the elevator two floors up and exited to her time zone. She continually pinched herself. Making sure this was real. And not a dream.

In the room, she considered calling Ted. Sleepy, she decided first to take a shower. That is when it hit her. She was exhausted and was asleep moments after climbing into bed.

CHAPTER 32

THE GROUP ASSEMBLED in the hotel's lobby after breakfast. "It is a short walk to the Vatican," said Mrs. Logan. "Just a reminder. Keep your valuables in your pouch. And your pouch inside your shirt or blouse." She looked around. Each gave a thumbs up.

"Did you enjoy the tour yesterday?" Mr. Craig asked. There was an uproar from the group. Then, everyone began talking at once.

Pointing to the door, Mrs. Logan said. "Well, off we go." Everyone headed out into the bright sunlight.

The streets are narrow and lined with Vespa motor scooters. A few small cars were scattered among the bikes and scooters. Surprisingly, the streets were not filled with litter. But many of the buildings had become canvasses for graffiti artists. The sidewalks were narrow, and they walked single file. The sidewalks were wide enough for two. But walking side-by-side meant ducking back into a single file. Allowing room for others to pass in the opposite direction.

The group noticed many cars honking as they approached a street intersection. Maureen asked Mrs. Logan and Mr. Craig about it.

"It's letting other vehicles know they are at the intersection. They have signals and stop signs. But motorists tend to ignore them," Mrs. Logan said. "Someone once told me signals actually do direct traffic in northern Italy."

Then, it was Mr. Craig's turn to explain local customs. "Here. Traffic lights merely suggest going on green and stop on red." He paused, then added, "They are considered mere decorations in Naples and southern Italy."

The laughter tickled down the line. But unfortunately, traffic noise made talking difficult. Thus, those in front constantly turned around. They explained what was said.

"Pedestrians have no rights," added Mrs. Logan. "So, be careful when crossing the street. And whatever you do, don't doddle."

They passed a McDonald's. Most stopped to look in. The one line for beverages included the usual coffee and soft drinks. However, it is possible to get a beer with your Big Mack in Italy. The only food item they recognized was the Big Mack on the food side. The other choices were unique to Italy. For example, they learned Italians called French fries patatine fritte.

When they arrived at Vatican City, two things were apparent. First was the forty-foot wall surrounding much of the city. Part of the ancient wall surrounding Rome was seen. However, it was not as impressive as this Vatican wall. Second, they noticed a long line. It started on the left, to the doors of St. Peter's. It stretched down the steps and throughout St. Peter Square. Finally, it disappeared around the corner.

Pointing to the line, Mrs. Logan said. "Without a private tour. That would be us." Then left to find their guide.

Mr. Craig pointed to the upper right of St. Peters, "You all know when a Pope dies or resigns. Until a new Pope is elected. They lock the College of Cardinals in a room." All said they knew the process. He pointed again to the window. On the right side of the building. He said, "That window is where they are locked. Black smoke comes out if the ballot was unsuccessful.

One of the groups said, "And white if they have elected a new Pope."

Mrs. Logan was back with another woman. "This is Isabella Russo. She will be our guide."

"Buongiorno," she said. "Welcome to The Vatican. This is the world's smallest country. Vatican City is its only city." She pointed to soldiers dressed in blue and gold costumes from the 17th century. "Beyond that gate is the Pope's residence. Those are the famous Swiss Guards who guard the Pope. Don't let their uniforms fool you. You do not mess with them."

Everyone jockeyed for an opportunity to get a picture of the guards.

"I am sure Mrs. Logan told you a private tour of St. Peter's Basilica does not mean you are alone in the church. It simply means you have a dedicated tour guide–me. So, you must stay together." Handing Mrs. Logan tickets to distribute, "These are your tickets to get in. You will need to give it to the guard to gain entrance. Any questions? Then, let's go!"

No one was prepared for they saw. From Michelangelo's Pieta. To the glass case with a mummified Pope.

"There are five chapels," Isabella said, pointing around. Then, indicating the altar in the center. "This is the Pope's altar. Don't be fooled by the appearance of the altar candles. They are six feet tall." Then, pointing to the gold canopy over the altar, "Your Statue of Liberty will easily fit under that canopy. The extravagance and beauty of the inside astounded everyone. In the Sistine Chapel, there were three or four guards on elevated platforms. Visitors were shoulder to shoulder. Several private tours in the chapel, and each guide pointed out various elements to their group.

"Silencio," the guards would say above the melee when the noise grew too loud. After that, most guides simply stopped and took a breath. And then continued.

"What is that?" Maureen asked, pointing to a black square in the ceiling corner.

"That, my dear," said Isabella. "That is a reminder. It reminds us to take care of what we have. It is how this magnificent ceiling looked before restoration."

About halfway through the tour, Ted spotted a gift shop. Ted and others started to go to the shop. The guide discouraged stopping at the gift shop. "Don't buy anything here. It is too expensive. I will take you to a gift shop afterward. There, you can buy the same merchandise. And it will be much less expensive." The group moved on.

While impressed with the ceiling, Ted was more enthralled with the "Wall of Souls." It depicted the second coming of Christ. Noticing Ted's gaze on the wall, Isabella explained that the figures were initially painted without clothes. When there was a movement to clothe the figures, Michelangelo objected. "I paint souls, not bodies. Souls do not wear clothes." Pope Julius II finally forced Michelangelo to clothe the figures. When finished, she said. "The man being eaten by the snake. That is the face of Pope Julius."

Maureen was mesmerized by the Hall of Tapestry. "Look," she said to Ted and pointed to the tapestries hanging in the hall. "The eyes of Jesus. They are always on you. No matter where you are." To prove her theory, they moved through the hall. Maureen stopped and pointed to the face of Jesus. He was, indeed, looking at them.

After they exited St. Peter's, Isabella led them to a gift shop. It was a block beyond the Vatican wall. Ted and Maureen recognized the same or similar items for sale in the Vatican. And at a much lower cost. The store had some things not available inside the Vatican's gift shop. And vice versa. They did not have everything Ted wanted. Especially the book Ted wanted. Everyone spent money in the shop buying souvenirs for themselves. And for friends back home. Before leaving, Ted confirmed they did not have the book he wanted.

"No," said the clerk. "That book is only available inside the Vatican."

Outside, Mr. Craig announced the tour had concluded. "You are on your own to explore the city." He said not to be late getting to the hotel. To collect their things and check out. He stressed being on time for the train ride to Florence.

"I want to find the book about the Vatican's history. The one I saw at the Vatican shop. The gift shop did not have it."

Pointing in the direction of McDonald's, Maureen said, "That little red sign. On the other side of McDonald's, Negozio di Libri. I believe it is a bookstore." Ted was duly impressed with Maureen's ability to read Italian. "Let's go and see if they have your book. We can even stop and get an Italian Big Mac."

They stopped for lunch, not wanting to pass up the opportunity to try an Italian McDonald's. But unfortunately, there was no Dr. Pepper, so they settled for a generic cola, a Big Mac, and patatine fritte. Then, with their hunger pangs and curiosity satisfied, they moved to the bookstore.

The store clerk said, "non parlo molto Inglese." Ted and Maureen understood the clerk did not speak much English. A customer offered to help. Ted and Maureen managed to learn the book Ted wanted was not available. With more help, they learned the book is sold only in Vatican City. They did not have a copy, and no, they do not sell used books. They thanked the clerk. And the other customer. Outside, Ted proclaimed, "Well, Amazon, here I come. I'll try to find a copy online when we get home."

"Good idea," said Maureen. "Let's get back to the hotel. We don't want to miss the train."

It would take more than three hours getting to Florence. It traveled up the western coast of Italy. The countryside was green and lush. The houses appeared tiny but well cared for. Painted with vibrant colors. The western coast was beautiful, and the train passed through small farms and vineyards. There were small factories. But no hustle and bustle. Not as found back home. Everything seemed to be smaller and moved slower. Of course, there were big rigs. But even those appeared smaller.

The train arrived a little after six. The three vans were waiting for their arrival and carried the group and their luggage to the hotel. People were waiting to check in. Many asked about dinner.

"You are on European time now. Restaurants don't open for at least another half-hour. Unpack and relax. The hotel has wi-fi. If you brought your computer, you may log in and email your family back home."

"What about Zoom?" Trudy asked. Like Ted, Trudy was a business major.

"They don't have the same bandwidth as Americans," explained Mrs. Logan. "Stick to email. You could call if you bought an overseas plan. That will cost you about $10 a minute. Double that if you call without a plan."

"I don't have a personal laptop. Is there a business center I can use?" asked Ted.

Mr. Craig took Ted to the business center. He helped him log on. Ted typed in addresses for Elliot, Pam, Jack, and Ruthie. "We just arrived in Florence. We have had a fantastic time. The tour of the Vatican was awesome. Normal dinner time here is around nine. It is just 8:30. We will go as a group to a family-owned restaurant for dinner. In Rome, Maureen and I were on opposite ends, with two floors between us. Was that your idea, Ruthie? This is a smaller hotel. It is not as busy. We are all on the same floor. But Maureen and I are on opposite ends of the hall. Again. Hope the project is going well. I will check in again before we leave. Ted."

Ted, a touch-typist, would have taken less than a minute for him to type. Tonight, it took more than fifteen. European keyboards are not set up like the ones Americans used. He had to hunt-and-peck his way through the message. Ted also checked his email, and there were no urgent messages or catastrophes. Ted felt a quick pang of something. Jealousy maybe? Ted was relieved and anxious. As for the crews. Ted believed no news was good news!

The restaurant was small, quaint, and off the beaten path.

"This is not a tourist destination," said Mr. Craig. "This restaurant is owned by the Berlusconi family. It has been in their family for generations." Mr. Craig stopped and nodded in the direction of the owner. "My wife, Mia, is a Berlusconi. She is related to Carlo and Angelica Berlusconi." The couple smiled and waved. "They understand a little English." Then, turning to a young girl with raven-black hair, "This is Concetta. She is fluent in English and can help you with your order. She can answer just about any question you have."

Concetta stepped up next to Mr. Craig. "Thank you, Mr. Craig. As he said, my name is Concetta, and welcome to my family's home. Yes, this is our home. We live in the apartments over the restaurant." Concetta pointed to the ceiling. "Our menu is not like yours. It is one page and has three choices. Since this may be your first visit to my country, may I suggest one of the tortellini? We have cheese and shrimp. Tonight, we are also serving tagliata. This is a skirt steak, sliced diagonally with greens. We also have calamari. Let me know how I may help you."

Ted opted for the tagliata while Maureen went with the cheese tortellini. Each sampled the others and had an enjoyable meal. Several ordered wine. Concetta suggested red wine, and it came in a water pitcher. Ted and Maureen stuck with their water. They quickly learned water in Italy was served in bottles. Guests are asked, "gas or no gas. Bubbles or no bubbles." Ted and Maureen opted for no bubbles.

Everyone cleared their plates. Except for Mitchell. He was the odd-man-out and ordered the calamari. Mitch expected small, spongy, breaded rings. Something resembling small onion rings. It is what he got back home. Instead, he got a plate full of tentacles. Each is about a half-inch long. They were neither breaded nor fried, as they are in the States. Instead, they were boiled. He said they weren't bad. Just not what he expected. To his credit, he finished more than half his plate.

It was after 11 when they reached the hotel. Maureen was too excited to sleep and called Ted. Unfortunately, Ted did not share her excitement. It wasn't until the fifth or sixth ring before he answered.

"Did I wake you?" Maureen asked, knowing she probably had.

"No, I was in the shower," Ted lied. And Maureen knew it.

"I can't sleep. Want to go for a walk?"

Ten minutes later, they met up in the lobby. After confirming their room key would allow them back in the hotel, they set out on their midnight adventure. The hotel took up an entire city block, and they walked around the hotel. Twice.

Ted looked at his watch. "It's midnight. I must get some sleep. Otherwise, I will not be worth much in the morning." Maureen agreed. She had calmed down sufficiently to get some sleep. They held hands while they rode the elevator in silence to their floor. They kissed and went in opposite directions.

CHAPTER 33

MAUREEN AND TED were up early and sat at a sidewalk café drinking coffee. They shared a small artisan loaf of bread. They reviewed their experiences thus far. While Maureen was excited about her assignment, Ted was even more excited. His passion was history and art. And here he is. In this magnificent little town. Filled with both. Florence is a city filled with historical landmarks and an abundance of art. It is impossible to go anywhere in Florence. Not without encountering compelling art.

Florence, Ted discovered, was a walking paradise. Except for delivery vehicles, cars and trucks were prohibited city's center. This allowed Maureen and Ted to leisurely walk along the narrow streets. Finally, they found themselves at the Plaza Della Signoria, the most famous square in Florence. It is filled with original art and replicas.

"That is David," said an old man. He was sitting on a bench in the square. "He is essential. That is why we moved him to the Accademia Museum. The other guy is real. No one knows who he is. So, we left him here." The square was filled with marble, stone, and bronze statues. Maureen was drawn to a bronze map. Opposite from the David replica.

"Look, Ted. It is a map of the city. Isn't it beautiful?"

"Everything here is beautiful. If I didn't have to go. I could spend the whole day here."

"What's this?" Maureen asked. Pointing to what she assumed was a church. "It is larger than anything else."

"That is El Duomo," said Ted. He turned her and pointed to a red dome towering over the landscape. "That is El Duomo."

"It is enormous." It was all Maureen could say. "I wonder if we'll get to see it up close."

"Trust me," Ted said with a smile. He was standing behind her with his hands around her waist. "You will definitely see it up close."

"That," said Ted, pointing to another building, "is the Pitti Palace."

"The what palace?" Maureen asked.

"Ever hear of a book called The Prince?" Ted asked.

"Sure. Written by Machiavelli, I think. The writer, not the rapper."

Ted laughed at the explanation. "Well, it is where his family lived when writing that little book."

Ted walked over to the bronze statue of Perseus holding the head of Medusa. Ted and gone around to the back. He called Maureen to join him. He told Maureen to look at Perseus' back, he said. "There is a second face. Is that amazing?"

"Yes. But why two faces?" Maureen wondered.

"According to legend," said Ted. "The artist believed the government was corrupt. It had two faces."

"So, the artist," Maureen started.

"Yup. The artist put two faces on this statue as a political statement."

They walked over to the Arno River. There could see a covered bridge with colorful panels.

"That," pointing to the bridge, "is the Ponte Vecchio Bridge. It connects Florence's Town Square with the Pitti Palace. There are several shops there. We will have to pay it a visit before we leave."

Maureen looked at her watch. "Speaking of leaving, I have to leave now. Or I will be late getting to the hospital. And you can't be late. Enjoy your day at the museum." They kissed, and each headed off to their assignments.

The Galleria dell'Accademia di Firenze, or the Gallery of the Academy of Florence, is primarily famous for its collections of Michelangelo's sculptures. Ted arrived and showed his credentials to the guards. He was directed to a desk. There, a young woman reviewed his credentials and made a call. She ushered him into the office of the curator, Umberto Collini.

Ted told Umberto he preferred to be called Ted, not Winston. His given name was on the papers the school provided. These provided an introduction. The two visited in the curator's office. Umberto then took Ted on a brief tour. Ted had seen pictures of David. None of what he studied prepared him for this experience.

"Magnificent, is it not?" Umberto asked, while admiring the statue himself. "This depicts David when he was a teenager, probably around 15 or 16. The sculpture is 17 feet tall."

"Wow," was all Ted could say as he moved around the sculpture.

"Most amazingly," Umberto said. "Michelangelo used a flawed slab of marble to create this masterpiece."

"Flawed?" asked Ted in amazement.

"Yes, there was an imperfection. A weakness. Many older and more experienced sculptures had determined the slab of marble was unusable. It was not fit for a sculpture. Not of this magnitude."

"How old was Michelangelo? When he did this?"

"We believe Michelangelo was 26 when he sculpted David. The year before, when he was about 25, he sculpted the Pieta, which I believe you saw earlier this week."

"Yes. It was magnificent. Both are beyond words to describe."

"The Pieta is the only sculpture Michelangelo ever signed."

"Really?" Ted said in astonishment.

"Yes. I understand Michelangelo overheard two gentlemen discussing the sculpture. They both agreed Michelangelo could not be the sculpture. He was too young."

"Who did they say created that masterpiece?"

"I do not think they settled that question. Then, however, in the dark of night. Michelangelo snuck in. He signed his name on the back."

"Wow," is all Ted could say.

"Do you know the link between the Sistine Chapel and David?"

"There is a link?" inquired Ted.

"The legend says Pope Clement VII commissioned David's sculpture with his slingshot, ready to face Goliath. After completing the sculpture, Michelangelo requested payment for his work. His requests went unanswered."

"Michelangelo never got paid for David?"

"Slow down. Don't get ahead of me. Pope Sixtus IV had the chapel built. But Pope Clement got Michelangelo to paint the ceiling. Michelangelo protested, saying, I am not a painter." The Pope did not budge. He made painting the chapel's ceiling a condition of payment for David.

"And that is a beautiful painted ceiling."

"Ah," Umberto said, interrupting Ted. "The ceiling is not painted. At least not with paint. It is called fresco, where colored cement was used to create the painting. So, you see. The painting is not on the ceiling. It is the ceiling."

Ted was acquiring a new appreciation for Michelangelo and Italian renaissance art. They toured the museum. Umberto commented on the Museum of Musical Instruments and the Hall of Prisoners. The final stop was the Hall of Colossus. They were preparing an exhibit. It focused on the importance of wood and textiles in Florentine art. It would be Ted's assignment while at the museum. He would help prepare the museum for this exhibit opening in about four weeks.

◆ ◆ ◆

Maureen arrived at the Ospedale Santa Maria Nuova and was shown to the Director of Nursing office. Her name was Tessa Ricci. The two talked about the care provided at this hospital. Maureen explained she had spent several weeks learning Italian. However, she was by no means fluent.

Tessa spent a few moments talking with Maureen in Italian. Tessa basically asked questions a patient might ask or giving directions a doctor might give in the area where Maureen would work.

"You'll do fine," Tessa assured Maureen. "Most of our staff speak English. Some are better than others. Between your Italian, which is actually quite good, and their English. You should have no problems."

"Where will I be working?"

"We have two day hospitals. I have you assigned to the oncology hospital. Patients come in for a consultation, examination, various treatments, and follow-ups. It is more, how do you say? Oh, yes. It is more laid back."

"Let me take you on a tour. As you probably noted when you came in, it is an old building. Even by our standards. The hospital opened its doors in 1288."

"1288? In the States, hospitals erected in 1900 are considered too old to use."

"Yes. We laugh at how you Americans build and discard buildings so easily. It could be. Since some of our buildings took many years to build. Sometimes, hundreds of years. On the other hand. I like to think we respect their hard work. Therefore, we are reluctant to discard them."

They walked the halls, and Tessa introduced Maureen to various department heads, doctors, and nurses. "We are the oldest hospital still operating in Florence. We are also the oldest and most important Florentine welfare institution. Our patients are among the oldest. And the poorest."

Maureen and Tessa ended up at the oncology day hospital, where Maureen was introduced to Andrea Columbo, the hospital's head. Dr. Columbo was about Maureen's mother's age, with thick grey hair and a quiet demeanor. They visited in both English and Italian.

"Well," said Tessa. "I'll leave you two to get better acquainted. And get to work with your patients. Good luck, Maureen. I think you will enjoy working with Dr. Columbo."

It was after eight when students returned to the hotel. Many students ate dinner in small groups. Ted and Maureen opted for a quiet meal alone. They exchanged notes from the day. They were impressed by what they had seen. And what they were able to do.

"That Babel Italian course, along with my course work, sure came in handy," explained Ted. "My co-workers did speak English. But it was nice we could carry on a conversation in Italian. They seemed happy I had made an effort to learn Italian. At least a little before coming over."

"It was my experience as well," said Maureen. "The doctors and nurses spoke English. The patients did not. I was able to help them and explain what was happening in their language. They were apprehensive when they first saw me. However, they relaxed when I greeted them in Italian."

"All in all," Ted said. "This has been an awesome experience."

Maureen uttered, "Uh, huh," but did not say anything else. She was exhausted.

The morning shift was more relaxed, and no one really had any significant responsibilities. Ted strolled through the museum and visited with the other workers. He was trying to learn as much as possible about the museum. His last stop was with the museum's development director. They shared problems unique to each other's country and their jobs in fundraising.

Maureen spent the morning observing surgical techniques and would occasionally ask a question. The results were pretty much the same. However, there were some procedures very different from what she had experienced.

At the appointed time, the group met on the steps of El Duomo. Umberto met Ted on the steps. He would be their tour guide.

"This is not a tourist destination. It is a church. We will be alone inside. I would ask you to respect this building. You may take pictures. But please, no flash photography. You can talk in quiet voices. You will be free to walk around. Again, do not touch anything. This is an ancient church. What is inside is priceless." With that, he opened the doors, and the group filtered in.

Without Maureen noticing it, Ted slipped Mrs. Logan his phone. Stunned by what she saw, Maureen was unaware the entourage had filled the pews. They were sitting on both sides of the aisle.

Ted stopped, and Maureen stopped. She turned to him. He took her hands in his and said, "Maureen Kathleen Rittenhouse."

"Oh, no!" she blurted, and began trembling in anticipation.

"As beautiful as this church is," Ted gestured at the surroundings. "It is no match for the beauty which is yours."

After each sentence, Maureen said, "Yes." In a barely audible voice.

"And as huge as this is, it cannot begin to hold the love I have for you today. For tomorrow and beyond. Just as this building has endured centuries. So will my love and devotion to you will endure." Ted reached into his pocket and pulled out a little blue box. He knelt on his right knee, opened the box, and held it up to her. "Will you make me the happiest man on earth? Will you be my wife?"

Maureen gasped and, ignoring the request for a subdued talk, was very loud and very definite in her answer.

Each yes Maureen said during Ted's proposal grew louder. Now, there was no holding her back.

"Yes! Yes! Yes!" Maureen exclaimed, watching Ted get up. He never let go of her hands.

Maureen was both nervous and excited. Ted had difficulty keeping her hand still as he put the ring on her finger.

Maureen admired the gem once the ring was on and began kissing Ted non-stop. He eventually had to put his hands on her shoulders to calm her down. "Now, look at the camera. You are on candid camera. Show the camera the ring. Now everyone knows it is official."

The girls rushed Maureen to give her hugs and to admire the ring. The guys pounded Ted on the back. They all shook his hand. Umberto knew what was about to happen. He stood to the side. He grinned from ear to ear. "This is one for the ages," he said in Italian.

Mrs. Logan came up and gave Maureen a kiss on the cheek. She handed Ted his phone. "Absolutely perfect." She gave Ted a hug and stepped out of the way.

Mr. Craig came up and gave Maureen a hug as well. He shook Ted's hand and held up his own phone. "I got it as well. Just in case Logan's hands were shaking too much."

Throughout the trip, Maureen and Ted could never sit next together. However, everyone ensured the newly engaged couple were together on the train ride and flight home.

Ruthie, Jack, Mack, and Melinda were waiting outside customs. As soon as Maureen saw her mother, she ran and gave her a huge hug. It took Ruthie's breath away. When Ted saw the four of them, he gave a thumbs-up. The guys applauded. However, Ruthie and Melinda were preoccupied with Maureen. And her excitement.

Tears of joy and excitement ran down Maureen's face, explaining how Ted had surprised her in the most beautiful church in the world. She was bouncing on her toes throughout the explanation.

After a quick welcome home celebration, Mack and Melinda dropped Jack off at his place on their way home. Maureen told Ted she would spend the night at her mom's.

"That's great. But I need to tell you something. It's about the ring."

Maureen looked at him in confusion.

"This is the ring my dad gave to my mom when he proposed."

"Oh," Maureen said. She looked at the ring. Unsure what was happening.

"Hank gave Mom a new ring. That meant this ring was sitting around gathering dust. Mom thought it would look perfect on your little finger."

"Um-hum," Maureen said, lifting her hand and admiring the ring.

"Dad's secret trip was to get the ring. Not knowing how you would react; I was sworn to secrecy. The three of us: Mom, Dad, and me. We will understand if you would prefer a brand-new ring as opposed to."

"Not on your life!" Maureen interrupted. "It took me forever to get a ring out of you. This ring is on MY finger now. No way, under any circumstances, are you getting it back!"

Maureen kept kissing him as he tried to make his way out the door. Finally, Ruthie said in a mock stern voice, "Maureen Kathleen. If you don't stop, you will suffocate him. Then where will you be?"

Blushing slightly, "Sorry," she said. And allowed Ted to leave.

After Ted was gone, Maureen sat at the kitchen table with her mother. "Do you think it's too late?" she asked.

"Too late?"

"Too late to call Marie?"

"No, honey. It is a perfect time."

Marie answered on the second ring. "Thank you, thank you, thank you. The ring. It is so beautiful. It is so much more. More than I could ever wish for."

Marie put Maureen on speaker, and Hank joined the conversation. They congratulated Maureen on the engagement. And, yes, they knew it was filmed. Ted sent them the video. And they have watched it. At least two or three times.

The phone call ended, and the adrenaline rush subsided. Maureen sat at the table with her mother. She admired her new bobble. "Isn't it absolutely gorgeous?"

"Yes, dear. It is gorgeous. But unless you are planning on sleeping at this table, I suggest you get to bed. You are way beyond me carrying you to bed."

They kissed, and Maureen went to bed. She fell asleep. The last thing she saw was her ring through the glow of her nightlight.

CHAPTER 34

AFTER RETURNING FROM Italy, the newly engaged couple found alone time elusive. The patient load at Maureen's surgical clinic had increased. Ted found keeping everything going at the Southtown Project was becoming difficult. Oasis Grocery and the gardens were running smoothly. The medical clinic's opening was to be the month. However, the youth center placed unexpected demands on Ted's time.

As he gained control of his life, Ted and Maureen invited Jack, Mack, and Melinda to an informal Italian dinner. Ruthie agreed to host the dinner at her house.

"I have absolutely no idea what these two international travelers are cooking up," Ruthie insisted. "Ted and Maureen's instructions were to have you here no later than seven."

"So, it is 7:22. Where the heck are they?" Jack wanted to know.

"Punctuality was never one of Maureen's strong points," Ruthie admitted.

"Ditto for Ted," added Mack.

Ted walked in carrying two pizzas from Uncle Dan's at that precise moment. Maureen followed, closing the door. She toted a McDonald's sack."

"Couldn't pull the Italian thing off?" asked Melinda.

"No. It's all here." Maureen said and joined Ted in the kitchen. "Please have a seat. Dinner is about to be served."

Maureen addressed those seated and awaiting their meal. "In Italy, pizza is generally served with a knife and fork. They also frown on sharing. Tonight, we will break with that tradition. The pizza is sliced, and you are expected to share."

Ted found two platters large enough for the pizzas. He entered, a pizza in each hand. "There is one other curious thing about Italian pizza. They add the toppings after the pizza is cooked."

"They start with a traditional cheese pizza," announced Maureen. Ted placed the pizzas on the table.

"Then they add the toppings. So, for tonight, we are having what Italians call Pizza Americana." With that, the McDonald's bag was opened, and Ted placed French fries on one pizza. Maureen put French fries on the other.

"Dig in," they said with smiles on their face.

"A fellow traveler saw this on the menu," said Ted.

"So, he ordered one," said Maureen. "His reaction was pretty much the same as yours. As it turns out, the combination is bad."

Everyone laughed and began pulling the pizzas apart. Then added fries to each piece.

"Well," Jack started, "let's get down to business. We are all here and well-fed. Now to the topic at hand. The wedding. When and where?"

They all laughed.

"Well, Jack. That is one way of getting the ball rolling." Said a bemused Ruthie.

"Just trying to be helpful," grumbled Jack.

Ted and Maureen looked at each other. It was Ted who started the conversation. "To answer you directly, Mr. Kelley."

"Getting all fancy or formal now, are we?" Jack said, grinning.

"As I started to say. We have not yet determined the where. Or when our nuptials will take place." His hands raised at Jack in a stop fashion, "We are working on it. We have a couple of places in mind, and we have to check availability. When we know where. We can determine when. And work back from there."

Maureen's turn to speak. "It will be at least three months down the road."

"Three months?" Jack hollered in mock exasperation.

"You guys can put a suit on and be done with it. But a woman must find a dress. Get it fitted to her girlish figure. And she must have her hair and nails done, work with the bridesmaids."

"Ok, ok, ok?" Jack said, raising his hands in a gesture of surrender.

"Maureen, dear," Melinda asked. "Have you begun looking at dresses?"

"No, mam. Mom and I are looking at dresses on Tuesday. I could use another pair of eyes. Want to come?"

"No. That is really a mother-daughter thing. I don't want to intrude."

"Nonsense," Ruthie said. "We'll look at dresses until early afternoon. Then we'll grab a quick bite. After that, we will enjoy an hour. Maybe two at the spa. We all deserve to pamper ourselves now and again."

"Are you sure I am not intruding?"

"Please come," pleaded Maureen. "It will be fun. The three of us will enjoy doing girly things. Without the fuddy-duddy guys hanging on!"

This led to laughter and a barrage of alternate plans from the fuddy-duddy guys. Finally, the girls informed the guys they were not invited. It is a girl-only day!

◆ ◆ ◆

"Did you get a dress?" asked Ted when they talked the next day.

"Wouldn't you like to know?" teased Maureen.

"I guess you could make a statement showing up in your underwear," Ted said.

"Or. I can make a bigger statement. By not wearing anything," Maureen shot back.

"Nah. The police would arrest you. And I don't know if I have enough savings to bail you out."

"Mom will do it if you won't," Maureen said.

They both had a laugh and continued with their wedding plans.

"I was thinking," said Maureen.

"That is always dangerous," retorted Ted.

Maureen slapped Ted's arm. "Shut up and let me finish. I was thinking we need someplace to live when we become Mr. and Mrs."

"What's wrong with my apartment?"

"Nothing, if you are a guy. It needs a woman's touch," Maureen said thoughtfully. "We both live in the same complex. Let's switch apartments. That way when we start getting wedding gifts."

"You think we'll actually get gifts?"

Ted ignored the comment. "As I was saying, when we get gifts, I can put them in our apartment, and we won't have to move them later."

"I can do that," countered Ted.

"The bride gets the gifts. So, it only makes sense I start organizing them in our new home."

Ted admitted it was a good idea but stuck to his guns. He insisted on staying put where they were. Maureen would remain in her apartment and Ted in his. "You know," Ted said by way of a compromise, "you can bring the gifts. That is, assuming we get some. Bring them over, and we can work as a team. We can organize our new home together." Maureen grudgingly agreed to the compromise.

The decision was to have the wedding at The Reach, with Pastor Gladstone officiating. The reception would be at Moore Hall. They hired "The DJs," a local band. They decided their first dance would be the Elton John song, "Your Song." Alcohol would be served, but it would not be an open bar. After much consideration and discussion, the couple chose blue and yellow.

Maureen told her mother she had one more thing to take care of. So Maureen got in her trusted Soul and drove over to Jack's. Surprised to see her, Jack invited her in.

"Ted's not here," he said. She took a seat on the sofa across from Jack. "Good. I don't want to talk to Ted. I am here to talk to you."

"Me?" Jack was surprised.

"Mr. Kelly,"

"Jack," he corrected.

"Mr. Kelley," Maureen continued, "It is customary for the father of the bride to walk his daughter down the aisle." Jack was nodding in agreement. "My father is not available. I am sure he will be watching over the ceremony. But he cannot walk me down the aisle."

"Ok. Your dad can't walk you down the aisle. So, why are you here? How can I help?" Jack asked. Began to get a little nervous.

"You and Mom have become really good friends. Right?"

"Yes," Jack answered.

"And. You are the closest thing I have to a father."

"I am?"

"You are. So, would you do me the honor of walking me down the aisle?"

"Well, I don't know. It is a long walk. Don't know I can make it!" Jack said. Then went over, bent down, and kissed her cheek. "It would be my honor to walk you down the aisle."

Maureen got up, did a victorious fist pump, and hugged Jack. This was the one part of her wedding that gave her the most concern.

"What does Ruthie think about this old coot walking her daughter down the aisle?" Jack asked.

"She doesn't know. Nobody knows. I wanted to ask you first. I'll tell her when I get home."

The following months were filled with the grind of work. And the excitement of planning the wedding. Although money was no longer an issue, Ruthie and Maureen settled on a modest budget and vowed to abide by it. Melinda had a friend who owned a bridal shop. Together with Ruthie, they found Maureen a stunning beaded gown with a traditional veil. It fit Maureen almost perfectly. It would require very little alterations. Melinda offered to get them a generous discount.

Before looking at dresses, Maureen and her mother set a budget for the dress and the whole wedding. "Just because you have the money doesn't mean you have to spend it. I am not saying you need to hoard it. But don't blow it either."

"I know, Mom," Maureen said while she hugged her mother. "Do you think Melinda will be upset when she finds I didn't need the discount?"

"No. Melinda never had a daughter. She is excited. Being part of all this. I talked with her about what your dad left you. She's fine."

"Great. I want to remember this day. For what it is. Not for what it cost."

Ted managed to get all three enterprises of the Southtown

Project open and operating. First, St. Michaels AME closed its food bank and donated food, money, and time to Oasis. Next, residents were given something resembling a credit card. They presented it when they purchased food and groceries at Oasis. The card provided an appropriate discount based on the residents' ability to pay. No longer were they going to the church and receiving a handout. Instead, they were able to go to a grocery store with dignity. And purchase what they wanted and needed. Often, the residents' cards allowed them to receive groceries for free.

Reverend Jacob Roberts worked with Ted to find additional resources to keep the new grocery store open and prospering. Stocking and clerking were done by volunteers. Malachi and Jamal are the only paid employees.

Maureen helped organize a staffing plan for the clinic. Nurses from the various clinics signed up. They will work on their off days. The chief of surgery at the hospital helped organize a cadre of physicians, physician assistants, and nurse practitioners. They will cover the clinic the three days it is open. The clinic never charged more than Medicaid or Medicare would allow for the services. Lew Diamond, the owner of Diamond's Pharmacy, filled any prescriptions at wholesale. Whatever Medicaid and Medicare did not cover would be donated.

Education majors at Southern State volunteered at the youth center and the Lions, Sertoma, Optimist, and Kiwanis clubs. In addition, the county library brought the bookmobile to the center once a week. This allowed neighborhood residents-adults and youth access to books and magazines.

The big day was upon the couple. Two years previously, Ted walked in with Jack. Maureen immediately fell head-over-heels in love with the handsome stranger. It took more than a bit of pressure from this formidable redhead to convince this tall, skinny dude destiny brought them together. Maureen had her gown and her entourage. Ted had his groomsmen. Everyone was decked out in a dark blue tux with yellow and blue bow ties and a yellow comber bun.

Everyone was in their place. The groomsmen stood behind Ted, and the bridesmaids were lined opposite. The Reverend Gladstone stood with a white stole streaming down his black robe. The organ suddenly changed tunes. The thunderous chords announced the ceremony was about to begin. Ruthie rose. She turned and looked back. Everyone followed suit. During the bridal march, Jack, in his blue tux, guided this beautiful bride down the aisle. Pam watched, recalling when he walked her down the aisle.

To guests watching Maureen walk down, it appeared Jack was holding her down. Without his holding on to her arm, she would indeed have floated. Ted was struck by the beauty of his bride. And for the first time. Ted realized how lucky she chose him.

When Maureen had arrived where Ted was waiting, Jack handed her off to the reverend. Maureen handed her bouquet to Wendy, her Maid of Honor. Reverend Gladstone held their hands and symbolically tied a rope around them.

"Who gives this woman to be married to this man?"

Ruthie stood with the biggest smile in her life and announced, "I do."

At the back of the sanctuary, Mr. and Mrs. Winston James greeted the guests. Ruthie and Jack stood next to Maureen. Mack stood alone next to his son.

Marie and Hank were first through the receiving line. Marie hugged and kissed her son. Mack shook Ted's hand and offered words of wisdom and encouragement. Mack held out his hand to Maureen. She pushed it aside and gave the big man a hug.

"Strangers shake hands," she said. "We're in-laws now. We're family, and families hug." She squeezed one more time and reached up and kissed Hank on the cheek.

Maureen hugged Marie and was reluctant to let her go. "Thank you for everything," she mouthed.

Marie kissed Maureen's cheek, gave a tight squeeze. "You are most welcome."

Melinda was next and gave the newlyweds a hug and kiss. "Just because you're now married doesn't mean you get to be strangers," she said, smiling through her tears. Holding Maureen's hands. She looked admiringly at Maureen. "You are the most beautiful bride I have ever seen,"

To Maureen and Ted, the handshakes and hugs seemed an eternal event. More than a hundred people came to share the couple's blessed event. Malachi and Jamal from Oasis were there. Reverend Roberts gave a hug and a blessing. In addition, many came from Southtown. They adopted these two as their own.

The ceremony, the photo ops, the receiving line, and the reception were a blur. Maureen and Ted danced to the DJ's rendition of *Your Song*, never taking their eyes off each other. Maureen had arranged the traditional father-daughter dance to be with Jack. They danced to the Bobby Darin song, *18 Yellow Roses*.

There were toasts and congratulations. Everyone had a champagne flute. They had the option of toasting champagne or, following Maureen's choice of bubbly grape juice. Ted was the lone ranger. He toasted with Dr. Pepper.

There was a buffet. While people ate. The couple worked the room. The newlyweds greeted everyone who was sharing in their celebration. Before the party was over, they departed. Maureen and Ted were happily celebrating their first night as husband and wife.

◆ ◆ ◆

Their honeymoon was a ten-day cruise on Royal Caribbean's *The Allure of the Sea,* out of Ft. Lauderdale. Ruthie and Jack were driving the couple to the airport in Ted's Sportage in the morning. Ruthie and Jack stood back as the happy couple checked in and checked their luggage. There were more hugs, kisses, handshakes, and tears, and then Maureen and Ted began their entangled trip through airport security. Then they were gone.

Maureen had an inside seat, and Ted was left on the aisle. They talked while the plane filled with other travelers. The door closed. The flight attendants went through the safety checklist and made sure everyone had their seats in an upright position and seatbelts fastened. Then the plane began taxiing down the runway. After liftoff, there was a mechanical sound indicated the wheels retracted. When the plane leveled off at 33,000 feet, Maureen and Ted began to relax. The first time in several days. Maureen slipped her arm through his and laced her fingers with his fingers. She leaned into him and said, "I love you, Mr. James."

Ted was leaning into Maureen. When he heard her message, he kissed the top of her head and said, "I love you more, Mrs. James."

Several minutes had passed without either of them saying anything. Then, in a voice barely above a whisper, "A dog. I think we should have a dog. Can we get a dog when we get back home?"

"Sorry, my love," Ted said quietly, "our complex won't allow pets.

Several more minutes passed. Then using the same voice. Maureen asked, "Do they allow babies?"

Maureen felt Ted shake with a slight, muffled laugh. "Yes, my dear. They do allow babies," and kissed her head again.

More minutes of silence passed, then Maureen made the proclamation. "Good. I want a baby."

He leaned further into her. Ted said simply, "We'll see."

He then squeezed her hand three times in their now familiar, discreet way of saying, "I love you."